TOBY CLEMENTS
Kingmaker
Winter Pilgrims

arrow books

Published by Arrow Books 2015

6 8 10 9 7 5

First published in Great Britain in 2014 by Century

www.penguin.co.uk

A CIP catalogue record for this book
is available from the British Library

ISBN 9780099585879

Typeset by Palimpsest Book Production Ltd, Falkirk, Stirlingshire
Printed and bound by Clays Ltd, St Ives plc

MIX
Paper from
responsible sources
FSC
www.fsc.org   FSC® C018179

Penguin Random House is committed to a sustainable
future for our business, our readers and our planet.
This book is made from Forest Stewardship Council®
certified paper.

To Karen, with all my love.

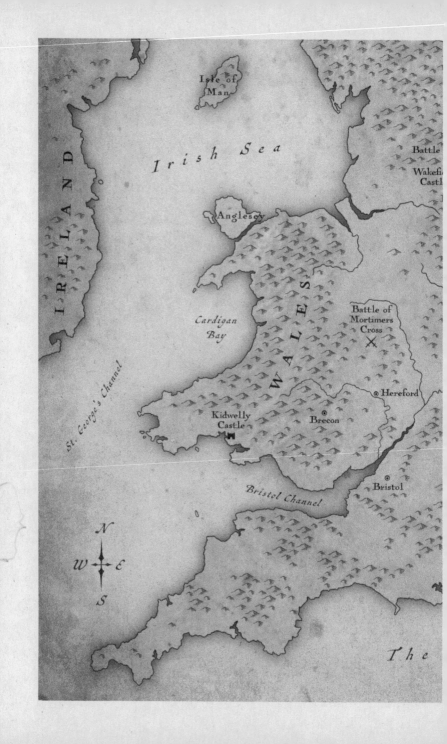

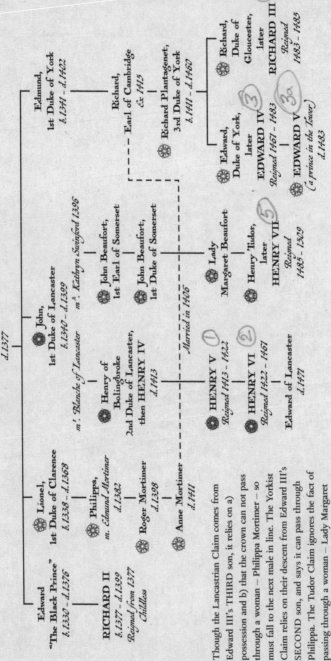

EDWARD III
d.1377

Key: ● York ● Lancaster ● Tudor

Edward "The Black Prince" *b.1330 – d.1376*
— RICHARD II *b.1377 – d.1399* Reigned from 1377 *Childless*

Lionel, 1st Duke of Clarence *b.1338 – d.1368*
— Philippa, m. Edmund Mortimer *d.1382*
— Roger Mortimer *d.1398*
— Anne Mortimer *d.1411*

John, 1st Duke of Lancaster *b.1340 – d.1399*
m.¹ Blanche of Lancaster   m.² Kathryn Swinford 1396

Henry of Bolingbroke 2nd Duke of Lancaster, then HENRY IV *d.1413*
— ① HENRY V Reigned 1413 – 1422
— ② HENRY VI Reigned 1422 – 1461
— Edward of Lancaster *d.1471*

John Beaufort, 1st Earl of Somerset
John Beaufort, 1st Duke of Somerset
— Lady Margaret Beaufort
— ⑤ Henry Tudor, later HENRY VII Reigned 1485 – 1509

Married in 1406

Edmund, 1st Duke of York *b.1341 – d.1402*
— Richard, Earl of Cambridge *Ex.1415*
— Richard Plantagenet, 3rd Duke of York *b.1411 – d.1460*

Richard, Duke of Gloucester, later RICHARD III Reigned 1483 – 1485

Edward, Duke of York, later ③ EDWARD IV Reigned 1461 – 1483
— ③ₐ EDWARD V *(a prince in the Tower) d.1483*

Though the Lancastrian Claim comes from Edward III's THIRD son, it relies on a) possession and b) that the crown can not pass through a woman – Philippa Mortimer – so must fall to the next male in line. The Yorkist Claim relies on their descent from Edward III's SECOND son, and says it can pass through Philippa. The Tudor Claim ignores the fact of passing through a woman – Lady Margaret Beaufort – or that John, Earl of Somerset, was born illegitimate.

Factions in the Wars of the Roses

Principal Yorkist leaders in 1460

Richard Plantagenet, Duke of York, senior Yorkist claimant to the throne (died at the Battle of Wakefield, 1460).

Edward Plantagenet, Earl of March, son of the Duke of York (to become King Edward IV).

Edmund Plantagenet, Earl of Rutland, second son of the Duke of York (died at the Battle of Wakefield, 1460).

Richard Neville, Earl of Salisbury – powerful magnate (executed after Wakefield, 1461).

Richard Neville, Earl of Warwick – Earl of Salisbury's son, later known as the 'Kingmaker' having helped Edward IV to become king.

Lord Fauconberg – Earl of Salisbury's brother, a fine soldier.

William Hastings – Earl of March's friend and pimp.

Principal Lancastrian leaders in 1460

King Henry VI – Son of Henry V, weak willed and possibly insane.

Margaret (of Anjou) – Henry VI's strong-willed French wife.

Henry, 3rd Duke of Somerset – Margaret's favourite, good soldier, louche.

In addition almost every other magnate in the land, including the Dukes of Buckingham, Exeter, Devon, the Earls of Shrewsbury, Wiltshire, Northumberland, as well as Lords Scales, Roos, Hungerford, Ruthyn and Clifford.

Prologue

During the 1450s England was in a sorry state: her hundred-year war in France had ended in humiliation, law and order had broken down in the towns and shires, and at sea, pirates were everywhere so that the wool trade – which had once kept her coffers brimming – had withered to nothing. Meanwhile her king, Henry VI, was prey to bouts of madness that robbed him of his wits, and with no strong leader, his court had become riven by two factions: one led by the Queen – a strong-willed Frenchwoman named Margaret from Anjou; the other by Richard, Duke of York, and his powerful allies the Earls of Warwick and of Salisbury.

Relations between the two factions first broke down in 1455 and each summoned its men to arms. In a short sharp action in the shadow of the Abbey of St Albans in Hertfordshire, the Queen's favourite, Edmund, second Duke of Somerset, was killed, and the Duke of York and his allies won the day.

But York's ascendancy was short-lived. By the end of the decade the King had regained his wits and the Queen her control of the court, and the sons of those killed at St Albans sought vengeance for their fathers' sakes.

In 1459 the Queen summoned the Duke of York and his allies to court in Coventry, where she was strong, and, fearing for his life, the Duke once more raised his banner and summoned his allies. The Queen – in the King's name – did likewise and on the eve of St Edward's Day in October that year, the two sides once more took the field, at Ludford Bridge, near Ludlow, in the county of Shropshire.

But the Duke of York and the Earls of Warwick and Salisbury were betrayed, and so, finding their position hopeless, they fled the country: the Duke of York to Ireland, the Earls of Warwick and Salisbury across the Narrow Sea to Calais.

And so now while those of the Queen's faction strip the land of all that is left, men in England are waiting, waiting for the spring to come, waiting for the exiles to return, waiting for the wars to start once more.

PART ONE

Priory of St Mary, Haverhurst, County of Lincoln, February 1460

1

The Dean comes for him during the Second Repose, when the night is at its darkest. He brings with him a rush lamp and a quarterstaff and he wakes him with a heavy prod.

'Up now, Brother Thomas,' he says. 'The Prior's asking for you.'

It is not time for prime yet, Thomas knows, and he hopes if he is asleep, the Dean will let him alone and wake one of the other canons: Brother John perhaps, or Brother Robert, who is snoring. A moment later his blankets are thrown back and the cold grips him fast. He sits up and tries to gather them to him, but the Dean casts them aside.

'Come on now,' he says. 'The Prior's waiting.'

'What does he want?' Thomas asks. Already his teeth are chattering and there is steam rising from his body.

'You'll see,' the Dean says. 'And bring your cloak. Bring your blanket. Bring everything.'

In the lamp's uncertain glow the Dean's face is all heavy brows and a crooked nose, and the shadow of his head looms across the ice-rimed slates of the roof above. Thomas untangles his frost-stiffened cloak and finds his worsted cap and his clogs. He wraps the blanket about his shoulders.

'Come on, come on,' the Dean urges. His teeth are chattering too.

Thomas gets up and follows him across the dorter, stepping over the huddled forms of the other canons, and together they go down the stone steps to the Prior's cell where a beeswax candle shivers in a sconce and the old man lies on a thick hay mattress with three blankets drawn up to his chin.

'God be with you, Father,' Thomas begins.

The Prior waves aside the greeting without taking his hands from under his covers.

'Did you not hear it?' he asks.

'Hear what, Father?'

The Prior doesn't answer but cocks his narrow head at the shuttered window. Thomas hears only the Dean's breathing behind him and the gentle rattle of his own teeth. Then comes a distant rising shriek, pitched high, thin as a blade. It makes him shudder and he cannot help but cross himself.

The Prior laughs.

'Only a fox,' he says. 'Whatever did you think it was? A lost soul, perhaps? One of the lesser devils?'

Thomas says nothing.

'Probably caught in the copse beyond the river,' the Dean suggests. 'One of the lay brothers sets his snares there. John, it is.'

There is a silence. They ought to send for this John, Thomas thinks, the one who set the trap. He should be made to go and kill the fox. Put it out of its misery.

'Quick as you can then, Brother Tom,' the Dean says.

Thomas realises what they mean.

'Me?' he asks.

'Yes,' the Prior says. 'Or do you think you are too good for such a thing?'

Thomas says nothing, but that is exactly what he is thinking.

'Do it like this,' the Dean says, miming with the staff, jerking its tip down on the skull of an imaginary fox. 'Just above the eyes.'

The Dean has been to the wars in France, and is well known to have killed a man. Perhaps even two. He passes the staff to Thomas. It is almost as tall as him, stained at one end as if it has been used to stir a large pot.

'And be sure to bring the body back,' the Prior adds as the Dean guides Thomas from the cell, 'for I shall want the fur, and the infirmarian the flesh.'

The Dean's light leads Thomas down more stone steps into the fragrant darkness of the frater house where he is drawn to the warmth of the fire's embers glowing under their cover, but the Dean has already crossed the room and pulled aside the door's drawbar.

'God's blood!' he exclaims as he opens the door.

Outside it is the sort of cold that stops you dead, the sort that drops birds from the sky, splits millstones.

'Go on, young Tom,' the Dean says. 'The sooner it is done, the sooner it were done. Then get back here. I'll have some hot wine for you.'

Thomas opens his mouth to say something, but the Dean shoves him out into the cold and closes the door in his face.

Dear God. One moment he is asleep, almost warm, dreaming of the summer to come even, and now: this.

The cold sticks in his throat, makes his head ache. He gathers his cloak, hesitates a moment, then turns and sets out, picking his way across the yard to the beggars' gate, his clogs ringing on the ice.

He unbars the gate and steps through. Beyond the priory walls the dawn is already a pale presence in the east and the snow lying over the fen gives off a light so cold it is blue. To the south, where the river curls around itself, the millwheel is frozen in mid-turn, as if opening its mouth to say something, and beyond it the bakery, the brewhouse and the lay brothers' granges stand deserted, their walls frosted, their roofs bowing under the weight of snow. Nothing moves. Not a thing.

Then the fox screams again, high and sharp. Thomas shudders and turns back to the gateway, as if he might somehow be allowed back in to return to bed, but then he collects himself and turns again and forces himself to move. One step, two, carefully keeping close to the priory walls, following them around to where the dark line of the old road comes into view on its way through the fen towards Cornford and the sea beyond. There was a time when it might have been busy, he thinks, even on a morning such as this. Merchants might have been making their way to Boston with their wool for the fleet sailing for the Staple in Calais, or pilgrims might have been coming to the shrine of Little St Hugh in Lincoln. These days though, with the land so lawless, anyone abroad at this time of day is either a fool or a villain, or both.

By the time he reaches the sisters' cloister Thomas's shins are scorched, his chilblains throb and his fingers are already so thick and clumsy with the cold he knows he will not be able to hold a quill all day, knows he'll make no progress with his psalter. Even his teeth ache.

He stops at the sisters' gate, pauses a moment, glances at it though he knows he must not, then he leaves the shadow of the priory's wall and cuts away, down across a field where the lay brothers will plant rye in the distant spring. There is an old path on the snow, a line of footprints he follows through the furlong and down towards the dung heap by the river. Here the path ends in a confusion of dimples in the snow and broken ice, as if someone has been fetching water.

Thomas climbs down the low bank on to the ice where a mist unfurls around his ankles. He steps on to it, testing it though he knows it to be strong enough to bear a cart and ox, and he hurries across in a few quick strides to thread his way through the ice-rimed reeds on the far side. Just as he is scrambling up the bank, the fox shrieks once more, rough-edged, filled with pain. Thomas pauses, frozen. The scream stops abruptly, as if cut off.

Thomas wavers again, looks back to the priory, at the low clutch of stone buildings that huddle around the stump of the church's tower. He sees the frater house roof leaking smoke into the pale sky and he wishes he were safe behind those walls again, readying himself for prime, perhaps, or even still asleep and dreaming again of the summer to come.

Curse the Prior. Curse him for waking him. Curse him for sending him on this errand.

And why? Why him? Why not this John who set the snare in the first place? Thomas is a scribe, an illuminator, not a lay brother, no longer some farm boy. He'd meant to pass that day applying leaf to one of the capitals, burnishing it with Brother Athelstan's dog's tooth tool. But now his fingers are like sausages.

This is the Prior's design, of course. Thomas understands that. The Prior means to knock the pride from him. He said as much the night before, when he'd preached against the sin during supper. Thomas had felt the old man's eye settle on him more than once during the meal, but had thought little of it. He hadn't looked contrite enough; that was it. A lesson there.

He carries on to where the snow is deeper, undisturbed since it started falling the day after Martinmas this last year. He breaks through the snow crust up to his knees, stumbles, flounders. Soon he is sodden. On he goes, up the gentle slope until he is only a few footsteps from the tangled borders of the copse. It hurts to breathe. He peers through the lattice of unruly branches. He sees nothing, only darkness, but something is in there. Again the hair on his nape bristles. He raises his stick to hook aside a bough.

There is an explosion. A rattling boom. There is a cry, a tearing sound, the beating of wings. It comes at him, soot-black, straight at his face, at his eyes.

He bellows. He ducks, swings the staff, throws himself to the snow.

But the crow is gone before it is really there.

It flies off with a dismal caw.

Thomas's heart is pounding. He hears himself blubbing, making no sense. When he gets to his knees, his hands are blue, his cassock quilted with snow.

The crow has settled on a snow-capped post by the dung heap.

'Bastard bird!' Thomas calls, shaking the staff. 'Bastard bloody bird!'

The crow ignores him. The bell begins tolling in the priory, and from the river a mist rises, thick as fleece. Thomas turns back to the copse, resolute now, but he can find no way in through the tangle of brambles. He hacks at them with his staff, circles the copse until he finds a track; the lay brother John's prints, he supposes. He ducks under the first low branches and fights his way in. The brambles pull at his cassock, snow tips down on him from above. He steps over a fallen trunk and finds himself on the edge of a tight clearing and something makes him stop. He eases aside a branch, and there it is: the fox, a slur of matted red fur in the gloom.

He steps forward.

Its neck and foreleg are caught together in a loop of wire, and the wire itself is hooked over a spur of hornbeam. The fox is on its hind legs, half-hanged, half-frozen, its narrow snout sunk on its blood-wet chest. The snow below is scraped to the frozen black earth and blood-stains and clumps of russet hair are everywhere.

Thomas makes the sign of the cross, and stands stock-still, listening. He can hear something. Then he realises it is the fox, still alive, still breathing, each breath a high bubbling drag followed by a racking exhalation that subsides in a hoarse whimper.

After a moment it seems to sense him and lifts its head.

Thomas gasps and takes a step back.

The fox is blinded, its eyes gone, each glistening socket weeping a tag of thick blood.

The crow caws from beyond the thicket.

'Bastard bloody bird,' Thomas breathes. Again he makes the sign of the cross.

After a moment, the fox's head sinks wearily back on its chest.

Thomas steels himself. He steps forward, raises the staff just as the Dean suggested, then brings it down. Crack. The fox jerks in its noose. There is a delicate patter of blood on the snow. The fox shudders. It gives a long rattling sigh; then it is dead.

Thomas pulls the staff from the cup of broken bones. It is smeared with a dark-veined soup of grey brains that he wipes in the snow bank below the hornbeam. Once he has done this he stands for a moment, then makes a final sign of the cross over the fox, blessing it as one of God's creatures, and is about to turn and go when he remembers the Prior's instruction.

With a sigh he sets aside the staff and begins following the line of the snare back from the branch on which it is caught, pinching it between thumb and forefinger, down through the wet spray of traveller's joy to the base of the tree. It is awkward. His fingers are so numb, and the knot is set in the ice, pulled taut by the fox's struggle.

He gropes forward, on his knees now, his ear pressed against the rough bark of the tree. He cannot pick apart the strands of the knot. He needs his knife, he realises, and is cursing his forgetfulness when he hears the shouts of men and the sudden drum of horses' hooves on the road beyond.

2

Daylight is almost come by the time Sister Katherine brings the pail down from the Prioress's cell. She comes out into the yard where the cold clamps her chest.

'God keep you, Sister Katherine.'

It is Sister Alice, the youngest of the nuns, newly come, wrapped in her thick cloak, her breath a rolling plume before her face.

'And God keep you, Sister Alice. I see you are not in chapel?'

'A walk, first,' Sister Alice says this as if this is the most natural thing. Katherine frowns. She has made the same journey every day for seven years now, and not once has anyone come with her. In truth she is grateful. An animal has been screaming in the night, and she feels the residue of anxiety.

'I'd welcome the company, Sister Alice,' she says. She holds the bucket away from her thigh as Alice helps her with the drawbar of the gate. Something slops within, and a tongue of warm steam rises to lick her wrist. Her skin crawls.

Beyond the gate their feet break the new crust of snow hard frozen in the night and a thick mist is rising from the river. A crow leaves its perch on a pole.

Alice stops.

'I have always hated birds,' she says. 'It is the feathers.'

Katherine wonders what it would be like to have time for such luxuries.

She carries on, her steps loud in the frozen stillness. When they come to the tangle of the previous day's footprints by the dung heap she sees someone – one of the lay brothers probably – has been out since yesterday, and has crossed the river. She sets aside the bucket and opens the barrel lid with a snap of ice. It is the one advantage of winter, she thinks, when the cold seems to keep at bay the lazy flies that usually hum around the barrel's open mouth and the stink of the process makes you gasp. Sister Alice tries to pass her the bucket. She slips and nearly drops it.

'Let me,' Katherine says.

'But I want to help.'

Again Katherine wonders why Alice is there. Not standing by the river and holding a bucket of the Prioress's slops, but in the priory at all. She is too young and too pretty to have come here to wait to die like the other sisters. She is too thin, that is true, but so is everybody these days, except perhaps the Prioress and Sister Joan. Nevertheless, even standing there holding that bucket of shit, even with that dew drop on the tip of her pink nose, Alice seems other-worldly, more than merely one of the sisters. Her clothes have no patches or stains and her rosary beads are finely wrought from ivory – a gift from a loving relative perhaps – and there is a lightness about her, as if she barely touches the ground at all.

'Why are you here, Sister Alice?' Katherine asks.

'I told you,' Alice says. 'I want to help.'

'No, no,' Katherine goes on. 'I mean here. Here at the priory.'

Alice smiles.

'Oh,' she says. 'I am a bride of Christ.'

She even holds up her hand to show the gold ring on her finger.

'What about you? Are you not a bride of Christ too?'

Katherine cannot tell if Alice is making a joke, but she thinks of herself: left at the almonry as an infant, with only a purse and some letters, and now the one to empty the Prioress's slop bucket every morning.

'Me?' she says at length. 'I am like this.'

And she pours the slops into the barrel, careful to keep back the solids for the dung heap. After she has done it, she empties the heavy bucket on to the heap, three or four very brown turds on the snow. The two nuns step back and Alice shivers.

Then they turn and begin their walk back across the fields towards the priory.

'Why is it always you who empties the Prioress's night bucket?' Alice asks.

'It just is,' Katherine says.

Alice opens her mouth to ask something more but then closes it. Perhaps she has too many questions and cannot choose the right one. They walk on in silence, listening to their footsteps, and the click of Alice's rosary, and their ragged breathing; Katherine is lost in thought, and so it is that she doesn't hear the horses on the road above them until it is too late.

When she does, she stops mid-stride. Her heart lurches.

Men on horseback. More than one. More than two.

'Quick,' she whispers.

She gestures to Alice, and they lift their skirts and run. She hears a man shout. Dear God. They've been seen. She keeps running. The men are urging their horses off the road, cutting down across the frozen river, aiming to meet them before they reach the beggars' gate.

There are only a hundred steps to cover, but Katherine and Alice are floundering in their clogs and skirts, and the bucket is heavy and she dare not drop it for fear of what the Prioress will say. Then Alice falls with a cry. Katherine drags her to her feet. The men are in the field now, hollering as if at sport, ploughing their horses through the snow, one pulling ahead of the others.

Katherine turns and starts running again, but in a moment the first horse is on them. She cowers even as she runs, ducking the expected blow, but the rider overtakes them, thundering past. Then he stands tall in his stirrups and hauls back on the reins. He sets the horse on its hind legs and blocks their way.

The horse is huge, brown, with flailing hooves, a beard of filthy icicles and eyeballs as big as fists. The rider is young, but strong, and his face is bright with delight at what he's caught. He is laughing. Without thinking Katherine takes a step to one side and then, using every muscle in her body, each one honed by punishing years of labour, she swings the heavy bucket. Lets it fly.

It hits the horseman with the crack of a falling trap door.

He flies back over the croup of the horse, hands clapped to his face. Alice screams. The horse launches itself forward again. They throw themselves aside as it barrels past them.

The man is screaming. He rolls on his back, knees drawn up, hands pressed to his face, blood pouring between his leather-gloved fingers. It is everywhere, staining the snow and his white tabard.

But now the other horse is on them, a grey, ridden by a man in a long red coat. He has a sword.

Katherine steps in front of Alice and faces him. She is beyond fear now.

The rider comes at her, arm raised. She stands to face him. But then something happens. Something comes through the air, a dark blur. It catches the horseman, hits his head with a slap. He falters, drops the sword, then collapses, as if filleted. He rolls from the saddle and crashes to the snow. The horse turns, canters away.

And suddenly there is someone else there with them. A man on foot, in a black cloak, clogs on his feet. It is one of the canons, running from the direction of the river. He is waving his arms and shouting, and his skirts are riding high around his bare knees.

The third rider turns to face the new threat, and the fourth rider, a giant of a man on a carthorse, dithers too.

Katherine snatches Alice's hand and they turn and bolt for the gate. The canon hesitates in mid-stride, swerves, nearly slips, and then follows them. The third rider pulls a long-handled hammer from his pack and jams his heels into his horse's flanks. The fourth rider – the giant – jumps from his horse and comes running at them on foot. He has no shoes, but is as fast as a wolf, and he has a monstrous axe, and he is roaring as he comes.

Katherine finds the beggars' gate and pulls Alice through. Then the canon comes hurtling through. She heaves the oak door shut in the giant's face and drops the locking bar. The planks rock and the bar bulges under the impact of the man's shoulder, but the door holds, just.

Katherine stands back. She can hardly breathe. She can feel her pulse in her teeth. She makes the sign of the cross, but she cannot help steal a glance at the canon. He is bent with his hands on his knees, gasping with the effort, a long funnel of breath rolling from his gaping mouth. At that moment he stands and he looks at her and for an instant they stare at one another. He has blue eyes, reddish hair.

Then Alice speaks. She is on straw-flecked ice of the yard, pointing at the canon's clogs, shrinking back, shielding her eyes so that she cannot see the rest of him.

'He must go!' she says.

It is true. If he is seen, Katherine can scarcely imagine the penance the three of them will face. But then a voice drifts over the wall.

'Brother Monk?'

It is a refined voice, nasal and strong. The voice of a man used to ordering others about.

'Brother Monk? Sister Nun? I know you can hear me. You've grievously mishandled my boy, Sister Nun, and you have knocked me from my horse, Brother Monk. By my honour, I cannot let that pass. Come out now and we shall do our business and then I shall ride on my way as if none of this ever happened. Do you hear me, Sister Nun? Brother Monk?'

His voice is close, just the other side of the door, a mere hand's span away. There is a pause of two or three beats of the heart and then the voice comes again.

'Well, Sister Nun and Brother Monk, since you're not going to come out then I shall have to come in. And when I do, I promise you this: I shall find you. I shall find you first, Brother Monk, and when I do, I'll let my man Morrant here do you to death. Then I'll come for you, Sister Nun, you and your snivelling girl. After Morrant's done with you, I'll nail your bodies to this very door here, see, the one you're hiding behind, and then I'll set a fire under you. I'll see you beg the Almighty to take you. Do you hear me?'

Then there is a quick turn of hooves on the other side of the gate and the horsemen are gone. Katherine stares at her wet wooden clogs under the snow-thickened hem of her cassock. Alice is whimpering.

'I must be gone,' the canon mumbles. 'Must go.'

She looks at him one last time. He is a big man, a half-head taller than she, with broad shoulders, the reddish hair cropped short, a disc of skin shaved bald. Apart from the horsemen beyond, he is the first man she can ever recall having seen. She almost reaches out to touch his face.

He turns and hurries across the courtyard to the wall that divides the priory and scrambles up on to the roof of the wood store. His clogs send the snow sliding, but he catches the top of the wall and hauls himself up and over. He pauses, looks back, and then is gone, back into his own world. Only then does she wish she'd thanked him.

'We must tell the Prioress,' Alice wails, still on the ground. 'We must warn all the sisters.'

'No!' Katherine says, helping her up. 'No. We cannot. We cannot. We must tell no one. No good can come of this.'

She is looking around them at the windows and the apertures. Has the canon been seen? She thinks not. There is no one about.

'But what of those threats?' Alice counters. 'Those things said?'

'They can do nothing,' Katherine says, 'so long as we remain within the priory walls. Let us thank God for that canon, whoever he was, and let us pray that he was not seen here in our quarters.

'We will do our own penance, Sister,' she adds. 'A thousand Aves and two thousand Credos before the Shrine of the Virgin, and we will forgo bread until the feast of St Gilbert.'

Alice nods uncertainly. Only Katherine knows that the feast of St Gilbert is but a few days away.

'I am sure that will please the Lord,' Alice says at length, and seems to be about to say something else, but just then the bell begins ringing for prime. They look at one another before they brush the snow from their cassocks, adjust their veils, fold their hands into their sleeves and walk towards the cloister and the safety of church.

Neither hears the soft tap of a shutter being pulled closed above their heads.

3

'Alarm!' he shouts. 'Alarm!'

It is just after first light and the canons are gathering for prime in the western arm of the cloister. They react as a herd of cows might to a barking dog. Only the Dean steps forward.

'What is this, Brother Thomas?' He stands with his hands on his hips and a scowl on his face.

'There are horsemen without.' Thomas points. He can hardly breathe for running. 'They are armed. They are coming for us.'

The Dean snaps into movement, as if this is something for which he had planned.

'Brother John!' he barks. 'Brother Geoffrey! Secure the main gate. Brother Barnaby, sound the bell to summon the lay brethren! Let it ring sharply now. Brother Athelstan, have the Prioress secure the postern gate in the sisters' cloister and shutter every window. She must gather the sisters in the chapel. Brother Anselm, bring reed and ink and some paper to the Prior in the secretarium. Brother Wilfred, have the ostler saddle a horse. And tell Brother Robert to come.'

Three canons are sent to take the books from the library to the secretarium, and two more to take axes to the buttery, ready to open the barrel and let the wine run to waste if the priory walls are breached. The bell in the belfry begins an urgent peal.

'How many, Brother?' the Dean asks.

'Four, I believe, although one has been sorely treated.'

'You harmed him?'

Thomas hesitates. He does not wish to mention the two sisters.

'I did, Brother, may God forgive me.'

'Good man,' the old soldier says. 'I am sure He will find it in His heart to do so.'

The Prior stands before the iron-bound door of the secretarium, frowning at the sound of the bell. He is dressed only in an alb, and the white circle of hair around his head is in disarray, and he blinks.

'Why is the bell ringing so, Brother Stephen?'

'We are under attack, Father. Brother Thomas here was waylaid while without by four armed men.'

The Prior's gaze switches to Thomas.

'What was their purpose?'

'Their captain threatened to invest the priory and to have me killed.'

The Prior turns to the Dean.

'You have alerted our sister the Prioress? Good. And secured every gate and window?'

'All is done, Holy Father, although I have not yet sent for aid from Cornford.'

The Prior looks thoughtful.

'It is difficult to know what to do in that regard,' he says, more to himself than the Dean or Thomas. 'I am not yet sure of where Sir Giles stands in respect to his obligations to our house.'

Brother Anselm arrives with the reed and ink and this decides the Prior.

'Nevertheless,' he says, taking the nib and paper. 'Let us do so, and see what results.'

'Brother Robert can deliver it.'

The Prior nods and the Dean turns to Thomas.

'Climb the belfry, Tom, and see if your men are still there.'

Thomas hurries through the secretarium into the nave, where Brother Barnaby is tugging the bell rope in sharp jerks. Thomas has never been up the ladder. His clogs are clumsy on the rungs and he clings to the risers so tightly that sections of bark come loose and spin down on Barnaby below.

'*Ave Maria, gratia plena, Dominus tecum. Benedicta tu in mulieribus . . .*'

After almost a hundred rungs the ladder emerges through a trap door on to a bird-shit-splattered, roughly adzed wooden floor. The bell swings close above him, deafening. He crawls across to the snow-capped sill of the window set in the northern wall and looks out.

Nothing.

Beyond the priory walls a milk-white dawn mist has risen above the fens, a membrane that floats over everything so he can hardly tell where the earth below meets the sky above. Only the stark branches of the hawthorn trees are prominent, though here and there the mist eddies and thins under the tutelage of the freshening wind, so that vague shapes appear for a moment, then are gone.

He watches from the other windows of the tower, each facing a different point on the compass, and through each the view is similar. There is no sign of the horsemen. Down below he can see the beggars' gate open and quickly close again to admit numerous lay brethren, summoned from their granges by the din of the bell.

At length it stops ringing, though his ears continue long after.

'Brother Thomas!'

The Dean is standing in the middle of the garth, framed by the cloister.

'Anything?'

'Nothing, Brother!'

From below comes the clop of iron shoes as a horse is brought across the cobbled yard. Perched atop is the reluctant Brother Robert.

The Dean calls up again.

'Is the road clear?'

Thomas waits before replying. A clearing in the mist is drifting across the land, a window through which he can see the snowfields below. He waits until it reaches the road, bulking out and flattening against the dyke before rising and passing over, revealing only the weals left by the tracks of long-gone travellers.

'No one,' he calls down.

The Dean signals for the gate to be opened and Brother Robert urges his horse through the gate. The Dean blesses his back with the sign of the cross, but already the gate is slammed shut and the locking bar dropped in place. Thomas watches as Robert trots away up the road, head down, shoulders hunched, vanishing into the mist.

Thomas has never been up here in the belfry before, never seen the priory from above. He sees how the whole is halved by the dividing wall, so that the canons' cloister is kept apart from the sisters' cloister, only touching in the window house, the octagonal brick building set in the wall that houses the turning window through which the two halves of the priory communicate. The charge of this is given to the oldest canon of the community, and it is through this screen, designed so that neither brother nor sister ever see one another, that food and laundry passes from the sisters to the canons, while in the wall bisecting the nave of the chapel is a smaller version through which the consecrated host is passed during Mass. In this way the two communities might be said to feed one another.

He watches Brother Barnaby making his way through the cloister. Barnaby waves up at him, a rude gesture of alliance. Thomas cannot help but smile. Barnaby is the closest thing he has to a friend in the priory, a good-natured boy, the son of a wool merchant, who cannot hold his ale and who will confide almost anything in anyone.

His thoughts turn to the morning. He had only heard the horsemen when they'd spurred their horses along the road and his first reaction had been to fling himself to the ground. It was only when he'd regained his feet that he saw the two sisters, and again, his first instinct had been to look away, following the Rule of St

Gilbert, and so he could not then explain, even to himself, what had taken hold of him.

Why had he run at a man – at men – on horseback? He cannot understand it. It was madness. He is an illuminator, a draughtsman. He is used to working bent-backed over his psalter, pricking out the designs, shaping the gesso, applying inks and paints, burnishing shivering gold leaf. That is what he does; that is what he is.

Nevertheless he had felt some savage fury grip him and from the moment he broke cover and let that staff fly, he knew that it would hit the man on the horse, and hit hard.

Now he remembers the horseman's threats, delivered through the gate. There is something about them, something more than merely the grisly specifics, something that made them all the more pressing. But what is it? What were the words he used? Thomas tries to reconstruct them, but finds he cannot.

How long he stays in the tower, on his knees below the bell, he is unable say. The life of the priory is disrupted and the observation of the Hours stalled while the canons maintain their stations at the walls and the sisters remain within the nave below.

He thinks about the two sisters. He had only seen the face of one of them: the one who had thrown the bucket. She looked fierce; that is the word that occurs to him. The other sister he would only ever recognise again by her beautiful rosary beads. He'd not dared look too closely at her face. They are the first women he has seen for five Eastertides.

Soon his stomach is like a stone for want of food and he needs to relieve himself. He is about to call out for help when he stops. He has heard something.

What is it? The wind? No. It is a distant and regular drumbeat, coming from the east. He can make nothing out in the mist, but the noise is constant now, and getting louder. It is solidifying into something like – like what? It is a confusion of scratching, shuffling, and grinding.

And then he sees it.

First comes the suggestion that the road is firming, becoming darker and more distinct, but then there comes one of those gaps in the mist as it hurries across the marshland. It slips over the road and with a start Thomas catches the fleeting glimpse of a man on horseback.

No sooner has he seen him than he is gone. He begins to doubt himself.

But no. There he is again. Less distinct, but surely there?

Then the rider emerges from the mist again. This time he is close enough so that Thomas can make him out. On a grey. His coat red. Behind him comes a huge man on a dray horse, then a cart loaded with hay, then another two men riding alongside one another and then more, in pairs, until Thomas cannot judge their numbers, for he cannot see the rear of the line where it vanishes into the mist. It might go on forever.

They all wear the same white livery coat; some carry long spears in their stirrups, others hammers and bills over their shoulders. One is carrying a banner that hangs in frozen swags.

Thomas tries to swallow but his mouth has gone dry. Then he is on his feet. He seizes the clapper of the bell and begins hammering it against the bell's brass lip.

The Dean appears in the garth.

'They are without!' Thomas cries. 'A host!'

'How many?'

'I cannot say. Many hundreds.'

The Dean seems to shrink. Thomas turns back. Had he not recognised the man in the red coat, he might entertain the hope that the soldiers will pass them by, that they might be bound elsewhere; but there he is, astride that grey horse, and behind him the giant, and now Thomas sees a man is lying on the straw-filled bed of the cart. His hands are pressed to his face and he twitches every time the cart jerks.

The man in the red coat spurs his horse ahead of the column and disappears from Thomas's view behind the wall by the gatehouse.

There is some shouting and then the lay brethren manning the gate turn and stare back over their shoulders, looking for an order from the Dean. Thomas cannot hear what is being said, but the Dean seems to have frozen. Then he motions that the gate should be opened and so the locking beam is removed.

What are they doing? The fools.

'Stop!' Thomas shouts. No one looks up. He is forgotten.

The gates swing open, admitting the man with the red coat and the giant. The lay brethren shrink back and the riders stop in the courtyard in front of the gatehouse. They sit there, apparently in silence. Then the Prior emerges and approaches, and the first horseman swings his leg over the saddle and dismounts. It is an awkward movement: perhaps he is carrying an injury? The horseman speaks to the Prior for a minute, gesturing and once touching his face. The Prior is listening hard and then turns and speaks to the Dean. The Dean shakes his head. Then he looks up at the belfry where Thomas is still kneeling. The giant walks out through the gate and a moment later returns, leading the carthorse by its bridle.

Then the infirmarian appears from his quarters. He approaches the back of the wagon and climbs up into it and crouches over the prostrate man for a moment. He tampers with the bandages and instantly the man in the hay gives a spasm. The infirmarian gestures and a lay brother runs for something from the infirmary.

Thomas continues watching, unable to understand.

Then the first horseman follows the Prior to the almonry and, after they have gone in, the door is closed. A moment later the Prior appears again and speaks to the Dean, who is waiting outside.

Then the Dean shouts up:

'Brother Thomas! Come. Your testament is required.'

Thomas feels his way to the hatch, his cassock now smutted with bird shit, and begins the descent. His heart is pounding irregularly and he feels so faint he can barely cling to the ladder. His feet slip on the rungs.

The Dean is waiting for him in the cloister.

'What have you got yourself into, Brother?' he asks. 'Sir Giles Riven is here, and that's his boy in the cart. Says a canon attacked him on the road this morning. Can only be you.'

Thomas shakes his head.

'As God is my judge I have done nothing wrong.'

The Dean says nothing and leads the way across the garth. As they walk, the other canons stare, and rumour flies fast in hand signals. Thomas can hardly place one foot in front of the other. Together they pass the giant, who watches them with vacant eyes. The Dean knocks on the door of the almonry, and they go in.

Sir Giles Riven is warming himself by a newly lit fire, a mug of something steaming in his hand. To a man used to tonsures and faded workaday cassocks, Riven appears exotic. His short, padded coat glows in the dark, the colour of rose petals in the summer sun, and his hose are made of finespun wool the colour of lapis. His leather riding boots are turned down to his knees and at his hip hangs his sword.

He stands as tall as the Prior, with his hair hacked short above his ears, but he is much bulkier and more powerful. He has horseman's thighs and broad shoulders, and he stands on the balls of his feet, ready to move.

He turns to Thomas. His skin is rough and reddened from travel, and his teeth are ruined by the sweetmeats and the dried fruits that only the rich can afford, and there is a bruise on his cheek and one eye socket is puffed and dark. The other eye is dark, unreadable in the singular.

'This is Brother Thomas, my lord,' the Prior says. His hands flutter to his pectoral cross. 'He was beyond the priory walls this morning.'

'Hmmm,' Riven says. 'Doesn't look very fierce, does he?'

'No, my lord, he is an illuminator. His skill is a gift from God. He is creating the most wonderful psalter.'

Riven grunts and drains his cup and puts it on the table.

'Ought to save time and kill him now, I suppose,' he says.

The Prior looks startled.

'Should we not get to the truth of the matter?' he asks.

'See no point,' Riven replies. 'I know what I saw.'

'Well. Now, Brother Thomas,' begins the Prior, gabbling almost, 'Sir Giles Riven has avowed that he and his men were attacked this morning by a common robber on the road beyond our walls. He says that this robber was dressed as a canon of our order and that he and his associates – of which we will talk more later – gravely injured his son, Edmund.'

His son. His boy. That is it. That was why the threat had carried such weight. Thomas stands in silence, as must a canon of St Gilbert, and the Prior dares not look at him as he speaks. Riven claps his hands together over the fire as the flames begin to pick up around the logs.

'Well?' the Prior asks. 'Is there anything you have to say?'

Thomas can hardly speak.

'It is a lie,' he manages.

Riven smiles.

'You accuse me of falsehood?' he asks.

Thomas can think of no answer that will not directly insult him and make the situation graver yet.

'Yes,' he says at last.

'Well, well,' Riven says. 'Well, well.'

The Prior opens his mouth to say something but seems unable to think of anything worthy, so closes it. The room seems to darken. Riven helps himself to more wine.

'Let me tell you what will happen now,' he says. 'If my boy dies tonight then I will have Morrant – the big fellow out there – pluck out your eyes and rip out your stones at dawn tomorrow, then I shall have you burned to death, starting with your feet, and I will have this done in the very centre of your cloister for all your monks to see and smell.'

'But, sir! He is a cleric,' the Prior bleats, the least he can do. 'He is in cloister. He must at least be tried in an ecclesiastic court.'

Riven flicks his wrist.

'I have no time for your ecclesiastic courts,' he says. 'I am riding to join the Queen in Coventry and I will see this done by Mass tomorrow and then be gone.'

'And if your boy lives?' the Dean asks, sensing hope.

Riven pauses.

'If my boy lives, well then that will be a happy occasion, and to celebrate his delivery I will have the satisfaction of a trial by combat. What do you say to that, Brother Monk? This I do to accord you the honour of dying like a man, and to prove to you, Father, that God's justice will be done.'

The Prior opens and closes his mouth, can think of nothing to say, and turns to look at Thomas for a fraction of a moment. Then nods his head.

'So be it,' he whispers.

And just then the bell in the church tower rings again, a slow reassuring clap to signal all is well, and that order has been restored, but Thomas knows that in the space of less than a hundred beats of the heart, the Prior has condemned him to certain death.

'And of course' – Riven smiles – 'I must keep my promise to those two sisters, mustn't I, Brother Monk?'

The Dean escorts Thomas from the building, across the yard to a stable, the nearest room they have to a cell, and he is locked in with a mug of ale and a sorry shake of the head. Thomas spends the rest of the day on his knees in prayer. He tries to pray for the life of the boy Edmund Riven, but every time he closes his eyes he sees the Prior's face at the moment he decided in favour of the boy's father. He can't stop his fists balling. How could a man sell a soul so cheaply? Without protest? Without anything?

Some time after vespers, it starts to rain. It takes him a moment to recognise it for what it is, for he has not heard its sound on the tiles since the autumn, around Martinmas, when the snows first came. Now though, just as the bell rings for compline, rainwater comes seeping in and he is forced to spend the night standing in the wet straw.

By morning his stomach is cramped for want of food and his mouth thick with thirst. He shuffles through the dirty straw and pulls himself up so that he can peer through the close-barred aperture in the eaves above. There is nothing to see, only the dawn and the rain. After a moment he drops back and resumes his pacing. The stable is three strides wide, ten long.

A while later the Dean brings a clay bowl of bean and fish soup and a leather tankard of ale balanced on a trencher of four-day-old black bread.

'Will he live?' Thomas asks.

'He'll live. Lost an eye, but the infirmarian says he'll live.'

'Thank the Lord,' Thomas says.

'Yes,' the Dean says. 'Praise Jesus. Now, eat.'

Thomas begins scooping the soup into his mouth. The bell in the tower begins ringing again, calling the canons to chapel. He looks up. Strange to think of life carrying on as normal.

'Some advice, Brother Thomas,' the Dean begins, returning and squatting next to him. He is an old man, about thirty-five perhaps, and his knees crack.

'Thank you, Brother Stephen,' Thomas replies, swallowing a lump of bread. 'I would welcome it.'

'You must flee.'

'Flee?'

'Flee the Priory. This morning, during the chapter meeting when no one is about.'

'Why?'

'You can't fight Sir Giles Riven. He's a soldier. Fighting – it's all he's ever done. God knows the man cannot hold a reed as you can. He cannot burnish gold as you can. What he can do, though, is fight. As you cannot.'

Thomas swallows.

'But if I do not face him,' he says, 'then God's justice will not be done.'

The Dean stands.

'God's justice,' he says. 'What is God's justice?'

Thomas looks about for an answer, but the Dean carries on.

'I know this is hard for you, Brother Thomas. I know things have gone against you, and that none of this is your doing, but these are bad times. Justice is no longer worth the candle lit to see it done. Everything is in turmoil beyond these gates and the Prior needs the protection of a man like Riven if the priory is to remain safe. He cannot afford to deny him any wish.'

'Whatsoever it may be?'

'Whatsoever it may be.'

'Then there is no justice within these gates either.'

The Dean sighs.

'If I were the Prior, Brother,' he says, 'I would tell you that since the Lord is on your side then there is nothing you need fear, and that you will win through this, and that justice will be done. But I am not the Prior. I lack his certainty. I lack his faith. And I know men like Giles Riven.'

Thomas chews his bread. The Dean continues.

'So you must take a staff and some clothes and as much food as you can carry and get away from here. Take your psalter of which everybody talks. Go back to wherever it is you come from. Your family.'

'I have no family to speak of,' Thomas says. He thinks of his father: dead. His mother: dead. His sisters: likewise. He thinks of his brother, eking out a life on the farm in the shadow of that great granite cliff. He'd always liked his brother, but his brother's wife had come between them, and all three knew his future was not there.

'Then see if you cannot join another order,' the Dean continues. 'Any abbot would be glad to have you.'

'They would know that I am a religious. They would suppose I was apostate.'

'Then all that remains to you is an appeal to the Prior of All,' the Dean says. 'Take him your psalter. Show him your art. State your case. He will give you justice.'

Thomas thinks.

'Where would I find him?' he asks.

'Canterbury.'

Thomas has heard of Canterbury, but he has no idea of where it is.

And besides, why should he run? If God is with him?

'But what then of God's purpose?' he asks.

The Dean loses patience. He strides across the stable, picks up the bread and the nearly empty soup bowl.

'God's blood, Brother Thomas,' he says, 'you are a stubborn young fool, and you eating this is a waste, for you'll be dead before you've garnered its goodness.'

Thomas scrabbles to his feet.

'Do not despair of me, Brother. Please.'

The Dean looks at Thomas. He pauses and thinks for a moment and then comes to some decision.

'All right,' he says, handing the dish back. 'You're right. Finish it. You'll need your strength.'

Thomas takes it.

'Thank you, Brother.'

'I must go now. Riven's men are camped in the fields beyond and are demanding what little food we have and the Prioress has sent word that one of the sisters has absconded.'

Thomas is gripped by the fear that he is saying goodbye to the Dean, that this will be the last he sees of him.

'You have been kind, Brother,' he says, 'and may God go with you.'

'You too, Brother. I fear you will have need of Him more the soonest.'

He leaves the door unlocked, but Thomas does not move. He has made his mind up. He will face whatever he must, and with God's grace, he will come through it.

Sometime later, when the chapter meeting is ended, the door is opened again and Brother John and Brother Barnaby stand there, pained to see Thomas has not fled.

'You are to come with us,' John says. 'The Prior has sent for you.'

The bell begins a slow clap, a rhythm like that of the passing bell, and for a moment Thomas considers refusing. Already he feels nostalgia for the time he has spent in the stable. But then he follows them out across the cobbled yard into the north arm of the cloister proper. The rain has melted away the snow, leaving the world lichen-grey.

The rest of the canons are gathered in the eastern arm, a knot of black cassocks and white scapulars against the grey stone walls. Giles Riven stands bare-headed in the middle of the square as if he owns it. He is exercising, flashing his black-bladed sword this way and that, stretching his powerful shoulders, working the heat into his right arm, the sword's tip a thrum in the confines of the garth.

Thomas is pleased to see his cheek is livid and his eye sealed with the swelling from yesterday's fight.

Next to Riven, a little way off, is the giant, that dreadful axe in one hand like a child's stick, and in the other two newly stripped quarterstaffs. He is a head and a half taller than any man there, and twice as broad. His grey-streaked hair falls in long hanks down the shoulders of his greasy leather coat and he is still bare-footed, like the meanest sort of peasant. When he sees Thomas he begins to laugh, a deep chesty boom that makes Riven stop and turn.

'Brother Monk,' he calls, his crooked smile apparently genuine. 'Good news.'

'What is that?' Thomas asks. He will not call Riven 'sir'.

'The good news is that my boy will live,' Riven replies. 'The bad news is that you will not.'

The giant laughs louder, and two others sitting on the wall join in. One of them is wearing a white jacket as Riven's son had been wearing, with a black bird that looks like a crow as a badge. The hem is made up of black and white checks, and the same device is repeated on a square banner that the other man has propped against the cloister wall. This other is in a thick padded coat, dyed blue, with long boots and a dark cap. Both have swords at their hips. Both are drinking from leather tankards, and Brother Jonathan stands by with a pitcher of something that steams.

The Prior and the Dean are together on the far side of the garth with Brother Athelstan. Athelstan is telling them something to which they continue to listen even while their eyes follow Thomas. The Dean looks angry – that Thomas hasn't fled the priory perhaps – while the Prior looks haunted, as if he has not slept, and his owlishness, which Thomas had once taken as a sign of learning, now looks like weakness. The old man turns back to Athelstan, who is waiting for an answer to some question he has asked.

The Dean leaves them and crosses the garth to intercept Thomas, taking responsibility where the Prior is too ashamed to do so.

'Your accuser has chosen the weapon with which you are to fight,' he says.

Riven interrupts.

'The quarterstaff,' he says, motioning to the giant to pass one of the staffs to Thomas. 'You're broadly familiar with it, I believe, Brother Monk? An uncomplicated sort of weapon. Two ends. A middle.'

The giant tosses Thomas one of the quarterstaffs. Thomas catches it and places its end on the ground and waits. He is familiar with the quarterstaff from long hours fighting with his brother when they were children, then adolescents. He knows the tricks, he thinks, and, looking at Riven's swollen eye, he permits himself to wonder. Without thinking he removes his cowl and hitches the skirts of his cassock as the men working in the fields do.

'Begin then, shall we?' Riven says, passing his sword to the giant and taking the other staff in return.

'A prayer first, sir, surely?' the Prior pleads, finally finding the strength to divert if not resist Riven's will.

Riven sighs.

'Very well, Prior. But make it quick.'

All kneel in the mud as the Prior begins the prayers with a paternoster. When it is over Riven stands, just as the Prior is drawing in breath to continue with an Ave.

'Thank you, Prior,' he says, 'that will be all. Now, let's get to it, shall we? In the absence of any formal arrangements, I suggest we clear this area and assume no quarter. Before I kill you, though, I shall permit the Prior here to administer the viaticum, so you're provided for on your final journey. Agreed? Anything to add, Brother Monk?'

'Only that this is not justice,' Thomas tells him.

Riven pretends to be shocked.

'Not justice, Brother Monk? Not justice? Yet here we are, quite equal before the Lord.'

'You are a trained knight.'

This is what the Dean had called him. Riven is sidling towards him across the grass, weighing and measuring the staff, testing its properties.

'Perhaps the good Lord knew I'd be called on to face this sort of thing, hey? Perhaps He instructed my father to instil in me a skill at arms? Perhaps that's it. Perhaps He knew you'd turn out to be a miserable sinner and so made your father a cowardly little runt who would rather teach his son to fuck a pig than fight a man?'

'My father died in France, facing the French, at Formigny.'

Riven straightens.

'Did he? Well, I am sorry to hear it, but you are not alone in losing a father in battle. My own died at St Albans.'

As Riven mentions St Albans he flicks his wrist and the tip of his quarterstaff flashes past Thomas's nose. Thomas remains motionless.

'I am a canon of the Order of Gilbert of Sempringham,' he says. 'If I am to be tried for a crime that I did not commit then it should be done in Court Ecclesiastical, not this mockery.'

Riven lowers his quarterstaff and looks comically disappointed. The giant laughs again.

'I cannot fight you, Brother Monk,' Riven says. 'Unless you strike me first. Now what will it take to get you to fight? I have impugned you and your father already, so now what about your mother? What can I say about her? A whore whelping in a ditch? No, no. I sense I am on the wrong track here.'

Thomas shakes his head, not in denial but in pity, and the gesture instantly brings the tip of Riven's staff within a finger's breadth of his right eye. Thomas blinks. Riven lowers the staff.

'Still nothing,' he says, and he turns his back and walks away. Then he clicks his fingers.

'Of course,' he says, turning back. 'I know! I have it! Louther!'

'Aye?' one of the men sitting on the wall answers.

'The beads,' Riven says, clicking his fingers again and holding out his cupped hand. 'Hand me the beads.'

Louther digs in his coat and pulls out a string of beads. He tosses them over. Even before Riven catches them Thomas knows what they are.

'Where did you get them?' he asks. His throat is blocked. He can hear pounding in his ears.

'Oh, I think you know, don't you, Brother Monk? Found them this morning. Just after sun-up, and only after a struggle, I'll admit, but they often start out that way, don't they? She enjoyed it for a bit, but Morrant here is a passionate creature, aren't you, Morrant? Tend to take things too far, don't you?'

The giant laughs and nods his head in cheerful agreement.

Now the quarterstaff feels light in Thomas's hands, just as it had the day before, and he feels a surge of energy, an empowering rage. He steps forward and flicks the staff up.

Riven steps back, avoiding the blow. He laughs and tucks the rosary inside his shirt.

'So,' he says. 'Now you'll fight.'

The first blow comes in low and hard and fantastically fast from the right. It clips Thomas's staff aside and cracks into his knee. Pain shoots up his leg. Before the next blow comes, Thomas throws himself backwards and Riven's staff hums through empty space.

'Ha!' Riven laughs. 'Not bad, Brother Monk. Quicker than your father, hey?'

Before Riven has even finished speaking, Thomas has to fling his staff up to catch the next blow. He grunts with the effort, but his clogs slip under him. He falls to his knees. Riven leaps forward and kicks him in the chest. Thomas falls back. Then Riven is on him. Thomas gets his staff up in time to stop Riven pressing his own across his throat. He is pinned to the mud though. Riven is a bulky man, his skin pitted, his breath smelling of salted pork and wine. His eye is puffed and purpled, the eyeball, barely visible, red. Thomas bucks and crashes an elbow into Riven's bruise. He brings his knee up with a jerk that makes contact.

Riven grunts and rolls clear.

Thomas is on his feet fast but Riven is faster still. Before Thomas has grounded himself, Riven charges. Thomas shoots his staff out, but Riven's move is a feint. The next second Thomas is face down in the sodden grass with his head ringing.

'Too easy,' he hears Riven say and then he feels the sole of the knight's boot on the back of his neck. For a moment he can do nothing about it, does not know what to do about it. He looks across at the Prior whose mouth is open in the shape of an egg. The Dean is frowning and his fists are clenched.

Then Thomas thrashes smartly, like an eel in the mud. He catches Riven's other heel and pulls. With a bellow of surprise Riven goes sprawling on to his backside. Thomas is up on his feet but Riven is still the faster and Thomas feels a blinding pain above his ear and he crashes to the grass again.

This time he rolls. He picks up his staff and is on his feet to use it to block the next blow, a simple chop delivered from above, and the next, a swing that comes from the other end of the staff that would have caught him between his legs.

Riven is still smiling as he makes another move, but Thomas sees it coming and steps inside. He takes the sting out of the blow with the tail of his own staff and then manages a glancing rake across Riven's fingers.

Both step back.

Riven's smile has gone. Thomas can smell his own blood.

Riven comes at him again, a flurry of feints, then two blows. Thomas stops the first but is too slow with the second. Riven brings his staff up under Thomas's arm and in a practised move he turns him, stamps on his clog and smashes the heel of his hand into Thomas's throat.

Thomas sags, drops his staff, and for a moment he cannot breathe for the pain. He falls backwards but lands with a jolt that rouses him in time to duck. Riven's staff passes over his ear. Thomas snatches it and uses Riven's strength to right himself, jerking Riven off balance. In one move he collects his staff from the mud and swings it around in a short sweep that Riven does not see it through his half-closed eye. It catches Riven behind the knee and he leaps backwards with the pain.

'Not bad, Brother Monk,' Riven says, 'but this has gone on long enough, hasn't it?'

He makes a feint that Thomas sees, then another that he does not, and then the full weight of his staff whirls around in a blurring arc and crashes across Thomas's skull as he tries to duck.

He is face down in the mud again and with the pain comes the blood. It is hot and blinding. He gets to his knees and wipes the blood with his sleeve in time to see Riven come at him again. He manages to parry the first blow and evade the next, but then he takes a short arm punch that rattles his teeth. He feels sluggish and his sight blurs.

The fight is leaving him and Riven is circling him, ready for the end.

He blinks the blood from his eyes, triggering another attack, a rolling series of blows that would have killed, but this time Thomas trips on his sodden cassock, drops on one knee, and ducks his head as Riven's staff passes over. Then he lunges. Again Riven is blinded in the malfunctioning eye and Thomas gets through the mêlée of Riven's pumping arms and into the soft area below his sternum. He feels the contact, doughy and soft. He rams the staff up.

Riven stops, gasps. His eyes bulge, then swim, then roll. He staggers, falling back, tipping on his heels, powerless. He drops his quarterstaff and thumps to ground and lies there with his tongue out; his face is grey-green, his breath a groaning wheeze.

Thomas gets to his feet and pulls his muddy cassock down.

He glances across at the Prior who has still not moved, his mouth still gaping. The Dean is urging him to do something with his staff. Bring it down.

Thomas plants his legs either side of Riven's body. He raises his staff vertically. He can bring it down now directly into Riven's unguarded face and it will be the end. God's will be done. He pauses. Blood drips from his wounds on to Riven below. Riven's face is puckered with the pain and almost babyish.

Thomas leans in to lend weight to the blow, bunches his muscles, lifts the staff and plunges it down, driving it with all his might, deep into the mud, a finger's width from Riven's ear.

Then he turns and walks away, leaving the staff upright in the ground.

The Dean meets him with a cloth and a smirk.

'You are wasted here, Brother Thomas,' he says, mopping his face. 'Fooling about with your psalter when you should be fighting the French. But why didn't you kill him?'

Thomas can think of nothing to say. He flinches when the Dean touches the weal on his skull.

'Probably wise,' the Dean mutters, 'but then I wish you'd let him kill you. We've a pretty problem now.'

Riven's three retainers are gathered around him, helping him to his feet while the infirmarian hovers. Riven is hacking something up and cannot stand straight.

'Brother Stephen,' Thomas asks, 'when you brought me food this morning, did you say one of the sisters has gone missing?'

The Dean nods. He looks grim.

'Found her now, though.'

'Is she well?'

The Dean lowers his voice.

'Dead,' he says. 'So the Prioress says. We'll bury her tomorrow.'

It takes a moment for this to settle in.

'Riven has her rosary beads,' Thomas says.

The Dean stares at him, calculating the value of the news, then he lunges suddenly, shoving Thomas aside.

'Look you!' he shouts. A sword blade hums through the space where Thomas had been standing, and the man Riven called Louther staggers among them, off balance. The Dean grabs his padded coat and hauls him onwards so that he crashes over the cloister wall, dropping his sword as he goes. Thomas turns, sees the giant lolloping towards them with that axe, a cruel confection of pick, spike and blade that might have been better employed to murder an ox.

'Run!' the Dean bellows at Thomas. 'Run, Brother Thomas.'

He snatches up Louther's sword and charges at the giant, aiming a savage cut to his face.

The giant bats the blade away with a simple chop of his axe and the sword is wrenched from the Dean's grip. The giant raises the axe to kill him, but Thomas has found Riven's staff and runs at him. The giant sees him and diverts his axe to catch Thomas's clumsy blow. He flicks his wrist, catching the staff under the steel pick, smashing it from Thomas's grasp. Then he swats Thomas with a backhand punch that sends him scrabbling in the mud.

Strange whirling lights fill his vision. The giant moves towards him.

The Dean takes up the staff, cracks it against the fourth man's skull, who reels away, and then he flies at the giant, diverting him while Thomas rolls out of his reach. Riven is up, but still bent and clutching Thomas's planted staff for support. Thomas shoves him backwards, unplugs the staff and turns back, just in time to see the giant block another of the Dean's attacks. The giant takes the blows on the fleshy part of his arm without even flinching.

The Dean steps back, looking up at the giant with something like awe.

'Run, Brother Thomas!' he shouts over his shoulder. 'For the love of God, just run!'

Then he wades in again, hacking at the giant, and again the giant parries the blows with ease. The giant has a blank smile on his lips as he aims a swipe that would have taken the Dean's head off. But now the fourth man is up again, coming at the Dean from behind. Before Thomas can move he smells wine and feels something touch the skin below his ear. The point of a knife.

Riven.

'See what happens, shall we, hey?' Riven says. 'Against the law to kill a bull without first baiting it, you know?'

It is over soon enough. The giant feints. The Dean doesn't fall for it. The fourth man swings at him and the Dean blocks it and even pushes him back, but then the giant feints again. This time the Dean is drawn. He dives forward, aiming his staff at the giant's throat, but the giant steps aside and swings his axe blade down and there is a noise like that of a shovel in dirt.

The Dean's bellow of rage turns into a wailing scream. He staggers forward with blood guttering from a gash from throat to sternum. He manages a few steps before dropping to his knees in a slew of blood. His wrist hangs to his knees. Blood is everywhere. He falls forward into it, and it seethes on to the muddy grass where he lies twitching. A moment later he is still, the blood slows and its smell drifts in the breeze.

There is silence. The canons stand in a row, their faces a line of pale coins.

'Well, that went all right,' Riven says. 'Now it's your turn.'

Thomas feels the knife prick his skin, but he no longer cares. If he is to die then let it be now, and let it be quick. He brings his wooden clog crashing down on the toe of Riven's boot. Riven roars and Thomas turns and crashes his elbow into his open mouth. Riven tumbles back, his shirt open, the rosary beads sliding into the mud. Thomas bends to take them.

The giant starts towards him.

'Stop!' It is the Prior, his arms raised, his voice high with emotion. 'Stop in the name of God! Stop in the name of all that is sacred!'

Without breaking stride the giant chops him in the face with the back of his hand. The Prior collapses and the giant kicks his body aside like a child's plaything and advances on Thomas.

Thomas stands a moment before finally doing as the Dean instructed. He tucks the beads away and turns and runs for the cloister roof, hauling himself scrabbling up across the slates.

'Kill him!' he hears Riven scream, and he feels the giant's fingers on his cassock. He kicks out and pulls free. The giant tries again but misses and Thomas scrambles away, up over the roof of the refectory with a clatter of his clogs, the tiles warm beneath his palms, and then down heavily in the yard. He staggers to his feet.

Through the door behind him he can hear the crash of someone running through the frater house. He unbars the beggars' gate and hurries through. The rain has softened the ground, and the millwheel is turning again. Smoke rises from blackened circles where Riven's men lit cooking fires the night before, but they've moved on and now the furlong is deserted save for two of the lay brethren, shovelling something down by the river's bank by the ford.

Thomas stops. Where to? He cannot think. He turns and the giant is in the yard, ducking through the gateway after him, moving fast on his bare feet, that great axe still in his hand. Thomas catches a glimpse of someone moving down by the river, near the mill, where the ferryman's lighter lies still upturned on the bank. He cuts that way.

'Help!' he shouts. 'Help me! Jesus!'

Whomsoever he'd seen there is gone now or maybe had always been a flit of his imagination. He grabs the lighter. It is a rough-built, flat-bottomed thing, turned over, and heavier than he'd thought. He bends and tries to right it, but isn't strong enough. He looks for the ferryman's boat pole: if he cannot use it to lever the boat over, then at least he can use it as a weapon.

The giant comes on.

The pole is nowhere to be found.

There is nothing for it.

He turns and faces the giant.

'Why?' he shouts. 'Why me?'

The question seems to hold no meaning for the giant. His face betrays the same emotion a man might feel milking a cow or washing a bowl. He holds the axe at his side as if he has no need for it now. He towers over Thomas. Thomas throws a punch. The giant catches it, his hand hard as a plank. He twists Thomas's fist over and forces him to his knees.

'Why?' Thomas cries again. 'What did I do to you?'

The giant says nothing, but puts aside the axe and seizes Thomas's shoulder. He lifts him as if he were a doll of plaited corn. Thomas kicks him between the legs. There is no reaction. It is as if he does not feel pain. The giant grabs his throat and Thomas can feel each fingertip. The giant forces him backwards on to the upturned boat. Thomas struggles and kicks but it is no use. The hand tightens. He feels the giant stroke his cheek, and he sees there is an almost tender look in the giant's eyes, but then Thomas sees the ball of his filthy thumb coming down on his right eyeball.

He screams.

4

When the bell rings the alarm, the Prioress ushers the sisters into the chapel and locks the iron-bound door behind them. The candles have already been lit for Mass and the flames shiver as the women kneel in uncertain silence and pray.

Katherine watches Alice in alarm. Her earlier resolve has leached away, along with all colour in her face, and she rocks on her knees, weeping incoherent prayers while her fingers punish her rosary beads. When at last the sedate tolling of the bell signals the end of the crisis, the sisters rise as one and clutch each other's hands. They are forbidden to speak in the church, lest they interfere with the prayers of the canons beyond the wall that bisects the nave, but gestures are enough. Alice puts her thin arms around Katherine and crushes her with a hug.

At length they return to their places and kneel again and silently give thanks to God for delivering them from they know not what. Katherine gives Him thanks not only for the delivery from the horsemen, but – perhaps more heartfelt now that the former danger is passed – that the canon has not been seen in the cloister.

She cannot imagine what her punishment might have been had he been seen, for since the day she had joined the Priory, all those years ago, the Prioress had forever been inflicting ever crueller punishments. Katherine had still been warm with the memories of her mother's love when she had come, or so she now imagined, and the sudden change in her life had seemed almost unendurably hard, but as the years passed, she'd come to see that the cloistered life needn't be so harsh, only that the Prioress went out of her way to make it so.

In the early years she had spent weeks at a stretch alone in her cell subsisting only on rye bread and lentils. If she were lucky: salted fish. She passed the hours on her knees, praying for she knew not what, to a God of whom she was unsure, but as her life progressed from one hardship to another, each visited upon her for something she did not understand or did not do, she began to wonder if God was the merciful deity that the priests espoused. She began to wonder whether He was not an absent God, or perhaps a powerless one, for she could not believe he was a vengeful one, who wished her to suffer this way.

When she spoke of her thoughts to one of the other sisters, a girl to whom she believed herself close, the Prioress heard within the hour and that evening the whole community was called to witness Sister Joan holding her down while the Prioress thrashed her with a scourge, grunting at each stroke. The sin of Pride was deadly, the Prioress had gasped, and it needed eradicating. This was the first of many beatings Katherine received over the years and now, more than a decade later, the skin on her back and legs is capped by a hardened matt of needle-fine scars.

Only later was she entrusted with the daily task of taking out the Prioress's nightly soil and her pisspot, but when Katherine had complained of it, had suggested the lay sisters should deal with it as they did the rest of the nuns' excrement, she was beaten, and made to carry the bucket away while the blood dried against her cassock.

Now she leans forward to gain a view down the line of the sisters to where the Prioress kneels in profile, her heavy hands resting on the prie-dieu in an effigy of piety. She is not a pleasure to look upon, with a big jaw and heavy brows that glower even in prayer. She is immensely strong though, with a man's shoulders, and when inflamed it is possible to see the blood of her Viking forefathers running through her veins.

Katherine watches as she rises now, her prayers at an end, and with a chopping gesture she instructs the sisters to rise too, to fall into their customary lines. After a pause she leads them across the nave to where Sister Joan stands at the north door. Katherine and Alice fall in beside one another and walk with downcast eyes, but as they pass Sister Joan, the older nun leans forward and pinches Katherine's elbow to make her look up.

Joan's eyes are like slits, and her tiny, pointed teeth are bared in a grin. She is laughing at something and pointing at Katherine. Katherine feels cold wash over her.

Of course the canon has been seen.

Almost blind with despair, Katherine follows the sisters through the cloister to the chapter house. Stark within, the room is dominated by a dais on which the Prioress sits like a queen, her head bowed in prayer. The stone floor is spread with rushes that sigh underfoot as they enter and take their places on the low bench and still without speaking each sister raises her hood to cover her face in prayer. When the Prioress has finished her own prayers she would ordinarily read to them from the Martyrology, but today she reads from the Rule of St Augustine, chapter four.

'The fourth chapter of the Rule', she announces, 'deals with safeguarding chastity.'

Katherine feels something twist inside.

'What should you do,' the Prioress asks, 'if you notice within your sister a wantonness of the eye? Would you admonish her so that the fault does not multiply, but stands corrected? Or would you treat it as an infirmarian might treat a wound?'

The Prioress looks around as if for an answer. There is none. She closes the book and steps away from the lectern.

'Let me tell you this remarkable thing,' she says, 'for it is an example that might inspire you. During the time of Bishop Henry there was a convent of virgins at Watton in the province of York, to the north of here, and they took in an oblate, a girl of five. She

passed her girlhood happily enough, in prayer and silent contempla-
tion, but as she grew older, she began to show signs of girlish
abandon.'

The Prioress pauses to let her words sink in.

Katherine's eye is drawn to the tight-shut door.

'Now one day,' the Prioress carries on, 'when some lay brothers
were brought into the cloister to carry out some works, the eye of
this girl fell upon one of their number, a handsome boy in the full
bloom of youth.'

There is a stirring among the sisters, all of whom can imagine
such a thing, though few have seen it for themselves. Alice at last
seems to have understood what is being said, for she begins moaning
and swaying again, as she had in the nave.

The Prioress continues, her gaze avoiding Katherine: 'And this
youth noticed the girl, too, and so it was that each watered in the
other the seeds of desire, and soon their nods turned to gestures
and they sought one another out in the secret darkness of night.'

The sisters gasp.

'Block your ears, oh brides of heaven!' the Prioress pronounces,
enjoying herself, 'for that night this girl walked out a virgin of
Christ and in the next moment she was corrupted in the flesh as she
had been in the spirit!'

'Shame,' a sister mutters. 'For shame!'

Others agree. The Prioress lets them calm themselves before she
begins again: 'Soon the evidence of the nun's wickedness was all
too clear,' she says, 'and when the truth emerged that the girl was
with child, the shocked virgins of the community clapped their hands
together and fell on her, ripping the veil from her head. They
whipped her without mercy! Some argued she should be tied to a
tree and burned over charcoal. Others cried out that she should be
skinned alive!'

Alice clutches her rosary to her mouth, kissing the crucified Christ.

'But mercy prevailed,' the Prioress soothes, 'and the sinner was put in a cell, with her hands manacled to the wall, while chains were attached to her ankles and passed through a window to a heavy log of yew, so that all that night she was stretched by its weight.

'The next day the sisters asked the canons to lay hands on the youth who had occasioned these ill deeds. One of the canons – a slight lad with a girlish frame – was dressed in the sister's veil and sent to sit in the appointed place at the appointed hour for their meeting. Sure enough the corrupt youth approached her and fell on him whom he thought a sister!'

Again the sisters gasp.

'Burning with lust, he was as a stallion brought to mare! But then those canons present, concealed in the undergrowth, jumped out and administered a bitter antidote to this lust with their staffs, beating him mightily so to extinguish his fever.'

Alice is delirious now, mumbling an endless prayer, dropping to her knees, righting herself, and all the other sisters are murmuring and chanting.

Katherine can think of nothing but escape.

The Prioress holds out a hand to calm them.

'If it had ended there,' she went on, raising a finger, 'if it had ended there, then this shining example of zeal in defence of chastity might have been obscured for ever, but the virgins of the community asked the canons to hand the wretch over, as if to glean some information from him, and when they had him in their hands, such was their clamour for virtue's reward, that they laid the youth out and, summoning their sister from her cell, they placed in her hands a knife taken from the kitchen and they forced her to unman the monster!'

A sister screams. Alice pitches against Sister Maria, who staggers and cannot hold her. She slips and falls to the ground, her head bouncing hollow on the flagstones. The infirmarian scuttles over and the sisters mill around her fallen form. Katherine steps back, and while the others are clustered around Alice, she turns and rushes for the door, not pausing to glance at the Prioress, who remains standing at the lectern.

Katherine throws open the heavy chapter house door and hurtles out into the cold white of daylight. From the tail of her eye she sees a blur of dark cloth. She manages two more steps until she feels a barking pain on her shin. She is tripped and goes sprawling in the snow. She tastes blood in her mouth. She looks up to see Sister Joan stepping over her, raising a staff and crashing it down on her, and after that, nothing.

She wakes on her back in one of the stables. Her feet are tied to an iron hoop set high in one wall, and Sister Joan is looming over her, tying her hands together above her head. When she is happy with the knot, Joan runs the rope from her hands through another hoop set on the wall behind Katherine's head and she pulls on the rope, stretching Katherine so that she is lifted off the ground. The cords burn her wrists and ankles but she will not cry out. She will not let Sister Joan see her weep.

Joan ties off the rope and leans over her for a moment.

'We ought to peel your skin,' she says, 'like they wanted to do to that nun.'

Katherine feels the older nun's rough palm sweeping over her leg, from ankle to thigh, pushing away the skirts of her cassock so that they hang bunched around her waist. Katherine can hear her breathing thicken. After a moment Joan turns and leaves, locking the door behind her. Katherine lets out a sob and her tears run to meet the fine strands of hair at her temples. There is no air or light in the stable and she is unable to hear the ringing of the bell that has until that morning ordered her life, so she cannot say how long she is there. It feels like a lifetime and Katherine has soiled herself twice before the door is opened and the light from a pair of rush candles spills in. Two sisters – one of them Joan – step aside to admit the Prioress.

She sniffs in disgust.

'Sister Katherine,' she begins, 'the sisterhood is roused and wonders what to do with you for the shame you have brought on our community.'

Katherine tries to speak but her throat is constricted.

'I have asked them to let you leave the priory,' the Prioress continues, 'to go your own way in the world, but they respond that you will only broadcast our failure abroad and bring yet more shame on us.'

A silence lasts. The Prioress looks Katherine over, exasperated.

'The nun of Watton cried out, child,' she says. 'She cried out to be beaten. She cried out that she deserved to be punished! Yet you lie in silence, as if your sin is worthy of neither comment nor shame.'

'Holy Mother,' Katherine whispers, finding her voice, 'I spoke but three words to the canon. He came to my rescue as I was being pursued by men on horses beyond the walls. Had he not done so I would now be dead.'

'Ha! Even now the devil disports in your mouth, child! For you make no mention of our Sister Alice.'

Katherine cannot stop herself gasping. She did not want Alice mentioned, to be blamed, to be involved at all.

'Sister Alice said nothing to the canon. Not one word! She did not even look at him!'

'But the canon looked at her! She will be reciting one thousand Credos in the chapel all night tonight and in the morning she will be taking up your penitential task of carrying the bucket from my cell to the dung heap—'

'No!'

Katherine writhes but the Prioress launches forward so that her broad face fills her vision. Her breath is septic.

'No?' she asks. 'No? You dare command me?'

'Holy Mother, you cannot send Sister Alice out to the river tomorrow. Those men will be there. I know it! They will be waiting for her. For all that is holy, I beg of you!'

Her voice rises in a scream as the door is slammed.

The long night passes. Katherine wakes three or four times – never conscious for more than a few instants – and each time she hopes she is waking from a nightmare. Sometime towards the morning she is roused with a bucket of water sluiced over her body by a figure in the doorway. Her body arches, pulling on the muscles that have cramped in the night, grinding the ropes deep into the wounds in her wrists and ankles. Sister Joan is there with a knife and she slashes through the cords that bind Katherine's hands to the wall. Katherine crashes to the ground. She does not scream. She has nothing left to give. She lies there as the Prioress comes in and looks her over again.

'Is she alive?' she asks.

Joan nudges her body with a clog.

'She is.'

'Get her on her feet and have her carry two buckets of water to the infirmary. She has a job to do.'

The Prioress leaves and Joan picks Katherine up by her armpits.

'Walk,' she says.

She takes her hands away. Katherine collapses. Joan tries again. Katherine collapses again. Joan hauls her to her useless feet and drags her from the room. As the blood begins to circulate Katherine cries out and throws herself down with pain. Sister Joan half pushes, half drags her outside into the yard.

It is dawn, and rain is falling. The snow has turned to slush.

The bell above is ringing a slow clap, like a knell, and she pulls on the well rope so slowly Sister Joan loses patience and helps with the bucket, pouring the water out into two small ones and even helping her to her feet. But then she walks behind her, cursing her, calling her a devil, a whore and worse.

The stone steps are the worst. The pain makes her dizzy. At the top Joan opens the door of the infirmary and pushes her staggering across the rushes. She has never been permitted to visit the whitewashed room above the calefactory. It is long and low, lined with two rows of six straw mattresses on each side and at the far end of the aisle, like an altar in a nave, a broad table dominated by the infirmarian's bottles of tinctures and bags of herbs and her pestle and mortar.

At this far end of the room the Prioress stands hunched like a bird of prey over one of the mattresses. She glances up and then turns back to the mattress.

'Here at last,' she says.

Joan pushes Katherine, who hobbles down between the beds, the sound of her clogs softened by the rushes. Someone is lying on the mattress, covered in a linen winding cloth.

It is Alice. She is dead. Her veil is gone and her pale hair lies in a slack clot on the sheet beside her. Bruises cover her neck and her right eye is swollen. Her chin looks as if it had been rubbed with the same sand they use to clean the floors and there are what look like animal bites across her throat.

Katherine feels as if something had been pulled from inside her. Her spirit hurts as much as her body. She feels rage bloom within.

'I told you—' she starts, but the Prioress cuts her off.

'If the child has come to grief it is through her own fault. She was once a fair and virginal example to us all but some corrupting malignity overcame her in the last days of her life, and she chose the devil over the Lord.'

'No,' Katherine says. 'You did this. You caused this.'

'Silence,' the Prioress says.

Joan hits her.

'Sister Alice was lured away from the path of righteousness by the many-horned legions of the devil.'

Joan hits her again, harder. Katherine staggers forward and puts the buckets down. The three women look at one another over Alice's dead body.

'It was you,' Katherine says. 'You did this just as much as those men.'

Before Joan can hit her again, Katherine turns and catches her fist.

'Enough!' she says and she twists the arm with a strength that surprises her. Joan flushes red and pulls free.

'Anger is a deadly sin, my child,' the Prioress murmurs. 'And for your penance you can now wash our sister for burial. I will send some of the lay sisters with a coffin. The sooner she is buried the better.'

When they leave, Katherine stands over Alice, and, now that she is alone, her tears pour down her cheeks and fall on the rough material of Alice's winding sheet. At length she takes a cloth from the infirmarian's table and, kneeling by the head of Alice's bed, she dips it into the bucket and begins gently to wipe her forehead clean.

As she does so, she begins to envy Alice. Her time in this world is done. She has journeyed ahead to a place where there will be neither tears nor suffering. Death is a release.

The bruises and welts on Alice's face only become more livid as Katherine wipes away the dried blood and spit and tears. She smooths the cloth across her unblemished eye and it is then that the doubt begins. She puts the flannel aside and presses the tips of her fingers against those bruised lips.

Is it her imagination?

She puts her ear to Alice's chest and thinks she hears something but cannot be sure. She hurries to the table where the infirmarian keeps her medicaments in neat rows, the largest jars at the back. She does not know what she wants or needs and the jars and bags are labelled with words she cannot read. She unstoppers one, then another, removing the pig's bladder seals and sniffing each until in one – a large green glass bottle – a sharp smell brings tears to her eyes, sets her coughing and clears her head. She hurries back to Alice and pours some of the black viscous contents on to the cloth. She reseals the bottle and drops it on the mattress next to Alice's, then holds the cloth below her nose.

There is an instant reaction. Alice's eyeballs flutter.

Alice is alive.

A moment later she opens her eyes and stares at Katherine. The clarity of her white eyeballs against the bruising all around is astonishing. Then her hand moves. The fingers creep out to touch Katherine's.

'Stay here,' Katherine says. 'I'll get Sister Infirmarian.'

Alice moves her head an inch and coughs.

'Be still,' Katherine says. 'Don't move.'

She crashes down the stairs and out into the cloister. Beyond, the Prioress stands by the well in conversation with Sister Joan. Both turn.

'She's alive,' Katherine says. 'Alice is still alive. Where is the infirmarian?'

The Prioress is startled.

'She is in the almonry,' she says. 'Quick, girl, summon her.'

Katherine stumbles across the garth and out across the yard to the almonry. But here the door is locked. She hammers and pulls at the handles. There is no give. She shouts. There is no one there.

She retraces her steps. The cloister is empty and the Prioress and Joan have gone. Another sister sits in her carrel poring over a page. Katherine makes her start.

'Sister, have you seen the infirmarian?'

'She goes to the library after Mass,' the sister tells her.

The library is on the other side of the cloister, up a small flight of steps above a storeroom. Another room Katherine has never visited. The infirmarian is there, standing at the lectern over a large book.

'Sister Meredith,' Katherine breathes. 'Come. Sister Alice is alive.'

The infirmarian looks puzzled.

'I am glad to hear it, Sister,' she says.

'Then come. She needs you.'

Sister Meredith leaves the book and follows Katherine out of the library and down the stairs. Katherine holds the door for her at the bottom and guides her across the garth.

'Where are we going?' she asks.

'The infirmary, of course.'

'What is Alice doing there?'

'She has been attacked. I thought you would have known?'

Something is wrong. The old woman mutters as they make their way up the steps to the infirmary. The Prioress and Sister Joan are there already, beside Alice. When the door opens they both step away.

Something inside Katherine goes cold.

Sister Meredith hurries past them and kneels by Alice. Her hands play over the girl's face and neck. Alice's eyes are closed again and her hair is messed up on the sheet behind her head. Sister Meredith fetches a small copper bowl from her table, places it on Alice's chest and pours in water from an earthenware jug. Then she stops to watch. After a moment she turns to Katherine.

'But she is dead?' she says.

The Prioress and Sister Joan are both staring at her.

The infirmarian leans forward and opens one of Alice's eyelids.

'Yes,' she says. 'You see? These marks? A sure sign that she died unable to breathe.'

But Katherine is not looking at Alice. She is staring at the long scratch on the side of Sister Joan's neck.

'Your neck,' she says.

Joan touches the scratch and then looks at the bloodied tips of her fingers. She smiles nervously, sharp teeth on her thin lips, a furtive expression.

Katherine cannot endure it. She lunges and before Joan can raise her hands she is on her. She knocks her back over on to the mattress and her hands seek out the neck, her thumbs in the doughy throat. But Joan bucks. She arches her back and screams and after a moment the Prioress grabs Katherine's shoulders and hauls her off and throws her across the room. Katherine lands badly, but Joan still screams. She is thrashing and scrabbling as if trying to get something off her back. And then there is blood frothing from her mouth and nose. It is staining her teeth, pouring down her chin.

The Prioress is frozen where she stands, hands clapped to her cheeks. Joan is choking on something. She rolls face down on the mattress and all three women see the shards of green glass driven into her back just as the stench of the medicine rises up and washes over them. It catches in their throats and burns their eyes and sends them coughing back up the infirmary.

This time there is no one to stop her. Katherine is through the door, down the stairs and across the yard, staggering past the very spot where she'd seen the canon, and out of the beggars' gate. She has no plan in mind, only flight, and she no longer cares what happens to her next.

Snow remains in patches across the fens, but there is more grass and mud, and there are black fire circles on the fields, and the sweet smell of cold wood smoke and human shit hangs in the air. She limps out across the furlong, making for the hamlet at the river ford. Two lay brothers are there at the river's edge with shovels. She turns from them to the ferryman's lighter, on the riverbank below the mill. If she can right it and somehow get it into the water, then she might follow the river's current wherever it will take her.

She crosses the furlong and tries to lift the boat, but it is too heavy. Vestiges of ice cement it in place. She finds the ferryman's pole, a long staff of ash. She is about to try to use it to lever the boat upright when she sees a movement by the canons' beggars' gate. Someone running. A man. At first she thinks he is coming for her. She panics and looks for a place to hide in the shelter of the water-mill, behind a pile of millstones. It is a canon, she sees, running desperately. Then she sees another man emerge.

'Dear God!' she says aloud.

It is the giant from the day before. He is still barefooted, still with that axe. She looks again at the canon. It is him. He runs towards her. He is also making for the boat. He tries to roll it over but gives up just as easily as she had. He goes looking for something and then starts with panic as the giant approaches.

'Why?' he shouts. 'Why me?'

The giant ignores him.

The canon tries to punch him, but the giant catches his fist and twists his arm. He falls to the ground.

'Why?' the canon cries out once more. 'What did I do to you?'

The giant plucks him up without effort. The canon kicks out but the giant has him by the throat. He is carrying him at arm's length. The canon struggles, still kicking, tearing at his hands, but he is forced backwards and pinned against the upturned boat. Still he kicks but it is no use. The giant leans forward and switches hands, so that he is holding the canon down with his left hand while his right moves up to the canon's face. The canon tries to pull away but the giant is too strong. He seems to stroke his cheek and look into his eyes and then he places his thumb over the canon's eyeball. The canon screams.

Without thinking Katherine leaves the stones and rushes the last few paces to the boat and, with all her remaining strength, she brings the ferryman's pole down on the back of the giant's head. It makes a crack she feels in her knees.

The giant lets the canon go and stands, as if he has just thought of something he ought to do. He turns and looks down at her. He is confused.

She takes a step back, lifts the pole again. The giant takes a step towards her. He stretches his hands out. She is about to bring it down on him when his face seems to go blank, his eyes roll up into his head, he cants to one side, staggers, then slips, and finally falls to the ground.

After a moment he is still.

The canon is gasping, muttering some prayer, his hands clapped over his eyes. After a moment he stops, removes his hands and now he too looks at her. Then he lifts himself to peer down at the giant's body.

'Is he dead?' she asks.

The canon gets up and looks at the giant more closely.

'I don't think so,' he says.

She is only partly relieved. There is a pause. A breeze has picked up. The rainclouds have retreated, and the sky is a scrim of white clouds again. They look to the walls of the priory, then at each other.

'Are you expelled?' he asks.

Katherine nods.

'I was seen talking to you,' she says.

She looks back at the priory. Three figures have appeared in the canons' beggars' gateway, one limping, coming down towards them. All are carrying swords. The men from the day before.

'Brother?' she points.

'They will kill us this time,' he says. He stoops for the giant's axe. It is a fearsome thing: four feet of chamfered oak pole with long steel points at both ends, its axe blade balanced by a vicious pick. It is crusted with dried blood, as if dipped in brown lace, and it looks oddly light in his hands.

'You cannot fight them,' she says. 'Not three of them, not even with that thing.'

'God is by my side,' he says. 'He will provide.'

'Where was God when he was about to put out your eyes?' she asks, pointing at the giant.

The canon flinches. He stares at her open-mouthed.

'Besides,' she says, hurrying him on past her blasphemy, 'God has provided. Look. We must take this boat. Come. Help me.'

She slides the boat pole under the lighter's edge and tries again to right it. Still it will not move.

Seeing her struggle, he joins her, pushing the axe under the boat's side and helping her lever it over, revealing grey grass and a family of dead rats. He puts the axe aside and helps shove the lighter across the mud and down into the water where the river is running high, thronging with brown meltwater, the ice long gone.

The men from the priory are running now, down across the furlong. They are shouting.

He stands with his feet in the water and holds the boat steady while she throws in the pole and then clambers in after it.

'Come!' she says, holding out a hand. 'Come!'

Still he hesitates. Is he mad?

'You cannot fight three,' she shouts. 'They will kill you! Then me! They'll kill us both. Come!'

This decides him. He collects the axe and slides it into the boat. Then he launches himself in after it, sending the boat out into the rolling current. The boat staggers, dips as if it will sink, then rises and spins in the water.

The men are near now. She can see their expressions. One has blood on his face. They are shouting. They run past the giant and the one in a white shirt comes down the bank and wades into the water up to his thighs. They are too late and they know it. The man in the water smacks its surface in frustration.

The canon plunges the boat pole into the water and heaves, sending the boat off into the current as the two men on the bank start following them. After a few moments the one in the water wades back on to dry land and shouts after the canon. She cannot make out his words and in a little while the boat crosses the ford and the man in the river is lost to sight.

Katherine stares back over her shoulder long after, though, watching as first the roofs and then, finally, the priory's church tower slip away until at last, for the first time in her memory, she is beyond its sight, floating in a land unknown.

PART TWO

Across the Narrow Sea,
February—June 1460

5

The sister sits ahead and keeps watch with the giant's axe across her knees. She is rubbing her blistered feet and Thomas can think of nothing to say to her.

Finally she speaks.

'Where shall we go?'

It is a good question.

'We must make our way to Canterbury,' he tells her with more certainty than he feels. 'We must seek redress from the Prior of All. He will hear our case and see that justice is done.'

The sister turns to him and studies him as he talks. Her eyes are blue, her face paler than vellum.

'Where is this Canterbury?' she asks.

Thomas does not know.

'It is where the Prior of All is,' he says.

There is a pause.

'So you do not know?' she says.

'No,' he admits.

She nods and turns her back on him again. He feels only confusion. To think that the day before he had been looking forward to rubbing gold leaf over a letter T he'd built up from the page with gesso. She says nothing more and after a while the mist begins to clear and a flock of gulls wheels above them, wings black against the pale clouds.

'More snow,' he says, and thinks of the night to come.

Then there is a crash in the rushes, and a shout from the bank.

'Oh Great God above.'

It is the giant. He comes pushing through a stand of reeds and is almost on them before Thomas heaves on the boat pole and sends the boat lurching across the river.

'Leave us be!' the sister cries. 'For the love of the Trinity, leave us be!'

The giant comes down at them, but stops at the water's edge. He looks about wildly and shouts something unintelligible. He seems stuck.

'Merciful Mary,' Thomas breathes. 'He's scared of the water.'

The giant stares at them, deciding what to do. Then scrambles along the river's edge, ripping his way through the thickets. Ahead of him a bittern takes flight with a slow clap of wings.

If Thomas can just keep up this rhythm with the boat pole, and if he can stay on the right-hand side of the river, then he need think of nothing else, need think of nothing that has happened and of nothing that might yet happen. His feet throb with the cold and his head rings from Riven's blow, but he goes on, letting the water run down his arm as he pushes and lifts, pushes and lifts, and all the while the giant crashes along the riverbank beside them.

Then, suddenly, the giant stops. He stands in the bulrushes and the sedge where the wind makes a tuneless song among the sodden seed spikes. But now Thomas can hear something else. The giant points ahead and shouts. There is something almost sorrowful in his expression. He shouts again and waves his arms.

'Brother?' the sister says. She is turning and pointing ahead. 'Have you seen?'

Ahead of them the banks of reeds part, and the river on which they have been travelling meets another, and this new water is broad, swollen with rainwater and snowmelt, heading south in spate. The lighter joins it and they are sucked into its turbid current. Water laps over the lighter's sides, pooling under their feet. The sister begins trying to scoop it out with her hands.

'We're sinking,' she says. 'We must reach the other side.'

But the river pulls them on and the farther they go, the wider apart the riverbanks become. They pass fishponds and eel farms and all along the banks the rushes have been clubbed and harvested. Two men in russet hoods stop digging in a field with a mattock and watch them as they go, as does a third on horseback, who turns and stares, a hunting bird perched on his wrist.

Thomas uses the pole as a rudder, guiding them towards a small hamlet dominated by a church tower, but as they approach a handful of boys leave off throwing stones at a cockerel and start trying to hit them in their sinking boat. By now they are standing up to their ankles in water and the boat is slipping away under them. There is nothing for it though: Thomas leans on the pole and the boat slews towards the river's western bank. Just as its bows dip under the water for the last time, it noses into a broad stand of reeds and Thomas jumps out to drop up to his thighs in the icy water. He holds the boat still for the sister, but by now she can hardly move. She inches across the prow and half falls into the brown water. Thomas hurries around, his clogs lost in the mud. He takes her arm, hesitating at first to touch her, but when she shows no sign of resistance, he helps her out of the boat and up the bank. He goes back for the pollaxe, just as the boat is tugged backwards by the current.

At the top of the bank he twists the water from the skirts of his cassock and looks around. There is nothing: only a broad stretch of reeds and mudflats. In the distance, a wood. Is there smoke in the air beyond? A village perhaps.

'We'll have to walk,' he says, gesturing downriver. 'We will surely come to something that way. We can ask the way to Canterbury from there.'

The sister looks doubtful. He sees she has wounds on her wrists and ankles. She has lost a clog too, and they both know they will never be able to walk far.

'We could say we are travelling on monastic business.'

'Together?'

Thomas frowns. She is right. They ought to part. He looks away upriver. A single swan comes towards them. He watches it for a moment. Then another appears from the rushes and joins the first and together they sail past and on out of sight. Thomas recalls words that he has written on parchment.

'"Two are better than one,"' he says, '"because they have a good reward for their labour. For if they fall, the one will lift up his fellow."'

'"But woe to him that is alone when he falls,"' the sister continues, '"for he has not another to help him up."'

He looks at the sister properly for the first time. She is sharp and fierce-looking, all angles.

'Ecclesiastes,' she says. 'I don't know the verse.'

He manages a smile.

'Nor me,' he says. 'But we should walk together, at least for a little while.'

She nods. He picks up the pollaxe and swings it over his shoulder. It is a good thing to have. It feels curiously natural in his hands, and now that the blood has been washed from it, he can see it is finely worked, with the tracings of an ornate pattern etched in its blades. No wonder the giant wanted it back. It must be worth something.

'We can always sell it,' he says.

They set out, following the river along its bank, the cold so raw it makes his bones ache, his feet throb. The sister's teeth are chattering. As they walk he goes through every stroke and strike of the fight with Riven and he tries to imagine it in a way that does not end in the Dean's death. He cannot. He finds his hands are gripping the axe so hard his head is hurting.

What would he give now to have Riven at his feet?

After a while a single flake of snow appears, drifting on a swirl, then another, and another, until they start down like feathers in a chicken coop.

They see the tumbledown cottage at the same time and increase their pace, both hoping to find something within. When they get there the sister hangs back while Thomas puts his head into the gloomy interior. He imagines bread on the table, a bowl of pottage, a leather mug of ale and – praise Jesu! – a fire. Instead it smells of cold ash and there is something dead in one corner.

'Anything?'

He shakes his head. The sister wipes her nose on the back of her sleeve and shrugs. He looks at her again. What is it that troubles him about her? He remembers her words. 'Where was God when he was about to put out your eyes?' He shakes his head. Tries to clear the thought. Where was God? What did that mean? That He was elsewhere? Not there?

As if she knows he is thinking about her, she turns and looks at him. He finds neither can hold the other's gaze. And they trudge on for a few more paces; they are approaching the wood when she stops and holds out a thin hand. Thomas is about to say something when she puts a finger across her mouth and draws it up and down. It is a sign common to all religious communities that eat in silence but still need to communicate among themselves: be quiet now. She raises her hands quickly in the air and touches the side of her nose with her right index finger: Smoke. Smell. She can smell smoke.

Thomas is not sure, but perhaps there is a fleeting scent above that of the snow and his own body. They move in silence along the path's edges until they pass under the leafless canopy of elm branches. Here the tang of smoke is stronger, sweet and definite.

And now in the darkness there is a hesitant glow. A little way off the path, in a glade. A fire. Thomas signals the sign for fire. Two hands, palms out, then rubbed together. The sister nods. Even in the dark he realises she's seen it long before he has. They slide through the trees, the soft cloth of fallen leaves muffling their steps. Through the trees is a circle of cautious light thrown by a small fire. A horse or mule stands whickering in the darkness beyond, its eyes occasionally reflecting the flames. Above the fire is a tripod from which hangs a small cooking pot. Intermingled with the smell of wood smoke, Thomas tastes fish.

His stomach churns.

He has not eaten since the Dean brought him bread and beer that morning. He begins to breathe a little faster, and can hear the sister do the same.

Where is the owner though?

They crouch in the darkness behind a fallen tree. The sister is very close now. He can feel her knee against his, and her breath on his cheek. He can hear his heart beating, perhaps hers too.

'Stand up.'

It is a man's voice, and the order comes from the darkness behind. They slowly stand and turn their backs to the flames to face the darkness. Thomas can see no one.

'Step back into the light,' the voice comes again. 'But I warn you, I have a bolt pointed at your head, Monk, and if you do not drop that axe, I will pin you to the tree.'

Thomas drops the axe. There is a moment of silence.

'Who are you?' the stranger asks.

Thomas swallows.

'Sir,' he begins, 'we are two ecclesiastics. We mean no harm. We are travelling. Travelling on monastic business.'

'On monastic business?'

The voice is softer already, as if the first command has been bluster, and now a note of incredulousness creeps in.

'Yes, sir,' Thomas says. 'We are of the Order of St Gilbert of Sempringham.'

There is another pause.

'And how come you to be travelling with one another? A canon and a sister of that order?'

Thomas looks at the sister in the dark. He can think of nothing to say.

'Well?'

'It is a long story, sir,' the sister says.

'I would hear it.'

'May we beg your charity before we explain ourselves?' the sister asks. 'We have not eaten and we are frozen to our marrow.'

There is another pause.

A tall man in a padded coat with a cavernous hood appears in the fringes of the fire's light. He has a crossbow in his hands, but even in the dark Thomas can see it has neither string nor quarrel. The man is as frightened of them as they are of him. More so, if anything.

The man bends to pick up the pollaxe and it is clear that he is no longer young.

'So who are you to be travelling abroad?' he asks, straightening up, inspecting the weapon. 'With no shoes and in one another's company?'

'I am Thomas Everingham,' Thomas says. He still cannot see the man's face. 'I am a canon of the Order of Gilbert. My cloister is at Haverhurst.'

He gestures into the dark, imagining the priory to be that way.

'And you, Sister?'

'I am Sister Katherine,' she says. 'Of that same priory.'

It is the first time Thomas has heard her name. He turns to her. She has a hard face, and in the firelight her eyes are quick and suspicious. She glances at him, and again he looks away.

'And you're hungry, you say?' the man asks.

'Famished, sir.'

'*Fabas indulcet fames.*' He laughs quietly, and he sets aside the crossbow in the shadow of the tree. 'Hunger makes everything taste good. My pot is small and my provisions few, but what I have you are welcome to share. In return for your tale.'

His voice is quick and learned, like the Prior's or one of those visiting clerics. He puts the axe by the crossbow and he passes Thomas some hawthorn sticks.

'Feed them in slowly, Brother Thomas, won't you?' he says. 'So as not to kill the fire. It is wet enough in these parts to drown a Jew.'

He has on short boots that bunch around his skinny shanks and, despite the crossbow, Thomas can see he is no soldier. He rummages in the shadow of the tree and brings out a leather bag from which he takes a flask and a canvas packet. He passes Thomas a small piece of bread. Thomas breaks it and hands half to Katherine. Their fingers touch in the dark and a curious jolt goes up his arm. He pulls back his arm, noticing that she does the same. While they chew, the man opens another bag and brings out a blanket and a coat.

'Here,' he says. 'It makes me cold just looking at you.'

'Thank you, sir, with all my heart,' Thomas tells him, still chewing, passing the blanket on to Katherine and pulling on the coat himself. It is heavy and padded, the finest thing that Thomas had ever worn, with buttons, a belt and a lambswool collar. A rich man, then.

'You did not tell us your name, sir?'

This is from Katherine. She has wrapped the blanket around her shoulders and though she is leaning into the warmth of the fire her eyes remain deep in shadow.

'I am Robert Daud, of Lincoln,' the man says, and then after a hesitation: 'A *quaestor*.'

There is a moment's silence.

'A pardoner?' Katherine asks.

'As was,' he answers with an emphasis Thomas does not understand.

'But why are you sheltering in these woods, sir?' he asks, finally swallowing his bread. 'When you might be happier at an inn, or staying with an abbot in a monastery?'

The pardoner looks from one to the other for a moment before replying. It is as if he is coming to a decision. Any number of answers might now come from his lips, none of them the truth, but at length he says:

'I have scrofula. The King's Evil.'

Both Thomas and Katherine stop chewing. The mule stamps in

the dark. The pardoner sighs, puts down his own piece of bread, and then reaches up to tug his hood from his crown. The light of the fire falls on his face. Roiling down his neck, from ear to collar bone, is a whorl of clustered growths, the largest the size of a ripe damson.

'You see?' he says, pulling his hood back up, casting his face into shade again. 'So it is that I avoid the company of men. Last night I approached a village to the west of here, to buy some ale. The alewife mistook these for buboes.'

He crosses himself, as if this might ward off the plague.

'She raised the hue and cry and I was lucky to escape with my life, let alone with my mule and baggage. The men must have been away hunting, or at the wars perhaps, for it was only boys who came after me, throwing stones mostly, though one of them had his bow. In the end I thanked St Sebastian that I looked to have the plague, for at least they were too frightened to approach.'

'Though you have that weapon,' Katherine says.

'Yes,' the pardoner laughs. 'It is antique, and quite useless. I bought it from a man who claimed it belonged to Joan, the French witch. Can you imagine?'

The pot begins to steam. The pardoner leans forward and crumbles pieces of dried fish with long fingers and drops them in.

'How do you know your affliction is not the plague?' Katherine asks. She seems unwilling to let the matter drop.

'If it were the plague, I would be long dead,' the pardoner says. 'These signs have been with me a year or more now, growing steadily larger, like old friends, or a family.'

'Do they hurt?' Katherine asks.

The pardoner shakes his head.

'No,' he says. 'They are cold though. To the touch, I mean. Though that is no strange thing this winter.'

'We will pray for you, sir,' Thomas offers, and Katherine murmurs something vague.

'Thank you,' the pardoner says. 'Thank you both. With your prayers and God's blessing I shall find a cure, in France.'

'In France?'

Thomas can hardly believe it. All he knows of France is that it is where his father was killed, and that it is a land so badly ravaged that when the alarum bells ring, even the stock animals know where they must gather to shelter from the English. Men and women threw themselves in the river rather than be caught. It does not seem the sort of place one might find a cure for anything, other than life itself.

'It is where I am bound,' the pardoner explains. 'First across the Narrow Sea to Calais and then south to Chinon, to the court of King Charles, to seek the cure of his touch.'

He speaks quickly, as if unwilling to dwell on the details of his journey, or the cure. Thomas is thirsty now, and pleased when from the shadows the pardoner opens the flask and pours more ale.

'But what is your story?' he asks, changing the subject. 'What brings you from your cloister? That is the tale I wish to hear.'

'We were set upon,' Thomas began with his eye on the cup, 'set upon by men belonging to a man named Giles Riven.'

'Sir Giles Riven?' The pardoner stops pouring the ale and sits forward, his face lit by the fire.

'You know of him?' Thomas asks.

'There is no one north of Stamford who has not heard of Giles Riven. I heard he took the castle at Cornford after old Lord Cornford was killed at Ludford Bridge this last year, claiming it on some slight connection. It is also said that he killed Cornford himself, putting a dagger through his eye, and that now he means to marry his son to the dead man's daughter.'

Thomas closes his eyes and sees Riven, smiling, holding out the dead sister's beads.

'We know nothing of this,' Katherine says. 'We have been in cloister for these past years.'

The pardoner nods, and finishes pouring the ale.

'How long have you been in orders?' he asks, passing the cup to Thomas.

'Eight years,' Thomas replies, before draining the cup and handing it back. 'Since I was twelve.'

The pardoner nods.

'And you, Sister?' he asks, pouring more ale.

There is a momentary pause before she replies.

'Since being a child,' she says. Thomas and the pardoner look up.

'You were taken in as an oblate?' the pardoner asks.

Katherine is hesitant.

'I was,' she agrees.

'I thought they had abandoned that practice?'

Katherine opens her mouth to say something and then shuts it again. She does not seem to know.

'And how many Eastertides have you seen in the priory?' the pardoner presses.

She shrugs.

'Ten?' she supposes, and then looks desperate. 'Fifteen?'

That would make her about twenty, Thomas thinks. About his age. There is a silence, disturbed only by the hissing of a damp log on the fire, the susurrus of the river through the trees.

'Do you receive news of your family?' the pardoner asks. Thomas passes her the mug of ale. Their fingers do not touch this time and he sees she is careful to wipe the mug's rim with her sleeve before she frowns, then shakes her head, and drinks. Thomas is about to ask a question of his own but the pardoner catches his eye. Enquire no further, he seems to be saying, and he changes the subject.

'How came Riven to attack you?' he asks.

Thomas explains. The pardoner grunts.

'These are unquiet and scrambled times,' he says, adjusting the fire to make the branches burn more strongly, taking courage from their company. 'Everywhere men are taking what they may, with no consideration of God, or the laws of the Holy Church.'

'Why?' Thomas asks. 'Why is it so?'

The pardoner sighs.

'I am a humble pardoner,' he says. 'And I know nothing of this first hand. But I talk to people. I listen to what they say.'

'And?'

'And most agree that the fault of it lies with the King,' he says.

'The King?'

'Yes. It seems strange to be talking about the King in a wood at night with strangers, doesn't it? But yes. The King. Henry, the sixth of that name, of the house of Lancaster.'

'And what has he done to bring this on the country?'

'They say that he's a simple man, without crook or craft, you know. Not like his father. Not like Henry the Fifth. D'you remember him? No. Before your time, of course. He was a proper king, that one. Beat the French time and time again.'

The pardoner stares into the flames. He grows wistful.

'What happened to him?' Katherine asks.

'Hmmm? Oh. Died too soon. They all do, the good ones.'

There is a long silence. The pardoner continues gazing into the fire. Men became like that with flames, Thomas thinks. Behind them the mule shifts.

'So the son is nothing like the father?' Katherine prompts.

The pardoner collects himself.

'That is right,' he says. 'He has fits. Seizures. When he goes limp, and cannot recognise anybody, not even his own son. And some say this is an affliction sent down from God.'

In the silence he stirs the pot with a stick.

'But what has he done to deserve such a thing?' Katherine asks.

The pardoner takes the mug from Katherine and fills it again.

'The fault lies with his grandfather,' he says, 'also called Henry. Henry the Fourth. They say he usurped the throne from King Richard who had had it before him, and then had him murdered. They say that the troubles tormenting the realm now spring from that crime, and that for however long the House of Lancaster keeps the throne, this land will see only war.'

'War?' Thomas asks. He thinks of the Dean's stories of sieges, of slaughter and rape. But that was in France. He cannot imagine it in England.

'There has been war, yes,' the pardoner answers. 'And there will be again. For while the King was shy of his wits, two factions have arisen at court, you see? One is led by the Queen, a she-wolf called Margaret from Anjou in France – a Frenchwoman! – and the other by the Duke of York, a cousin to the King.'

It is easy to see where his sympathies lie.

'And who is winning this war?' Thomas asks.

'The Queen is in the ascendant, for the moment. Her army routed that of the Duke of York outside the gates of Ludlow last St Edward's Day. This time the King was present at the fight, and a faction of the Duke of York's men would not take up arms against his royal standard, however ill gotten the gain. *Rex non potest peccare*, you see? The King can do no wrong. Even though he is a usurper, the King is still the king.'

'Strange,' Katherine says.

'Indeed,' the pardoner agrees. 'And the people of Ludlow paid dearly for the principle that day, let me tell you, for after York's soldiers had lain down their arms and slipped away, the Queen let her own troops into the town. It is said they broke every hogshead of wine they could find and by the eve they were so sodden with drink they would only drop what they'd stolen to rape the women. It is in this confusion that Lord Cornford was killed, by your man Giles Riven himself.'

He takes a sip of ale and stares into the fire again. The pot is steaming, the water plicking around the greens.

'But Queen Margaret is queen of the realm,' Thomas begins. 'Why would she let her subjects suffer so?'

'She is French for a start,' the pardoner says, 'and furthermore she has no money so must pay her troops with promises of plunder. Besides, many of them are from the north: wild uncultivated brutes, almost as bad as the Scots, and their love of plunder is second to none.'

'And so where is this Duke of York now?' Thomas asks.

'He is in Ireland, attainted and called a traitor, while his great well-wisher the Earl of Warwick is in Calais, across the Narrow Sea, and likewise condemned.'

The pardoner's voice has changed now, and he looks up from the fire as if inspired by some memory.

'He will be back though,' he carries on, 'for never was there such a man as the Earl of Warwick.'

Thomas thinks the pardoner speaks the Earl of Warwick's name as if it has holy weight to it, like that of a saint, or one of the martyrs. He drains the cup.

'But until he returns,' the pardoner continues, 'we have those of the Queen's affinity peeling us for what little we have and disinheriting rightful heirs of what's theirs. Your Giles Riven, for instance. He is of the new Duke of Somerset's affinity, you see? Able to provide him upward of a hundred mounted archers, I dare say, fifty billmen and a handful of men-at-arms. And so long as he continues to do that, the new Duke will back him in any dispute, and who now in the county would go against the Duke? Not a man.'

There is a moment's silence.

'Riven said he was moving south,' Thomas says. 'To join the Queen.'

The pardoner nods.

'Yes,' he says. 'The Queen is summoning her army. It will be spring soon, unbelievable as that now seems, and with the spring comes the campaigning season, and with the campaigning season comes the Earl of Warwick, back from France, and I believe he will want more than merely his rightful place in the King's council.'

He unhooks the pot from the stand and sets it by Thomas's feet. He passes him a carved wooden spoon. Thomas murmurs his thanks and then a prayer before eating. The pottage burns his lips and tongue but he carries on, scooping in the leaves and the slippery fish and beans. When he has half finished the bowl he passes it to Katherine, who takes it and eats in quick suspicious spoonfuls.

While she eats, the pardoner relieves himself in the dark. Thomas puts another branch on the fire. It is a luxury of which he has long dreamed, being able to sit by a fire with his hands so close that the flames can scorch his palms.

When Katherine has finished she murmurs a quick thanks be to God, sets aside the bowl and retreats under her blanket. She says no more. The silence is not oppressive. Neither is used to speaking more than fifty words of their own device in a day, and silence, when not interrupted by prayer, is their natural state. Yet he is conscious of her, and finds his gaze drawn to her.

After the pardoner returns Thomas finishes his interrupted account of Riven's false accusation. When he describes the fight in the garth the pardoner can scarce contain his glee.

'By the saints! You fought Giles Riven with a staff?'

Thomas nods.

'And won?'

Again Thomas nods.

'I suppose,' he says. Though it had not felt that way.

'By the death of Him who died for us!' the pardoner laughs, 'there is either more to you than meets the eye, Brother Thomas, or you talk of a miracle!'

He pours more ale and passes it over. Thomas drinks it at once. Then Katherine follows with a curt description of being accused of harbouring him in the cloister, and of the imprisonment that followed, before touching on Alice's death.

'Perhaps Riven and that giant of his did the damage,' she says, 'but it was the Prioress and Sister Joan who together choked the life out of her, to that I will swear an oath on all that is holy.'

The pardoner is watching her closely.

'What happened then?' he asks.

Katherine shakes her head and says nothing. She pulls the blanket up around her face and a long silence follows. After a moment, she settles herself more comfortably, and, then, despite the cold, she begins to snore softly.

'The ale is strong,' the pardoner observes.

He leans forward and tugs the blanket over Katherine's ravaged foot, and then he pours the last of the ale to share. He sits back, turns to Thomas, and speaks confidentially.

'How long do you think it will be before it is known that you are apostate?' he asks.

'But we are not apostate!' Thomas says.

The pardoner waves his hand.

'I know that now,' he says. 'But when first I saw you, I naturally assumed you had fled your priory for the love of one another. It is what everyone will think.'

Thomas cannot help glancing at Katherine. Despite her snores he is certain she is listening.

'But—' he begins.

'But nothing. A monk and a nun. The moment your flight is known, you are excommunicated. Your sin will be broadcast abroad, even in Boston by tomorrow if you are unlucky, and then no one will help you. All are forbidden to do so, and who would willingly offend the Church? No man. The friars will start looking for you first, and then the Justices will come after you with their writs of apostata capiendo.'

'But the worst they can do is take us back to the priory, surely?'

'But you left the priory accused of common assault, and now, no doubt, the charges will be magnified a hundredfold. And your prior will only hand you over to Riven again, and this time he will take no chances. He will kill you. And her.'

This is a bitter truth. Thomas feels his spirit, so cheered by drink, curdle.

'We are making our way to Canterbury,' he tells the pardoner. 'The Dean of the Priory says our only chance is to find a sympathetic audience with the Prior of All, the head of our order. He will hear us and give us justice.'

'And you hope this Prior of All will go against a man like Riven?'

Thomas has not thought of it like that.

'I suppose not,' he says, thinking on what the pardoner has said about the Duke of Somerset. 'Yet what else can we do?'

'Remember Deuteronomy,' the pardoner tells him. 'An eye for an eye.'

Thomas feels something stir in his chest: a flutter of excitement. The offer of some alien freedom.

'You cannot mean me to find Riven myself?'

The pardoner shrugs.

'Why not? You have shown how capable you are.'

It does not bother Thomas that the pardoner has suggested the opposite only a moment earlier.

'No,' he says. 'I cannot. I am a canon of the Order of Gilbert of Sempringham. I shall seek justice with the Prior of All. I shall put my faith in the Lord for as St Paul tells the Romans: Do not take revenge, but leave room for God's wrath. It is His to avenge. He will repay.'

The pardoner raises his eyebrows slightly.

'Yes, yes,' he says. 'I am sure you are right to do so.'

There is a pause. Thomas feels foolish quoting the Bible to a man so learned, but the pardoner does not seem to mind.

After a pause the pardoner asks, 'Tell me: how did you hope to get to Canterbury?'

Thomas hesitates.

'I had not thought that far,' he admits.

The pardoner's eyes stray to Thomas's feet.

'The best way to Canterbury from here would be by ship,' he says. 'From Boston. You might pay a ship's master to take you to

Sandwich, on the Kent coast. Were he on his way to Calais, I mean. It is not so great a diversion.'

'We have no money,' Thomas says.

'Listen to me, Brother Thomas,' the pardoner is saying. 'I have paid for bells to be rung in the cathedral at Lincoln, and I have offered up prayers to St Nicholas for the success of my venture, but what if I now pay for you to get to Canterbury? If I provide you with clothes and shoes? If I pay for your food?'

'Why ever would you do such a thing?'

The pardoner says nothing for a moment. It is as if he is framing his argument.

'We are all three pilgrims,' he says at length, 'in our way. Pilgrims help one another. They help one another to help themselves, so yes, helping you helps me. Do you see?'

Thomas can think of nothing to say. The reality of walking any distance with no shoes or clothes or money has suddenly become fearsome.

'I would thank you for your offer, sir, with all my heart.'

The pardoner nods as if this is happily agreed. He sits back. Thomas has another, final draught of ale. The hem of his cassock lets slip tendrils of steam in the warmth of the fire and his feet are chilblained and sore, but the ale is now so soothing he hardly cares.

'But you know,' the pardoner goes, his eye ranging over Katherine's sleeping form, 'if you are being sought by the friars, it might be as well to disguise yourselves. They will be after a man and a woman. I wonder if we might find some clothes for you and Sister Katherine here that disguise first your calling, and then her womanhood. She is a skinny thing, with not a curve in sight. I feel sure she might pass as a boy.'

6

Katherine wakes before dawn. Her limbs ache from her beatings over the previous days and the cold that has crept into her bones in the night. Before she can stand she has to kneel and then sit on one of the pardoner's bales to let the pain pass. She finds herself in a small clearing in some woods, with a mule and two men gathered around a small circle of ashes where the fire has burned out. The mule regards her charitably, while the men, the canon Thomas and the pardoner, lie wrapped together in the mud under a grey travelling blanket.

This is her chance. She must get away from this canon Thomas. She can never go to Canterbury. She can never see this Prior of All, for what justice could he be expected to give to someone who has broken the fifth commandment? When she shuts her eyes Katherine sees Sister Joan in her last moments and she knows that every step she takes towards the Prior of All is a step nearer the gallows.

She stands. Her knees are agony, her feet like blocks of wood. But she must move. She can leave now, walk back the way they came. The canon will never follow her, not that way. She stretches her hands out to gather her possessions, but then realises that she has none, and that already it is too late.

Thomas is waking. He opens his eyes and looks up into the canopy of the trees, and then at her, and then he closes them again and shakes his head.

She sits back down. She will have to wait, she thinks, to seek the right moment.

'Good morning, Sister,' he says.

'Good morning,' she answers.

She takes a moment to look at him, to see the difference between him and the pardoner. Thomas is tall, broad in the shoulder and long in the arm and leg. His hands and feet seem enormous, too, and he reminds her of a young dog, a puppy, in whom one can see the size of the adult to come. Next to Thomas the pardoner, waking now, is a pinched and dried old thing, all his colours faded, his skin creased and worn.

'God in heaven,' the pardoner says, and he clambers slowly to his feet, huffing in the cold morning air. When they have said their prayers, they eat the last of the pottage and load the pardoner's bales on to his mule. The pardoner notices the blood clotted in the hair above Thomas's ear.

'I have a salve,' he says and he digs in his bags to produce a clay jar. He unstoppers it and the glade is filled with the scent of the infirmary. She thinks of Sister Joan and the thin blood on her downy chin. The pardoner smears a dab of the contents on Thomas's wound, making him flinch, but after a moment Thomas says it feels numb, then warm. She watches the way the pardoner applies the salve, the way he strokes it along the wound.

'What is it?' she asks.

He is pleased by her interest.

'A mixture of thirteen herbs,' he says, 'mixed with pig fat and elder buds.'

He holds the jar for her to see the dark paste within.

'It cools wounds and cures almost everything,' he says.

Then he tucks it away in a leather pack, and sets the leather pack inside another one, and this he places very carefully on the mule's pack, as if it is valuable. Thomas stands with the giant's pollaxe, looking uncertain what to do with it. Does he carry it? Or put it on the mule? Eventually they decide on the mule and they set out, following a path where the wood thins and out on to a broad expanse of fog-haunted marshes.

'By the blood of Mary,' the pardoner laughs as they walk. 'Will you look at us? Two thieves ripe for the hanging and the third a victim of the plague. Thank the Lord for this mist or they'd have raised the cry and chased us away by now.'

To Katherine's eye the pardoner's clothes appear garish. He wears a long russet habit, not unlike Thomas's, but over it a blue fur-trimmed cloak with a tightly fitting hood that has been dyed bright green. A low-crowned round hat of black-fringed felt holds the hood in place and she can see that between his hat, hood and beard, it is almost impossible to see the whorls on his neck.

Next to him Thomas looks like a crow, but she knows she is the worst: her patched cassock is crusted with mud; she has only one clog and no headgear, not even a cloth to cover her hair. She looks the sort of beggar the Prioress would turn away from the gate.

'I will lend you my hat,' the pardoner says, passing it to her. 'And there'll be a fripperer at the market from whom we might buy something more suitable. It should not be too far now.'

Ahead of them they hear the steady din of bells, and she can smell coal smoke. They join a road and as they walk, its surface improves. Stone replaces mud, and other travellers pass with loaded mules and curious looks.

'Sir, by the grace of God, good day to you,' the pardoner sings out each time he feels their glances settle too heavily on one or other of them, and each time the traveller nods and returns the greeting and moves on with a blessing, as if all were well.

Katherine stares back at them resentfully, and after a time the pardoner touches her elbow.

'We're strangers here, Sister,' he says. 'If someone takes against us, they will denounce us for some crime, and without our friends to vouch for our good name, we will end up like this poor fellow.'

He gestures towards a tree where a crowd of birds mob something hanging from the branches. It is a man's body, hanging near naked, mottled and erupting with decay, his braided guts spilling out like fistfuls of grey string. A bird with glossy feathers clings to its face and with each peck the corpse twitches on its rope. The smell of rotting meat is thick and sweet.

'Been there about ten days,' the pardoner guesses.

'But why doesn't someone bury him?' Katherine asks through her fingers.

'He's posted as a warning to others.' The pardoner shrugs. 'Were it a witch they would just strangle her at the roadside and leave her for the dogs. In the south when they catch a thief they nail his ear to a post and give him a knife to cut himself free.'

They walk on through mist that is shrinking towards the river, leaving a sodden, level landscape interrupted by meagre stands of trees, a low-beamed cottage and a herd of oily sheep. Ahead the town is a gathering of church spires and roofs under a pall of dark smoke.

'The town of Boston,' the pardoner says. 'Home to a thousand or so souls. We must get through it to reach the harbour.'

She hesitates.

'Come on,' the pardoner encourages. 'Walk on the far side of the mule, so the captain of the gate can't see you. And hold its rope, so that if he does, he'll think it belongs to you, and that you're worth something after all.'

They join the other travellers queuing behind a carter trying to get his oxen on to the bridge.

'*Hoc opus, hic labor est*,' the pardoner mutters. He is looking anxious.

At the far end of the bridge a fat man in a stained leather jerkin and an iron helmet stands under a wooden awning, while another with a bill takes coins from those crossing the bridge.

'Good day to you, sir!' the pardoner calls when they reach the second man, and he presses a coin into the outstretched hand. The man says nothing but frowns and shows the coin to the first man. The first man holds up his arm to stop the flow.

'Never seen you before, master?' he says. His gaze travels over the mule, to Katherine, to Thomas, then back to the pardoner.

'I am Robert Daud,' the pardoner says. 'A merchant, of Lincoln.'

The man tips his chin and stares down his broad nose.

'Take your hood off.'

There is a moment of silence. The pardoner looks very old. He begins fiddling at the ties below his chin. His fingers are trembling. But then the mule lifts its tail and shits. A man with a sack of beets on his shoulder cheerfully sets them aside to gather the steaming lumps.

'Hands haven't been this warm since Martinmas,' he calls, and gets his laugh. Someone behind shouts and all around them people urge the Captain of the Watch to get on with it, and just then the pardoner discovers the knot is tighter than he thought, and at last the captain shrugs as if in the end he could hardly care less. He gestures at the mule and rolls his finger in a circle for another coin.

'Pontage,' he says. 'Another penny to cross the bridge with a mule.'

The pardoner cheerfully digs in the pouch on his belt and produces the coin. The crowd surge forward. When they've turned a corner, the old man slumps against a wall and runs his fingers under the band of his hood.

'Thanks to the blessed St James for that,' he breathes.

When he is recovered he leads them along the narrow street to the marketplace, where the ground underfoot is cobbled and houses of every shape and size tower above them, each with glazed windows, and at one end is an edifice of ash poles and scaffolding indicating that something grand is being built.

But it is the business of the people that startles Katherine most. She has never seen so many men and women or children gathered together at once, and they are all shouting. Traders proclaim the value and virtue of their wares while rivals bellow disparagement, and money is changing hands, and everyone seems to be arguing with good-natured passion. In the middle of it all is a bear, a creature at once both human and alien, sitting glumly while a man nearby eats a pie.

'We must eat something before we go about our business,' the pardoner is saying, tying up the mule to a rail and handing a boy a coin to tend it. He leads them down a covered street to a cookshop where he buys them each a bowl of pottage, dark stuff, much tastier than Katherine can believe, reinforced with bacon and strips of yellowing kale. Then comes a loaf of dense brown bread still warm from the oven as well as an earthenware plate on which three pasties are actually greasy with butter. The cook's wife hands them mugs of ale and they eat and drink sitting on the step with their backs against the shop's wall. After they've finished the pardoner buys each of them a baked apple with wrinkled skin, too hot to hold.

'You were hungry,' the cookshop owner says. He is foursquare with short legs and sly eyes. His woman stares at them from the darkness of the kitchen.

Fabas indulcet fames,' the pardoner replies, half turning. 'We have had a long voyage, goodman, from foreign shores, much delayed by wild weather. Now that we are replete, we are bound for the fripperer and then the shoe-maker.'

'And the barber too, I hope,' the man says, nodding at Thomas's tonsure. 'There are plenty in town'd turn you in for the way you look.'

'Quite so,' the pardoner allows, swallowing the rest of his ale. He pays the man and hurries them on their way.

Katherine feels sick.

'We must find our vessel,' the pardoner announces, though this is news to her. 'It won't be long before the friars get about and they'll know you've left your priory. First though: some clothes.'

They find the fripperer beyond the tailors' stalls on the far side of the market, next to a man dealing in horsehides and urine. He is seated on the ground with his legs crossed, surrounded by a shin-high pile of rags of every kind of colour and cloth. He is working on some stitching, but when he sees the pardoner looming into view, he throws aside the work and is on his feet.

'Master,' he says, 'may God make you prosper.'

With quick eyes he grades the value of their clothes, deducting from the total the price of every tear and abrasion, and though he is pleased at the thought of the money a man like the pardoner might possess, he grimaces when he sees Thomas and Katherine's cassocks. The pardoner explains what he wants and the clothes-mender begins casting uncertainly through his stock, looking for something that might do.

'I cannot furnish this chit with anything at the present,' he says, indicating Katherine. 'Women tend to their own clothes, see, or if they do leave me a garment, they come by to collect it. They don't seem to get caught up in other things, as men do, or get themselves killed so often.'

'I am not interested in anything for the girl,' the pardoner tells him airily. 'She can take her chances. I need clothing for him, and for my other servant. A lad smaller than this one.'

'Much easier, that,' the fripperer says and he begins pulling garments from different piles again, holding them up and then discarding them. Eventually he hands Thomas two piles.

'Should sort you out,' he says.

The pardoner pays the man and they retreat to an alley behind the marketplace.

'You can change here,' he says, dividing up the piles of clothing. 'And mind where you step.'

The smell in the alley is powerful, and at its end they each turn a different corner and begin to try to make sense of their new clothes. For Katherine it is a strange experience. She needs to hold them up first, to see what they are. Then she pulls on the linen braies, followed by the woven hose. She rolls them over at the top and ties them off around her waist. Then she quickly takes off her cassock, and plunges her naked arms into the undershirt. It is rose-coloured, faded in parts, mossy at the pits and slick with wear. Then comes the tunic, russet-coloured as most men wear, then the coat, green and quilted, but worn and smelling of horses. Down its front on one side is a row of rough horn discs with which she is not familiar, and down the other stitched slits that mystify her. The garment gapes over her bosom and feels wrong. She's spent her life in a cassock that hangs from her shoulders and these new clothes grip her body in unfamiliar places. Still, she is able to move more freely unhampered by the heavy skirts, and so long as she does not get her feet wet, she imagines she will be warm.

She meets Thomas in the alleyway and they stare at one another for a moment. His jacket is blue and his hose green on one leg, red on the other. His tunic strains where he had done up the buttons on the front. When Katherine sees this, she understands what the bone discs on her own jacket are for and she clumsily presses them home.

'These are men's clothes,' she says.

Thomas nods.

'It is safer,' he says. 'They will be looking for a canon and a sister.'

She nods. Unsure. He too looks askance.

'Why is he doing this?' she asks, pulling on the felt cap she's been given. 'He has no need to show us such kindness.'

'It is a penance, I think,' Thomas says. 'If he helps us, things will go well for him in France. And if he hopes to benefit from it, then we may take these favours in good conscience, surely?'

She sees he too is in need of persuasion.

'We would have had to take them from someone, at any rate,' Katherine says, 'or we would be dead.'

It is a hard point, and Thomas is silenced.

'Look,' he says. 'I took these from Riven. You should have them.'

He proffers her Alice's rosary beads. She does not take them for a moment.

'I did not even know her,' he says, pressing them on her.

Katherine does not want to gain from Alice's death, but she takes them, puts them over her head and tucks them into her shirt. For a moment they are cold against her skin.

When the pardoner sees them he laughs.

'Not perfect,' he says, 'but what is perfect?'

He is holding two pairs of brown leather boots. They slide them on and stand in them. She stares down at herself. She can hardly believe what she sees.

'Good God!' Thomas says. He is wriggling his toes and smiling broadly. She smiles too. The pleasure is almost too much to bear. Warmth begins to thaw her feet and though the boots are too long, so that they smack the cobbles as she walks, they are not half so bad as the clogs she is used to, not half so bad as going with one foot bare.

'Thank you, master,' she says. 'Thank you for all your kindness.'

'It is nothing more than my duty as a Christian soul,' the pardoner replies, 'but perhaps we had better not linger.'

Two friars are hurrying across the marketplace, and there are many more behind, spilling from one of the churches.

'Your hat,' the pardoner murmurs to Thomas. Thomas pulls it on, quickly covering the patch of shaved skin. Katherine can feel herself stiffening as they pass. She realises she is holding her breath. One of them is ruddy-faced, a drinker, with eyes that linger on Katherine's crotch, and she feels horribly naked, and steps behind Thomas.

When the friars have passed, the pardoner takes them to find the mule, and when he has paid the boy off, they pass down a narrow road to a grey sweep of sea-slimed stone staithes. Ahead is the sea, under a huge stretch of pale sky, and boats and ships of every imaginable size bob in the puckered waters.

It takes her breath away.

'Dear God,' she murmurs.

All along the quay men are busy among the stacks of sarplers and bales, the casks of wine, piles of logs, coils of thick ships' rope and canvas-covered heaps of only the Lord knew what. The smell is a mixture of salt and fish guts and something else.

They walk along the quay a little way until they come to a quiet spot by a pile of conical wicker baskets leaking green water back to the sea.

'Look to the mule,' the pardoner instructs, 'while I find the harbour master, and, Thomas, you'd better cut our sister's hair so that she looks less like a Katherine and more like a Kit.'

So in one thoughtless stroke, Katherine becomes Kit, and Thomas borrows the pardoner's knife and cuts her hair, dropping the hanks on the ground around her feet. She can feel his fingers on her scalp and her skin prickles with ill ease. She can feel her back arching, her shoulders rising, as if to escape his touch. Then he sits while she takes up the knife and attempts the same with him. She starts slowly, trying not to touch him, chopping at his thick hair until she sees she will have to hold it to cut it. She can feel his discomfort too. She stops to examine the wound above his ear. She flakes away some of the pardoner's salve and sees the wound is livid under it.

When the pardoner comes back he shouts with laughter.

'Saints above! He looks like a madman!'

She says nothing, but she too cannot help laughing at Thomas's piebald head. He pulls on his cap.

'Have you found a ship, sir?'

'I have. The carrack *Mary* leaves for Calais on the next tide.'

'Calais?'

'Yes, but have no fear. Master Cobham is happy to put in at Sandwich before he crosses the Narrow Sea. Sandwich is in Kent, scarcely a day's walk from Canterbury. So that has fallen well, thanks be to God. Not that the *Mary* is as comfortable as I should like, and Master Cobham is rather brusque, but there you are: *non licet omnibus adire Corinthum.* It is not given to everyone to visit Corinth, you see?'

The pardoner takes Thomas back to the market to buy bread and whatever else they might find. Katherine remains alone among the baskets.

Now is her chance. She begins going through the packs on the mule's back, looking for the one where the pardoner keeps his money. Is this it? The one with the jar of salve. Where is it? She cannot find it. She stops, sick with shame, as a boy with half an ear leads past a train of mules, and then a man follows holding a dead badger, never quite happy with the way he is carrying it.

Dear God! Where is the pack? Her fingers are numb as she struggles with the knots. There. She finds it. It is inside a rough sack, a disguise. She is pulling it out when the pardoner and Thomas return in a hurry. They've bought cheese, bread, a sack of apples and three wineskins apiece, and they've even managed to sell the mule for a good price. Now they keep glancing over their shoulders and the old man misses her returning the pack.

'We must be quick about it,' he says. 'The friars are astir over something and it is more than two apostates.'

The pardoner glances at Katherine, and she looks away. He shakes his head as if to clear some thought and she knows he knows. She wonders when he will tell Thomas.

'Come on,' he says, and they hurry to find this Master Cobham, who is standing with his hands on his hips watching a long-beaked hand crane swing a bale of something heavy on to the deck of a three-masted ship.

This is the carrack *Mary*, about twenty paces long, and low in the water. Cobham turns when he sees them and watches them approach without a change of expression. Up close he is solid, with sandy hair and the sort of face that mottles in the wind. He touches his hat in an ironic salute.

'Day to you,' he says.

His glance lingers on Katherine, and she feels herself warm under it, but after a moment he turns and shouts to the men on the crane to load the pardoner's bags. The pardoner is especially careful about the pack with the salve in, and he will not trust it to anyone else. She sees Cobham's pale eyebrow cock and her doubts about the man harden to mistrust.

'Yours, my boy,' the pardoner says, handing Thomas the pollaxe. 'Best not let it stray.'

Then the horse-dealer's boy arrives with a bag of coins and when everything is aboard, the pardoner turns and strokes the mule's nose. There are tears in his eyes, though the animal stares back without emotion.

'Goodbye, old friend,' he says. 'Perhaps we shall meet again when I come back through this way, a new man?'

As the boy leads the unprotesting mule away, Katherine follows the pardoner across to the carrack via a gangplank. She does not think to let Thomas take her hand even though it is offered and after a moment she steps down into a curious world that shifts beneath her feet.

Hardly an inch of the ship's planking can be seen for sacks and barrels and bales and all manner of wooden spars. There are coils of rope, canvas sheets and two huge and badly rusted anchors. In one corner a dark-skinned man sits on an upturned bucket and warms his hands on a fire that smoulders in the middle of a broad slab of stone. Other men linger in the ropes, staring at the newcomers. There must be about seven or eight of them, each as wiry and wild-looking as the next.

'You'll be stopping in there, if you've a mind,' Cobham says, nodding to a plank door below the raised deck at the stern of the ship.

'Very good,' the pardoner says and he picks his way across the deck to prise open the door. An insistent stink billows out, stronger even than that of the sea: an unholy combination of vomit and the privy.

'Gets mighty cold out here at night,' Cobham continues with a smirk.

It begins to snow again, fat wet flakes that settle on the pardoner's hat. Katherine looks along the wharves to where the mule is disappearing in the gathering gloom. Two black-robed friars have stopped the boy. Benedictines.

'Let us try the cabin,' she says.

The pardoner catches her glance.

'Indeed,' he agrees. '*Ignis aurum probat, miseria fortes viros.*'

There is no light, only slatted apertures, and the floor is sodden and the walls are crusted with something that has long set hard. The pardoner pulls the door shut after them.

'We need only stay until we set off and are out of reach of the friars,' the pardoner tells them as they hold their breath. He peers through the gap in the window.

'Or until that man hands us over,' Katherine says.

'Yes,' the pardoner agrees, 'he looks like the worst sort but I have only paid him half what we owe, with the promise of the other half on safe delivery in Calais, where I have said I am to be met by associates with the balance. He will not let us go to the friars without collecting that, but knowing we are wanted might make the journey more awkward – and more expensive – than need be.'

They sit in the sulphurous dark, listening to the voices outside. At length there is silence. It seems the friars are gone.

'Thanks be to God for that,' sighs the pardoner. They can only see his eyeballs in the dark. Footsteps fall on the ladder beside the door and someone shouts and then more feet fall and there are more shouts and suddenly the ship shudders and lurches and seems to come alive. Katherine impulsively grabs Thomas's arm. She feels him stiffen.

'We're casting off,' the pardoner says. Above them on the rear deck they can hear Cobham bellowing rhythmically, as if encouraging some physical effort.

She lets go of Thomas's arm, just as the pardoner claps his hands to his cheeks.

'Dear Christ on His cross!' he exclaims.

'What? What is wrong?'

'We have made no offering to St Nicholas,' he says. 'We have made no offering for a safe journey.'

7

The wind comes from the east, bringing with it ranks of lace-topped swells that roll under the carrack, lifting her and dropping her nearer the lee shore. Master Cobham, standing on the aft deck, legs spread and his leather hat pulled low over his brow, swears.

'God's wounds!' he bellows. 'God's holy wounds!'

On the deck the pardoner and Thomas crouch together, heads between their knees, clinging to the ship's listing side with raw hands.

'We shall be wrecked,' the pardoner shouts over the wind. 'We should have said a Mass. Should have said a hundred of them.'

He retches again and wipes his mouth with the back of his hand. In the night he has pulled a muscle from all the vomiting and now his face is yellow, his eyeballs bloodshot, and his beard slimed with something not even the rain can wash away.

By the evening he is too weak to sit and, with the help of Katherine and the ship's boy, Thomas carries him back into the cabin and hoists him into a stained canvas hammock.

'By all the saints,' the old man murmurs when he is settled, 'have I not suffered enough? They said take a medicinal bath. They said that would suffice. So I sent a servant, a good girl, to drown a litter of puppies for me: fox terriers. Then I had her gut the little things, *Jesu Christe*, and boil them up to make a soup. Yes. A soup. Dog soup. Enough to fill a bath. In which I sat for four hours with two—'

He retches again, a long fruitless spasm.

'Two newly cut goat-kid skins – one on my head and the other on my chest – so that I shouldn't catch a chill. They told me that would be enough, that that would cure me, but no. No. God wants to kill me this way. With seasickness.'

The ship's boy is lingering in the cabin door, glad to be out of the rain for a moment.

'Master Cobham says no one ever died of seasickness,' he pipes.

'The thought of dying is the only thing that keeps me alive,' the pardoner groans.

The boy laughs and hurries off, balancing against the slant of the deck, letting the door bang behind him.

'A good lad,' the pardoner says. 'Reminds me of my own boy.'

'You have a son?'

The pardoner shakes his head.

'Buried him three years ago,' he says. 'Plague.'

The weather lasts for two more days. They are not wrecked and when it is over, life on deck begins again. Gulls resume station, their wings snowy against the blue sky, and the sun shines, warming the skin if not the bones. The cook lights a fire on his stone and makes soup from fish the boy catches with a hook. Though the ship still dips and surges, the crew set about repairing the sails and everything wet is hung out to dry, including the pardoner.

The next day the land recedes to their right, and there are boats on the horizon. The water under the ship's prow changes colour, becomes a choppy brew littered with broken barrels, scrubby feathers, filthy rushes, a dead dog.

'Crossing the estuary,' the boy explains, gesturing westwards. 'Up there to London.'

Master Cobham is more watchful and the boy is sent to climb the ratlines and sit on a spar lashed to the mainmast's crown.

'Worried about pirates,' the pardoner murmurs. 'Something else we have to be watchful of these days.'

Thomas hears himself grunt absently. It seems to him that he has not slept since leaving the priory, for every time he closes his eyes, he sees Riven, or the giant in that moment before he felt his thumb press on his eyelid; or he sees the Dean being killed in the cloister, and all these images come afresh, just as if they are still happening, not things that have happened, and every time he lurches into wide wakefulness, his heart racing and his fists clenched.

He has tried to pray for release, and he asks God to take vengeance on his behalf, but as he prays, he cannot help but imagine himself as God's chosen instrument. He imagines that it is he seeking Riven out, just as the pardoner suggested, and he imagines it is he landing the blows on the man, cutting him, pounding him, breaking bones, gouging flesh. Each time he must catch himself, calm himself, and return to prayer.

He hears the pardoner sighing on the bale beside him.

'It must be hard,' the old man is saying, gesturing to Katherine in the boat's bow, her back turned on them. 'Thrust from her cloister to be among us rough-skinned men.'

Thomas looks at her again: her straight back, stiff shoulders. He says nothing.

'And what about you, Brother Thomas? Will you return to the cloister?'

'One day,' he says. 'It is a good life.'

'It's a good life,' the pardoner agrees, 'though I cannot see that it will last too much longer.'

'What do you mean?'

'The monasteries are too rich,' the pardoner starts carefully, gesturing towards the shore. 'Think of the ends to which our dukes and earls go to find their children advantageous marriages, and yet the finest match in all England would be that between the Abbot of Westminster and the Abbess of Sion. With wealth like that, such men as your man Giles Riven, well, they will find a way to get hold of it, by hook or by crook, and when they do, all the monasteries and convents and priories and friaries will be snaffled into someone's hunting bag before a single summer is out.'

The pardoner is interrupted by a shout from the mast. The boy has seen something. All the sailors stop what they are doing.

'What is it?' Cobham shouts up.

'Balinger,' the boy calls down. 'Moving fast, maybe ten oars, maybe more. Mainsail up, making for the foreland.'

Thomas rolls to his feet and joins Katherine at the bow. Across the water one of the boats is moving fast, with a bank of oars that dip rhythmically and propel the craft forward in definite steps. Cobham shouts orders and the sailors run to new tasks, easing the sails to let them slip the wind. The ship relaxes under their feet. They wait.

'Changed course,' the boy shouts down. 'Coming towards us.'

Cobham swears again and shouts more orders. The crew reset the sails and the carrack lurches. Cobham jams the tiller over so that she slews eastwards, out to sea.

There is another long silence. The sailors are tense.

'Well?' Cobham shouts.

'Coming on after us,' the boy cries.

There is a groan.

'Bloody pirates,' Cobham says. 'No good, this. Th'Earl of Warwick's supposed to be keeping the seas clear and look at this. Unless . . .?' An idea strikes him. 'Who are they?' he calls up to the boy. 'You make 'em out?'

'Sun's shining on a quantity of metal.'

'Harness?'

'Could be. Helmets, anyway.'

'Might even be Warwick's men,' Cobham supposes.

They look up at the patched sails, and the next minute they watch them sag as the wind dies. The carrack loses way. Cobham swears once more and begins pumping the tiller as if this might speed them on their course.

'You!' he shouts. 'Cook! Stop eating your bloody biscuits and whistle up the bloody wind!'

The cook – the pardoner says he is a Genoese – begins whistling. A light air riffles the heavy sail.

'Keep whistling, you whoreson! Keep whistling!' Cobham storms around his deck. 'Saxby! Saxby there! Let go what we don't need.'

Saxby is the master's mate, a bully with dark curly hair and a gold hoop pressed through his ear. He grasps the cook's still warm firestone and hefts it and staggers with it to the ship's side. He shunts it over and it hits the sea with a kerplunk that shoots a fountain of green water above the ship's rail. The cook doesn't pause in his whistling. Then Saxby and three others tip the anchors over, each one disappearing with a deep booming splash.

'Christ on His cross,' Cobham mutters. 'Cost me more than a penny.'

'Gaining on us, master!' the boy cries down.

'Right,' Cobham says. 'We need to lose all this if we are to get clear. You there! Master Daud and your boys! Lend a hand. Everything overboard.'

Thomas and Katherine set to, joining the sailors as they begin hauling bales and packages overboard, tipping them over the carrack's side into the sea below. The pardoner can hardly stand to watch but mews 'no, no, no, no' as his bags go over with the rest. Some sink, others float. Cordage, sailcloth, buckets, bales, boxes, anything not fastened down goes over. In the carrack's wavering wake they leave a stream of bobbing wood spars and planks and canvas-wrapped bags.

One of the men emerges from the cabin with the pardoner's sack-covered pack.

'Master!' the pardoner cries, springing into action. 'Not that one! That is all I own!'

The sailor looks at Cobham, who narrows his eyes.

'All right,' he nods. 'Put it back.'

The sailor lobs the pack back in the cabin, but everything else goes over. The cook's pots and pans, a wooden chair, every scrap of rope, every lump of tar, all the food, all the ale. All that remains are the men, the sails, the pardoner's bag and the weapons: four rusted swords, a long-handled bill, a hammer used for breaking chains and the giant's axe. Each member of the crew has a knife on his belt and one hidden in his clothes. Thomas has the pollaxe and one of the sailors passes Katherine a length of rope with its end tied off in a knot that looks like a large fist. Within is a weight and together they make a lethal club.

'I am expected to fight,' she whispers to Thomas. She swings the weight and flinches as it flies past her nose.

'Foof!' Thomas says. 'Be careful.'

She stares at the knot. He moves to stand in front of her, to protect her from whatever will happen next.

'Still gaining, but slower now,' the boy calls down.

He need not have bothered. Every sailor is ranged along the ship's side watching the balinger come battering across the water. Cobham watches from the stern deck.

'Fuck,' he says. 'Should've kept the firestone. Drop it on 'em from up here, it'd take the whole stinking lot of 'em with it.'

Thomas sees something flicker in the sky. Then there are two sharp thuds in the carrack that make every man jump.

'Christ Jesus!'

Two fat arrows quiver in the deck. Both a yard long and as thick as his forefinger. One instant they aren't there, the next they are, buried in the deck in a corolla of grey splinters. Dust rises from each like smoke from a candle wick.

'Christ!' Cobham shouts. Then he calls up to the boy. 'Oi! Boy! Warn us when they're about to loose those bloody arrows, will you, you little—'

He breaks off and shields his eyes from the glare. He stares up into the rigging.

'—bastard,' he concludes quietly. An arrow pins the boy through his chest to the mast. He looks around. Then: 'Saxby! Saxby there!'

he shouts. 'Stop your fuckin' gawkin' and get rid of the dead wood.'

He nods his head and Saxby leaves off his post at the ship's rail with something like a leer and on quick feet he crosses to where the pardoner stands, pale and old and frightened. Before Thomas can move, Saxby grasps the old man around his arms and rushes him backwards, toppling him over the ship's rail and into the sea. The old man has no time to cry out.

Saxby steps back.

Thomas runs to the ship's side. There is nothing there, just the green sea, peaking, troughing, frilled with foam, unreadable to the horizon. There is no sign of the old man. The pardoner is gone. Thomas cannot believe it.

Next to him Saxby smirks, self-satisfied.

'He was slowing us down, mate,' Cobham calls out. 'And didn't look able to fight none.'

Thomas wants to lash out, to hurt Saxby.

Saxby sees his expression change. A blade appears in Saxby's hand and he is quick with it. He flicks it at Thomas's face and makes a grab for the pollaxe. Thomas throws his head back, feels the knife pass.

Saxby is laughing, coming at him again. But Thomas thrusts the spike of the axe at him. He means to fend Saxby off but Saxby is too fast, and is not expecting it. There is a gristly crunch. Thomas feels resistance give and something soft slip. Saxby gasps; his eyes turn round as pennies. Thomas cannot help himself. He pushes. Saxby's face changes colour and his tongue sticks out. He gasps for breath.

Thomas steps back. There is a neat sleeve of dark blood on the axe's poll. Saxby falls to his knees, his eyes rolling back into his head.

It is so quick.

'Oh Christ!' Thomas cries. 'Oh Christ! Forgive me!' He drops the murder weapon and grabs Saxby's arms, as if holding him up might save his life. 'I didn't mean it. You saw! By all the saints I swear to you!'

But Saxby is already gone. His dead weight passes through Thomas's grasp to slump on the deck.

'Dear God!'

Thomas steps away from the body, looking around for help, for credence. Katherine is staring at him, her mouth open, her face pale. It has been so quick. So sudden. So easy. There are dark ropes of blood across the deck and on Thomas's boots, and a pool of it is forming under Saxby's body.

'Christ's sake!' Cobham roars from his deck. 'What're you doing? You lot! You lot! Kill him. Kill 'em all, by Christ! Kill 'em and then bloody put 'em overboard!'

Thomas's vision seems to waver. Sound is muffled. Time slows. All he can do is look at those hands of his, those murdering hands.

Dear God! He has killed a man.

Then Katherine slaps his shoulder.

'Thomas!' she shouts. 'Thomas!'

Sound and light come back to him with a roar. Men are running at him. Running at Katherine. He stoops for the pollaxe and pulls her behind him. The first sailor is on them with a rusted blade. Thomas catches it with the axe. He staggers back under its weight. The sailor is red-faced and ugly, spitting with fury. Thomas shoves the butt end of the pole up into the man's groin. It seems light in his hands and such an easy thing to do. The axe seems to move for him.

The sailor shouts something, drops the sword and throws himself back. He trips on his heels. Without thinking Thomas steps after him and drops its blade into the falling man's face. The man screams and clamps his hands to the mess of his nose and teeth. He writhes on the pitching deck; a moment later he is choking on his own blood.

The second sailor is there already, big with a wind-burned nose and a thick leather jerkin. He's behind Thomas and aims a slash at

Katherine with a chipped cleaver. She flinches out of the way. The blade whistles past but snags her sleeve. Thomas turns and drives the crown of the axe into the sailor's armpit, breaking his ribs and sending him staggering over to the ship's rail where he collapses on his backside, blood all over his hands and his chest, his bare feet scrabbling on the deck. He is gasping; then he too is dead.

'Oh God Oh God Oh God.' Thomas's face is very pale.

'For fuck's sake!' Cobham bellows.

There are still three sailors left: men with scarred knuckles and expressionless eyes. One takes up the rusted sword from the deck. Thomas watches him circle to his left, just as the other comes from the right. He wonders how he will fight two at once.

But then another flight of the arrows from the balinger hits the ship's deck like a ripple of thunder. Five shafts, suddenly there, like a fence, buried up to their shoulders in the deck. The last one catches the sailor's heel, nailing it to the boards. He throws up his sword, bellowing, flailing at the arrow's fletch.

Just as the second digs his blade at Thomas. Thomas catches it against the steel languet of the pollaxe, steps into him, and, copying Riven, smashes his left fist into the gristle of the sailor's nose. Two fangs of blood sprout on his face and Thomas wheels around to drive the axe into the sailor's knee. The sailor goes down in a tangle on the deck. Thomas drops the fluke on him. It is a wound that won't kill him for days yet.

The third man comes at Thomas, circling, his blade held low, but he is half-hearted now, and backs off as soon as Thomas levels the axe at him.

'Help me!' the sailor with the arrow in his heel keeps crying. 'Help me! For the love of God! Help me for the love of all that's holy!'

Now Cobham has had enough. He abandons the tiller, storms down the ladder. He scoops up the rusted sword and advances on the sailor with the arrow in his heel. The sailor looks at him imploringly, then changes expression and tries to scrabble backwards. He holds up his hands.

'No!' he screams.

Cobham chops the blade through the meat of the sailor's throat. There is a spray of blood and the sailor goes down with an awkward bounce, as if he has fallen from a tree, still pinned by the heel while blood seethes across the planks.

'That's how you do it, by all that's bloody holy,' Cobham roars. 'That's how you bloody well do it, see?'

He turns on Thomas.

'I had you for apostates,' he spits. 'I should've handed you over to the friars when I had the bloody chance.'

Even before he's finished the sentence, he lunges at Thomas. Thomas smashes the blade away. Then Cobham darts at Katherine. Thomas jabs at him. Cobham catches the axe on the blade of his sword, a clash of sliding steel. Cobham is strong, stronger than Thomas, stronger than Riven maybe. He pushes Thomas back, then spins and crashes his elbow into Thomas's cheek. Thomas's knees ooze, his vision wavers and the axe seems too heavy to hold.

Cobham smiles. He is about to hit him again when Katherine catches him with the rope maul.

Now it is Cobham who staggers. His hand flies to his collar where she's struck him. He checks for blood. Only a little. He tries a quick underhand thrust at her body. Thomas drops his axe on the blade, knocking it from Cobham's hand. Cobham shouts in pain and the blade rattles across the deck towards Katherine. She bends to pick it up. A knife appears in Cobham's hand. He leaps at her, catches her collar, pulls her to him, bends her around, shielding himself and exposing her neck to his blade. Thomas recovers.

He swings the axe, just missing Katherine. There is a dense thunk of steel on bone, and he buries the long spike of the axe into the flesh under Cobham's chin. Cobham dies instantly, his body converted to dead weight that pulls the axe from Thomas's grip.

Together axe and man crash to the deck. The stink of blood is ferrous and intimate.

Katherine staggers free, her knees weak. She is holding her throat. Thomas bends and twists the axe from Cobham's body, ready for the next attack. He is breathing heavily, hardly able to see straight. He holds out the axe and stares at the men gathered on the deck.

They do not move. They stand watching him, pale-faced, incredulous. Then they drop their weapons and step back. Thomas can scarcely believe what has happened either. Katherine is looking at him as if he is someone else.

'I must sit,' he says. He drops the axe and sits just before his legs give out. He cannot stop his face from creasing and the tears silently pouring down his cheeks. He grips his hands together to stop them from shaking.

'What now?' Katherine asks. Her face is also pale, a smudge of blood above her lip.

'We wait,' the Genoese cook answers for Thomas. 'Hope they don't kill us.'

Thomas has almost forgotten the pirates.

There is a small crump as the balinger hits the side of the carrack, out of sight below the ship's rail, and a moment later two more men come springing over the ship's side. They have swords in their hands, steel helmets on their heads and heavy padded coats. The first is tall, and moves lightly on to the deck in high leather boots more suited to a horse than a ship. The second is small, wiry, like a terrier, with ginger whiskers and a big nose, often broken. Both wear red tabard coats, sweat-ringed and salt-rimed.

They stop and look around.

'Fuck me!' the second one says. 'Looks like we're late for the harvest.'

The first of the two, taller by a head, sheathes his sword and takes off his helmet.

'Saints,' he says, disappointed. 'What's gone on here?'

He has dark hair cropped short above the ears, like Riven, but he is younger, with an open, handsome face, the sort Thomas trusts. Three more men join them, clambering slowly over the carrack's sides. They do not look at ease with the swell of the sea, and Thomas recognises their sort from home, long ago: beefy, well-fed, deep-chested boys with backs warped by work in the fields and butts. Each carries a short sword, except for one, who carries a longbow and a bag of arrow shafts. They wear the same red livery coat as the first two, with a small star marked in white cloth on the right side of the chest. When they see the dead bodies each crosses himself.

The first man runs a hand through his hair.

'My name is Richard Fakenham,' he announces to the sailors, 'of Marton Hall in Lincolnshire, and on behalf of my lord the Earl of Warwick, the Captain of Calais who is entrusted to keep the seas, I am claiming this boat for his purposes.'

'You are not pirates?' the Genoese cook asks.

Fakenham looks insulted.

'No,' he says. 'We are soldiers. Now, which one of you's the master?'

One of the surviving sailors – the ferrety-looking one with a widow's tooth, older than the others – points to Cobham's body.

Fakenham grunts. 'His mate?'

The man points again. This time at Saxby.

'All right,' Fakenham says. 'Which of you knows how to sail this thing?'

Again the older man volunteers.

'What's your name?'

'Lysson,' he says. 'John Lysson. Of Falmouth.'

'All right, John Lysson of Falmouth, can you sail us to Calais? Across the Narrow Sea?'

After a moment's hesitation Lysson nods.

'Get to it then.'

Lysson looks at the other sailors, as if for permission, then clambers up the ladder to take control of the tiller. He shouts an order that the other two sailors and the Genoese cook start to obey. As they pass the smaller of the two soldiers, the second man aboard, he bares his teeth and growls at them like a dog.

'Don't kill any of them unless you absolutely have to, Walter,' Richard Fakenham calls. 'We need them to help sail this damned thing.'

Then he turns to his own men.

'You lot,' he says, 'tie the other boat alongside and when that's done, let's get my father aboard.'

One of them shouts down into the other boat and a rope is thrown up and caught. Fakenham looks around as if he has forgotten something. Then he sees Thomas sitting and Katherine standing among the bodies.

'What's gone on here?' he asks.

Thomas swallows. He can say nothing. He knows if he tries, he will start to weep again.

Katherine answers for him.

'They threw our master overboard,' she says, gesturing towards the ship's stern. 'And then they tried to kill us.'

'So you killed them?'

Katherine nods.

Fakenham raises his eyebrows.

'But who are you?' he asks. 'Why are you on board at all? You aren't with them, are you?' He indicates the sailors.

'No,' Katherine says. 'We were his servants.'

'The dead man's? Who was he?'

'His name was Robert Daud. He was a pardoner. Of Lincoln.'

'Of Lincoln? Wonder if I met him? We're from Lincoln way. Walter? Did you know a Robert Daud? A pardoner? From home?'

There is an impatient grumble of denial.

'Well, I'll ask my father. Though he has no time for such things. Indulgences and so on.'

Fakenham notices the giant's pollaxe, lying where Thomas has dropped it, glazed with blood. He bends to pick it up.

'Is this yours?'

Thomas can nod.

'Nice,' Fakenham says, and he swings it, checking the balance. 'Very nice.'

'We are going to Canterbury,' Thomas says, as if that explains everything.

Fakenham hardly hears him.

'Have someone's eye out with that,' the man he has called Walter says, appearing at Fakenham's shoulder and regarding Thomas carefully. He rubs his bristles on his chin and frowns. Then his eyes travel up and down Katherine for longer than is comfortable. There is something about her he does not seem to like.

'Get shot of these will you, Walter?' Fakenham asks, indicating the dead bodies. 'Overboard. And clean the place up a bit, too. Then let's have some action. We need to get to Calais without attracting any more attention.'

Walter crouches over the dead sailors and begins going through their clothes. He is mumbling to himself, a disappointed burr. There are some coins in a pouch around Cobham's neck that he keeps for himself, three knives of inferior quality that he leaves on the deck for anyone to take, which Katherine does, and a pouch in which one of the men kept the wooden beads of his rosary. Thomas watches in silence.

He has killed a man. More than one. He understands he has done it to save himself, and Katherine, but he can smell their blood on his hands, and on his boots, like a stain on his soul.

'You there, servant! Lend a hand here.'

Walter is standing holding Saxby's heels. He wants Thomas to take the shoulders. Thomas stands and grasps the mate's leather jerkin and lifts, and together they swing the body towards the side.

'Should we not say the viaticum?' Thomas asks. The thought of even a man like Saxby going to heaven or hell without some blessing and prayers is shocking. When a canon or a sister died, the prayers lasted three days.

Walter looks at him as if he is a simpleton.

'No,' he says.

And that is that. They swing Saxby over and let him go. Thomas watches his body splash into the sea. Then Walter calls and Thomas returns to collect the others and together they bundle their corpses over the ship's rail. Thomas murmurs a blessing each time, and as the men go over they are just meat, more solid in death than they had been in life. One of the remaining sailors climbs the ratlines to the mast. A moment later the boy's loose-limbed body tumbles down, catches on the stays with a fumbling bounce, and then goes over the side with a small splash.

'Only a lad,' Fakenham says, peering after him. 'Shame.'

The sailors start hauling in the flapping sails and the ship stiffens under them and begins to make headway. The horizon steadies. Two more men from the balinger climb aboard and begin helping an older man up over the ship's side. He is red-faced and snowy-haired, with a long grey feather in his blue velvet cap. He wears a fur-trimmed coat and on his feet very fine, muddy leather boots, which might once have been the colour of a polished conker. When he reaches the deck, he hobbles, as if in pain.

'God's nails,' he mutters. There are tears in his pale blue eyes and he stands for a moment, swaying, as if he knows his next step will hurt, and he looks for the shortest route towards somewhere to sit.

'Can you get my chest, my boy?' he asks Fakenham, who crosses the deck and shouts down to the boat below. A moment later two more men bring up a chest – a fine red leather brass-bound trunk – and put it against the cabin wall. One of them is fat, fatter than any man Thomas can recall ever seeing, but he has powerful arms, each one like a shaved piglet, and he is as broad across as a church door. While the older man waits, breathing heavily, Richard Fakenham opens the trunk, removes a large red cushion, and shuts it again. He places the cushion carefully on the trunk and helps the old man lower himself on to it.

'There you are, Father,' he says.

'Thank you, my boy,' the old man says. 'Thank you. What would I do without you, hmmm?'

When he is settled and has set his cap in a particular angle, the elder Fakenham looks about.

'Not a bad little ship,' he approves. 'Young Warwick'll be pleased.'

His eye falls on Thomas and Katherine, standing there.

'Who are you?' he asks.

'We are servants, sir,' Thomas begins. 'Of Robert Daud, a pardoner, lately of Lincoln.'

'Not old Master Daud?' the old man says, brightening at the mention of a familiar name. He turns to his son. 'Once tried to sell me a chrism for my 'plaint, you know? Often wondered if I should have paid its price, but when his boy died a year or so back, I thought, well, if he can't cure that with his toe bone of St Cecilia or his scapula of whomsoever, then what chance has he of curing me?'

'Here, Father.'

Richard Fakenham hands him a beaker that he drinks with a shudder.

'So where is he? Master Daud?' he asks, dabbing his mouth with a cloth.

Thomas tells him.

'Drowned? Is he now? Poor old bugger.'

Sir John pauses a moment and looks up, his eye drifting across Thomas's bloodied clothing.

'But you would not go so quietly, hmm?'

'They killed five of them,' the younger Fakenham says, showing his father the giant's pollaxe. 'Five and half if you include that one.'

He nods at the sailor with the wound in his belly, still alive in the shadow of the ship's rail.

'Lord, Richard,' the old man says, whistling at the axe. 'Look at it. Lovely piece of work. I'd not like to be on the receiving end of that. Who are you?'

'I am Thomas Everingham of— I am . . . a servant.'

There is a moment's silence while the old man looks at them both thoughtfully.

'A servant, eh? And yet how many men have you killed this morning? And not a scratch on you. It is almost, what? Miraculous? Don't you think it miraculous, Richard? Geoffrey?'

He is addressing his son and the fat man. Neither says anything, but both allow for the possibility.

'Perhaps the good Lord is keeping an eye on them, eh? Perhaps He has some special purpose in mind? Some higher calling?' He is joking, and he turns back to Thomas. 'You are a big lad, aren't you?' he says. 'Not much muscle, but . . . You ever shoot an arrow?'

'Not for a few years,' Thomas calculates. 'I lost the practice after my father went to France.'

'Ah. France, eh? And he did not return?'

'No, sir.'

The deck pitches under their feet and the old man is distracted by pain for a moment. His eyes water, but he recovers and takes another drink.

'Well,' he says, 'I am indentured to provide my lord Fauconberg with fifteen archers. I had fifteen until one of them ran back to his fields the moment he saw the sea, and so I am short by one man.'

'They say they are on their way to Canterbury,' Richard puts in.

'Well, that is another happy coincidence. So are we, just as soon as we are able.'

'You will take us to Canterbury?' Thomas asks.

He can hardly believe his luck.

Sir John laughs.

'We are not hauliers or carters, man,' he says, 'but if you are prepared to join my company as an archer then I will see you to Canterbury, and beyond.'

He glances at his son as he says this. Richard smiles slightly.

'But—' Thomas begins. He is about to tell them of his vows. Katherine shakes her head slightly. The old man misinterprets.

'You don't fancy it?' he asks. 'Then we'll have to see if the Lord really does have a special purpose in mind, won't we, for you'll have to swim ashore, here and now. I will not take you to Calais only to see you run off and join the Duke of Somerset in his stinking castle. You are altogether too able with that pollaxe of yours, and I should not like to find myself facing you across some sodden field in the future, regretting that I did not have you killed while I had the chance.'

Thomas turns to Katherine. What choice do they have anyway?

'We will do our best,' he says.

'That's more like it,' Fakenham says. Then he turns to Katherine. 'And how old are you, boy? Fourteen? Fifteen? Ever shoot a bow? Not by the look of you. Well, I dare say we can use you for something. Until you acquire a bit of muscle, that is. Perhaps you might act as a squire for my son? Richard? What do you think?'

Richard nods. He seems pleased at the thought. Katherine says nothing.

'I cannot afford to pay you the same as one of my archers, but I can promise you four marks a year, better cloth than you are wearing now, food most days, and the chance of a share in whatever might come our way. What do you say?'

They can but nod, and so it is agreed.

8

For three days and nights the carrack *Mary* stands off the coast of Kent, pinned back by an unflinching wind that comes up the Narrow Sea. On the cliffs to the north they can make out the two towers of the shrine of Our Lady, but no amount of prayer brings a let-up in the weather and by the third day every man watches with a tinge of envy as the sailor whom Thomas wounded finally dies.

'All right, Thomas,' Walter says, 'another notch on that axe of yours. Chuck him over and then help these others with the sail. And you! Girly! Clean all this up.'

At the sound of the word 'Girly' Katherine stiffens. She turns away, hiding her face in the loose folds of her hood, feeling her cheeks flush and her heart hammer. The fat man Geoffrey touches her arm.

'Don't mind him, Kit,' he murmurs. 'He's got a vile tongue, but he's kind at heart.'

She nods, grateful for the big man's compassion, but she cannot meet his eye. She ducks away and begins sluicing seawater over the dead sailor's blood, conscious of Walter's boot caps as he stands watching her work. Afterwards she helps Geoffrey bring the sick men mugs of rainwater, just as the ship's boy had done, until at last on the fourth day the wind backs around and releases them. The sailors reset the mainsail and the ship begins to forge across the heavy waters.

The fat man, Geoffrey, is, as far as she can tell, the one who makes sure the men are fed and clothed, the one who worries about where they will sleep the coming night. The other one, Walter, is the man who organises the fighting, who enforces the discipline. Old Sir John is happy to leave them to it, while his son Richard is more concerned with his own affairs, and says little. Unlike Geoffrey, who is disposed to talk, and speaks quickly and quietly; in this way she learns something about Sir John Fakenham and his company.

The story, as far as she is able to pick up and later relay to Thomas, is that Sir John has been to the wars in France. He's fought at the siege of some town the name of which she forgets even before Geoffrey has finished telling her the tale, but while he was there, the army was ravaged by a sickness Geoffrey calls the bloody flux, which in the end took the King Henry, the fifth, too, and this seems to have marked a turning point in the fighting.

The names of the battles that follow are lost on her but Sir John survived them all, though only just, and was captured and ransomed at one, where the French used cannons and someone of whom Katherine pretends to have heard was killed and beaten so badly with an axe handle while he lay trapped under his horse that his herald only recognised his body from a distinctive gap between his teeth.

After that the impoverished Sir John had returned home to England to find his manor house near Lincoln seized by a local knight, who claimed some legal right to it, but in reality had none save he knew he could count on the support of the Duke of Somerset should Sir John try to reclaim it.

'Sir John appealed to his cousin, who was Lord Cornford, wasn't he? He hoped he might do something for him at court, seeing as Sir John'd managed to betroth young Richard there to Lord Cornford's daughter. But there wasn't much Cornford could do for him while the Duke of Somerset was so strong at court, was there? And then any hope was lost when old Cornford found himself on the wrong end of dagger at Ludford Bridge last year. Stabbed in the eye, he was, poor old bastard, and after the battle, such as it was, was ended.'

The coincidence is impossible.

'Who stabbed him?' Katherine asks, though she knows the answer.

'The self-same man who stole Marton Hall. A man called Riven. Sir Giles Riven, though no one knows when he became a knight. If you're from Lincoln, you'll know of him.'

Katherine nods.

'Notorious throughout Lincolnshire, Riven is,' Geoffrey goes on, 'and beyond now, since he's not only managed to get himself into Lord Cornford's castle at Cornford, but he's gone and made Cornford's daughter his ward.'

'What does that mean?'

Geoffrey is puzzled by how little she knows.

'Only that he has broken off the planned marriage between Richard and the girl!'

Katherine is little the wiser.

'Which means old Sir John's lost his manor, and young Richard doesn't get his hands on Cornford Castle.'

Geoffrey spits in disgust.

'And so there is Giles bloody Riven,' he goes on, 'sitting in the castle, in the lap of bloody luxury, with an army of archers, kept warm by the thought that his son will inherit the place with an income forever, while here we are, sick as pigs out on the Narrow Sea, just fifteen of us, attainted and stripped of everything we own, including our names, and me with my wife and daughter still at home.'

Katherine goes to stand next to Thomas where he is bent over the ship's rail, peering back at the coast of England hidden somewhere in the sea mist. He's wrapped a piece of sailcloth around his shoulders and his eyes are red-rimmed with lack of sleep. The souls of those dead men lie heavy on his conscience, she supposes, and he has spent the last few days sitting by the dying sailor, wringing his hands and praying for his life.

'Sir John knows Giles Riven,' she says.

Thomas starts.

'How?'

After she's told him he throws off the sailcloth and stalks away across the deck. She watches him for a moment. He is so drawn and thin next to the other men. She can see every bone. The sooner he returns to the cloister, she supposes the happier he will be. But she feels a breeze of panic when she thinks of parting from him. What will she do then?

When he comes back he looks even more disturbed. There is something in his eye that reminds her of Alice, or perhaps one of the other sisters after they have been at prayer too long.

'It is the will of God,' he says. 'There is no other way to explain it.'

She says nothing, but she feels something sinking within her.

'Why would He send those winds?' Thomas is asking. 'If not to hold us back, so that we would meet these men? Why would He preserve us through the fight with – with Cobham? Surely it is as Sir John says? He has some special purpose for us.'

Katherine does not believe God has in mind a special purpose for anyone, for if that were so, then why not for everyone? She cannot believe His special purpose for her was to endure the Prioress's torments for so long. She cannot believe that His purpose for Alice was to die like that. Were she to believe that, then she could only conclude that this God was a vengeful God.

'It is God's will that we go to Calais,' Thomas is saying.

She shakes her head to distract herself.

'Why?' she asks. 'Why Calais?'

Thomas is momentarily flummoxed. He glares at her. Then softens.

'We can go from there to Canterbury,' he says. 'Where we will seek out the Prior of All and plead our case.'

'Oh,' she says. She does not want to think about Canterbury.

'What is wrong?' he asks.

Now it is her turn to be flummoxed. It is the question, and the way he looks at her when he asks it, because it seems he wants to know what is wrong with her so that he can put it right. The experience is new.

'Nothing,' she says. 'Nothing.'

And now she looks away over the ship's rail, across the dipping waters at the banks of sea mist and fog that have congealed around them. She has been putting off the moment but now she knows she must tell him that she can expect nothing but a noose from the Prior of All. She knows she must do it now. Tell him that she cannot come with him to Canterbury, she cannot return to the priory. She looks up, ready to confess, but a sailor in the ship's bow gives a shout, Thomas turns away, and the time for confession is gone.

Hearing the cry the men in the ship's waist roll to their feet and Richard Fakenham appears to seek out Lysson, the ship's new captain.

'What's up?' he asks.

'Ship,' Lysson says, nodding towards the French shore.

The men begin to crowd the ship's side, staring across at the waters to this new vessel's hazy outline. She looks to be a carrack like their own, but she is moving faster, with her sails filled and her bow throwing up white water.

When Richard Fakenham is anxious he clenches his jaw and even under the ten days' of bristle it is possible to see his muscles at work.

'Where did she come from?' he asks.

'Dunkirk, prob'ly,' Lysson says.

'You sure?'

'Came from inshore, so.'

'But it could be anyone?'

'Can't make out the standard yet, but they ain't merchants.'

'No?'

'Look at them castles,' he says. ''S a fighting ship, all right. Pirates, most like.'

The new ship is built up at both ends to give her crew the advantage of height when it comes to loosing arrows and throwing stones.

'Could be French. Spanish. Breton. Could have come from Sandwich. Stuck there with the wind and that. Could be from the English fleet.'

'Best be ready then,' Richard says, and turns to the men gathered on the deck. 'Walter?' he calls.

Walter is already ushering the archers into the cabin to collect their bows and put on their quilted jacks. They emerge cumbersome, strapping leather bracers on their wrists, pulling leather tabs over their draw fingers. Each man straps a short sword around his waist and hangs a small circular shield over the pommel. The bows are taken out of their bags last and the hemp strings nocked.

'Lids on, lads,' Walter says.

They slip their helmets on, close-fitting steel shells each fastened with a leather strap under the chin.

Richard stands at the ship's prow while Geoffrey straps a piece of plate armour across his back. Despite being so large, Geoffrey has agile fingers, and he fastens the hidden straps before Richard's father appears on deck.

'Richard,' he calls to his son. 'Better stand elsewhere, eh? No sense making yourself a target.'

Richard is pale and keeps swapping his drawn sword from hand to hand. He ignores Sir John and peers at the ship ahead. The plates of his armour tap and scrape as Geoffrey secures them.

'Walter,' Sir John calls. 'Get the flag up.'

Walter leaves the rail and fetches a large square of fabric from Sir John's trunk. One of the sailors takes it and climbs a few yards up the ratlines.

'Go on. Farther. Up there. Look.'

Walter points. The sailor climbs up and ties the top corner to a stay, then pulls it taut. The flag – a large black star on a white background – catches in the breeze. There is a tentative cheer from the men.

'Can you make out her standard?' Sir John asks the sailor. The man pauses with his bare feet on the ship's rail and peers across the waters at the other ship, shields his eyes, then, after a moment, shakes his head.

'Never mind the standard,' Walter mutters. 'Has she got any cannons? Any bombards?'

At the mention of artillery the sailor quickly climbs down. The rest of the archers are quiet.

'I can't see anything,' Richard is saying. 'This mist. God's blood! Is that smoke? Look! Yes! They have a fire going. They mean to use fire arrows.'

He turns on Thomas and Katherine who are standing spare before the cabin door.

'You two! Find a bucket each. Get some water on board.'

Since Cobham and his men have thrown everything overboard there is only one bucket from the balinger.

'I said we should have brought a friar,' Geoffrey says, his voice slightly higher than usual. 'We need someone to lead us in prayer.'

Thomas opens his mouth but closes it again and instead they drop a bucket on a rope down into the green seawater and let it fill, hauling it up as the archers kneel and begin a muffled chant of the paternoster. Each archer makes a sign of the cross on the deck where he kneels and then bends to kiss it.

'All right, on your feet,' Walter says when they're finished. They keep glancing at one another and fiddling with their equipment and one of them yawns with nerves.

'Put your arrows in your belts,' Walter says. 'Make every one count 'cause we ain't got no more. Pick your aim and look for faces. Look for faces, understand? Faces. Anything pale. This ain't the butts. This is the real thing.'

They are still well beyond bowshot, but the other ship is approaching fast. Geoffrey stands next to Katherine. He is carrying a long-handled hammer with a pick on the reverse, like Thomas's pollaxe, only shorter, designed to be used with one hand.

'Can you make out her standard?' he asks.

Thomas shakes his head. Katherine cranes forward just as the wind gusts and backs a notch, and the ship's banner spreads itself red across the grey sky.

'It is a picture of something,' she says.

Sir John hobbles over and grips the ship's side.

'Of course it is a picture,' he barks. 'Of what though?'

Katherine cannot be sure. The boats plough towards one another, dipping in the green waters so that the flags flap and buckle. Then the banner stretches and looks to be some sort of creature, and she remembers the bear she saw in Boston.

'Could it be a bear?' she asks. 'Gripping something?'

'A stump?'

'A tree stump? Perhaps.'

'You're sure?' Sir John asks.

She nods.

'Ha!' Sir John claps her on the shoulder, nearly driving her to her knees. Then he cups his hands and tries to shout across to the other ship. 'A Warwick!' he cries. 'A Warwick!'

The archers groan with relief but then hurry to the ship's side to join the shouting, and soon across the dipping waters they hear the same cry returned. There is the sound of men sighing with relief. Soon the other vessel is alongside. The men across the water are almost identically dressed, in red coats and jackets, and they watch as their captain climbs the ship's rail, one hand raised in salute.

'Where are you bound?' he shouts.

'Calais!' Richard shouts back. 'We are the company of Sir John Fakenham!'

Even at such a distance Katherine can see this means nothing to the other man.

'Godspeed!' he calls. 'And keep you safe!'

Their sail shudders as the carrack passes and takes their wind, and then it is gone, away into the mist, southwestwards on a soft air.

'All right,' Walter begins, 'excitement's over, let's get everything put away.'

'God gave you good eyes, Kit,' Sir John says. Katherine flushes and hides herself in fiddling with the handle of the bucket. The old man hobbles back to his cabin.

'What's wrong with him?' she asks Geoffrey.

'Fistula,' Geoffrey says. 'Spent too long sitting on his horse in the rain, see, wearing heavy armour and looking for a Frenchman who'd give him a fight.'

The archers begin unstringing their bows and putting their swords and bucklers back into their packs. Only Richard looks anything but relieved.

'He's yet to be blooded,' Geoffrey says quietly. 'And it weighs on him more heavily than on the rest of them.' He nods towards the others, who are teasing one another, elated now that the danger has passed. 'You nearly shat your pants, Dafydd, when you thought they'd fire a gun at you.'

'No, I never,' the Welshman replies in his impossible accent. 'Been in tighter spots than that, haven't we, Owen? Being shot at by a couple of drunken sailors from England, I don't know.'

Dafydd and his brother Owen are from somewhere in Wales, though perhaps by different fathers, for Dafydd is compact, with dark brows and a lick of black hair as coarse as a horse's tail, while Owen is big-boned and blank-faced under sandy hair. Dafydd has an argumentative streak, but Owen says almost nothing, except to repeat that of which he approves. He smiles most of the time, and sits in silence staring at his brother, his massive hands curled in his lap. Geoffrey says he is simple, but there is something reassuring about his company.

'Sir John was doubtful about taking him on after Ludford,' Geoffrey tells her, 'but Dafydd says he can spit a mouse at two hundred paces. Yet to see him try, of course, but he's been no trouble so far.'

Dafydd and Owen often play dice with Black John. Black John is one of the six Johns in the company, called black for the colour of his hair. There is also Red John, who has wild red hair and freckles; and Little John Willingham who had been the smallest in the company until Katherine arrived. Then there is Brampton John, who comes from a village called Brampton, near Sir John's manor; and Johnson, son of John, from Lincoln, whom they call Johnson in honour of his father, and finally Other John, also from Lincoln, whose father is also called John, and who looks so like Brampton John and Johnson they can think of no way of distinguishing him from the other five Johns except to mark that he isn't one of them.

Along with another archer called Thomas – who remains just Thomas, while Thomas has become Northern Thomas because of the vestiges of a northern accent – there are two Roberts and a Hugh, also from Lincoln. Most have spent every Sunday and feast day learning to shoot arrows in the butts behind the churches in their various villages, and they've worked together in the fields since they were boys too, and there is an easy familiarity among them.

Of the others, sometimes Simon Skettle of London joins Dafydd and Owen and Black John in their dice game, but no one seems to like Simon, and though he talks a great deal, he tends to silence any conversation he joins.

Walter's disgust is reserved in the most part for Hugh. Hugh is a long-limbed youth with fleshy lips and eyes like a girl's, and he is always on the brink of tears.

'More like a friar than an archer,' Walter tells him. 'You sure you've spent your time in the butts? Show me your fingers again.'

Hugh manages to look misused and is made to feel it, like some kind of self-fulfilling prophecy. As they sail on towards France he stands alone, staring mournfully as the mist begins to dissipate and they sight the coast.

As they near the shore Katherine smells the tang of coal smoke and human excrement. The archers are crowded at the ship's rail peering over the waters towards the coast where a wavering smoke stack rises above a town.

'Calais,' Walter spits. 'The last piece of France we have to call ours.'

'Looks like a bit of a shithole,' Dafydd says.

'You could say that,' Walter agrees, 'but it's our shithole. Or at least, it's the Earl of Warwick's.'

This gets a laugh. The remaining sailors start to reduce sail. They can hear the waves on the shore and the ship begins to slow.

'That's Fort Risban.' Walter points, nodding across the water at a castle looming on the end of a long low spit that curves around the port. It is a squalid building, salt-stained where it is not caked in gull shit, and from its lower walls protrude three squat black barrels. There are soldiers on the castle battlements and behind them a fire is sending up smoke, as if the wood they are burning is green.

Lysson gives an order the sailors have been waiting on. A rope is thrown out to a smaller boat with oars, and the carrack is towed along a green-watered reach between Fort Risban on one side and Calais Castle on the other.

Beyond the castles the town sits behind its limestone walls, a jumble of church steeples and the gabled roofs. Along the quay is a broad skirt of lean-to shacks and fish-hangers where women and children are gutting fish and mending nets while men hurry past pushing carts laden with bales, bundles, caskets and barrels.

The *Mary* is brought into the murky waters of the crowded harbour beyond, finishing her voyage by grating against the weed-slimed timbers of the quay. While the sailors tie her up, the gangplank is run out and dropped with a bang. Sir John Fakenham emerges from the cabin. He looks grey, more ill now than he had when he boarded the ship, and he hangs from Geoffrey's thick arm.

'Let us thank St Nicholas for a safe voyage,' he says, and then he catches sight of Thomas and Katherine and stops. 'Though I know that not all would see it in that way,' he admits.

Simon and Red John are lugging Sir John's chest out on deck and Richard emerges from the cabin behind his father. He turns to Thomas and Katherine.

'What about this?' he asks. He holds up the pardoner's pack, the one he had valued so highly. It is stained now, but it has been carefully tied so that its contents look to have survived the journey. She sees Thomas about to speak.

'It is his,' she interrupts, nodding at Thomas. Thomas glances at her, then nods and stretches his hand to take it. Richard hardly cares one way or the other, and tosses Thomas the pack. Thomas slings it over his back, and together they step up on to the gangplank. She follows him across, trying to imagine what the pack might hold that the pardoner valued above all his other possessions.

9

Thomas sits next to Katherine on a millstone on the quayside. She is staring at the grit beneath her boot soles.

'Did you ever think you'd come to France?' he asks.

He stamps on the ground, as if to make sure it is real. This is the land where his father died, but it is also the land apart, where Englishmen come to make their names and their fortunes. Despite himself, he feels a slight thrill, as if the earth is communicating something to him. Katherine is less excited.

'I did not ever think I'd leave the priory,' she says.

He is quiet after that and together they watch Geoffrey haggling with a traventer over the cost of hiring an ox and cart to take the company to find lodgings in the Pale.

'You'll find no room in the town,' the traventer says. 'Every man in England who owes his living to the Earl of Warwick is here. More attainted traitors than you'd dare shake a fist at.'

He is an old soldier with a worm of pink scar tissue crawling across his nose. His mate, who holds the ox's ring, is drunk and grins distantly while the archers pile their equipment into the cart. Thomas carries an iron cauldron that leaves his hands covered in black grease while Katherine has a leather bucket crammed with wooden spoons, plates and mugs, and a set of leather bellows. There is a grindstone and a massive roll of canvas that the Welsh brothers carry between them as if it is a dead body. There are tent poles, a lance, another bucket of broken arrows, a pile of grubby sheepskins imperfectly cured and there are more boxes and bales and lengths

123

of canvas and some spare bows and some bags of arrows, a number of bills with rusted heads, three dented breastplates, a kettle helmet, a roll of rondel daggers and a falchion, as well as a collection of lead mauls kept in a broken barrel. Lastly the archers throw their own bags up.

'Right, boys,' Geoffrey calls, 'that's the lot.'

The carter lashes the ox and they pull off across the wharves towards Calais's Seaward Gate. Thomas and Katherine walk shoulder to shoulder behind it, hanging back from the other men; the pardoner's pack is heavy on his back. They cross the drawbridge and go through the fortified towers in a crush with the porters hurrying under the spikes of the portcullis. The Stand Watch are there in quilted, buff-coloured jacks, each man with a cross of St George on his chest, a polished sallet on his head and a bill in his hand.

'Ordinaries,' Walter states, gesturing at the soldiers as they crowd under the gates. 'Posted to the garrison here. Can't do a day's work on the land and shoot an arrow afterwards like us.'

'Walter,' Geoffrey cautions.

'I'm just saying,' Walter replies, spreading his hands, all false innocence. 'And anyway, even if they can do all that, they can't be expected to remember on which side they're meant to be fighting.'

His voice rises as he speaks. A heavyset soldier's hand goes to his sword. Two more shift their bills.

The Watch Captain appears.

'All right,' he says. 'All right. Calm down. Let's move it along there.'

Walter smirks.

'Say anything like that again though,' the officer says as he passes, 'and I'll prick you myself, you little shit.'

Walter laughs. They follow the cart out along a narrow street towards the marketplace, its wheels grinding on the cobbles. All around them are wool-houses, great blank-sided stone buildings where the merchants store their sarplers.

'What was all that about?' Thomas asks Geoffrey. Geoffrey glances at him with a mixture of irritation and surprise.

'Don't you two know anything?' he asks.

Thomas shakes his head.

'It was their mates who swapped sides at Ludford Bridge last year,' Geoffrey says. 'Went over to the Queen. The King, I should say. Their captain was the Master Porter of this place, bloke called Trollope. Andrew Trollope, a northerner. Meant to be a good friend to the Earl of Warwick, only when it came to it, he wasn't.'

'So what happened?' Thomas asks. 'Were you there?'

'Me and Walter were. We were with Lord Cornford's men, in the Duke of York's battle. We had the men of Calais with us, and the Earl of Warwick in command, and though the King had three times the numbers, we were in a good spot, with a fortified wall and even some bombards and guns. And no one thought much of the King's troops. They were northerners, see? Rather steal a candlestick from a nun than go toe to toe with a man.

'So on the night before the battles were supposed to meet, we said our prayers and slept in the field where we were. Next morning, even before Mass, it was clear everyone'd left. Turned out that the Calais men had gone over to the King in the night. And so, seeing as he knew our disposition, and how the enemy now had four times as many men as us, the Duke of York and the Earl of Warwick gave up hope, and to spare the bloodshed of the commons, or so they said, they fought with their heels.'

The traventers lead them into the marketplace, where the gabled houses seem to take a step back from the cobbled streets and there is glass in every window. Above them the towers of St Mary's and St Nicholas's rub shoulders with the Staple Inn, the stone-built hall where the Captain of Calais conducts his business. Even here Thomas can smell rotting meat.

'God's blood!' Katherine mutters next to him. 'Another one.'

She has her hand over her mouth and turns her head from the sight, but Thomas cannot help himself. Four mottled quarters of meat hang on grimy ropes from a stone cross: a man's arm and his legs, covered in fat black flies, and the rack of his ribs where the executioner's axe has passed.

'Wonder where his head is?' Dafydd asks.

They walk on, leaving the market square for a street full of taverns and cookshops, bath houses and a cock pit.

'What I wouldn't give for a drink,' Walter mutters.

A woman without a headdress watches them pass from the door of an inn. Then another, from a window above, who stares down at them in a manner Thomas knows to be brazen. Walter licks his lips.

'A harlot,' he says, addressing Katherine, who has been pretending not to see them. 'Better not let Sir John find you with one of them though, Girly, or you'll lose a month's pay.'

'And the wench'll have her arm broken for her troubles,' Geoffrey adds.

Katherine moves closer to Thomas. He finds he likes it when she does that, but her proximity confuses him, muddles his mind, makes him uncertain what to do with his hands. He glances down at her. She is not looking his way. They walk on, she in his shadow.

The alleyways between the houses are dark and noisome, little better than blocked sewers. Some are choked waist-high with every kind of refuse and worse, leaving only narrow slips at the centre for men and animals to pass. Here there are stables and sties, tanneries and pelterers' workshops, each adding their signatures to the stink and noise of the streets.

'Gah,' Geoffrey exclaims as they pass a dyer's yard where a great vat of urine and dog shit simmers. 'Right strong, isn't it?'

Worst are the shambles, where butchers bleed their animals and leave offal to rot in the streets. Here is a pile of rotting cows' hooves.

Another Watch guards the fortified Boulogne Gate, but this

afternoon they are more interested in throwing stones at a man hanging in a basket suspended from the castle walls.

'Get on with it!' one of them shouts as he launches a half-brick over the moat.

'Cut the rope, you dozy bastard,' another bellows. 'Then we can all go home.'

'What's he doing up there?' Dafydd asks.

'Don't you worry about him,' the soldier laughs.

The moat's waters are turbid with all kinds of rubbish, and rats compete with seabirds for scraps. Two soldiers are stationed in a boat below the man in the basket though whether they are there to drown him when he falls or pull him out it is impossible to tell.

Beyond the gate sprawls a vast village of rain-damp canvas shelters in a broad sea of pale mud that stretches as far as the eye can see. The roads are raised on dykes over drainage ditches and the water in the canals reflects the dull skies above. It reminds Thomas of the marshes around the priory, and he feels a leaden depression settle on him.

'Welcome to the parish of St Anne's,' Walter spits. 'What we call the Scunnage.'

Wordlessly they follow the cart up an avenue between the tents. Some are grander than others, with standards hung from long lances thrust into the mud, and within them it is possible to see chunky sheepskin beds where the better class of captain sleep. From other tents bored men stare at them. They are not precisely friendly, not precisely hostile, and there is nowhere for anyone to sit.

Everywhere is crowded with rough-looking women and boys acting as porters, carrying jugs of ale and water, armfuls of pimps and faggots for the cooking fires. The boys are filthy and malnourished, and more than one is missing an ear. Beyond are more women, eyeing them with weary speculation. Walter waves to them, all false jocularity.

'Whores,' he mutters.

They move on.

'I always hate this bit,' Geoffrey mutters. 'Looking for the best place to set up and everyone looking at you like you've got the pox.'

'And you always end up exactly where everybody's been shitting since a month back,' Walter adds.

They move on through the camp until they come to its edges. Sure enough a shallow scoop has been gouged in the earth and the stench of human waste is almost unbearable. Chickens and geese and pigs are everywhere.

Then there is a priest on a grey donkey.

When he sees him, something in Thomas lurches. He has been so long at sea that he has almost forgotten his state as an apostate. Now it comes back to him. He ducks his head and hurries to the other side of the cart. Katherine is already there, her eyes wide with anxiety. Her hands still shake long after the priest has gone.

The sooner they see the Prior of All, he thinks, the happier she will be.

'I think we'll head around there,' Geoffrey says and urges the carters off the road and across a sodden compression towards where the armourers and arrow-makers have set up their stalls. The acrid smoke from their fires does something to mask the smell of the camp, but the din of their hammers is insistent.

'You'll soon get used to that right enough,' Walter says, 'and, anyway, they can't work after sunset.'

There are long hovels where the horses, oxen and asses are kept and there are more boys in cast-off clothes bringing hay from the barns. There are pens for geese and sheep and sties for pigs and efforts have been made to make a road using willow hurdles laid across the mud. Some boys are piling up slender logs for the fires and thick-armed women are trying to wash clothes in water that has never been clean. Every now and then a Watch rides past, back from one of the other castles in the Pale, their horses' hocks yellow with mud.

'Not much of a place,' the other Thomas points out, shaking his head so that the line of water drips scatters from the fringe of his cap. He is a quietly spoken boy, about Thomas's age.

'It'll be better when we've had something to eat,' Geoffrey asserts. The rest of the men begin unloading the wagon while the carters look on and Geoffrey shows them how to set the battens and canvas and tie the loops off to keep the tents upright. They use broken arrows as tent pegs, hammering them into the mud with mauls that might properly have been used to stave in a man's skull.

Two of the Johns return with a pile of sticks and lumps of coal, which they light with some baked linen, a good black flint and a steel, and they soon produce a new source of discomfort as foul black smoke fills the tent.

Geoffrey then gives Thomas five silver coins, a sack and four jugs and sends him with Katherine to buy bread and ale.

'Don't spend it on pretty clothes, Girly,' Walter calls as they leave.

When they are away Thomas asks her how long she thinks it will be before her sex is discovered.

'I don't know,' she admits. 'But what else can I do but keep up the pretence? Besides, if you are right that God has a special purpose in mind for us, well, we shall see.'

It is on Thomas's tongue to remind her that Joan of Arc was burned not for being a witch, but for disguising her sex under a man's clothes, against the strictures of Deuteronomy. Does she even know who Joan is? He doubts it suddenly. And whatever will they do to her when they do? He thinks of the man hanging in the tree outside Boston, or the wretch quartered in the marketplace in Calais, with his head sent elsewhere, or the pardoner's story of the man with his ear nailed to a post, and the whore with her broken arm. There seem to be any number of ways to punish a man, or a woman.

'Besides,' she goes on, 'Walter only calls me that to hurt me. It seems that is how he is.'

Thomas nods. He supposes she is right.

'He is like a dog my father once had,' he says. 'He used to nip the sheep's heels, and we lost more than one lamb because of it, so in the end my brother took him out and drowned him. After he'd done it, we regretted it.'

Katherine glances at him, but says nothing, and Thomas wonders why he has told her the story. He has never talked of home to anyone since he left. He does not often think of the place now. He had been happy to leave the farm. It was a harsh life, always cold, usually dark, and every day mutton. His brother too, and his brother's wife, pregnant with their first child, always looking at him. He knew that being away, being in cloister, was the best thing that could have happened to him.

They walk on until they find some women willing to sell them ale and bread. By the time they return to the tent a cauldron of beans hangs over the fire.

Geoffrey has also spent money on new-made clothes. He hands Thomas and Katherine each a linen shirt, two hoods – one blue, one red – two pairs of blue hose that look as if they might fit Thomas but not Katherine, a travelling cloak such as the other men wear, and a thick quilted jacket each.

'Won't stop an arrow or a blade,' he says as Thomas shrugs his on, 'but then almost nothing does. Leastways, nothing we can afford.'

Thomas has never had new clothes before. The jack hangs stiffly from his body while Katherine's reaches below her thighs and she pulls it tight about her, so that it becomes more like a long coat than a jacket. Geoffrey hands Thomas the giant's pollaxe.

'Keep it somewhere safe,' he says.

Just then Richard Fakenham comes into the clearing by the fire.

'Any news?' Geoffrey asks.

'The Earl of Warwick has sailed for Ireland,' he says, throwing his helmet through the doorway of the tent and on to a pile of sheepskins. 'Gone to see his grace the Duke of York. Means we'll be stuck here awhile.'

Geoffrey groans. Walter spits a fob of white mucus into the fire.

'Still, at least we'll be able to prepare ourselves,' Richard continues. He sits on the pile of sheepskins and unties the spurs from his boots. 'The boys haven't loosed an arrow in a week.'

Walter nods.

'Where is Sir John?' Geoffrey asks. 'Is he lodged in town?'

'He is. With old Lord Fauconberg. They were in France together, and you know how it is with them. He'll take supper and sleep there, I suppose.'

'Is that soup ready?'

After they have eaten dinner, Walter leads the company through the sprawl of tents to the butts. Thomas and Katherine follow along, a step or two behind, not yet accepted.

'Right,' he says. 'Let's get busy.'

The men begin unfastening their bows, shaking out their arrows on the mud. They nock their strings and begin stretching their arms and shoulders, limbering up ready to shoot.

'You ever use a bow?' Walter asks Thomas.

'Not for a few years,' Thomas says. 'Not since—'

He stops. He has not used a bow since he joined the priory. Until then he had spent every Sunday after Mass with the other villagers on the butts behind the church, sending sheaf after sheaf of arrows into the sky. He had been thought a promising bowman, and when Walter passes him a spare bow, the weight and balance of it bring his childhood back.

'Take a cord,' Walter says. 'Nock it.'

Thomas loops the string around one of the horn nocks and then places it against the side of his foot to help bend the bow and loop the other end over. It is a big bow, fat and long, witch hazel, but old and tired, and probably never a really good one.

'Seen better days.' Walter nods at it.

There are dark pricks in the wood and signs of cracking from long use. Yet with the string nocked it comes alive in his hands and he itches to find an arrow to put it to use.

Walter has turned back to the men and Thomas watches as they strap on their bracers and slip their fingers into the leather tabs that protect their drawing fingers. There is something timeworn and easy about this routine, the manner in which they joke together and mock one another, and he can easily imagine them back at the village butts. But then instead of taking turns to loose their arrows down the range, as they did at home, the men form a loose harrow formation, standing in three ranks, so that each has just enough room to shoot. They have arrows stuck in the ground and in their belts and some wear their bags on their belts. They stand waiting for Walter's command.

'Nock,' Walter says, and they nock their arrows on to the bowstrings.

'Draw.'

They haul the strings back as they lift their great bows into the pale sky.

'And loose!'

They send their arrows off with a roll of thrums, each shaft oddly elegant as it whips sighing out of sight. As he lets fly, each archer grunts, as if in satisfaction, and staggers a pace or two forward.

Then they pick up another arrow each. Walter repeats the command.

'Nock, draw, loose!' he snaps, quicker this time. 'Nock, draw, loose.'

After they've shot about a dozen shafts each Walter stops them.

'All right,' he says. 'Time for a laugh. Thomas here is going to have a go.'

The men let Thomas through.

'I have not shot for some time,' he says, preparing them for the worst.

'Just get on with it,' Walter grumbles. There is a low murmur of well-meant mockery. Thomas cannot help but smile.

He picks an arrow, nocks it on the cord and places it on the shelf the knuckles of his left hand make where he grips the bow. It is a bodkin head: a war arrow. He begins the draw, but the bow now seems horribly stiff. He knows he has to get his body into the bow, so that his back muscles take the weight, not his arms, but still, after so many years in the priory attending to not much more than his psalter, his muscles have withered, and though he has the technique, he has lost the strength. He can hardly get the string to his left shoulder. Sweat breaks out on his brow, his arms begin shaking and the string cuts into the soft fingers of his right hand. He cannot hold the string any longer. He looses it with a twang and the arrow shoots forward about a hundred paces to land in the mud.

Walter cackles.

'I reckon young Girly can do better than that,' he says.

Richard is watching and gestures that Katherine is not to be put to the test.

'All right,' Richard says. 'You've had your fun. Now let's stop messing about. Collect your arrows and then we'll have a sheaf each. Fast as you can.'

The men grumble as they fetch their arrows, but are silenced on their return to find the men of the Gate Watch that Walter abused earlier that morning standing fanned out along the back of the butts, each man at ease with his bow, waiting, watching. No one says a thing. The atmosphere thickens.

'All right, boys,' Walter mutters, pretending to ignore the newcomers. 'Let's see if we can't put on a show to remind this lot not to switch sides in the future, shall we? Remember this is for the pride of Sir John Fakenham's company, so go fast, but make each one count. I don't want to be able to see the butts for the fletches. Understand?'

The men gather their arrows together, and get back into position.

'Not you, Northern Thomas,' Walter says. 'Right. Let's go. Nock! Draw! Loose!'

For the next few moments the men work fast, each one drawing and loosing his bow twenty-four times. Dafydd is the last to finish. The arrow storm has been brief but nearly four hundred arrows have been loosed, and it is possible to imagine just what that might do to an enemy.

When they've finished, they are all flushed and breathing heavily and they are steaming in the chill air. They look satisfied enough, but Walter's eyes are shut. The Watch officer begins a slow hand clap and his men begin murmuring, then laughing.

Walter turns on the captain.

'Think your boys can do any better?' he asks.

'I know they can,' the captain says. 'But let's have a bet, shall we?' The captain has tired eyes, creases either side of his mouth, and wears a scarf to warm his throat. 'A barrel of ale?' he suggests.

Walter cannot get out of it. They shake hands and the men of John Fakenham's company shuffle to one side to let the Watch take their places. Thomas cannot help thinking that even without their livery and quilted jacks, these men look more like soldiers than Fakenham's. They are older, grizzled, and their equipment more accustomed to use. They move with a muscular ease, too, certain of themselves.

Others have turned up to watch now: other archers, billmen, some women and boys and a dark-skinned man in a wool-lined travelling cloak, sitting on a rouncey with a baggage train behind him.

'Right,' the Watch Captain says in a nasal drawl. 'Butt on the left-hand side. A sheaf apiece. Nock. Draw. Loose!'

The soldiers erupt into action. It is measurably smoother and faster than Fakenham's men and it seems each one has sent his third arrow off before the first has hit its target. Before Thomas can count to one hundred it is over. They all level their bows as one.

'Fuck me,' one of the Johns mutters.

Everybody else is silent for a moment. The two companies walk down to the butts, one on either side of the range. The Watch's arrows are without exception buried up to their shoulders in the earth of the left-hand target. Those of Fakenham's company – distinctive because of the green-tinged twine that has been used to secure the fletches – are scattered over the ground: some have fallen short, some have overshot, some are wayward to the left, others to the right.

'Tcha!' the officer says, clapping his hands together with a bang. 'We'll have that barrel delivered to the garrison, if you please.'

They collect the shafts and walk back to their tents in silence, shame trailing them like a pall.

'I'm glad they're on our side,' one of them mutters.

'They are for now,' Walter snarls.

When they get back to their tent, they put away their bows and sit in silence. None can look another in the eye.

'So what are we going to do?' Richard asks.

'Can't go back there again,' Walter says.

'Chuck away our bows? Become billmen?' This is from Simon the Londoner.

'God's nails!' Dafydd says. 'I'm not becoming a bloody billman. Don't get paid as much, for one thing.'

'We'd best be selling our bows anyway,' one of the others says, 'to pay for that bloody barrel of ale.'

'Walter should pay for it. He made the wager.'

This is from Simon again. The others look at him.

'Walter backed us,' Red John says. 'We let him down. Least we can do now is help him out.'

Walter nods his thanks. One or two of the men dig in their purses for small coins and pass them to Walter.

'Simple fact of the matter is that we aren't good enough,' Richard says.

'We are,' Simon says. 'We're as good as any of those northerners, and much better than any Scot, or any bloody Frenchman.'

'But when we go back, we won't be fighting Frenchmen, will we?' Red John says. 'We'll be fighting . . . You know. Fighting . . .'

He cannot bring himself to say that they will be fighting Englishmen.

In the silence that follows, Richard stands up.

'By God,' he says. 'You might as well be a billman if that's the way you look at it. I don't want to stand and fight with men who aren't as good as someone else. I only want to stand and fight with the best.'

All eyes are on him. What is he going to do? Desert them and join the Calais garrison?

'The thing is,' he starts again, quieter this time, piecing his thoughts together, 'they are fast and they are accurate. That comes not from fighting, but from practice.'

'And any fool can practise,' Geoffrey chips in.

'Even you lot,' Walter adds.

Each man is silent for a moment, trying to imagine the comments they'll have to endure when next they appear at the butts.

'We need to get away,' Richard goes on. 'Somewhere we can put in the hours without the garrison troops turning up every few minutes to show us how it's done.'

'Not back in the boat again?' This is from Hugh.

'No,' Richard says. 'I'll see if we can't volunteer to garrison the fort at Sangatte. On the higher ground over there.' He gestures westwards, back towards the sea. 'Nothing's going to happen here, anyway. Not until the Earl gets back. No one will miss us.'

10

The next morning the same men who'd watched them erect their camp the day before watch them break it again. While Walter goes in search of the carters and their ox to first take a barrel of ale to the ordinaries at the Seaward Gate, then to carry their gear up to Sangatte, Geoffrey takes Thomas and Katherine to buy more supplies, including arrows from the fletcher.

'So what are we going to do?' Katherine asks him as he loads her arms with three sheaves in their linen bags.

'We'll spend every moment in the butts,' Geoffrey supposes, passing the fletcher a large handful of coins, 'until the Earl of Warwick returns, and then, when he does, we'll be the best archers in his affinity.'

Richard has bought a horse, 'with money borrowed from a Genoese banker' according to Walter, and he leads them out of the camp with his cap low, hunched in his travelling cloak. Cows graze in the waterlogged furlongs, low-bellied pigs rootle along the baulks, and the wind from off the sea presses cold wet cloth to cold wet flesh.

After half a mile or so, the road passes through a complex of earthworks where sluice gates corral a river and send it under a stone bridge and around the walls of another forbidding stone fort.

'Newnham Bridge,' Walter says. 'See them sluice gates? If the French come, the garrison can close them in a moment and flood the whole Pale.'

'Why would they do that?' one of the Johns asks.

'So the fuckers can't get their bombards and whatnot up to the walls,' Walter says, jerking his head back towards Calais. 'Whoever controls the sluice gates controls Calais, see, and whoever controls Calais, well . . . that's a question, isn't it?'

There is a sizeable Watch on the bridge: more men in the Earl of Warwick's red livery coat with that white badge on their chests. Each carries a bill except the sergeant, who carries a pollaxe like Thomas's, and he steps out from under a slate awning to greet Richard.

'May God send you to prosper, sir,' he says, touching the rim of his sallet. 'Mind telling me where you're bound?'

'Sangatte,' Richard replies. He hands him a pass, signed and sealed by Lord Fauconberg, but the sergeant can't read, so he sends for the castle's captain, and while they wait, he looks them over.

'Who are you?' he asks. 'Don't recognise the badge.'

'My father is Sir John Fakenham,' Richard tells him. 'He is Lord Fauconberg's indentured man and we are his company.'

The sergeant pauses and then smiles, as if he has remembered something.

'Heard about you,' he says. 'You're the archers, aren't you? Ha! The archers what can't shoot arrows.'

The men on the bridge laugh with their sergeant. Walter reaches for his sword, smiles vanish, four bills come down and the point of the pollaxe swings up.

'Easy, there,' the sergeant says. 'If your fighting's like your shooting you'd best not get into it with us.'

There is the tap of metal against stone and through an aperture in the castle wall Katherine sees a man peering at her over the top of a crossbow.

'Walter,' Richard says, 'step back.'

Geoffrey pulls him back. A moment later the runner returns with the Captain of the Watch.

'God give you good day, sir,' he says, taking Richard's hand. In his dented leg armour and faded livery he looks every inch the old soldier, and Katherine watches Richard covertly studying him.

'You are garrisoning Sangatte?'

'We are.'

'The captain up there. Walden. He's a drunk. Sleeps all day and roars all night. As a consequence there are no women up there, or boys. You may need to provision yourselves accordingly.' He nods to the village beyond.

Richard thanks him.

'I'll bid you good day, then,' the captain says and then: 'Oh. Sorry. Nearly forgot. Wonder if this'll be any use to you?'

The captain is holding out a boy's practice bow.

The men of the Watch begin laughing again.

Richard exhales loudly, touches his helmet and nudges his horse on. Across the bridge is a village with two churches and a cobbled marketplace where roads meet: one leads southwest to the French port of Boulogne, the other to the castle at Guisnes. Another, theirs, leads westwards, up on to the headland and the fort at Sangatte.

They follow it through steep banks around the cesspit and then on up towards the high ground where its muddy surface becomes sandy and stands of leafless poplars close around them. They carry on up the hill, sweating now, helping the cart along until at length they emerge from the woods to breast the rise. Sangatte Fort stands on the foreland before them like a solitary tooth in an old man's jaw and beyond is the sea, clean and grey, vanishing in the distance, and the wind is sharp in their faces.

They find the relieved garrison already gathered on the grass, waiting to take their cart. They are glad to get away from the place and it is soon clear why. The garrison captain meets them in the fort's courtyard with a mazer of ale in his hand. He has a grey beard streaked with food and his clothes, likewise stained, stretch across his bulbous gut. He is drunk already.

'Day to you,' he says, addressing Richard. 'You're to be my lieutenant then, are you?'

Richard nods and introduces himself.

'Well,' the man says, 'I am Gervaise Walden, Captain of Sangatte Fort, and so long as you keep yourselves tidy, and out of my way, you'll hear no word of complaint from me.'

He drains his ale and leads them back through the gatehouse. The fort consists of a circular tower of limestone blocks surrounded by an outer wall, both topped by flint-capped battlements and a deal of bird shit. Within the tower are four rooms, the one above the other, each linked by a spiralling staircase canted so that anyone mounting them exposes their sword arm to those above. On the ground is a cistern for fresh water, a sewer that gives out on to the dunes below and, under one smoke-blackened patch of rough-built wall, a pile of spindly firewood and damp coal.

'We had a woman,' Walden says. 'But she went.' He lets out a ringing burp and leaves them, saying, 'If you need me I shall be in Newnham.'

The men stare around.

'Homely,' Dafydd says.

'Like Wales, you mean?' Walter laughs.

They climb the steps to the battlements. Seagulls wheel overhead and the wind is strong. On some days, when the weather clears, they'll be able to make out the low profile of England herself, but for now it is not easy to tell where the sea ends and the cloud begins. Down below, in a trough between the sedge-topped dunes, someone has built an archery butt and broken arrows and fletches litter the sand.

By the time they descend Geoffrey has got the fire going and has set about making dinner. They begin unloading the wagon, carrying the tent canvas up to spread across the top floors to dry, and then after dinner the men troop down to the butts, leaving Katherine to keep watch from the battlements.

'Keep a good watch that way,' Richard instructs, pointing over the Pale towards a distant castle. 'That is Guisnes. The Duke of Somerset's taken it, and would love nothing better than to take this one too. If you see anything, anything at all, ring that bell.'

A verdigris-covered bell hangs from a strut cemented into the stonework. From the top of the castle Katherine watches the men spill out below and make their way through the long grass to the butts. She watches them form up, this time with Thomas in their midst, between Red John on one side and Dafydd on the other. He has that old bow of which he has complained but she sees he's managed to borrow a glove for his right hand and one of the leather sleeves to stop the string cutting his left forearm.

They loose some arrows and now that she has watched the soldiers from Calais shoot, even she can see how slow they are. Each man looses an arrow perhaps every ten seconds, and after they have each loosed twenty-four, the arrows, perhaps buffeted by the wind, are scattered over an area the size of the garth in a cloister. Thomas is the last to finish, and still has five arrows left to shoot after the next last, Dafydd, has finished shooting his.

She watches as Thomas and Dafydd are made to run up the butts to collect the spent arrows. When they have gathered them in their bags, they are made to run back down and distribute them among the rest. As soon as that is done, they loose them all over again. She can just hear the shouts carried by the wind.

'Nock! Draw! Loose!'

Again Thomas is the slowest. He takes off his jack and throws it on the ground. Walter shouts at him and he puts it back on and sets off up to the butts again, staggering through the sand. He gathers all the arrows together and starts running back with them. His legs are heavy and he falls over, drops the arrows, gets up, picks them up, falls over again. He delivers the arrows, then collapses on a grassy sand bank until Owen brings him a winesack to drink from. No one seems to think any the worse of him when he begins retching. The men carry on shooting.

A while later Thomas rejoins them, but by now he can hardly lift his bow, let alone draw it, and after failing to keep up he sits back on the bank and watches.

Katherine follows the walkway around the castle battlements, searching the land in all directions, watching the farmers and charcoalers, tiny dots in the distance, going about their business. Men are passing up and down the roads, some on horseback, others walking. There are a few carts rolling along, carrying barrels, and she watches a swineherd lose control of his animals as a galloping messenger scatters them under his hooves.

The archers continue all afternoon.

'They'll be stiff tomorrow,' Geoffrey says, joining Katherine on the tower. She does not mind his company any more. Despite his size and strength, he is a soft man, kind-hearted, who misses his wife and daughter, who should, he tells her, be married by now but is in England.

They stare out to sea. A ship lumbers through the heavy waters, heading westwards, to Ireland Geoffrey says, or around the coast and down to Spain. Beyond is England.

'I bet there are men in towers over there' – Geoffrey nods – 'staring this way, just waiting for us to come back and start it all again.'

'When d'you think it'll be?' Katherine asks.

'Depends on the weather,' Geoffrey thinks. 'The Earl of Warwick's got to get back from Ireland first, and I've heard of men stuck there for months or more, waiting for the right wind.'

'What's he doing in Ireland?'

'He's with the Duke of York, coming up with a plan, though it is clear to all what that plan'll be: Warwick and his men – that's us – we'll land somewhere in Kent; the Duke and his men'll land somewhere in the west. Then each party will march towards London, hoping to raise the country as he goes. The men of Kent have reason to hold the Earl of Warwick dear, for he has kept the sea clear of pirates these last few years, and stopped any more raids on the coast, but the Duke of York, well . . .'

He trails off. It is clear the Duke is less popular than the Earl.

'But what will happen when we reach London?' Katherine asks. 'Surely they don't mean to kill King Henry?'

Geoffrey actually splutters.

'Course not. Course not. No one would wish that. It is just to free him from the crust of his advisers, see? They cling on, don't they? And take everything they can. And the Queen! Did you know she's a Frenchy? And that she organised the raid on Sandwich?'

Katherine has never heard of a raid on Sandwich. Hardly ever heard of Sandwich.

'Where've you two been?' Geoffrey exclaims again. 'You and Thomas. You know nothing. It's as if you've been locked away these past years.'

11

Days pass, each longer than the last. Catkins appear on the hazel branches and the elm blossom is purple in the woods. A blackbird calls loudly. Spring is coming. Katherine can feel it in her bones: a curious thrill.

Until it comes though, the men spend every day, wet or dry, in the butts with Walter snapping at them, comparing them harshly to their forefathers who'd fought the French to a standstill at Agincourt, Crécy and Poitiers, judging them just as harshly against the men of the Calais garrison. When they come in from the butts for supper they eat in silence before throwing themselves on to the floor to sleep, each man curled against his neighbour for warmth. They go off instantly, and the noise of their snoring is like bubbles rising through mud.

Meanwhile Katherine either keeps watch on the tower, or is replaced by one of the archers as his reward for having won one of Walter's competitions. Sometimes she goes with Geoffrey to buy more bread and ale in Newnham, where the farmers speak English and come to know them by name. Here she watches Geoffrey haggle and tries a little herself. She is pleased when she beats a woman down a few pennies. She learns the meaning of money. Other days she scours the beach for firewood. Then she helps Geoffrey cook the dinner and supper, turning the spit, watching the pot, stoking the fire, eating plenty herself, and for the first time she can recall, she spends more than two consecutive days warm and dry and full of food.

'I have never eaten so much meat in my life,' she tells Thomas when they are on the castle walkway one morning. 'I used to dream of it, when I was in the priory, but now I thank the Lord it is Lent soon and that all we will eat is herring.'

Thomas laughs, but then becomes serious.

'It is the same with Mass, isn't it?' he says. 'We have not been since we left the priory.'

'We should do so,' she agrees, though in truth she has not missed Mass, or the cycles of prayer, though she still wakes in the night and it takes a moment before she remembers not to rise and hurry silently to the chapel for matins or lauds. She feels relief, but also guilt.

'We should have a Mass said for the pardoner's soul,' she says.

Thomas nods.

'He was a good man,' he says. 'I remember him in my prayers.'

She nods.

'Thomas,' she begins, 'have you looked in the pack he left?'

Thomas has almost forgotten the pack. When they'd reached Sangatte, he had put it under a mouldy scrap of tent canvas and ever since has used it under his head at night in place of a log. It has never been far from Katherine's thoughts though, and its existence has given her a kernel of confidence, as well as something else: a distraction from the waiting at the very least.

'I could get it now?'

He brings it back up and together they crouch while he unpicks the bag's stubborn leather ties. When he has them loose he slips out the contents. There is the pottery flask of the pardoner's salve wrapped in a piece of cloth, but there is another parcel too, bulky and roughly square and stitched tightly into a canvas jacket.

'A book?' Katherine asks.

'A bible perhaps,' Thomas agrees, feeling the canvas. He is obviously excited. 'Though it doesn't feel valuable. There's no lock or anything by way of ornament. And how to get in? I'll have to cut the stitches.'

He finds his knife and slides its blade along the canvas. The cloth falls away. It is a ledger, with dangling seals, roughly bound. Thomas opens it. It is a series of what looks like lists written in black ink, in the usual two columns, entirely unadorned.

He is disappointed.

'What is it?' she asks. It is frustrating, not being able to read.

He studies the pages.

'A record,' he says. 'A record of service. A muster roll. Or something like that. From a garrison of troops, in a place called Rouen, here in France, I think. From St Aubin's day in 1440 to the last of August 1442. It's just a list of the soldiers serving and their movements in the country. Who was there, in which retinue, where they went, how much each was owed. Thousands of them. That's all.'

Disappointment settles on Katherine so that she feels bitter towards Thomas, as if it is his fault. She has no idea what exactly she'd hoped for, but it isn't this.

'Why would the pardoner think it so valuable?'

Thomas shrugs. He reads out a few names.

'Thomas Rodsam. Thomas Holme. James Lodewyke. Robert Bassett. Robert Barde. Nicholas Capell. Piers Dawn.'

'Who are they?'

'I don't know.'

The binding is cursory, the paper low quality and the lettering little better than functional. Thomas folds it open, hoping perhaps something will fall out. There is nothing. Katherine shakes the canvas wrapping. Again, nothing.

'And yet do you remember how he reacted when he thought it was going to be thrown overboard?'

Thomas turns it over in his hands again.

She stares at it.

'Is that all?'

He looks at the pages towards the back:

'"To Gaillard Castle on St Ives' Day: Thomas Jonderel with eight archers; Roger Radclyffe with five; William de Beston with six and five billmen. Each paid the sum of two marks.'"

'There must be something else,' she says. 'There must be something of value in it. Perhaps some piece of information that we don't yet understand?'

It is the only explanation.

Thomas nods. She watches him return the parcel to the pack with the salve and tie it up again.

'I'll keep it safe,' he says. Afterwards they are both quiet, disappointed.

On the following afternoon Richard returns early from the butts.

'Bring me my harness, will you, Kit?'

Katherine stiffens. She finds being with Richard unsettling. Geoffrey shows her where his armour is kept, wrapped in oiled cloth against rust. Bag by bag she carries it up to the room on the second floor and when she brings the last one, she finds him wearing only his hose and a linen shirt. She has seen all the other men naked, including Thomas, but she has always avoided looking at Richard while he is washing or changing his shirt. She is wary of looking, wary of the feelings he provokes.

She looks away now. Then back again. He is broad-shouldered, narrow-waisted and long-legged and there is something about him and the way he moves that catches her mid-stride. She gathers herself and waits, averting her eyes, confused by the sudden warmth.

'Come,' he says impatiently. 'Help me with this.'

He is crouched over one of the bags, trying to make sense of the intricate jumble of steel pieces, laying out the larger parts on the planks next to him. When they are all organised he stands and picks up a padded doublet, patched at the armpits, elbows and groin with links of chain.

Starting from the sabatons, the interlocking strips that cover his feet, he instructs Katherine how to attach each piece of his harness, carefully naming each part as they go so that she will in future know the difference between a pauldron – the piece of plate that protects the shoulder – and a gorget, the collar of steel that covers the throat. It is a complex business, involving the delicate interplay of many pieces of overlapping steel, each one fastened with leather straps.

As she moves about him, Katherine can feel his breath on her cheek and smell his body, but still she does not look him in the eye. Her head seems to throb as she puts her arms around his chest. At last she straps the sword belt about his hips and then helps him with his armet, the close fitting helmet with a visor that comes down to meet the gorget.

She steps back and watches him moving around the room, re-acquainting himself with the feel and weight of the armour. It is unnerving. He looks like a different order of creature entirely, and as he moves the metal slithers and scrapes and jangles.

After a moment he lifts up his visor with the knuckles of his glove.

'Now go and fetch Thomas, will you, Kit? And tell him to bring that pollaxe of his.'

Thomas is in the butts. He is still always last in any competition, but it is now only by the most slender of margins, often just one arrow, and in the last weeks he has acquired some bulk in his arms and shoulders so that his linen shirt is too small for him. He walks with that curious rolling gait all the archers have. But now he comes up the steps anxiously, the pollaxe in his hand, and when he sees Richard he steps back.

'Come,' Richard says, his voice muffled, 'I need the practice too.'

'But, sir, I—'

Richard swings his war hammer. It swishes through the air between them.

'Come on,' he says. 'I want you to come at me. With your axe. I'll not hurt you, I promise. This is practice.'

Thomas doesn't believe this is possible. For a moment they circle one another. Katherine can see the panic in Thomas's eye. He is scared. It must remind him too strongly of his fight with Riven, and Riven had not been encased in harness, or armed with anything more lethal than a stick. Richard swings the hammer all the time, slowly backing Thomas into a curve in the wall.

When he can move no more, Thomas raises his pollaxe and blocks the hammer, a ring of steel that reverberates in the low-ceilinged room. Richard spins and mimes a blow that would have planted the hammer's fluke into Thomas's back.

'You're dead,' he says.

They step apart and come together again in the same way and this time, when the first blow comes, Thomas brings the axe up to block it and then spins on his heel to catch the next. He takes his top hand off the pollaxe and waves his fingers as if the blow had stung. Gloves, she thinks. That is what he needs.

But Richard has turned again and tries to jab Thomas in the stomach with the handle of the axe. Thomas sways one way, lets it pass, and then pushes Richard back with the flat of his axe.

'Good,' Richard says. 'Now, come at me. Hard as you like.'

Thomas cuts at him, a half-stroke. Richard blocks it with an armoured arm, the blade ringing on the steel vambrace. Now Richard steps back, lifts his visor and looks at the dent in the plate.

'Damn,' he says.

But Katherine sees he is pleased with the mark. It makes him look as if he has been in battle. He articulates his wrist and winces. Then he lowers the visor again.

'Come on,' he says.

Thomas swings again. This time Richard catches it with his hammer shaft. Thomas tries again and Richard steps into the blow and uses his weight to push Thomas back. The hammer comes around again and stops short of Thomas's neck.

Again they stand apart. Three more times this happens. The first Richard hooks the hammer behind Thomas's knee and sends him sprawling, the second he hits him with his fist in the teeth, drawing blood. During the third mêlée Thomas only just manages to stop a chop that might have caved in his skull, even if he had been wearing a helmet. Thomas drops the axe and clutches his hands.

Richard steps back.

Thomas bends to pick up the axe.

Richard steps forward and brings his knee up to Thomas's face, but this time Thomas rocks forward, grabs Richard's other calf and then throws himself backwards, pulling Richard's leg out from under him. Richard crashes to the floor and loses his hammer. Before he can roll away, Thomas is on him, axe held like a spear, the point pressed under the rim of Richard's helmet.

'Stop!' she hears herself cry.

Richard is still for a moment, and then slowly moves his hand to lift his visor. Thomas puts the axe down. He is breathing heavily, his eyes wild. He stands up, shaking with effort, and he smells sour. He helps Richard to his feet and they stare at one another. Katherine stands by, her face held in her hands, all blood drained away.

Richard appears unruffled.

'Enough for one day, I think,' he says. 'Next time, we'll wrap our weapons.'

The next day there is a repeat of the fight, but this time they each tie long lengths of sacking around the heads of their weapons. Thomas borrows a sallet off Dafydd and a pair of leather gloves off one of the Johns and the fight lasts perhaps twenty minutes. By the end both men are red-faced and sodden with sweat. Again Richard has the upper hand, and not just because he is wearing armour, for though that gives him protection, it hampers his movements and Thomas is able to get behind him. Thomas learns to target Richard's more vulnerable points too, and though Richard always wears the padded doublet with the mail patches under his plate, soon his elbows and armpits are blue with bruising where Thomas has struck him.

Geoffrey comes to watch the third afternoon.

'Funny thing about wearing armour', he says, 'is that people tend to go for it in a fight. Don't know why. Seems to attract their blows, so they don't hit your flesh. Worth wearing a piece of it, just for that.'

The next afternoon Thomas borrows one of the rusted breastplates. It is so large it sits low on his hips and it ends up with a sizeable indentation just over the heart where Richard smashes it with the fluke of his hammer.

By the next week their fights have taken on a different sound: the constant clang and slide of steel on steel and with every hour of it, Thomas becomes stronger. No longer does he lash out or become overheated. He learns anticipation, craft and guile and soon the giant's pollaxe has come to look like an extension of his arm.

Richard's armour is scuffed and dented, but he too learns from his bouts with Thomas and by the third week their fights can last an hour or more, swift, vicious and exhausting. At the end of each one Katherine has to undress Richard, removing the armour, cleaning it with sand and vinegar before oiling it and returning each piece to the right bag. He stands by and drinks mug after mug of ale.

'Thirsty work,' he says. His eyes are bloodshot. He looks mad.

Then she has to help him with the sweat-soaked doublet. The smell and sight of his hair-covered body still frightens her, and she is glad that Thomas stands by, watching, though she wishes he would not wear that anxious expression.

It is Walter who worries her.

She can tell he is watching her, even across the crowded room. She can look up and find his gaze fixed on her. Sometimes he will look away instantly. Other times he will carry on staring. Every time it happens, her heart lurches. She knows she only makes it worse by tugging her jacket down to hide her hose, since that only emphasises her bosom.

One of the days when it is raining, Hugh's bow breaks in the butts, and one of the broken pieces nearly takes his ear off. Despite the boy's tears and the blood that pours from the wound, Walter sends him back up to the fort with a series of cuffs and kicks. Katherine finds him whimpering by the well, and she washes the wound with clean rags and cold water and then applies some of the pardoner's salve. Hugh rests his head against her shoulder and she puts her arm around him to soothe him as he weeps.

It is not the pain, she understands this; it is the misery of his life, so far from home.

'There, there,' she whispers. 'There, there.'

Just then Walter returns. He stares at Katherine.

'How come you don't stroke my hair like that, Girly?' he asks.

Hugh stiffens and she nearly drops the salve. Her fumble covers her shock, but she still doesn't know what he means. If he knows she is a woman, why has he not exposed her? And if he thinks she is a boy, then why does he look at her so?

She tells Thomas the next day while they are out on the beach together, scavenging for driftwood. It is St George's Day, nearly summer, and although a light mist is coming in off the sea, the water is millpond still.

He frowns.

'Walter knows you are a woman?'

He seems not to believe her and it makes her angry. She turns her back on him. Later she finds a charred piece of ship's timber, nuzzled by the tide, and she needs his help with it. They are carrying it up through the dunes, consciously not talking to one another. Thomas is leading the way, carrying his end of the spar behind his back.

'The sooner we reach England the better,' he says. 'Then we can go to Canterbury.'

'Yes,' she says. 'Canterbury.'

They walk on. The timber is heavy and she needs a rest. He gives her some water.

'Will you miss the world?' he asks. 'When you are back in the priory?'

He is making conversation, trying to apologise, but the question makes her stop. She still has not told him the truth about Sister Joan.

'I will,' she says cautiously. 'All this – it has been a revelation.'

He says nothing, and his head is cocked as if waiting for her to go on. A bee bumbles in the still air. The day is already warm and sweat prickles her eyes.

'Your people will be happy to hear you are returned at last,' he says. He is probing for something, but what?

'I have no people,' she tells him. 'Or none that I know of.'

'But everyone knows their people,' he says. 'Everyone must know where they come from. You have to. It is the only way to know who you are.'

Katherine is silent. She shrugs and after a while they pick up the log and carry on up the dune. Although she does have a vague memory of something nicer – warmer anyway – she only really remembers the priory and any other thoughts as to who she might be beyond the priory walls are something she's never had the luxury to pursue.

'All I recall of life before the priory is a hearth, with a fire,' she says. 'And of being warm beside it.'

'That's all?'

'I thought for a long time that the memory was just something I'd imagined, but there are odd details about it that I do not think I can have invented, such as a window filled with coloured glass. Yet I am sure I have not knowingly ever seen such a thing.'

'Do you recall anything about your arrival at the priory?'

They are on easier terms already.

'I can picture it so easily in my mind, that I may have invented it.'

'How does it go?'

'I was five, or thereabouts. It is snowing but I was not cold. Not then, anyway, and I have some letters the words of which I cannot read, of course, and a heavy purse, and whoever I am with – I think it is a man but I cannot be sure, and when I think of it now it cannot have been a man for they would never have let one into the priory

– but whoever I am with, they make me give the letters and the purse to an old lady in black, who must have been the prioress before the Prioress. I recall her being kind. Or having a kind face.'

'Then?'

'Then, nothing. I remember the person I was with leaving and then the Life began.'

She does not want to tell him about all the punishments and the beatings and the humiliations and the coldness of the place. She does not want to tell him about the Prioress. Or Sister Joan.

'The money must have been for your keep,' he says. 'Someone will still be paying it. Someone will be worrying about you.'

The idea that someone has been paying for her keep when all she ever did was work until her fingers bled makes her smile. The thought that there might be someone out there to care what happens to her though, that is beyond comprehension.

'Someone worrying about me?'

For a moment she is at a loss for more words. Then a flush rises within her. Someone is paying for her keep, someone who knows who she was; someone is worrying about her. It is as if some previously dead part of her body is coming back to life, and she cannot stop the tears. She drops the wood again and turns so Thomas cannot see her crying.

'Kit,' he says. 'Katherine.'

He takes a step down the dune towards her and tries to put his arms around her shoulders, but she flinches and stretches her hand to hold him away. Tears are spilling down her cheeks. She tries to rub them away and spreads soot on her face.

Unable to speak for a moment, she looks out to sea; then she turns back.

'Thomas,' she begins, 'I have something I must tell you—'

But before she can say more, the alarm bell in the fort rings out.

12

It was Brampton John who saw the Duke of Somerset's men first.

'About three hundred archers,' he tells the company. 'Maybe more. And about two hundred billmen. Coming up the Boulogne road.'

'Any horsemen?' Walter asks. Brampton John tries to think.

'Not so many as to make a difference,' he says after a moment.

Walter grunts and hurries to catch Richard. They are moving down the road as it passes through a pocket of dead ground and for the moment Newnham Bridge and its fort are hidden from them just as they are hidden from it. When they emerge over the rise and begin their descent again they hear a crack that splits the silence of the day.

The men duck as one.

'Lord above!' someone cries.

When Thomas raises his head he sees a sallow puff of smoke hanging in the air above the battlements of the fort.

'It's all right, lads. It's all right,' Walter says. 'It's one of ours.'

Nevertheless the noise of the gun is impressive, and for a moment they are so absorbed in the sight of the smoke drifting inland that none notice the mass of men moving in three blocks up the Boulogne road.

When they do, they swallow hard.

Banners are unfurled, and Thomas can hear the drums beating and the high pitch of a fife, and a trumpet blowing. Dafydd crosses himself. Walter licks his finger and posts it in the air, checking the wind.

'Whatever can they hope to achieve?' Richard wonders aloud. He is sitting on his horse, war hammer across his lap, with a better view than them. 'They have no siege weapons to break the castle and surely not enough men to invest it.'

'Must have run out of beans and women then,' Walter says. 'They'll take everything in the town that isn't nailed down, torch it and piss off back to Guisnes. What I'd do.'

'Will the Newnham garrison come out, d'you think?' Richard asks.

'Got to,' Walter says. 'But there aren't enough of 'em to stop that lot. Calais garrison'll have to come out too.'

They watch the last of the townspeople hurry across the bridge under the fort, trying to get away from Somerset's men. They seem to share Walter's opinion on what will happen next and they are pulling carts laden with everything they can carry. In the distance the Calais garrison are already emerging from the Boulogne Gate, moving up in order: archers, billmen and a handful of horsemen, all hurrying. Walter is more interested in Somerset's men though, who are arranging themselves in their own blocks on the far side of the town.

'Something funny about this,' he says. 'They're holding their shape. Normal men'd be in there, grabbing everything they can get their bloody hands on, finding a woman before anyone else.'

'And they can't have had it easy these last few months,' Geoffrey agrees.

Since the Duke of Somerset had taken Guisnes Castle the year before, he'd been cut off from supplies. He'd promised the garrison prompt payment of their wages just as soon as a relief force came from England, but when that fleet reached the coast of France, the wind had turned and the fleet had drifted helplessly into Calais harbour where its supplies had been snapped up by the grateful Earl of Warwick. Warwick had then lined up every man of the relief force and those he recognised as having switched sides with Andrew Trollope the year before at Ludford, he hanged on the quayside.

Another force was fitted out back in England, but that too was captured, this time in a dawn raid while it was still moored in the harbour at Sandwich. Warwick's men caught the admiral in bed, and brought him back to Calais as a prisoner along with some others the Earl had enjoyed mocking at the dinner board.

Since then Somerset's men have lived hand to mouth, scavenging, bartering their futures and begging off the local population.

Now here they are, though, positioned across the road just beyond Newnham, ready to make a fight of it. Thomas watches as a detachment of soldiers breaks ranks and runs forward into the town.

'Here we go,' Walter mutters.

A moment later a plume of pale smoke spews from a straw roof, then another, then another.

'Trying to draw the garrison out,' Walter says.

If this is their plan it is working. The Newnham garrison in their red livery are now crossing the bridge to take up position along the town road west of the bridge. Thomas can even make out the garrison captain and the sergeants shouting at the men, keeping order. They watch in silence for a moment, impressed by the display. Three men on horseback ride the line, scanning the houses ahead for any sign of the enemy.

'That's it,' Richard says suddenly. 'Where are his horse? Why hasn't Somerset brought his prickers? His scurriers? His scouts? Where are they?'

Walter nods.

'You're right,' he says. 'Don't tell me the nobs walked all that way?'

'Can you see any?'

'Where's Kit? He has the best eyes. Come up here, boy.'

Katherine hurries forward, pushing past Thomas. She still has no helmet for none would fit so small a head, even with a woollen cap beneath, nor any sword.

'Can you see any horsemen among them?' Richard asks.

There is a pause while Katherine scans Somerset's army. The men gather around, staring through the trees.

'None,' she says.

'Not even the banner-carriers?' Richard asks.

Katherine shakes her head.

'And if there are none on the field . . .' Richard begins.

'Then where are they?' Walter finishes.

They scour the flat landscape below. Thomas can see nothing of any note. There are various stands of trees among the furlongs and baulks, and there is the broad skirt of green-coated marshland down by the village, but not much else.

'Perhaps he has no horse?' Richard is suggesting. 'Perhaps he's eaten them?'

Walter doesn't look convinced.

'Can you make out the banners, Kit?' Richard asks.

'There is one divided into fourths,' she says. 'Red and blue, with some flowers or something, and the white one has what look like black marks on it.'

'Are they birds?' Richard snaps.

'I cannot say. They might be.'

Richard is sharp.

'Look again,' he demands. 'Look again. Is the edge of the white flag chequered?'

'I can't see. It is too far.'

'How many birds are there?'

Katherine counts them.

'Six,' she says. 'But they . . .'

Thomas is on his tiptoes, peering into the distance; his heart is pounding.

'It's Riven,' Richard says, turning to Geoffrey. 'Riven's here. I know it. It is him. Look.'

Thomas nearly shouts something. He too is sure Riven is here.

'What about the horsemen?'

'We can worry about them later. Let's go.'

Richard wrenches his bridle around, and is about to jam his heel in when Katherine starts.

'There,' she says, pointing. Richard stops, wheels around again, drags his nervous horse prancing across and follows her directions.

'Christ on His cross!' he breathes. 'Where did they come from?'

There are about fifty of them, filtering along a narrow path between two orchards, using the trees as cover, moving up like grey wraiths in a grey land, each carrying one of the long lances and each wrapped in a thick travelling cloak so the spring sun won't shine on their harness. Even their horses wear sackcloth.

As they come up on the Newnham garrison's flank, obscured from view by a copse of poplars, Somerset's archers and billmen are retreating back down the road to Boulogne, luring Warwick's men further into the trap.

'Must have moved up in the night,' Walter says. 'They'll wait until the garrison have shot all their arrows, then they'll get in among 'em.'

'The priests'll be busy then,' Geoffrey agrees. 'It'll be a slaughter.'

'We've got to stop them.'

'Hard to see how.'

Richard throws his leg over his horse and drops to the ground, his armour ringing. He turns to Katherine and passes her the reins.

'We can come behind them,' he says. 'That's what we can do. Tie her up, Kit, will you?' He nods to his horse. 'Then follow with the arrows. We'll need every one of them.'

Katherine pauses, her gaze still on the flat lands below. She opens her mouth to say something, but it is too late, Richard has hurried forward. Walter is rubbing his hands, his eyes shining like a ferret about to kill.

'All right, this is it, boys,' he says. 'This is it. We won't have time to cut stakes so we'll have to shoot quick and accurate and pray they don't catch us in the open.'

Thomas checks his bow, his arrows, his blade. He presses the helmet down on to his head and all sounds are muffled. He wishes he had found a buckler like the other men. He glances at Katherine, still unsettled by what happened between them on the beach. He had not meant anything by trying to hold her, only that . . . What? He shakes his head.

She is tying Richard's horse's reins to the bough of a tree. Yet he must say something. If he is going into battle and is killed – well, she must know what he meant and what he didn't mean. She turns and catches his gaze. He almost glances away, ashamed, but she hurries to him.

'Thomas,' she begins. 'Listen to me—'

'I'm sorry,' he interrupts. 'For earlier.'

Katherine waves it away. It is as if she has already forgotten it.

'It's not about that,' she says. 'Look. I've been watching the men in the butts. I've seen how you shoot. You form a pattern, like a block, don't you? And then loose your arrows.'

Thomas nods. It is exactly as she imagines.

'So?' he asks.

'So if you come up behind the horsemen, when you shoot at them they'll ride out of range, won't they? Or they'll turn and ride you down. They'll still be able to attack the garrison troops. But if you cross the marsh and follow the dyke there' – she steps up to the brow of the hill and points to a length of earthwork that runs beside the road – 'you might get alongside the horsemen as they charge the garrison. That way you'll get each and every one of them. That way Riven will not get away.'

Thomas sees what she means. The road along which the horsemen will ride is bracketed on one side by a steep dyke that holds back the marsh and the cesspit. If they can cross the marsh they might reach the dyke and from there they can cut the horsemen off before they reach Newnham.

'Tell Richard, will you?' she asks.

Thomas nods and sets off after the archers as they hurry down the slope. All chatter has stopped now. Faces are pale. Hands keep moving from bow to string to arrow bag to crown of helmeted head as each man checks his equipment over and over again. They run down the sandy lane until it bottoms out and then rises again between two muddy furlongs where onions grow. Here they pause so that Walter can sight the horsemen. Thomas crouches next to Richard.

'Godspeed, Thomas,' Richard says, fiddling with his visor. 'Remember our practice and we shall come through this with our smiles in place.'

Thomas repeats what Katherine has told him. He does not tell him it is Katherine's idea. Richard listens. Then he stands and studies the way the land lies.

'It is a good plan,' he decides, but when Walter comes back he isn't happy.

'No time,' he says, dismissing Richard. He turns to the archers. 'Now, the horses are in a stand of trees on the other side of the road, so we'll set up here. Harrow formation,' he says. 'Six in each rank.'

Richard wets his lips. 'We'll do it Thomas's way, Walter.'

Walter stops, turns, spits.

'Thomas's way, is it? Not how Sir John'd want it.'

'Sir John is safe in his bed in Calais. We are here. We'll do it Thomas's way.' Richard turns to the men. 'Take off your boots and jacks,' he says. 'Drop everything but your bows and arrow bags, and bring a dagger each. Hurry now!'

The men begin to remove their equipment. A moment later they are in shirtsleeves and hose.

'Fuck's sake!' Walter snaps, throwing his jack on the ground. 'No way to fight a war.'

'Walter,' Geoffrey warns.

They can hear the drums change now, signalling the Newnham garrison advance. A trumpet blows.

'Quick now! Kit! Help me.'

Katherine arrives breathing hard and begins helping Richard out of his armour.

'Come on! Come on!' Richard urges as her hands fumble with the leather points. 'That'll do! That'll do. Stay here with it, Kit, and keep a good eye on it. With God's blessing we'll be back soon.'

One by one the archers slip into the mud of the marsh, freezing water up to their midriffs.

'Christ on His cross!' Walter is saying as if staying dry is his right. 'We'll drown!'

The water in the marsh is rich and brown, brackish with seawater, its margins stippled with sedge and reeds. Birds' nests are secreted in the rush thickets and the mud draws and sucks at their legs. The smell is ripe. Thomas half gags.

They have about three hundred paces to go, each man carrying his bow and arrow bag above his head. To their left is the river, sluggish in the spring sunlight, ahead is Newnham. On their right, beyond the road, stands the copse of trees behind which the horsemen are hidden.

They go silently dipping through the stagnant waters. The sky ahead darkens briefly, as if a flock of starlings has come between them and the sun, and Thomas looks up to see a flight of arrows flit from the market square. Each shaft looks so delicate from that distance, like the most considered stroke of the best sharpened reed, but then comes the irregular flurry of thumps and cracks as the arrows hit stone, steel and flesh, followed by the cries of the wounded men.

'Quick!' Richard urges. 'Quickly now.'

The water is thickening, fouler still.

There is a salvo of arrows from Somerset's men in return.

'Hold on to some of them fuckin' arrows,' Walter urges, but more shafts fly. The archery duel will last only moments, until one side exhausts their arrows, and then they'll retreat to let the billmen or the men-at-arms take up the mêlée. Once their arrows are spent, the lightly armed archers will fall easy prey to the horsemen with their lances, hammers, swords, axes and God knows what else. They'll be driven into the river behind them.

'My foot!' Dafydd gasps. He's spilled his bow and shafts into the water, and is stuck fast in the silt. Thomas grabs one arm, Owen the other, and they haul him out of the ooze. Swirling clouds of black mud roll under the surface as he comes free and the smell makes them retch.

Thomas surges forward. The thought that Riven might be waiting beyond the dyke makes him numb. He wishes he had the giant's pollaxe with him now, but he's left it at the fort. Then he stops. The giant. Of course. The giant will be there. He will be protecting Riven again. At the thought of the giant and his thumb on his eyeball, Thomas wavers. What is he doing? Why is he here? He is a canon of the Order of Gilbert. He stops. The others catch him.

'All right, Northern Thomas?' Red John asks. 'Not thinking of turning tail on us now, are you?'

Thomas gathers himself. He thinks of the Dean. He hears that sound of steel in flesh. He thinks of Riven holding out Alice's beads and something comes over him, like a glove over a hand, the same feeling that made him throw the staff at Riven in the first place. He surges forward and finds himself at the front of the men once more.

The marsh shelves into grainy mud, with patches of slick green waste to one side, its edges crusted with lichen-green, stinking slime. They slip as they scramble across the reach, two of them going down into the ooze, neither dropping his bow, both emerging with eyes white against the brown faces. They struggle to the water's edge where it solidifies into land against the dyke.

'Keep down,' Richard calls.

The men are crawling out of the water and they lie gathering their breath on the side of the dyke. Thomas crawls to see what is happening, and is about to poke his head over the top when he feels them, through his knees and the palms of his hands. The horsemen have set off.

'God's teeth!' Dafydd hisses. 'They're close!' There is fear in his voice, echoed in the face of every other man.

'Keep down and spread out!' Richard calls. 'Come on, get ready! We'll have but one chance at this. Nock. Nock, damn you!'

Walter has his bow gripped sideways, an arrow nocked, three more tucked through the points of his muddy hose. The others fumble for their bows, nock their arrows and copy him, crouching in the reeds, giving themselves space to loose. Richard crawls up on the tussocky grass next to Thomas, peering over the dyke from behind a clutch of reeds.

'Here they come,' he says. 'Wait for it. Wait for it!'

Thomas can feel the weight of the horses through the ground. A stalk trembles before his nose. Then he hears them: their hooves on stone, the jangle of harness and the shouting of men gearing themselves up for the slaughter.

'Now!' Richard cries.

The archers stand.

'Draw!' Walter snarls.

One of the horsemen sees them at this last minute and flinches, hauling at his reins, trying to bring his lance around. Thomas's arm is fully cocked, the linen string to his ear. He cannot hold this pose for more than a long breath but he swings his bow along the line of the charging men, looking for anything that might identify Riven or the giant. There! A flash of that red coat. Or there! That white livery!

'Loose!'

He looses. He cannot miss. None of them can. Their arrows slam into the charging horsemen from five paces. The din and the violence are terrible. Riders are hurled from their mounts. Horses slew, or rear. They fall and throw riders. Man and horse scream together. A horse is upended and lands with a crack. Another cartwheels, its shadow flicking over a man below, sparing him, before landing on another, killing him instantly. One is trampled before he hits the ground in a drum of skittering hooves.

Thomas watches his arrow crash through the breathing holes of a man's helmet, so hard and so close that the steel visor opens in ragged flanges to admit the bodkin head. He is plucked from his saddle and vanishes from sight. His horse swerves, hits another, screams and crashes to the ground.

'Nock!'

Thomas nocks and seeks the man in the white livery.

'Draw!'

Where is he? Where is he? He is already down.

'Loose!'

Thomas lets the shaft go at another, whose armour is swathed in sackcloth. He hits him in the stomach and he jumps in his saddle and another arrow hits his horse and knocks it aside. The man goes down under it.

They loose three more salvoes. From that distance an arrow will pass through a man, armour or no. It will pin him to the ground, or his horse, or whatever is behind him. It will pin two men together. As they nock for the fourth time Richard raises his arm.

It is over. It is done.

The archers lower their bows.

There is no one left standing. There is only a single white horse, galloping into the distance, stirrups flying. The road is filled with the dead bodies and the stink of shit and blood and ruptured guts.

A horse is still trying to get up, but has lost the use of its back legs, and is dragging them behind as it crawls on, screaming with the pain. Geoffrey raises his bow and looses an arrow that fizzes across and catches the horse behind the jaw. It collapses. Another lies wheezing, its chest rising and falling, its eye suddenly enormous. Blood spreads from an arrow that is buried up to the fletch in its shoulders. The horse's black lips vibrate as it gasps for air. It seems this is the only thing left alive. Walter takes three paces from the top of the dyke, down into the road, steps over a dead man and smashes the animal's skull with a lead maul.

No one says anything. Everyone is breathing heavily. Owen turns away from what he has done. Dafydd puts his arms about his brother and holds him as he sobs. He soothes him in a language only they can understand before breaking into English.

'It's all right,' he says. 'It's all right. It's over now.'

One of the Johns vomits.

Another horse shudders and whinnies. It is trapped under the body of another horse. It raises its head, its neck arched, and stares at them. It is looking to man for help. Walter crosses to it, bends down, lets his hands drift over the heaving chest, down to where the animal's foreleg is trapped under the dead horse. It is bent where it should have been straight. Walter shakes his head sorrowfully, then stands and crashes the maul down again. The animal subsides. Walter peers over to look at the rider the horse has pinned to the ground.

He laughs. 'Like a bloody hedgehog.'

Richard is silent, pale-faced, unmoving on the bank.

Thomas feels weighed down with regret.

One by one they step down and into the road. Blood leaks from between armoured joints, clots in mail. Are any of the men alive? Does that one move? Does this one raise his gloved hand in a gesture? There is a gentle scrape, like a man breathing out, and a grate of steel on stone.

Each archer is drawn to the rider he killed first. Thomas stands frozen. Then: Christ! A man has caught his ankle. He can hardly see him for he is pinned by the weight of a horse.

Thomas pulls free.

The man's fingers go slack.

Walter steps past, over the bulk of the horse, peers down at the man. He bends and lifts the man's visor. He smiles. It is almost tender. Then he raises the maul and brings it down with a gristly crunch.

Walter tucks the maul under his arm and begins undoing the man's chinstrap.

'I'll have this,' he says.

Thomas turns away. He can still feel the man's fingers on his ankle. He finds the man in red, lying face down, crumpled against the far bank. Thomas thinks he recognises the coat. It is the same madder red. As he turns the body, it slips to the road. Thomas's arrow is broken, jammed in the visor. He inserts his knife into the hinge on the other side and levers it open.

It is not Riven.

It is a man with a thick moustache and a spider's web of blood spreading across his face. His eyes are open, curiously blue, looking into the far distance. Thomas waves away a blowfly.

'May God have mercy on your immortal soul,' he murmurs. 'And grant you eternal rest.'

He makes the sign of the cross over the man and then Richard appears at his shoulder.

'Let me see,' he says, and he stares into the dead man's face.

'It is not him,' he says. 'He was never here. Never here.'

He gestures across at the man in white, lying between his horse's legs.

There are black marks on the man's tabard but they are not birds. They are ornate, curlicued crosses, arranged in the same three, two, one pattern that distinguishes Riven's livery.

'Look,' he says. 'Kit mistook the banner.'

The dead man is fat, with leathery skin, quite elderly; he does not even look like an Englishman.

Richard is in despair. Geoffrey and the other men pass among the dead men, lifting their visors where they have not already been shaken loose.

'We will find him,' Thomas says. 'I know it.'

Richard nods.

They stand like that for a moment, shoulder to shoulder. They become aware of a presence. A man stands behind them. It is the captain of the Newnham garrison, the one who lent Richard the practice bow. He stares at them speculatively. Behind him stand his sergeant and three of the garrison ordinaries, bills in hand. They are the men who'd jeered at them as they had passed over Newnham Bridge. Now they are silent, staring at the carnage, counting the bodies. The bells in both churches in the village begin ringing again.

'It is you, isn't it?' the captain asks. 'You're the archers who can't shoot to save yourselves a barrel of ale.'

Richard stands up and wipes the blood from his palm on the front of his shirt. He is about to say something when his attention is taken by something else, over the man's shoulder. A party of men in costly burnished plate is walking towards them. One of them carries a blue and murrey battle standard emblazoned with a white lion, the others their pollaxes.

The captain turns to see what Richard is looking at. As soon as he sees who it is, he steps off the road with a slight bow. A huge knight with his visor raised to form a peak on his helmet leads the party. His armour is scratched and dented, and there is another man's blood over his plated lower legs. He stops in front of Richard and stares down at him.

'Who in the name of the great God above are you?' he asks.

Richard takes a breath.

'I am Richard Fakenham, my lord,' he says. 'Of Marton Hall in Lincolnshire. My father is Sir John Fakenham. He is my lord Fauconberg's man and we are his company.'

He gestures at the archers, who stand perfectly still. The man stares at him, then at them. He is very big, almost a giant, and very young, with wide blue eyes and fair hair.

'Then, Richard Fakenham,' the man says slowly, 'I owe you a debt of thanks. For you have saved many lives here today. I do not know how you came to be stationed here along this road, but without your famous action there would be many more widows and orphans and childless fathers alive today.'

He bends to pick up one of the spears the horsemen had been carrying. It is more than twice his height. He peers up at the tip to make his point.

'I shall not forget you,' he says, turning back to Richard. 'I shall not forget you, Richard Fakenham. You or your men, d'you hear? England needs men like you, Richard Fakenham. I need men like you. If ever you need a favour of me, I hope you will ask. I hope I shall be able to help you in return.'

Richard bows.

The man shakes his hand. Thomas whispers in Geoffrey's ear.

'Who is that?'

Geoffrey looks at him as if he has gone too far this time.

'Give me strength. Who is that? Who is that? D'you really know nothing?'

Thomas shrugs.

'That is Edward Plantagenet, the Earl of March. He's the Duke of York's son. He's the King's cousin. He's – oh for God's sake.'

13

The Earl of Warwick's fleet puts in to harbour five weeks later. It is a fine early summer's day and they see his ships' masts break the horizon just after dawn. When the news spreads, every bell in the Scunnage rings out. What it must have meant for the Duke of Somerset's men, beleaguered and decimated in their castle at Guisnes, Katherine can only guess, but for Sir John Fakenham and his company of archers it is reason enough to rejoice.

'Soon be home now, Owen,' Dafydd says, thumping his brother on the back.

'Home,' Owen choruses.

Instead of any celebration though, Walter makes them work harder, as if punishing them for something they haven't done. They spend every daylight hour practising in the butts. He picks on Thomas especially, so that almost all Katherine sees of him is as a lone figure in the distance, constantly running the length of the clearing to collect arrows, bring them back, loosing them, and running to collect them again.

The Earl's return brings with it an increase in the number of tents outside the town walls and an increase in the level of noise across the Pale.

'Very keen on guns, the Earl of Warwick, isn't he?' Dafydd moots, his hands over his ears.

'Big ones, little ones, you name it,' Geoffrey agrees. 'Keen on anything new, he is.'

They are taking a rare break, gathered on the walkway of the fort, leaning against the battlements. They are staring out across the Pale towards the town, where rolling puffs of grey smoke erupt from the butts. Burgundian handgunners are down there and the air crackles with the reports of their guns. Twice that first morning they hear an unusual crump as one of the bronze-barrelled weapons bursts.

'Don't see what's so great about them,' Simon says. 'Rather use a bow any day. Least when they break they don't kill no one.'

'You ever face gunfire, boy?' Walter asks him.

Simon shakes his head.

'Well, wait till you have before you say anything so bloody stupid again.'

Walter is still sour-tempered. He's been thus ever since the skirmish at Newnham. The others are happier, especially with rumours of their return to England circulating.

'Must be soon, eh? Did you see how many ships they've got in the harbour?'

'I can't bloody wait,' Dafydd says. 'You know what I'm going to do when I get there? I'm going to find a rich knight – you know, someone in the Duke of bloody Somerset's affinity – and I'm going to kill him, and take everything he has, I am. I'm going to take his lands, his horse, his armour, his squire, his missus and his dogs, everything, even his chickens, aren't I? Then I'm going to ride back home to Kidwelly with Owen here, both of us fully armoured up, see? And we're going to kick that no-good fucker Will Dwnn right into the bloody sea.'

'Who's Will Dwnn?' Red John asks.

'Will bloody Dwnn? Don't you know Will Dwnn? He's the fucker who's supposed to marry Gwen, isn't he?'

'Gwen,' Owen says. His voice is deep and so larded with affection that everybody stops and looks at him.

'Is Gwen your sweetheart, Owen?'

'Gwen's not his sweetheart!' Dafydd says as if everyone should already know. 'Gwen's our sister.'

Walter cackles.

'Heard about you Welshmen and your sisters.'

Before a fight can start, Walter holds out a hand. He's pointing at the woods.

'Now who the fuck's this?' he asks. A man in green is casting about in the scrub. He has a short-legged dog on a lead.

'Richard says he is a huntsman,' Katherine tells them. 'He had a boy with him earlier, but he sent him off back to town.'

'Must have found a scent,' Geoffrey guesses. 'The boy'll have gone to fetch the hunting party.'

Later that morning they watch a party of horsemen on the road to Newnham. There must be a dozen or so. Those at the rear are carrying flags and around the horses' legs run the tiny dots of dogs.

'A hunting party,' Walter says. 'All we bloody need.'

'You recognise any of the flags, Kit?'

'There is the red saltire,' she says.

'The Earl of Warwick,' Geoffrey says. 'Coming this way.'

'Better let Richard know.'

Geoffrey goes to find Richard. Katherine watches the party crossing the bridge. The riders stop at the fort and then emerge from behind the castle and ride through the village and start up the road towards them, along the road where they fought on St George's Day. The bodies are gone now, some buried behind the church in a piggery, some thrown in the river. The dead horses have been dragged away by a tanner and butcher.

By the time the horsemen come over the crest of the hill, Richard and Geoffrey are in the courtyard. There are about fifteen in the hunting party, including the standard-bearers, various grooms and servants. Trotting alongside are five or six greyhounds. One of the riders is a bishop in purple. He is swarthy-faced, wearing a long fur-lined cloak. It seems almost comical that he should be there. Katherine finds herself staring at him, ignoring the man in black behind him, a cleric of some sort, ill-at-ease on horseback, and the other huntsmen, each dressed in high boots and thick coats, each with a bow and a bag of arrows.

She remembers the nerves the sisters all felt when the Bishop of Lincoln paid the priory a visit. They had scrubbed their half of the priory for weeks beforehand, and each had washed their cassocks and their bodies so that nothing might offend him. And all the while they had known he would never see them, just as they would never see him.

Richard starts out as the riders draw up.

'My lord of Warwick,' he calls. 'Good day to you, sir, and may God guide you safe.'

The man at the front of the party raises his hand in salute. The clouds of yellow dust the horses kick up slowly settle. His is a black horse, ostentatiously beautiful.

'You are Richard Fakenham?' he asks.

'I am, my lord.'

'Then let me shake you by the hand,' Warwick says, swinging his leg forward over his horse and descending lightly to the ground. 'I have heard of your actions from my cousin the Earl of March.'

'It was no more than my duty, my lord,' Richard counters, shaking his hand.

'Nonsense, nonsense. You and your men are the talk of the town. I have brought his grace Bishop Coppini all the way from Milan to meet you.'

Richard kisses the Bishop's hand, who ignores him and keeps up a lively stream of chatter aimed at the large snowy-haired fat man sitting on the horse next to him. At first Katherine thinks this might be Sir John Fakenham come to see them from Calais, but where Sir John Fakenham's face is open and cheerful despite his pain, this old man looks sour-tempered.

'That's the Earl of Salisbury,' Walter mutters. 'Warwick's father. Right bastard.'

Salisbury takes Richard's proffered hand in a half-hearted squeeze and drops it quickly. Warwick ostentatiously steps back to stand with his hands on his hips and survey the fort and the men who are gathered at its battlements. He pretends it is a fine sight.

'So that is the famous Earl of Warwick, is it?' Dafydd asks, staring back down.

'Quite small, isn't he?' Red John says.

'No, he's not,' Little John Willingham snaps. A couple of them laugh.

'They say he never sleeps, you know? Not ever.'

'They say he never sits down, either.'

'And that he has his hair cut three times a week.'

'A peacock,' Owen says in his thick voice. Warwick is dressed in a deep purple, extravagantly puffed hunting coat that stops at his waist. His hose are lapis and his boots so pointed in the toe so that it is a wonder he can ride in them at all.

'To think he's our only chance of getting out of this shithole and going home.'

Warwick is asking something of Richard, who gestures to the other side of the fort where the huntsman with his dog paces impatiently through the long grass. A third man, whom none of them recognises, leans forward, both hands cupped on his saddle. Katherine thinks he looks slightly out of place, but she cannot say why.

'Who is that?' she asks.

'Hastings,' Walter says.

'Lord Hastings?'

'No. Just Hastings. William Hastings.'

'Stupid name if you aren't lord of the manor.'

'Supposed to be a good man, though. Good to his men and so on. Their wives.'

Katherine cannot tell what he means. She can see Richard is smiling at something this Hastings has said, nodding his head and then hurrying back through the gate.

'Geoffrey! Geoffrey there!'

Geoffrey has the horse saddled already. Richard is quickly on to it and he joins the party as they ride around the fort to find the huntsman.

'He loves his hunting, doesn't he?' Walter says. 'Misses those hawks of his.'

The archers in the top of the fort walk around to watch them taking the huntsman's directions and disappear under the canopy of the branches. Soon a trumpet is blown.

'All right, into the butts,' Walter says. 'Make it look good for when they come back. Northern Thomas, you stay here. They might stop and talk to us, and the last bloody thing I want is to hear you telling them cutting across the marsh like that was your idea, understand?'

Thomas knows better than to argue, and anyway he values any time away from archery practice.

When the others have gone Thomas sits in the sunshine and oils his new bow. His old one eventually broke in his hands, just as he always said it would, and from his own money Richard bought him a new one from a bowyer in Calais. It was meant as a reward for his part in the skirmish on St George's Day and, for a day or two, Thomas hid it from Katherine because he was anxious she would take offence at him being credited with the plan. She'd laughed when she found out.

She watches him for a moment, the way his new muscles move as he works. He is much bigger now than he was. It is all that food, and all the work in the butts. He looks like a soldier, almost like one of those hard-faced men who made up the Calais Watch, and he has taken to carrying the pollaxe around with him all the time, hanging it around his shoulders on a long leather strap pinned to the wood. She often sees him staring at the palms of his hands, frowning at them. She wonders what he is thinking when he does so.

Now, though, he looks happy, or at least content, carrying out a soothing task in the sunshine. She smiles to herself and carries on pacing. She has spent more hours on the walkways of Sangatte Fort than she cares to think about, and knows the land all about intimately. From up there she has watched spring give way to summer, watched the woods around them take on a green haze of new leaves, then spread into full dark leaf. She's also watched the daily skirmishes unfold on the Boulogne road as the Duke of Somerset's men continue to harass the Staple. She's seen the carts bringing back the bodies of men killed and wounded.

After a moment she turns and stares across the sea.

'What do you think he's doing now?' she asks.

'Who?'

'Riven.'

Thomas looks up.

'I suppose he is waiting to see what happens next,' he tells her. He is not good at imagining things.

She nods.

'I imagine him in that castle Geoffrey is always talking about,' she says. 'Cornford. With his son married to that girl whose father he killed. I can almost hear her screams in the corridors, can't you? And everyone looking away.'

Thomas looks anxious. He nods uncertainly.

'We will have justice when we see the Prior,' he says, missing the point. 'When we get to Canterbury.'

Canterbury. She opens her mouth and then shuts it again. It is so pleasant to be up here in the spring sunshine. And there is always some awkwardness about Thomas whenever they approach the subject of returning to Canterbury and the Prior of All. In another person she might think his evasions are a sign of duplicity, but this is Thomas. She assumes he becomes flustered because he is anxious at the prospect of appealing to the Prior.

He has moved on to the bowstrings now, pulling them between his waxed thumb and forefinger.

'There were no men like Riven in the priory,' he says. 'Or so it seemed, but out here in the world, you know, it's as if everyone is using one another for some gain, something they do not deserve.'

She feels her mood darken. Does he mean her?

'And yet, how much happier you seem to have left the priory so far behind,' she says.

Thomas stops his work.

'It seems distant now, doesn't it?' he says.

She nods again, but says nothing. The priory does not seem distant to her. She thinks about it almost every moment of every day: of Sister Alice and Sister Joan; of the Prioress. And all this: the plentiful food, the conversation, the days going by without the hours spent on her knees in the nave, sitting in the sun with a man in his shirt – it seems unreal, a dream, and there is a greater part of her feels the world of the priory, with its black and white certainties, *that* was the real world.

She has removed her hood, as she sometimes does when they are alone, and she is enjoying the sun on her face.

'Your hair needs cutting again,' he says, resuming his work.

'Perhaps you can do it when you have finished that?' She nods at the strings and the little flask of oil for the wood of his bow. He puts them aside and takes out his knife.

'What did you make of the Earl of Warwick?' she asks as he takes her hair in his hand.

'I don't know,' he says. 'Everybody speaks so highly of him. Men seem to love him.' He slices through a hank of hair and drops it over the edge of the wall to scatter in the breeze.

'But that is not to say he is a good man, is it?'

'No. That is true,' he agrees.

'Everything I hear of him makes me think he is no better than a man like Riven. Perhaps worse even, because his power is so much the greater.'

Thomas grunts.

But she does not want to think about the Earl of Warwick. It is a pleasure to be with Thomas, to have him touch her hair. She recalls the time he cut it on the shore at Boston, when it was so cold and she was ill with fright. Now she feels herself soften, relax. She hums with pleasure. She feels as if she should take his hand and hold its palm to her cheek. It is the sun, the warmth, the food, the lack of care.

'There,' he says. 'It is quite straight.'

She smiles at him.

'Thank you Thomas,' she says.

He smiles uncertainly back, hesitates as if he does not know what to do with his hands, then goes and sits with his bow again, but she can see him fiddling pointlessly. Her own heart is beating erratically and her limbs tingle. She feels dizzy. The feeling makes her anxious. She gets up, walks to the wall, places her hands on the warm powdery stone, tries to breathe slowly.

Eventually the feeling passes.

She watches the others in the butts below for a few moments. It is always Hugh who is last. He is not strong enough for the bow. She hears Walter barking at the boy as he is sent up the butts again and she turns and crosses to the other side, to look out over the woods to the Pale beyond.

Suddenly a scattering of birds take flight from the canopy of the trees with shrill calls of alarm. There is a drumming of hooves below and some shouting from the woods. Something is wrong.

'Thomas!' she calls.

The hunting party is back but they ride urgently, with the dogs at their hooves, heads down, riding fast, the horses white with sweat. They flash from the tree line and for a moment it looks as if they will not stop at the fort gatehouse.

Geoffrey is out to greet them straight away and Thomas and Katherine hurry down. Warwick is at the head of the little party as they pull up by the drawbridge to the fort. He looks grim, his mouth a downturned slash, all that morning's pomp gone. Next to him the Legate, Coppini, looks frightened and is having trouble keeping his horse in check. The Earl of Salisbury's face is mottled and clenched with anger. None of the hunting party gets down from their saddles, and Warwick's horse, caked in mud, bucks and prances, sensing its rider's desire to be gone.

'There has been an accident,' Warwick says. 'Richard Fakenham has taken an arrow in his back. He is coming in now.'

'He lives?' Geoffrey asks.

Warwick shoots a glance back towards the woods.

'Just,' he says.

'How did it happen?'

Close to, Warwick is clean-shaven with a long face, a wide jaw and eyes like polished brown pebbles. There is just one deep line down the side of his thin mouth, the work of nature rather than a wound, and there is no spare flesh on him at all, so that they can see every muscle at work below the thin skin of his face, trying to control his expression, and failing.

'Hastings brings him now,' he says. 'He can tell you. The hart got away, that I can say.'

He turns his horse.

'Are you not staying to see him home?' Thomas asks. He speaks before he has thought it through. Warwick turns his horse with a savage yank. He stares at Thomas. His lip is curled and his eyes have deepened in his head. He spurs his horse towards him. Thomas steps back.

'Who are you?' Warwick spits. 'Who are you to presume anything?'

Geoffrey intervenes, stepping between them. Thank the Lord he is so fat.

'Sorry, my lord,' he says. 'He forgets himself.'

'We will look to him,' Katherine says, meaning Richard, distracting the Earl. Warwick glances her way.

'Do so, will you?' He turns to the other men. 'Come, we have wasted enough time here.'

He makes it sound as if it is someone else's fault he's been hunting. He turns his horse, and with one last look at Thomas, he jags his spurs into the animal's belly and canters off, leading the party away over the crest without a backward glance.

'Bastard,' Geoffrey says.

Thomas and Katherine follow him around to the other side of the fort, over the earthworks and along a shaded track through the woods. A horse appears at the end of the charcoalers' track. Then two more. The first is ridden by the man Walter called Hastings. It was he who invited Richard to join the hunt and here he comes back, leading the second horse on a long rein; Richard is slumped over the horse's withers, his arms either side of the horse's neck, his face waxy and lifeless. Next to him trots the hunter with the short-legged dog. Behind comes the third horse, ridden by the cleric in black.

Despite her anxiety for Richard, when Katherine sees the cleric, she catches her breath. All the old anxieties grip her, and she hangs her head. The cleric ignores her, and rides by in silence. They lead the horses into the yard where Hastings slides from the saddle to help Geoffrey and Thomas ease Richard down and carry him to a grassy bank. They lay him face first on the turf. The arrow is buried deep in the muscles that divide his back. He is alive, but his eyes are closed and his face is sheened with sweat. He is breathing very quickly.

'Who shot the arrow?' Geoffrey asks.

'My lord the Earl of Warwick,' Hastings says. 'It is a broadhead, I'm afraid. I have mine made by the same man.'

He pulls an arrow from his bag to show them. It is a typical hunting arrow, with a chested shaft and a flat head that ends in two barbs, each about a finger's tip long and the same again wide.

'How did it happen?' Katherine asks.

'I cannot say,' Hastings says. 'I was looking elsewhere. I was . . . distracted.'

'We should send for a surgeon,' the cleric tells them. He has one of those voices she's heard countless times, floating over the wall of the nave back at the priory.

'A surgeon?' Hastings says, standing. 'Saints. That will certainly do for him.'

'His father, then,' Geoffrey says, 'for there is nothing we can do for him here. If we try to extract it, it will only take more flesh. It will kill him.'

'And yet we cannot leave it in.'

Geoffrey takes his knife out and slices through the jerkin and then the blood-soaked wool of Richard's coat and his linen around the wound. Richard's flesh is pale, mottled, like stained marble, and the flesh around the arrow is already turning purple.

'We can cut it out,' Katherine says. 'Find out which way the barbs are, and then slice the flesh ourselves, so that it does not tear.'

Hastings looks doubtful but Katherine feels a curious certainty. It takes her by surprise.

'I have heard of this thing done,' the cleric says. 'But with forceps. You have nothing like that here, do you?'

Geoffrey shakes his head.

'How can we tell where the barbs are?' Thomas asks.

'We can feel,' she tells them.

Hastings shakes his head.

'It is a hunting arrow,' he says. 'The barbs run along the line of the notch. Look.' He points to the fletched end of the arrow, carved across with the notch for the bow's string. 'A war arrow's notch runs the other way, across the barb.' He shrugs. 'Each is designed to slip through the target's ribs, you see. A huntsman is after a stag, an archer after a man. It is the way it is.'

There is a beautiful sense to that.

'I will do it,' Katherine says. She bends over Richard's body.

There is a long strand of material embedded in the wound. She tugs it. Richard stirs.

'Might be better done quickly, you know?' Hastings offers. 'Men asleep after a fall in the tilt yard feel no pain until they wake up.'

Geoffrey passes her his knife. She still feels entirely calm. Of course she will do it. She takes the knife. It is big, and dirty. She looks at it doubtfully.

'Here,' Hastings says. 'Use mine.'

Hastings's knife is beautifully wrought and perhaps twice as sharp as Geoffrey's. She puts the back of the blade against the arrow. The wound is bleeding freely now. She blows the hair from her eyes, then slowly forces the knife down into Richard's flesh. Blood wells from the wound and pools against the torn cloth of Richard's shirt. The meat under the blade is resilient. She imagined it might part easily, but no. Richard shudders.

'Hold him still,' she says.

The four men press down on Richard, pinning him to the grass. He moans. She feels the knife tip touch against the barb.

'It's there,' she says. She cuts away from the arrow a few tugs of the blade; the grain of Richard's flesh parts a little with each pass.

When she has repeated the process on the other side of the shaft she hands the knife back to Hastings, who takes it gingerly and goes to wash it in the trough.

'Shall I pull?' she asks. Geoffrey nods. She takes the arrow with both hands, gripping it just below its feathered fletch, then slowly eases it out. Blood fills the wound, dark and free-flowing.

'I pray the head does not come away from the shaft,' Geoffrey says.

'These are well-made arrows,' Hastings objects.

The arrow comes free with a tiny suck and a well of blood.

'We must stop the bleeding,' she says. 'Cut his shirt into strips, will you?'

While Geoffrey cuts the cloth, Thomas takes the arrow and joins Hastings at the trough. It can still be used.

'Thomas,' she calls. 'Fetch the salve.'

He turns and looks at her blankly. She is about to remind him it is in the pardoner's pack when she recalls that it is supposed to be his pack. She gives him the monastic sign for an old man, and then the sign for bag. She notices the prick of interest in the cleric, who leans forward to look at her more closely, and she feels her stomach turn. She flushes and busies herself by pressing one of the linen pads against the puckered mouth of Richard's wound.

He stiffens under the pressure and gasps with the pain. He is coming to. She presses gently down. The linen soaks up the blood quickly. She puts another fold of it over the first and holds it down again. She will not look at the cleric.

When Thomas returns she spreads some of the gritty salve over a clean pad and begins blotting the wound.

'What is that?' the cleric asked.

'A salve,' she says as if she knows, roughening and deepening her voice.

'And what is its purpose?'

'It is to prevent putrefaction.'

'And does it work?'

'I hope so.'

The cleric grunts.

'Is he still alive?' Hastings asks. 'Is he still breathing?'

'I don't know.'

She stops the pressure and blood fills the wound in small rises. She presses the linen back.

'Hold it in place,' she instructs Thomas. 'Press down.'

She moves and kneels beside Richard's head and holds her blood-wet fingers to his lips. She feels the faintest coolness. She nods.

'He's breathing.'

When she looks up, the men are staring at her.

'Saints,' Hastings says. 'That was neatly done.'

'Almost as if you've done it before,' the cleric says. 'Have you worked in a hospital?'

He is looking at her very closely. He has a long pale face and — visible now that he has removed his hat — sleek dark hair that lies flat on his pin head as if oiled or wet.

'No,' she stammers and pulls her hood over her head. Perhaps it is that exact action which confirms the cleric's suspicions, for then when she goes to the trough to wash, plunging her arms into the cold water up to the elbows and watching the blood float off her skin in delicate skeins, he comes to stand behind her.

'Sister,' he says.

She turns. Her heart is thumping, her throat blocked. She can feel the heat in her face.

'What do you want? Why're you calling me that?'

'I wanted to make sure,' he says.

'Sure of what? Who are you?'

'Sure of who you are,' he says. 'My name is Stephen Lamn. I am secretary to his grace Bishop Coppini. But I am a Lincoln man, you see? Of the Gilbertine Order.'

PART THREE

The Road to Northampton
Field, June–July 1460

14

Thomas groans when he sees the carrack *Mary* again. He'd hoped he'd seen the last of her, and her little master whose name he's forgotten, but as they trudge through the Seaward Gate and out on to the wharf, there she is, lying low in the water, and there he is, one tooth still in his head, standing at the tiller with his hands on his hips. As they come aboard he stares at them with undisguised contempt, not recognising them, quite as if he has come by ownership of the carrack through some proper process, and is now her legitimate master.

'Come on,' he caws, 'get yerselves set down. Tide's changing and we'll lose the wind if you don't get a move on.'

Thomas wishes Katherine were there to see him. It would have made her laugh. But Sir John Fakenham has asked her to stay and care for his son, and so she will be sailing later and for that he is glad. What could she have done anyway, if it came to fighting?

The archers meanwhile have climbed down into the ship's hold and now spread themselves in the waist. More archers come aboard, men in blue and white with Fauconberg's fish-hook badge over their hearts. Thomas's eye is drawn to the spot where he killed Cobham and Saxby and the other men. The arrow shafts have been broken off and adzed flat in the deck, like knots in the planks.

As soon as it is agreed they can fit no more men aboard, the sailors take in the gangplank and cast off. Two barges take up the hawsers' slack and their crews haul on their oars and the carrack labours out into the channel. Once she is in the deeper water, the barges let go and the carrack's new crew set a sail that fills with a crump. After a moment's hesitation, *Mary* gathers herself, quickens and surges out to sea on a skirt of milky froth to join the rest of the small fleet waiting to cross the channel, each tub filled with men in harness and helmets.

'Soon be there,' Geoffrey says.

'I've heard that one before,' Thomas tells him.

But they are. They are soon out on the green sea, butting through the choppy waters, a constant wind behind them. The sun shines on their backs and seagulls cry in their wake. They are one ship of six, each packed with Fauconberg's archers and men-at-arms: a fine sight.

Soon they can see the low line of England in the haze and then, not much later, even the chalk cliffs above Dover.

The thought of crossing the Narrow Sea again has so preoccupied Thomas these last few days that he has not given much thought to the fighting that lies ahead, but as they close with the coast of Kent, the mood on board changes. Fear makes one or two men more vocal others become quieter, mumbling their prayers, crossing themselves. Others fiddle with their weapons, retie bracers, stretch gloves, check arrows for trueness. One or two yawn uncontrollably. Dafydd whistles through his teeth. Thomas's mouth is dry, and his hands are trembling. He wishes for ale.

'Sandwich,' Walter says. He points out a distant huddle of pale roofs gathered around a dark stone church among a green swathe of marshland. 'Doubt we'd be trying this if the French hadn't already busted down the walls and burned the place to the ground.' He is gloomy, sour-tempered still, unenthused by the thought of what is to come.

'Good to see England again, though,' Geoffrey tries.

'Never had to come ashore somewhere I'm not wanted,' Walter continues. 'And I'll wager they've got guns this time. Guns and water. Guns and water. Worse combination there is, that one. If you don't get a stone in the face, you'll most likely drown. This is going to be fun, this is. Where's Simon?'

'Here.'

'About to see what's so bloody good about guns, you are, you ignorant bastard.'

They hear the first one go off as they breast the channel. Ahead of them are the docks and then the flint walls of the town. The gates are shut. Smoke rises from fires and all along the wall men are clustered at embrasures.

The first boulder thrums through the air and then falters and falls slushing into the turbid waters of the channel. There is a faint cheer from the first boat. The next gun fires. This time there are two separate noises that run into one: the report of the gun, then the longer sound of its boulder hitting the first tub amidships. The stone smashes through the wooden planks and tears into the men behind.

The boat staggers, loses way. Thomas hears bellows of rage and pain. Blood comes running down the boat's side. Bodies soon follow, dead and wounded men pushed overboard as those left alive struggle to find space to loose their arrows. Then a third gun goes off.

'See?' Walter shouts above the noise. 'See?'

Again the stone crashes into the tub, sending her shivering. There are more screams. Thomas hears men shouting at the defenders, men begging for mercy. Begging not to be fired on.

A fourth gun goes off. The archers in the first tub begin loosing their arrows at the men on the shore, aiming for the gunners, but they are too tightly packed and the gunners ashore are behind palisades and under tile roofs. Arrowheads spark on the cobbles. The defenders loose fire arrows, sooty trails arching in the sky, and soon the first sail is on fire, dropping in flaming black rags on to the heads of the men below.

Then a stone hits the carrack. It is a small one, about the size of a man's head. It comes with a thrumming sound and an explosion of splinters from the top of the ship's rail in the waist. It passes through the first man's chest, throws the second man into the air and then shatters the third's hips. Splinters of wood and man fly in every direction and others clap hands to their faces and suddenly blood is everywhere, a steady pink drizzle. It turns faces red. Gums eyes, lingers on lips, tastes distinct and coppery.

The *Mary* butts the first ship, now ablaze and listing against the quayside. Her deck is scattered with the corpses of the dead, and the wounded are scrabbling to get off before they are burned or drowned.

Thomas follows Walter across the gap, scrambling over the bloodied ship's rails; he slips on the gore, picks himself up before he is trampled by those behind. Men around him are roaring, and he realises that he is too. A steady thunder of arrows keeps coming at them. Arrows pick men off, spin them around, hammer them to the deck.

The man next to Thomas goes down, skewered by an arrow between the buttons of his jack. It is the other Thomas. Johnson takes an arrow through the thigh, too, a typical archer's injury. He doesn't scream, but throws down his bow and turns, limping away, where he is swatted aside by one of Fauconberg's men trying to make firm ground.

Another one of Fauconberg's men falls just as he's scrambling over the ship's side on to the harbour wall. He screams and Thomas feels his body give under the press of the boat against the dockside. He doesn't look down.

'A Fauconberg!'

Thomas makes it stumbling on to the dockside, getting the pole of his axe caught between his legs and tripping just as an arrow whispers over him to crash into the burning ship. Black smoke chokes them all. He finds his feet, swings the axe on his back and begins loosing his arrows without any thought, nock, draw, loose, nock, draw, loose, all those hours in the butts rewarding him now. He lets his shafts go wherever he sees the pale disc of a face.

The defenders are wearing the same livery as the men in Calais: murky linen jacks with the cross of St George. They are good archers, too. They keep the sky overcast with volleys and they are withering Fauconberg's men. Shafts boom down, men are killed and the wounded cry out. Friends drag friends away before they are hit again, and blood turns the cobbles black.

An arrow strikes his helmet. It seems to grab his head and throw it at the ground. His feet fly up above him. He sees a flash of green light and then finds himself lying staring up at the grey sky where smoke clouds billow and arrows flit from left to right and back again. Men step over him, trip on his lifeless legs. They are shouting. He can't get up. Darkness crimps his vision. Sound comes at a remove. Where is he? What is happening? He feels warmth stealing over him. He can feel a foolish smile covering his face. Then his view is blocked. Owen towers over him, a great paddle of a hand catches him under the arm and hauls him to his feet.

'Back,' Owen says. He is using his huge body to protect Thomas, and he pushes him. 'Go back.'

Thomas comes to. Power returns to his legs. He bends to recover his bow. Owen is still with him, back turned to the enemy. Dafydd arrives.

'All right?' he shouts.

Thomas nods. He still has arrows to loose and the guns by the town gate keep firing. One of the bombard barrels is sighted across the hard and Thomas can see men crouched over it, blowing on the wick to set the fire going. Then they all step back and clap their hands over their ears as the gun goes off with a jump. It belches a great spike of smoke and the noise itself is enough to drive a man mad.

The stone passes through a rank of men at the front; four of them are instantly cored. Bodies drop and sprawl. A mist of blood drifts in the air. Men wail. They try to turn and run but the vintenars are there with their pollaxes, driving them on with jabs and thrusts.

Then the second gun fires. But it explodes. Chunks of iron and oak hurtle into the gathered defenders, scattering them in a cloud of smoke and blood, ripping them to pieces. The invaders cheer. They take new courage and storm forward across the blood-slicked hard. More ships' companies debouch and join the assault; fresh numbers begin to tell and soon it looks as if they'll do what they came to do.

They move up into the town, one pace at a time, seeking the shelter of walls, barrels and coils of rope and carts, but the arrows still find them out, heavy bodkin heads landing with a distinct chunk, thumping into wood and daub, stone and flesh.

Thomas's muscles go on working without him thinking, until he is out of arrows. With his bag hanging limp at his belt and sweat in his eyes, he turns and pushes his way back through the press of men, twisting to let other archers take his place.

Walter is there, paused by a foul-smelling alleyway between two new-built cottages.

'We need to get around behind the guns,' he shouts. 'Bring that bloody pollaxe and come with me.'

Thomas sets off after him, but they are too late. The defenders have run out of arrows too, and now they throw aside their bows and draw their side weapons – the mauls, the daggers, the falchions, the pimp cleavers – and they swarm forward over their wall to engage with their attackers. Fauconberg's billmen move forward to meet them and so begins the mêlée, the cutting and hacking hand-to-hand fighting that will be decided not by skill but by the fear of being driven back into the sea.

For a moment it looks to be in doubt. The press of the defenders seems heavier than that of the attackers, but the drums are beating and trumpets are sounding and men are shouting for Fauconberg. The left flank gives under the pressure, and the axis of the fight pivots. But a knot of armoured men-at-arms under Fauconberg's banner surge forward and already the left flank is rallying, and then the right is turning the enemy.

It is over soon enough after that. It reaches that point when unannounced everybody knows what will happen next. The attackers take the first easy step forward; the defenders break and run. And now the rout can begin.

When it is over Thomas sits on a broken barrel with his head in his hands. His temples throb and his fingers are bleeding from the bowstring. He unties the leather strap of his helmet and studies its previously smooth surface. There is a star-shaped depression and a long gouge on the back where the arrow has hit and glanced away. He feels the puffy welt on the side of his head, his fingertips coming away damp. He puts the helmet back on again and ties the straps under his chin.

Smoke drifts across from a burning cottage roof, and the smell of it is mixed with blood and shit and saltpetre. The men-at-arms have pressed on into the town, after their slice of glory, but all around him, the archers and the billmen have broken off and most have fallen to looting. Corpses are scattered across the quayside as if they'd been flung away, piled the one on the other, some pinned by arrows, others bearing the marks of war hammers, glaives, daggers, axes. Some have been blown clean apart by the guns. Already there are noisy flies in the air and blood glistens between the cobbles, an oily slickness, viscid as phlegm. It is splashed on the cob walls of the houses and there are scraps of cloth ripped from banners and clothes; peelings of broken armour; discarded weapons; broken arrows; a dead horse. There is an arm lying alone on the cobbles, neatly dismembered through the elbow.

Thomas watches as two archers in murrey and blue begin picking through a pile of bodies thrown against the church wall, three or four deep. They haul them off as if they are grain sacks until they find a man alive. One archer shouts a warning to his mate. The man on the ground bellows something and throws up his hands in supplication. The second archer falls on him and stabs him in the face. The screaming is horrible. Men look up from what they are doing, and then look away again. The dead man stops thrashing, but the archer keeps on stabbing him, too terrified to stop. He has a short black dagger, and his arm goes up and down, up and down, as if he is pounding walnuts in a pestle. Thomas puts his hands over his ears.

Walter comes back down the road with five or six of the others. He has blood on the sleeves of his jack, a dent in his buckler and a small leather purse he is throwing up in the air and catching. He looks pleased with himself. Thomas is glad to see Dafydd and Owen and Red John with him. Dafydd's hose is ripped at the knee and there is blood all over the stocking. Owen has a black eye. But they are alive.

'Wait here, you lot,' Walter says. 'Take what you like off the dead, but don't touch anything else. Don't for fuck's sake go in any houses or I'll kill you myself.'

He turns and makes his way back through the town gate to the harbour. The rest of them gather around and find places to sit. They pass around a jug of ale.

'It's all right,' Red John says. 'I paid for it.'

'Ale,' Simon says. 'Saints, it's good to be back.'

But it feels wrong.

'Feels as if we're invading though, doesn't it?' Dafydd says. He gestures at the dead bodies. 'As if we're not wanted in our own country.'

'You mustn't mind all these bastards, Dafydd,' Simon says, taking a draught. 'They may be wearing the King's livery, but they aren't proper Englishmen. Bet you half of them are, you know, what-have-yous: Frenchies.'

'Still,' Thomas says.

'The people want us back. You wait and see. Soon as we get on the road to Canterbury, they'll be flocking to join us. And girls too. That's why they don't want us smashing the place up, nicking stuff. In case it scares them off. And to show we're better than those bloody northern bastards. Begging your pardon, Thomas.'

Men and women and children are beginning to appear now,

round-eyed, stepping between the grisly piles, stopping to stare at the bodies. Mothers hide their children's gaze. A merchant and his wife stand in front of their house and survey its broken windows, arrow-studded thatch, and a dead body slumped across their doorstep. There are bloody fingerprints on the plaster. Then the child gets blood on her shoe and starts to cry when her mother can't get it off.

'I saw Thomas killed,' Thomas says.

There are mumbles of regret and the others stare at the ground.

'What happened to his bow?' Dafydd asks.

Thomas's bow had been a beauty. Thomas shakes his head. Someone must have picked it up.

'And look what I found,' Little John Willingham says. He shows them a finely worked dagger with a badge on its pommel. A cockerel with its tail feathers raised.

'Wouldn't hang on to it, if I were you,' Dafydd cautions. 'Imagine his son finding you with it?'

'Well, I can't sell it back to him, can I? Cunt's dead.'

'Break the chicken off then.'

John flips the knife and bangs the decoration on a stone. After a while it breaks off, but now he finds he doesn't like it any more, so he throws it in the water.

They sit for a bit and watch the other archers going about their business, lifting visors, cutting the leather arming points, stealing rings, weapons, purses, anything. One laughs when another treads in a coil of blue guts that have spilled from a man who's come off worst against something sharp.

Hugh is sitting a little apart from the rest of them, looking out to sea. His face is the colour of goose fat.

Thomas calls over to him.

'You all right, Hugh?'

Hugh shakes his head but says nothing, just gestures to the nearest dead body. There are tears in his eyes, vomit on his livery and he is trembling. His arrow bag is full.

'Once we get to London, it'll be all over,' Dafydd says. 'The King'll get rid of whoever it is we're trying to get him to get rid of, and then we'll all be home for the harvest.'

'Got to be home for the harvest, anyway,' Brampton John says. 'Can't let my old ma get it in. I hate them fields, though.'

Walter returns with Geoffrey.

'Back to the ship, you lot,' Geoffrey calls. 'Fetch the stuff up. We need to get moving if we're to find somewhere dry to sleep tonight.'

They pick their way back across the market square, but have to wait by the town gate while prisoners are led down to the harbour. One of them is wearing fine armour, the bevor broken, obviously high-born.

'Who's that?'

'Fuck knows,' Walter says. 'Taking him back to Calais, anyway, so that's where he'll get his.'

He chops one hand on to the palm of his other to make the noise of an axe falling on a wooden block. The knight hesitates mid-step – he's no more than a boy really, with clear skin and big frightened eyes – but then an unshaven soldier in Fauconberg's livery pushes him from behind and on he goes.

By the time they are back aboard the carrack, Johnson is dead. He lies in a pool of blood to one side, the arrow still in his thigh, his head thrown back, lips blue, face as colourless as the moon.

'Saw he was still moving,' the master says with a shrug. 'Thought he was just wounded.'

They gather their gear and between them they carry Johnson's body in a hammock down the makeshift gangplank. They load it on to a cart. There are no oxen to be had so they have to wheel it themselves through the town. Once they are through they find a burial party at work with spades and mattocks in a field. Three priests and two heralds are counting the bodies. They unload Johnson, distribute his valuables, and swing him into the trench.

Beyond the graveyard is the common ground where Fauconberg is making camp. More men with shovels are throwing up earthworks while others cut stakes from the nearby woods. A fire is being lit near a red bell-shaped tent with yellow trim, and a man is erecting Fauconberg's banner on a spear. Others in unfamiliar liveries, are milling about, each waiting to speak to his heralds.

'See?' Simon says. 'Men're flocking to our colours now.'

They put up the tent in a corner of the camp and then scavenge some wood from a barn for their fire. They sit on their helmets by the flames and watch as men queue to join Fauconberg's army. There is every sort of soldier, from swineherds with rough iron bills and glaives all the way up to knights with liveried retinues. Some of the soldiers they've been fighting only that day are returning to join up. Companies and contingents bring with them carts laden with barrels and sacks and their women and children, and as evening descends the army has already doubled its size.

'Be invincible soon,' Dafydd laughs.

'Wait till we get to Canterbury before you say that,' Walter says. 'That's the first real test.'

Canterbury. Even mention of it hurts Thomas. He looks around for Katherine, but then remembers.

'How far is it?' he asks.

'A day?' Geoffrey guesses. 'Not far.'

Rain sets in. They retreat into the tent and stand peering out as the fires hiss and are slowly extinguished.

It doesn't stop for the next two days, and by the third the camp is a stinking quagmire. Men slip and fall; horses slip and fall. Armour and weapons rust; Thomas's jack doubles its weight. Men relieve themselves from the earthwork walls.

They are waiting on the Earl of Warwick, still in Calais.

'Why doesn't he just hurry up?' Dafydd asks. 'Seems I've spent half my life waiting for the bloody Earl of Warwick and a favourable bloody wind.'

'Favourable wind,' Owen repeats, rolling on to one buttock and farting.

It is still raining the next morning when the ships come in. Thomas is drinking ale with Geoffrey under the sodden straw awning of an alewife's house. She is looking at them because together they take up most of the space and there is little room for any other customers. They are talking about Hugh.

'He's a boy,' Thomas is saying. 'He should still be at home. Not seeing all this.' He gestures at the marketplace where now the rain has washed the blood from the cobbles, and all that remains of the fight are broken windows, starred stonework, arrows stuck in thatched roofs like pins in a cushion. One wall is still sooty and pocked where the gun exploded.

Geoffrey laughs.

'Listen to you, Thomas. Ha. Like the old soldier all of a sudden.'

Thomas thinks for a moment. Christ. Geoffrey is right. All the things he's done. The men he's killed.

Look at his hands! Blood in the creases. Dear God.

'And plenty been to fight younger'n Hugh,' Geoffrey is saying. 'I was in France when I was his age. And Walter? Well, how old was he when he first went to the wars? Three? Four?' The ale leaves a wet crescent on Geoffrey's upper lip.

'But Hugh feels things,' Thomas goes on. 'Did you see him after we'd landed? He'd vomited on himself and soiled his hose. He'd not loosed an arrow.'

Geoffrey looks away, as if it is somehow his fault.

'I'll make sure he has more ale next time.'

'It is not want of pluck, I think.'

Geoffrey shrugs.

'Perhaps you're right,' he says. 'Perhaps he shouldn't be here. Perhaps he should be in a monastery.'

Thomas opens and shuts his mouth. A boy comes through the harbour gate where the portcullis has been broken down and already taken away by a smith.

'The Earl of Warwick is come!' he shouts, and they begin drinking up. By the time Warwick has disembarked, word has got out. Men and women and children are ignoring the rain and have come to watch.

Warwick rides the same beautiful black horse he rode hunting that day, and he is wearing a travelling cloak with a cross of St George on a tabard underneath. It is a gesture to please the common soldier and to let the people know he has not come to make war on their king. As he passes, the crowd shout their greetings and thank him for coming. Men bless him.

'A Warwick!' they cry. 'A Warwick!'

'Why do they love him so?' Thomas asks. He remembers seeing Warwick after the hunt. Hastings would not be drawn on what had happened in the forest, but it was the Earl who shot Richard, and the Earl who rode away in haste.

'You can't blame them, Thomas,' Geoffrey is telling him. 'He's kept the Narrow Sea free of pirates these past years, free of Frenchmen. More than the King could ever do.'

They stand at the side of the road that leads up to Fauconberg's camp and as Warwick rides past them, his glance falls on them and his face twitches with recognition. His smile clouds; his eyes snap to the front. He rides on, his fist clenched by his hip.

'But he is a bastard,' Geoffrey says quietly. 'That much I will say.'

The Duke of York's son the Earl of March is next, much the bigger man, on a beautiful grey destrier. Thomas last saw him after the skirmish at Newnham. He is smiling and waving and laughing, and even from where Thomas stands he can see why. A little farther along the street is a tall young woman in a dark green kirtle. Her hat is high on her head and her chest is plump. One glance at her makes the spit in Thomas's mouth dry. As the Earl of March rides past her, he makes his horse skitter on the cobbles. Sparks fly. He makes a show of soothing the horse, patting its neck; then when the horse is calmed, he takes off his hat and speaks to the woman, who blushes, and all the while her husband stands at her shoulder smiling fatly. After a minute the Earl of March rides on with a long backward glance.

Next comes Warwick's father, the Earl of Salisbury, slumped in his saddle, glaring from under the brim of his hat where raindrops are gathered in a line. He looks at the people as if they are in his way, and somehow responsible for the rain; as he passes, the little crowd falls silent. Behind him, by some distance, comes Sir John Fakenham, his small pony being led by William Hastings. Hastings's face is green, as if he has not enjoyed the passage and does not trust himself swaying on the back of a horse. A lad wearing his black bull badge is leading Hastings's horse a few yards behind, and even the horse looks ill.

Sir John sees Geoffrey and Thomas and waves them over. They greet one another with handshakes.

'Thanks be that you are still with us. I hear they put up a fight?' Geoffrey nods.

'And what's the reckoning?' Sir John asks.

'Two dead,' Geoffrey says. 'Two boys from home.'

Sir John pulls a face.

'If you give me their names? Though I know not how I'll ever get word to their families. By all the saints, this is a bloody business. Englishmen killing Englishmen.'

'And what of Richard, Sir John?' Geoffrey asks.

Sir John's face puckers.

'He's with Kit, aboard some damned carrack that has been cruelly knocked up, with that old pirate as a master, but she sailed on the same tide and should be off the coast now. That friend of yours is a born surgeon, Thomas, but my lord of Warwick is sending his own man over, a physician, and just as soon as Richard is settled, he shall have the best attention money can buy.'

Thomas smiles to think of Katherine. He glances down towards the dock where her ship should be arriving. There are more horsemen coming up from the ships now and it takes him a moment to realise he is looking at a man in a bishop's headgear among them. When he sees him Thomas instantly turns his back on Sir John and disappears into the crowds.

'Thomas?' he hears Geoffrey call. 'Where are you going?'

It is not the Bishop he fears, but the man riding the pony behind him: the cleric Lamn.

15

Katherine is standing at the ship's rail when the *Mary* nudges against the dock at Sandwich for the second time in four days. The ship is now patched with bloodstained sailcloth and her timbers are scorched and studded with broken arrows.

'Stand by,' her master calls, and the Genoese cook, now promoted to sailor, throws a line for the boys on the dockside. Katherine returns to the waist where Richard lies face down, loosely tied to a softwood plank. He is asleep.

When she peers up over the ship's rail she sees Thomas and Geoffrey waiting on the dockside, and she feels the warmth of relief. Both are alive. The state of the carrack had given her cause to fear the worst, but now here they are, shoulders hunched against the rain, waiting with a carter and an ox.

Thomas looks older, strained somehow, and she sees the burned houses, the smashed windows, the pitted stones.

'Was it bad?' she asks when she is ashore.

'Nothing we haven't seen before,' Geoffrey answers for him. 'Though we missed you. Johnson's gone, dead, and the other Thomas, too, God keep their souls. The rest are fine though. How's himself?' He nods at Richard.

'I think he is through the worst of it,' she says. Richard still looks terrible. His face is fallen in and his skin tinged with a feverish rosiness around his eyes and mouth. She doesn't tell them how bad it has been, how close she's come to calling a priest.

They lift him up on his plank and together they carry him down the gangway on to the dockside. He groans as they load him on to the cart. Geoffrey sits with the carter while Thomas and Katherine walk behind.

'Lamn is here,' he tells her.

'I know. He sailed on the ship before mine. I thought I was unlucky not to be sailing with Sir John, who would at least have insisted Richard have some ale, but we were delayed and then the Bishop and his retinue joined Sir John's ship. After that I was glad.'

'And he's still said nothing?'

'Not so far.'

When he had accosted her by the trough at the fort, after Richard had been wounded, she had denied his accusation. Thomas had heard her voice raised and had loomed over the cleric and, with Geoffrey behind him, and the rest of the men returning from the butts just then, Lamn backed away and pretended to have made a mistake. He'd said no more and once they had carried Richard inside, Lamn had ridden away with William Hastings without a backward glance. As soon as he was gone Katherine had hurried up the steps to where they slept and had starting gathering her things.

'He will be back tomorrow,' she'd said. 'With the friars.'

Thomas tried to persuade her that no one in Calais was going to listen to Lamn.

'Warwick needs every soldier he can keep,' he'd said. 'No one will care if we are apostate.'

She'd known then that she must tell him she was more than an apostate, but still something held her back, and now here they are back in England with Canterbury only a day's march away.

'But who is he?' Thomas wants to know. 'The Bishop, I mean?'

'His name is Coppini. Sir John says he is a Frenchy from somewhere called Italy. He comes straight from the Pope himself.'

Thomas laughs.

'The Pope?'

She smiles too. Even the word Pope feels foolish on her lips. It reminds her of the night they met the pardoner in the woods and they found themselves talking about the King. Such people weren't for them to discuss.

The cart rumbles on through the town until they reach the camp. Here the mud has become thick and pale, the sort to pull a man's boot off, and the rain doesn't look like stopping soon – if ever. When they unload Richard from the cart he wakes.

'How was it?' he croaks. His lips are cracked and his breath foul. He cannot open his eyes properly.

'You didn't miss a thing,' Geoffrey soothes. 'They turned tail as soon as they saw us.'

'There was no fight?'

Geoffrey shakes his head.

Richard closes his eyes.

'Is Kit here?' he asks.

'I'm here,' she answers. Richard is relieved and drifts off again.

They take him into the tent where Sir John is already sitting on his cushion on his chest. After he has bent and kissed his son he turns to Katherine.

'I have good news, Kit,' he says. 'My lord the Earl of Warwick is sending his physician over this morning. A fellow called Fournier. He has a great reputation.'

Katherine can think of nothing to say.

'It is no reflection on your care,' he goes on. 'No man can have wished for a more attentive nurse and Hastings has been boasting of your skills with the knife far and wide.'

'He's a kind man, William Hastings,' she says.

Sir John agrees.

After Sir John leaves she crouches in the tent next to Richard and tries to make sense of it all. She still has no idea what to do. She will have to leave soon, before Thomas can take her before the Prior of All, but she cannot simply abandon Richard. Perhaps this physician will reassure her.

But when Fournier turns up, she is still unsure.

'Master Dominic Fournier,' his servant announces, holding open the tent flap as the physician steps in. He is wearing a velvet cloak, greasy at the worn lapels, and a sagging fur hat sprouting an array of damp goose feathers. He is poorly shaved and his dark eyebrows meet in the middle. He looks anxious, as if he might be unmasked at any moment.

'Do you have wine?' he asks. 'Any will do?'

'None,' she says.

He nods.

'Very well. Then let us make this short. Boy, expose the wound.'

The boy looks at Katherine for permission. He is grey-faced with a clipped right ear from which for a moment Katherine cannot take her gaze. She wonders absently how strange it is that one rarely sees men with clipped ears. What happens to the boys? Do only a few live long enough to become men?

She does not want the boy to touch the wound, so she bends and peels back the dressing herself. She hears Fournier suck his teeth. Then sniff the air. The wound is black-lipped, and slightly puckered, the skin around it rosy and delicate, fine as silk. Something glistens between its lips. Katherine knows that the wound is healing and she is pleased – no, astonished by what she has managed.

'Yes, yes,' Fournier says. 'It is as I feared. The wound has cured from the outside in. It has sealed in the hot wet humour. It needs cauterising. We'll need a fire.'

Katherine stands.

'You are going to burn him?' Panic makes her voice high.

'It is the only way,' Fournier says. 'We must clean the wound from within, with fire, then we shall bleed him. Such a wound, particularly in such a place, unbalances the humours. We need to make a small incision between the fingers, there.' He points at Richard's limp hand with the long point of his patten. 'It is connected to the functions of the liver. And the moon is in an auspicious quarter for cutting.'

He gestures upwards. Katherine stares at him a moment. Something begins growing within her, a physical force that shakes her narrow frame, fills her skin. It is always this way when she puts herself in harm's way. The Prioress once suggested it was the presence of the devil within her, and beat her for it, as if that might expel the demon.

Now she crosses to where Thomas has left the giant's pollaxe against one of the tent bracers. It is lighter than she remembers, but the weight of its head gives it fearsome impetus, and when she picks it up, it levels itself at Fournier's belly.

He steps back.

'If you so much as touch him,' she says, 'I will run you through.'

Katherine has never been more certain of anything, and yet – what is she doing? She is threatening the Earl of Warwick's personal physician with a pollaxe. Fournier takes another step back. Spots of high colour have come into his cheeks and his mouth quavers. He slips off his pattens as they catch in the mud.

'You are mad!' he squeaks.

She jabs the axe at him.

'Out,' she says. 'Get out.'

'You have not heard the last of this,' Fournier cries as he backs through the tent flaps. 'You have not heard – d'you hear?'

He is away before she can think of anything to say. His boy stoops to collect his pattens and runs out after him.

When Geoffrey comes to find her, Richard is asleep under a rug, breathing steadily.

They say nothing for a moment, but it is clear Geoffrey is exasperated.

'Sir John is upset,' he says.

Katherine says nothing. She does not know what to say. The shame weighs on her.

'Whatever were you thinking?' he goes on. 'He is the Earl of Warwick's personal physician!'

She shakes her head and closes her eyes to stop the tears. She can still think of nothing to say. Why can she not be content to let things pass? But then – he was going to burn Richard. That cannot be a right thing to do.

'You're an odd one, Kit, and no mistake. If you haven't been looking after Richard so well, then – well, I don't know. You'd've had your ear clipped long ago.'

She thinks of Fournier's grubby boy and nods tightly. She swallows.

'As it is,' Geoffrey goes on, 'keep out of his way for a day or two.'

Later that day the order comes to break camp.

'Thank the Lord for that,' Thomas says, but if he thinks breaking camp will mean getting away from Fournier, or Lamn, he is mistaken, for the news comes down that the Bishop is to travel with them.

'Warwick hopes to persuade him to excommunicate the King's army,' Sir John laughs while he watches them start clearing their tents in the rain. When they have the cart loaded, they leave the town of Sandwich and begin up the Roman road towards Canterbury, a thousand years old and still mostly passable. In the fields either side of them water lies in the hollows and anyone who leaves the road comes back with mud up to his knees.

'Never seen it rain so,' one of them says.

'Wheat'll rot if it goes on like this.'

'Everything'll bloody rot if it goes on like this. We'll bloody rot.'

They cross a river that has broken its banks. Swans sail on the fields. Still the rain comes down. But still men join them. Soon the towers of the cathedral break the skyline ahead.

Katherine is walking next to Hugh just behind the cart. Every step towards the city pains her, but she cannot think what to do. Panic has reduced her to indecision.

'I can't stand it again,' Hugh whispers to her.

She looks up.

'Stand what?'

Hugh looks about them, down the column, seeing if it is safe to speak. He sees something or someone and shakes his head. They walk on in silence until he stops again. Here the trees have closed in on the road, the bushes are thick with leaf. An archer is squatting over a ditch.

'Goodbye, Kit,' Hugh says and he holds out a slim hand. Katherine takes it. It is cool, like holding a fish.

'You're going?' she asks.

He nods.

'I am not strong enough,' he says. Then he steps off the road on to the grass verge. A moment later he is gone.

Katherine opens her mouth to call after him, to tell him to stop, to come back or to wait for her. She does not know which.

'Come on. Come on,' Dafydd says as he and Thomas push up against her from behind, and she turns again and walks on. Ahead of them the banners are hanging in damp folds. Men huddle within their cloaks.

Walter drops back from the cart. He is carrying four bags of arrows. He gives one to Thomas.

'Try to keep 'em dry,' he says. 'You'll need 'em first thing tomorrow.' He looks around for a moment. 'Where's that streak of piss Hugh?' he asks.

Thomas shrugs. Walter glances at her. She shrugs too, but differently, and Walter understands. He steps off the road and peers back along the lines.

'Silly fucker,' he says. 'Hope to God the prickers don't get him. They'll hang him from a branch soon as look at him.'

They walk on.

So that is Hugh, she thinks, gone, and will she ever see him again? Ever find out what happens to him?

Some cows in an orchard watch them pass.

'We should take one,' Dafydd says. 'Never know when you're going to need a cow.'

'Touch one of them and the Earl of Warwick'll have you drowned in a puddle.'

'What about a swan?'

'Same thing.'

'But look about you,' Dafydd exclaims. 'Look! There's so much here. I've never seen anything like it. It's all orchards, everywhere. Pear trees. Plum trees. Cherry trees. What's that? A bloody chestnut tree! And all those birds! Partridges and pea-fowls and pheasants – and that's without even talking about the sheep!'

'Sheep!' Owen says.

'And where is everybody? It's like it all goes on without anyone looking.'

There are fat chickens loose in every village, and well-kept inns where they serve beer brewed from imported hops and serve it in pewter cups, with cheese pies, and buttered peas, and every step she takes only brings her nearer the gallows.

Just then there is a blaring of trumpets and shouting from behind them.

'Make way! Stand aside there!'

It is the Earl of Warwick riding past in full armour, his visor up, followed by a body of men in armour, their hooves throwing up the mud as they pass. As they pass, though, men begin to lift their heads. They start to stride forward. Katherine shakes her head. Why they cannot see him for what he is, she does not know. A moment later the Earl of March rides past, languid, with less of the bustle, and then came the others, Salisbury and Fauconberg and their household men, their banners held stiff despite the rain. Then the Bishop Coppini, and last, Lamn.

'Late for their supper, I bet,' Dafydd sneers.

That night they camp on the common land outside the silver grey walls of Canterbury and in the still of the night, such as it is, Katherine gathers her things: her knife, her few clothes, the spare hood; and she puts them in her bag, and waits.

16

The sound of trumpets and men shouting in the dawn.

'Stand to. Stand to. Come on, you lazy dogs. Get up and stand to.'

It is Walter, at the tent flap. Fleeting shadows cross the canvas as men go about their business by the fires' light, scuffling and cursing in the gloom. Thomas rolls to his feet and straps the bracer on his forearm. He forces his still raw fingers into his blood-stiff glove.

Katherine is already awake, her eyes open in the dark.

'Good luck,' she says. 'And God be with you.'

'You too, Kit. You too.'

She throws her blanket off and stands, smelling of sleep and warmth.

'No, Thomas,' she says. 'I mean it.'

She grips his hand. He smiles. The way she behaves can still surprise him.

'Me too,' he says.

She is unblinking in the dark. He has to pull his hand free of hers and he feels her stare following him as he leaves the tent. Something is wrong, but what?

Outside Geoffrey is shirtless, his hairy belly silvery like a moon in the dawn. He is emptying a jug of ale into his mouth as two boys march past, one hoisting a banner, the other beating a drum like a heart, boo-boom, boo-boom. Men are falling in behind them, their faces black and smoke-smutted from the fires they've tended through the night. There is a strong smell of horses.

'Archers, to the front,' a man shouts from his saddle, though they all know what is expected of them. 'Archers to the front! Find your mark. Quickly now.'

Thomas finds his spot. They are in a grass meadow a little way off the road, the ground under their feet soggy, copses of elms and oaks to both sides. Behind them the men-at-arms and the billmen are forming up, rattling in their armour plate, five or six deep. Some of the billmen are carrying just farm tools: a hayfork, a knife lashed to a pole to make a glaive; all of them on the lookout for better weapons for the next time. These are the naked men, the scrapings of the recruitment barrel, the men who make up the numbers for the Commissions of Array.

Others are carrying bills, hammers, axes, swords, mauls, pikes and spears. Most have a helmet, and some have gauntlets. None of it matches and most of it has been looted at least once before, if not twice.

Gathered under their banners are the armoured knights and the men-at-arms, the household men of those who can afford to pay them. The men of the Earl of Warwick take the central division, straddling the road, and those of March take the left flank while Fauconberg's men occupy the right. It is easy to see March. He is the tallest man on the field, his banner long and fishtailed.

'A Fauconberg!'

'Come on! Lively now!'

The day comes slowly. What has been invisible in the dark becomes discernible in the light and they find themselves facing the town walls across a ditch and a stretch of broad water meadows. Before the gates of the city, to one side of the road, is a small hamlet clustered around the squat tower of another church, and beyond are some earthworks from which a man with a donkey and a spade moves off sharply when he sees what is afoot.

In the city men are moving between the battlements of the gate-house and there are more on the walls too. Thomas imagines them staring back out at the besieging army, trying to estimate their number and deposition, gauging their banners, waiting and wondering.

The bells begin a steady toll.

'Easy now, lads,' Geoffrey is telling them. 'Check your equipment. Take the time to make sure you've got everything you need. Check your arrows. Check your bow. Then take a drink.'

Ahead of them in the hamlet they can see a number of men in livery, some of them horsemen. They can hear the slide of harness and the stamp of horses' hooves.

'Here they come,' Dafydd says. He bends and makes a sign of the cross on the mud beneath his feet. Then he takes a piece of earth in his mouth and nocks an arrow. So do all the other archers. A priest walks ahead of them, intoning the paternoster, blessing them as he goes.

They all kneel. Thomas can hardly swallow.

'I hate this bit,' Red John says next to him. Even in the gloom Thomas can see John's eyes are unnaturally bright. He wishes he had a wineskin with him, or a mug of ale. It is easier with drink.

'Wait for the order,' Walter murmurs. He licks his finger and checks the wind. There is none.

A party of well-mounted horsemen ride forward from their lines up the road and into the hamlet.

'Who are they?' Thomas asks.

'Heralds,' an archer at the front says. 'Warwick Herald, there.'

They relax. Red John stabs his arrow back in the ground. The horsemen, about five of them in different coloured tabards, dismount and leave their horses for a servant.

'Parley, it is,' Walter says. 'See if we're going to fight.'

Thomas finds his lips moving in prayer. Time passes. The light grows stronger. Someone is sick. Men laugh. Thomas holds out his hand and watches it tremble. It will be better when it starts. He wishes he'd had something to eat and he still craves something to drink – anything.

Then, suddenly, instantly, he is no longer afraid: he is bored.

He thinks about Katherine. She has been behaving strangely since they returned to England. Perhaps it is being so close to Canterbury. He looks across at the spire of the cathedral and thinks about returning to orders again. He looks at his hands: how they have changed their shape. They are calloused and square now, firm with muscle, and all that remains to mark his former life is a dent in his forefinger where he held the reed. His arms must have doubled their girth.

Now he tries to imagine the Prior of All, just beyond the city walls, seated over some wine in a room very like the almonry. He can see him receiving Katherine back into the order, and then what? Here the picture becomes vague. He cannot imagine her standing before the Prior in her stained jack, her hacked-off hair, with her hose sagging around her ankles. He cannot imagine her bowing her head to some old man.

Perhaps he will have to find her some sort of dress and headgear? It will be the least he can do. And the last thing he can do, for once they say goodbye, that will be the end. He will never see her again. He remembers suddenly her feverish grip that morning, and her heartfelt wishes.

He hawks and spits on the ground. Dafydd has found something to eat and his fingers are greasy with meat juices. He offers a bone to Thomas, then quickly drops it as he sees something moving. He snatches up his bow again.

'Here we go.'

The heralds emerge from between two cottages in the hamlet and canter across to where Warwick waits with his men under his banner. There is a brief conversation. After a moment, Warwick forces his horse forwards so that he is alone in front of the army. Then he turns and faces them, stands in his stirrups and tips back his visor, so that they can see his face: a pale square. He raises his arm and gestures. Thomas cannot make it out but those who can begin cheering.

'Bloody hell's he up to?'

Trumpets and horns begin too, and then the bells in the cathedral begin a celebratory peal.

'He's done it!' someone shouts. 'They've opened the gates!'

Along the line the men begin cheering.

'A Warwick! A Warwick!'

Another party of horsemen ride out from the hamlet: more heralds. Up the road the city gates are pushed open from within. Canterbury and the Archbishop have declared for the Duke of York. There will be no fighting. Not today at least.

Thomas feels a mix of emotions. Relief, of course, but now he will have to say goodbye to Katherine.

They disperse back to their tents and Thomas goes to find her. His heart is heavy with what is to come, what he must say, but he has imagined this part many times: he thinks he knows what he will tell her, and how.

'Where's Kit?' he asks.

No one has seen her.

He helps Geoffrey with dinner, one eye out for her, but she does not appear. When the food is ready they sit on the earthwork wall, yawning with fatigue, spooning stewed mutton into their mouths. Above them their jacks hang from the branches of a hawthorn tree, drying in the weak sunlight.

'Anyone seen Kit?' Geoffrey asks. 'Richard's asking after him.'

No one has seen her since they'd been called to stand to.

'Probably found an inn somewhere,' Brampton John says, though there are none to be seen.

'See if you can find him, Thomas, will you? Tell him Richard needs him.'

Thomas nods. In the tent there is no sign of Katherine's pack.

Trumpets begin blowing in the camp again. Drums are beating. Horses cross the meadows. A Te Deum has been sung in the cathedral and the Earls have paid their respects at the shrine of St Thomas, and now Walter returns to the camp.

'Come on, come on,' he says. 'Let's get cracking,' and they get up and begin the wearying process of breaking camp once more.

There is still no sign of Katherine.

Carts are already starting to wheel along the road and in through the city gates when a handful of horsemen come riding through the chaos shouting that they are looking for Sir John Fakenham's company. They are Warwick's men, on good mounts.

'That's us,' Walter tells them.

'Found a boy of yours,' their vintenar says. 'Making his way across country. Hardly worth the trouble keeping him, he's so skinny, but the Earl wants examples set. Anyone slipping away gets theirs.'

He gestures towards a party of men threading their way through the breaking camp. Between them, Katherine, hands bound, dragging her feet. She looks so small, so round-shouldered and miserable, that even Thomas mistakes her for a boy.

Walter stands with his hands on his hips.

'Christ,' he spits. 'What d'you want us to do with him?'

'Hang him.'

Thomas feels a chill grip him. The atmosphere hardens. Colours spring to life; lines sharpen.

'Hang him?'

'What the Earl wants.'

Katherine stares at the ground. She has a bruise under one eye.

'What were you thinking, Girly?' Walter asks.

Katherine says nothing.

'He's just a boy,' Thomas tells the vintenar. 'You can't – We can't hang him.'

The vintenar looks down from his horse.

'Who're you to say?'

Dear God.

'Look, he's right,' Geoffrey says. 'Kit, how old are you?'

Katherine will still not talk.

'He's fourteen, for the love of God,' Thomas says.

The vintenar lifts his hand from the saddle.

'Could be two for all I care,' he says. 'The Earl of Warwick wants an example.'

The men look at one another. Others are stopping to stare.

'Oh Christ!'

'But there must be some – I don't know – mistake,' Thomas says. 'Kit's no reason to run.'

'He's nowhere to run to,' one of the men says.

'Why d'you do it, Kit?'

She will not answer.

The vintenar is growing impatient.

'You're not listening,' he says. 'There's nothing I can do about it. Either you do it, or we do it.'

One of the horsemen has a rope. He is surveying the hawthorn for a suitable bough.

'Thomas,' Walter mutters, 'go and find Sir John. He's the only one can get Kit out of this.'

'Where is he?'

'Try the Watch tent. He'll be near Fauconberg.'

Thomas tries to catch Katherine's eye before he turns and runs, tries to reassure her that he is doing something, but she remains staring at the ground, acknowledging none. He runs through the camp to its centre. Fauconberg, March and Warwick have all been to the cathedral to hear the Te Deum and are riding north together. No one has seen Sir John.

A bell rings in the city.

Time is passing.

He begins a prayer, his footfalls punctuating the Latin lines. He abandons it halfway through. He is sick with panic. Where is he? Where is Sir John?

He thinks of Katherine. A rope around her neck. Legs kicking in mid-air. Hanging in the hawthorn branches with the laundry.

Oh Christ! He cannot stand it. He runs through the lines and back again, looking where he has already looked. Where is the old man? Surely he cannot have gone far without Geoffrey's help?

'Thomas!' he hears a man cry.

Half the men in the camp are called Thomas, but Thomas recognises William Hastings's voice. He is at the head of a table with some men Thomas does not recognise. They are drinking wine and there is a pie on a board and a small dish of salt.

'Thomas Everingham! Hero of Newnham! Come and join us in a drink,' Hastings calls.

'I cannot, sir, I am looking for Sir John.' He explains his hurry.

'Not because of the surgeon fellow? I thought Sir John'd managed to sort that out.'

'It's not that. They've caught him trying to run.'

Hastings springs to his feet.

'But he's – Christ. What a waste. No. No. We can't have that. Lead me to him. My word counts for something, enough perhaps to delay the inevitable.'

When they find her again, Katherine is standing under a tree in her shirt with her hat pushed back. She looks pitifully thin and in the watery sunlight her skin is translucent. One of Warwick's men stands behind her, bending the damp rope to form a noose. Walter is still arguing with the vintenar. Katherine will still say nothing. It is as if she has already left them.

'Hold fast! Hold up there!'

When he sees Hastings, the vintenar touches his knuckle to his helmet.

'Sir,' he says.

'You can't mean to hang this boy?'

'Earl of Warwick's orders, sir. Caught him the other side of the village over there. Put up a fight. Saved us a deal of time and trouble if we'd killed him there and then but his lordship wants an example made. So.'

Hastings turns to Katherine.

'Is this true?'

Still Katherine says nothing. She will not even look at him.

'Kit, you must say something in your defence. Otherwise—'

'Get on and hang him,' someone in the crowd jeers. The soldier throws the rope over the tree above her head.

'Lucky he's a little 'un,' he says, finding the branches thin.

Hastings holds out his hand.

'There'll be no one hanged here,' he says.

The vintenar is surprised.

'You'll take responsibility?'

Hastings nods, but he is anxious. To countermand the Earl of Warwick is no small thing.

'I will,' he says. 'I will.'

Thomas feels his heart beat again.

The crowd is disappointed.

'Piss off, all of you,' Walter snarls.

The vintenar nods to his men. The one with the rope pulls it down again and folds it into a sack. It is difficult to read his face: is he disappointed or relieved? The others mount their horses.

'I don't suppose this is the last we've heard of this,' Hastings tells them. 'But keep an eye on the boy and don't let him wander off again.'

Walter nods.

'Thank you, sir,' he says.

'I'd better find old Warwick before he finds me,' Hastings says. His gaze lingers on Katherine, who will still not speak, and whose expression has hardly changed. 'A handsome lad, you are, Kit, if only you'd fill out a bit, but you'll never do that if you're hanging by your neck from a tree.'

Again there is nothing from Katherine and with one last nod to Thomas and Walter, Hastings parts the crowd and strides off back the way he has come.

Walter exhales.

'Christ on His cross, Girly. Christ on His cross!'

A single tear slides down Katherine's cheek.

'Don't do that again, d'you hear?' Walter barks. 'If you do, then we'll all bloody well hang, and I am not hanging for a strip like you. Understand?'

Katherine nods.

'Thomas,' Walter says. 'You keep an eye on him. Find out why the bloody hell he ran and make sure he doesn't do it again. Understand?'

They sit together on the bank under the branches where the clothes are still drying.

'Why?' Thomas asks. 'After all we've been through. When you are so close to Canterbury?'

She shakes her head.

'I will tell you,' she says, 'but first I must sleep. I am so tired I can hardly lift my head.'

She has been watching over Richard for more than a week with no proper sleep, he supposes, and relief at escaping the rope must have diminished her too, and so now she lies on the bank and sleeps so soundly that even the men packing up and taking their still damp clothes from the branches above do not wake her. Thomas fetches her blanket and drapes it over her. He sits by her and stares at her and tears well in his eyes when he thinks how nearly he lost her.

Later Sir John appears. He looks fretful and is leaning heavily on Geoffrey's arm, in great pain. Geoffrey too looks anxious. They have come from Warwick's tent and the news is not good.

'Hastings did what he could,' he says, 'but punishment must be seen to be done, or it ain't punishment. He wants Kit's ear clipped.'

Thomas closes his eyes.

'Well, now we'll see what he's made of,' Walter says. 'Wake him up, will you, Tom?'

Walter never calls Thomas Tom. No one ever has, except his father, and the Dean. He crouches over Katherine. She looks peaceful, snoring gently under her blanket. He rests his hand on her shoulder.

'Kit,' he says. 'Kit.'

She wakes and looks at him for a moment.

'I was having a dream,' she smiles. She sits up and stretches, then looks at him again.

The men are gathered around, looking at her.

'What is it?' she asks.

'The Earl of Warwick,' Thomas tells her.

She is still.

'What does he want?'

'Your ear.'

'My ear?'

She does not look especially frightened.

'He wants it clipped,' he goes on, gesturing, in case she has not understood.

Katherine frowns.

'Ah,' she says. Then: 'How do they do it?'

'Scissors.'

He hears her swallow. Her eyes are wide as she looks around.

'Will you do it?' she asks.

'Me?'

She nods. He stares at her. He feels sick at the thought. He cannot stop himself glancing at the pink tip of her ear.

'If you want,' he says.

She nods again.

'Get plenty of linen, will you? And keep the pardoner's salve to hand.'

Walter is standing by.

'Here,' he says.

He holds out a pair of iron shears still warm from the grinding wheel. Nearby Sir John stands whey-faced.

'Sorry it has come to this, Kit,' he says. 'My lord of Warwick is adamant though, and it is only through the good graces of William Hastings that you are not swinging from the tree. It will make a good story for your grandchildren one day, but I do not suppose it will improve your looks.'

The men watch silently.

'Do you want to take your shirt off, Kit?'

She shakes her head.

'Sit then.'

They take away Sir John's cushion and they sit her on the chest. A group of stable boys appear, summoned to witness the punishment, and one brings a drum he intends to beat until Walter threatens him with a knife.

Thomas looks at the shears in the palm of his hand and squeezes them together and lets them spring apart a couple of times.

'Put them in the fire for a bit,' Walter says, passing him a cloth. 'Get them good and hot. Helps seal the cut.'

Katherine sits there, and he remembers first cutting her hair back on the staithes in Boston. Then he bends and puts the blades over the embers for as long as he can stand it. His hands are shaking. Geoffrey stands behind her, ready to catch her, and over her head, he nods. She tilts her head, exposing the line of her throat and her small right ear. Thomas takes the shears and moves quickly, brushing aside her hair and cutting down across the top of her ear with a sharp snip. He feels the rubbery tag of the ear under the slide of the blades, a moment of toughness, then a give, and then the smooth snick of the scissors. He is through. Hot blood covers his fingers.

She stiffens and thrashes, kicking his shins, but does not scream. Geoffrey holds her tight. Thomas's nostrils are filled with the smell of burning flesh and hair. He drops the shears and turns away. Walter stoops and tosses the piece of ear on to the flames then kicks the shears out of sight. Geoffrey holds Katherine to him, soothing her, stroking the back of her head.

'It's all right lad,' he says. 'It's all right. It's all over now. The pain'll soon go.' He winks at Thomas. 'Well done,' he mouths.

'All right! All right!' Walter bellows. 'Show's over. Piss off, all of you.'

The men and boys drift away. Thomas applies the linen swabs to her wound. It is not bleeding as much as he'd have thought, and he wonders if perhaps Walter was right about the heated blades. Katherine is grey-faced where she is not gummy with her own blood.

'We'll stay here tonight, Geoffrey,' Sir John is saying. 'Give them time to get over all this. Let's turn in early, though, and only small beer, you understand?'

Geoffrey nods. A strange atmosphere lingers.

'We can hear Mass in the cathedral tomorrow,' Geoffrey says. 'Thank the Lord for small mercies.'

Thomas helps Katherine back to Richard's tent. He is asleep on good thick sheepskin now, bought from the sale of his horse, and Katherine lies down on his old mattress next to him. Thomas brings a bowl of water and some linen and he begins washing her face.

'Can I bring you ale?' he asks. 'It might numb the pain.'

She nods with her eyes only.

'Thomas,' she says. 'You know – you know—'

She stops. She glances at Richard where he lies in feverish sleep. Thomas thinks she is about to tell him why she has run.

'What?' he asks.

'You know I can never return to the priory now.'

He sits back on his haunches. Dear God! He has not thought of that. Then he dips the linen into the water and wipes away more blood under her neck. He needs time to think.

'By the saints, Katherine. I am sorry.'

She smiles.

'No,' she says. 'No. It is a good thing.'

He pauses.

'How can that be? Do you not want to go back to the priory?'

She places her hand on the bandage over her ear.

He feels a fool. Of course she does not want to go back the priory. 'But what will you do?'

'It seems I have no choice,' she tells him. 'Even if I had anywhere else to go, the Earl of Warwick wants me to stay.'

She smiles again. He smiles too and is silent for a while. She closes her eyes as pain grips her. She relaxes when it has passed.

'So you will stay?' he asks.

She opens her eyes.

'If you do, yes.'

A great weight is lifted.

'The wheel of fortune.' He laughs. 'Just when you think you are down, you are up.'

She opens her eyes and looks at him for a long moment.

'Yes,' she says, 'but then again, just when you think you are up, you are down.'

He grips her hand. She smiles once more, then turns over on to her side, her back to him, and goes to sleep.

The tears course down his face, and he wipes them with the back of his wrist.

'Bloody hell, Kit,' he says, 'bloody hell.'

17

The next morning they break camp and cross the water meadows and enter Canterbury through the gatehouse. The bells are ringing and people call out to them as they pass, wishing them luck in the name of St James. Thomas walks with Katherine. She takes short shuffling steps, gingerly, and leans against him now and then. She's pulled her hood up to cover her ear and face, and walks looking down at her feet rather than up at the cathedral. In the suddenly cramped confines of the town they are hemmed in by friars of every hue.

'I would like to go to Mass again,' she admits, her gaze rising quickly to the cathedral windows. 'I have not made my confession since we left the priory.'

Thomas hangs his head.

'And we have much to confess,' he says.

Katherine says nothing. They walk on.

'Will you confess to apostasy?' he asks.

'I have thought about it,' she says, 'and the truth is that I will not.'

'Then you will die unshriven? You'd be damned for eternal life.'

Katherine shakes her head.

'I don't believe leaving the priory was a sin. The Prioress used to beat me with a hawthorn broom. She used to starve me. She chained me to a log and stretched me for a night and the Lord knows what she had in mind for me had I stayed. Have you ever heard of a sister from a place in the north called Watton?'

Thomas is staring at her.

'No,' he says. She cannot tell if he believes her, but there is a curious, almost tender look in his eye. He raises his hand as if to touch her, then drops it. He shakes his head.

'Well, count yourself lucky,' Katherine tells him, 'in more ways than one.'

The crowds pat them as they pass, and wine flows and everywhere men and women are laughing. Thomas stops to buy some reeds and ink from an inkseller. She tells him he has paid too much, but what does either of them know? Then they are through the city gates again and out across the fields. The old road is dead straight, heading west where clouds threaten more rain. News spreads up and down the column that the Archbishop of Canterbury has thrown his lot in with the Earls of March and Warwick, and that he will be riding with them.

'Coppini says it is all his doing,' Sir John laughs from the back of his cart. 'Typical bloody Frenchy.'

Richard is sitting up. He is pale, very thin, still not talking much, just staring back at the cathedral's spires as the town drops away behind them. There are dark circles under his eyes and his skin is like that of a drowned man, but he no longer smells of contagion, or of the grave, and Katherine is sure he is on the mend. For his sake later that morning they let Katherine ride with them, but she is conscious that she remains under a shadow. Sir John ignores her, though she sometimes catches him staring at her with an expression she cannot read. Is it regret? Anxiety? Now and again he leans forward to try to see her wound, but she has it well hidden under her cap.

The cart creaks along, its wheels spinning through the long troughs of mud, jarring over the loose stones. Here and there the road has slipped away into the verge and the men behind must steady it as she rolls, or they must put their shoulders to the wheels when it becomes stuck. The threatened rain begins to fall. She covers

Richard in a travelling cloak and places a straw hat on his head and after a while she is sure he is asleep and she watches out for Thomas, walking behind with the others, a head taller than most of them. He smiles at her and rolls his eyes, and a smile breaks her own lips, and she feels a small thrill alike to that one feels with the first scent of spring.

Men are still joining the column as it marches west, and each evening the scurriers return with the news that such and such a place has declared for the Duke of York and the Earl of Warwick instead of King Henry. Soon the men no longer cheer as one after another the towns and villages along their way send archers and billmen to join them, each contingent led by mounted men-at-arms under a new flag, a new banner. Even those men raised by order of the King join them, and the army drifts along the road like a flock of sheep, numbering many thousands.

As the numbers grow, food becomes steadily more scarce. Despite the wealth of the land about them, ale isn't to be had. Not even in Rochester itself, where they camp under the stern walls of the castle before crossing the river. By then the column stretches for more than ten miles, and those at the back have less of everything than those at the front; everything, that is, except mud and shit, both horse and human.

Every night the column stops and a camp is built, earthworks and staves enclosing a town of tents. At the camp's centre a watch fire is lit and the lords compete to have their tents erected as close by it as they can. The camp is divided into four quarters by two roads that intersect in the centre by the fire, and these roads quickly become impassable because of mud and drifting soldiery. In the morning the camp is struck. Tents packed up, staves collected, fires doused and everything thrown into carts and off they move, leaving the earthen walls and ditches, soot-blackened fire pits and a telltale cross of mud to mark their passage.

And every day it rains.

On Sunday they say Mass in the open air outside Gravesend and the priest calls on the Lord to send them a let-up in the weather. It rains all that day, too, but the next day is bright, and they take this as an omen, and by evening they wind their way through the hills above Southwark and in the fading light, they see London for the first time.

The city is dominated by the spire of the Cathedral of St Paul, finer than an arrow's bodkin head, and so high Katherine thinks it must be a trick of the light. It is such a sight that the rest of the men line the hill and stare in silence for a while. The usual pall of wood and coal smoke hangs above the city, and the river is busy with all manner of boats, toing and froing on its dimpled surface or moored against the wharves that line both banks. Downstream on the other side is the Tower, a massive complex behind its serried walls and moats.

But Katherine is more concerned with the churches. The skyline is crowded with spires and steeples, and there are more in the fields and villages beyond the walls. There is even one balancing on the bridge below them that looks as if it might topple one way or the other any moment.

'The place will be overrun with friars and priests,' Katherine tells Thomas. 'The sooner we are gone from here the better.'

Thomas ignores her.

'Geoffrey says the main body of the King's army is in the north,' he says. 'Somewhere near Coventry.'

'Coventry?'

Thomas nods.

'Where Riven was bound?'

'Yes,' Thomas says. 'The King thinks the Duke of York will come that way, when he comes from Ireland, so he is there to meet him.'

'But now we are here, behind him. He will have to do something about that, won't he?'

'I suppose so,' Thomas admits.

Katherine pulls a face. It is the thought of much more travel.

'Will we go to them, d'you think, or will they come to us?' she asks.

Thomas doesn't know.

'Perhaps we'll meet halfway?' he says. 'It is all supposed to depend on tomorrow, and that if the aldermen of London close their gates to us, then we are sunk. Geoffrey says Warwick and March won't be able to borrow any money from the merchants there to buy us food or pay their liege men to keep in the field any longer.'

The following day men on horseback ride constantly through the camp, coming up from London with messages from the Mayor and the aldermen of the city, taking them back from the Earls of Warwick and March. By the next morning something has been settled, and the Earls appear at daybreak wearing their finest clothes, and they make ready to lead the army across the bridge into London.

The sense of relief is everywhere.

'The townspeople have welcomed us,' Sir John explains as they roll down the hill. 'But by Christ it was a close-run thing.'

'And what about the King's men?' Katherine wonders. 'Surely they must fight?'

'There are few enough of them left, and those that remain are expected to run, save perhaps Lord Scales, who has retreated to the Tower.'

Even as they pass through the fields outside Southwark they hear a distinct crack in the distance. Everybody flinches. After their experience at Sandwich, the men all fear the sound of guns, even Simon the braggart. A tiny finger of smoke erupts from the battlements above the donjon of the White Tower away down the river.

'What is that?'

'Lord Scales is firing on the city,' Sir John says. 'He always was mad.'

Even Walter is shocked.

'That's not right,' he says. 'He'll be made to pay for that.'

Those at the head of the column are met by cheering crowds as they enter Southwark. Men and women and children and pigs and dogs stream out to greet the Earls who are riding with the Archbishop and the Legate, but by the time Thomas and Katherine file between the lines of inns two hours later, boredom has set in and only the pigs remain.

They buy ale from a woman who lives next to an inn called the Tabard.

'Normally sell it to folk heading east,' she says. 'Pilgrims and that.'

They follow the cart across the drawbridge and on to the bridge itself, packing together to pass through the gatehouse, a squeeze so tight they are thrust together and men are injured. All eyes are involuntarily drawn to the grisly lumps on poles that line the battlements.

'Expect we knew half of 'em,' Walter says.

Birds mob the heads, pulling at what soft flesh they can find under the tar in which they are dipped. Farther along Walter points to the beams of the houses that are scorched and the stonework marked with the distinct pits left by arrows.

'From Jack Cade's time,' Walter mutters.

And Katherine sees that among the crowd there are some serious expressions, and that not everybody is pleased at the thought of having an army of Kentishmen march through the city. Once across the bridge the crowds thicken again. They are all so strange, these Londoners, not just to her, but to one another, from the finest merchants in their budge-lined cloaks on fine palfreys, right down to the roughest gong farmers with shit-caked feet. There are so many foreigners, too, terrifying men with dark skins and outlandish clothes who may not even be Christians, and men with pale skins, dark clothes and odd hats, watching them from narrow-set eyes as they follow the street up towards the spire of St Paul's.

Hereabouts the friars stand in groups: their grey, black, brown and white cloaks signalling their orders. Katherine seeks the shelter of Thomas's arm and she huddles in her cloak.

'It is all right, Kit,' he says. 'They are only friars. You are a soldier.'

Behind the crowds all manner of shops are shuttered against temptation, and every few paces a vintenar in Warwick's red livery stands looking grim. Each carries a pollaxe or a hammer or a sword, making sure the various companies keep their hands to themselves.

Walking underneath the steeple of St Paul's, she looks up, still scarcely believing anything can be so tall, or that the vast rose window set in the eastern end of the church can be so lavish. Thomas stares open-mouthed, tripping himself on the road. But soon they turn and pass along a street where the smell of rotten meat rises from the stones and the friars give way to butchers' boys and husbandmen. They queue again to pass through the Newgate, and then they are outside the city walls again, among priories and abbeys and smallholdings as they follow the road up the hill past various inns. The smell of cows is everywhere and the road is thick with their dung.

Soon they reach some worn-out pasture around a pond where once again they set up camp among the pigs and dogs and piles of every kind of filth. Geoffrey has to buy the wood for their fire from a local farmer and they eke it out with discarded rushes that burn without a flame or heat and send a column of dense grey smoke into the damp afternoon air.

'What a shithole,' Dafydd says.

Thomas finds his reed and a bottle of ink, and then unstraps the pardoner's ledger and begins copying the design of the rose window of St Paul's from memory in a margin. Katherine sits and watches. It is mesmerising, seeing his reed shape and shade the paper.

After a moment Red John joins them and is alarmed.

'What're they?' he asks, pointing at the names. He looks at them as if the words may have magical powers, as if they are a chant, or are somehow threatening.

'The names of Englishmen stationed in Rouen in 1441,' Thomas tells him, and he runs his finger along the crudely rendered letters. 'Look. There is the Duke of York mentioned, and his retinue.'

Red John is amazed.

'I thought it was just the Bible in words,' he says.

'No,' Thomas tells him. 'It is a record of men and their move-ments in France. It says the Duke spent the summer of 1441 in a place called Pontoise.'

'Where's that?'

'I don't know.'

Red John points to another column.

'And what are they?'

'The names of men who stayed in Rouen that year.'

'Read them out.'

'William Hyde. Hugh Smyth. John Rygelyn. William Darset. Robert Philip. Nicholas Blaybourne.'

The list is long. Who are these men? Katherine wonders again. Thomas has said they are long-dead soldiers, so why was the record of their movement important to the pardoner?

'Can you write as well?' Red John asks.

Thomas nods, and he writes two words.

'Look,' he says. 'That is your name.'

He writes Katherine's name too, and she smiles and tries to remember the letter K so that she will know it when she sees it again. Red John settles himself next to her and they watch while Thomas finishes the window's design. When it is done he nods with real pleasure.

'Very fair, Thomas,' Red John says. 'Very fair. But I still don't know why you've all them names writ in a book?'

Thomas shrugs.

'I don't know either. They were there when I got it. The book is supposed to be very valuable, though I cannot say why.'

Red John squints at him as if he is daft.

'And it isn't because – what? – it's made of gold or something?'

Thomas holds up the plain old binding, the rough-edged paper.

'No,' he says. 'It's not that.'

'So it must be what is written in it that makes it worth something?'

'I suppose so.'

'And it's just a list of who was where when? Nothing more?'

'No.'

Red John thinks for a while.

'Then it means someone whose name is writ in there as being in one place should have been somewhere else. Or he shouldn't have been where he was, when it says he was. D'you see? It's got to be one or the other.'

Thomas laughs.

'But there are thousands of names.'

'True. True,' Red John admits. 'So what you have to do is find out who it's valuable to. Who wants it, I mean. Sell it to them, then you'll not have to follow the Earl of Warwick about the place for the rest of your life.'

With that he gets up and leaves them and they watch him walk away with something like awe.

'Wrap it up well, Thomas,' she tells him, and watches while he does so.

Later that day a long line of carts comes out from London loaded with beans and peas and dried fish. There is ale, wine, bread and even bacon. There are pimps and faggots and great logs of ash. They eat well that night, gathered together around their fire, drinking ale, singing songs and watching the sparks fly up into the dark. They drink so much that most are unsteady on their feet, Thomas among them. Katherine has enjoyed the beer and drunk more than usual and now she feels warm and full and generous.

Thomas sits beside her and is silent for a moment as they watch Dafydd and one of the Johns enact a strange dance with one another while the tabor man taps the skin of his instrument at the speed of heavy rain. When it is over, everybody cheers and then there is a moment when people are smiling and laughing, and the evening could go in one of many ways.

'How is your ear?' Thomas asks. He is watching her in a way that unsettles her, but she is pleased by. She touches her cap that hides the missing tip. It still aches.

'I think this helps,' she says, raising her mug of ale.

They smile and drink and there is a comfortable moment between them, when they are alone despite the crowd.

'Why did you run, Kit?' he asks in a low voice.

She looks at him quickly, and she can see he fears he has spoiled the mood, but then she lets out a quick sigh and settles back. She stares into the flames for a moment, then comes to her decision.

'Thomas,' she starts. 'I should have told you this when we first left the priory. I kept meaning to, but – I was too ashamed of myself. I was frightened about what you would think of me, what you would do when you heard.'

'Heard what?'

'When I was at the priory, there was a nun there. Sister Joan. She was older than me, and a great favourite of the Prioress. It was she who used to hold me down when the Prioress beat me. She looked after the keys. That sort of thing.'

Thomas nods, but his mood has sobered.

'When I left – just before I left – we were in the infirmary. With Alice, do you remember? Well, I pushed her. Joan, I mean. On to a mattress.'

Thomas is puzzled.

'So?' he asks. 'It sounds as if she deserved it.'

'Yes. Yes. She did. But I'd left a bottle on the mattress. Or a jar. I can't remember now. It was made of glass.'

Thomas understands what she is saying.

'And she fell on it?'

Katherine nods.

'The bottle broke. The glass. The shards – they went into her back. Into Joan's back, do you see?'

'Was she hurt?'

Katherine nods.

'I threw myself on top of her. I did not know about the glass, but I was pressing her down on to it. I wanted to kill her, I admit, but didn't think I could. And then there was blood in her mouth.'

'Her mouth?' Thomas asks. 'You mean? The glass went through her . . .?'

He gestures towards his back. Katherine nods. She is shaking a little.

'Did you save her?' he asks.

Now she shakes her head.

'I did not even try. Did not know how, even if I'd wanted to.'

Thomas looks into the fire.

'So that is why – why the friars were so busy when we left Boston? Because they were looking for you?'

'The girl who killed Sister Joan, yes.'

There is a silence. Thomas takes a long draught from his mug.

'Dear God,' he says when he has swallowed the ale and wiped his lips with the back of his hand. 'No wonder you did not want to see the Prior of All. No wonder you ran. But – Jesu! – I wish you had told me.'

She nods again and looks at her hands.

'I wish I had too,' she says, 'but I thought you might turn away from me, to leave me to fend for myself. And I cannot – I just cannot go on, not without your help. Look what happens when I try.'

She touches her ear again. He nods again, but his face has softened. His gaze travels across her, from her broken boots, up her baggy hose, across the jack that is too big for her, to her hat that hangs over her eyes, and she can see that he is consumed with the same tenderness he showed on the shoreline that day in Sangatte, and for a moment she wishes he would lean forward and put his arms around her as he had tried to do that day.

Instead he asks a question.

'Do you remember that first day?' he asks. 'After the giant came after us and the boat sank?'

She does, but not exactly. A tear has found its way from her eye, and she wipes her nose with the back of her hand.

'"Two are better than one . . ."' he quotes. '"For if they fall—"'

'"—the one will lift up his fellow,"' she completes.

Katherine catches his hand in hers, and blinks away her tears. Thomas returns her grip. They let go at the same time.

'So,' he says. 'If you will not go back, what will you do?'

She looks around. The pipe and tabor are playing a new tune now, a slower one, and the men around her have become introspective, and it is possible to imagine them thinking about absent loves, or missed opportunities, or past regrets.

'I don't know,' she tells him. 'I just don't know. Whatever the Lord has in store for me is what the Lord has in store for me.'

18

It is past dusk and the rain is still beating on the canopy of leaves above their heads. Thomas huddles next to the tree, listening to Dafydd moaning in the dark.

'I can't believe this,' Dafydd says. 'We've been traipsing all over England for two weeks solid, in the pouring bloody rain, and now we've got here, we've got to stand picket?'

'Just give it a rest, will you, Dafydd?' Henry the new archer says. 'You talk so much. I don't know what you're like quiet.'

Henry is from Kent. He joined them in London, just as they lost Simon the braggart, who slipped off unmissed in the night. Henry is broad-shouldered and a fine archer, but his mouth pulls down at each corner and he glowers at the world from under heavy brows.

Nevertheless what he says is true: Dafydd has not stopped moaning since they left London. First they had marched north up the Cambridge road, following Lord Fauconberg in search of King Henry and his army that were rumoured to be making for the Isle of Ely in the fenlands. After two days' travel, never moving faster than the slowest cart, it was discovered that the rumour was false and so Fauconberg stopped them and they waited in the fields by the roadside for news as to where they should go next. Then they'd broken camp and made their way westwards on terrible roads towards the town of Dunstable, in Bedfordshire. Here at least Geoffrey found a new ox for their cart but there was no sign of the King's army. After another delay while messengers were sent and received, they moved northwards again, up along the old Roman road towards Coventry, but on the way they heard that the King was moving down from Coventry to meet them.

So now they are camped on a rise just off the old road to the south of the town of Northampton, and the Earls of Warwick and March have brought their troops up from London and Kent to join Fauconberg's, and at last they are ready to meet King Henry's troops.

'Settle this thing for once and for all,' Dafydd says, 'then we can piss off home, can't we?'

'Why are you here at all, Dafydd?' Thomas asks. 'I know you're after a fine suit of armour and that, but how did you come to fall in with Sir John?'

Dafydd tells him how he fought for Lord Cornford, who had land near their home in Wales, but when Cornford was killed at Ludford Bridge, rather than go home to face some trouble he does not want to specify, he joined Sir John Fakenham's company, also of Cornford's retinue.

'Happenstance, see?'

Thomas grunts. Happenstance. That was the force which seemed to guide them all: him, Katherine, the pardoner, Sir John, Dafydd. All of them save the Earl of Warwick, who seemed to bend the forces of destiny to his own will.

Time passes. The rain continues and in the camp someone throws more wood on a fire and sparks rise above the pointed roofs of the tents. Walter arrives through the darkness with a fresh tallow lantern. He is bristling with anger.

'Right,' he says. 'Come on, you idle bastards, up! Up you get! Come on. We've rounds to make.'

The men get to their feet and find their spears wet in the grass. They follow Walter swinging his light, Dafydd bringing up the rear with his own. Henry's greaves squeak as he walks.

'Get some bloody oil on them, will you?' Walter grumbles. 'That noise goes right through me.'

They tramp around the earthworks. Men are gathered in groups at the entrances to their tents, quietly sharing ale and stories around their fires when they should be sleeping.

'Funny to think some of them'll be dead tomorrow, isn't it?' Dafydd starts.

'I hope to bloody God one of them's you, Dafydd,' Walter snaps.

Since they heard the news the scurriers brought back with them that afternoon, Walter has been in a savage temper. The scouts had met the enemy in the fields just this side of Northampton. Two of them had been killed outright, another wounded and expected to die in the morning, but able to bring back the news that the King's men are encamped before the town with a river protecting their flanks; that there must be nearly ten thousand of them; that they are hard at work throwing up a defensive rampart, and that they have more cannons and bombards than either of the two survivors have seen in their lives.

It is this last piece of news that has made Walter so foul-tempered.

They walk on towards the road where Geoffrey and the other men are waiting by a hissing fire, their eyes sore with the smoke.

'Anything?'

'Nothing.'

'Waste of bloody time, this,' Walter says. 'We should be getting our heads down, not on guard duty. I bet they're all fast asleep behind their walls right now.'

'Nothing's going to happen tonight, that's for sure,' Geoffrey agrees. He holds his hand out to cup some of the rain. It has picked up again, drumming on their helmets and running into their eyes. A moment later the rushlight dies on them.

'Bloody thing.' Walter throws it away against the roots of a tree.

'We may not have to attack them, Walter,' Geoffrey says.

Walter is furious.

'They've just spent the best part of two days digging in behind that bloody wall and you think they're going to leave their guns behind and come out and have a pop at us, are they? Up a hill?'

'Warwick is still sending heralds.'

'And they keep getting sent back, don't they? And so long as the Duke of Buckingham's in the King's camp, they always will be.'

'There's still the Archbishop. If he gets involved, the King will have to listen.'

'Listen to what? It's you that's not listening, Geoffrey. Warwick says he wants to talk to the King. Fair enough, you'd say, but what does he want to talk about? I'll tell you. He wants to talk about getting his lands back and getting rid of bastards like Buckingham and Somerset and all the other turds the King's got hanging off him. So why would all those turds who're hanging off him want Warwick to talk to him? They wouldn't, and they won't. Warwick knows that. March knows that. Which is why we're here. A huge bloody great army that should be in France, beating the crap out of the bloody French, but instead we're waiting to charge down there into a load of other Englishmen who are waiting to blow us into goddamned purgatory with all those bloody cannons. It's bollocks, that's what it is. It's just bollocks.'

There is a long silence. Rain pits in the fire. Walter spits, then walks off and urinates loudly into a puddle.

Geoffrey raises an eyebrow and catches Thomas's eye.

'Ah, well,' he says, shrugging.

Walter stops pissing halfway through. Everybody turns to wait, unsettled by the hiatus, holding their breath.

'Saints,' he says over his shoulder, pulling up his hose. 'Someone's coming.'

Geoffrey throws more wood on the fire.

'A horseman,' Walter whispers. 'Maybe more than one. You lot, get out of the light. Nock your bows. Geoffrey, come with me. Henry, get the Captain of the Watch. Bring him here. Fast as you can.'

They can all hear the horse now, coming up the road from the direction of Northampton. It is coming slowly, picking its way through the dark. Thomas fingers the beak of his axe. The horse is a grey, the rider muffled in a dark travelling cloak. It stops on the fringes of light where the fire gleams faintly on his greaves and sabatons. Not a traveller then.

'Sir, you are very welcome to our fire,' Geoffrey calls out into the dark. 'Though why you're travelling on a night like this, I should dearly love to know.'

The rider kicks his horse forward one or two paces. The firelight still doesn't stretch to his face.

'I am here to see Richard Neville, the Earl of Warwick,' he says. He has the firm voice of the well born, though in his cloak it is impossible to make out what sort of man he is: young or old, fat or thin, well made or sickly.

Walter steps forward a pace and peers into the stranger's face.

'Can I tell him who you are?' he asks.

'He does not know me by name,' the man says, 'but he will want to hear what I have to say. Give him this, as a token.'

The stranger leans forward to hand something to Walter. He is wearing gloves. They still cannot see his face.

Walter accepts it, frowning.

'Are you armed, sir?' he asks.

The stranger pauses for a moment, as if considering this an insult; then he pulls his cloak back to reveal an empty sword scabbard at his hip. He wears a white livery coat.

'Thomas,' Walter says. 'Run and give this to Warwick Herald.'

'No!' the stranger snaps. 'No. Give it only to my lord the Earl.'

Thomas steps across the pool of light to take the token. It is warm in the palm of his hand. He turns and begins to walk away.

'You there. Wait.'

It is the stranger. Thomas stops.

The stranger leans forward in his saddle and stares down at Thomas. His face is hidden in the depths of the hood of his cloak.

A long moment passes. Thomas can hear him breathing, hear his mouth click open, then close.

Finally the stranger sits back and flicks his wrist.

'Go,' he says.

Thomas turns and walks on into the camp. In the scant light of the fires, the design of the token is hard to make out, but it is a small silver badge such as a man might pin to his jacket to show his allegiance to a particular lord. Thomas holds it in front of the watch fire in the middle of the camp and can see the badge is of a ragged staff, Warwick's own symbol. The Captain of the Watch meets him as he approaches, hurrying up the path with Henry trailing behind.

'I have something for his lordship the Earl of Warwick,' Thomas says.

'Give it me,' the captain says, holding out his hand. Thomas shakes his head.

'It is for the Earl alone.'

The captain raises his eyebrows.

'I hope you know what you are about,' he says and he turns and gestures across the clearing to the largest tent, lit from within by numerous candles so that he can see the shadow of a man sitting in his bath. Another shadow pours a bucket of water that sends up swirling clouds of steam. A large awning extends from the front where two more men guard the entrance.

Thomas explains his mission and while one of the guards watches Thomas the other puts his head through the tent aperture and mutters in a low voice. Thomas hears the Earl barking.

'Send him in,' he shouts.

The guard emerges and jerks his thumb.

Thomas slips through the tent flap.

The Earl of Warwick sits in his bath while a servant pours water over his back, his knees like islands in the cloudy water. The smell of herbs is strong but that of the candles – tallow – is stronger still.

Warwick's hair is plastered to his head.

'You,' he says, recognising Thomas despite the feeble light. 'What in the name of all the saints do you want?'

Thomas is surprised Warwick recognises him. He has only glimpsed him that moment after the hunting accident.

'There is a rider at the edge of the encampment who bid me give you this token, sir.'

Thomas steps across the rug on the ground to hand it over. Warwick takes it with a wet hand and turns it over a couple of times. A frown gathers on his brow.

'Who is this man?' he asks Thomas.

'He will not say his name.'

Warwick grunts.

'Wait for me.'

He stands up, letting the hot water cascade from his body, and holds his arms out. The servant hurries to rub him with a length of linen.

'Hurry, man!'

Warwick dries and dresses quickly. He makes Thomas wait, and Thomas stands and has to watch him as he slides into his travelling cloak and riding boots. Thomas has never seen a man so full of energy, so certain in all that he does, and there is a sort of concentrated ferocity in the way he moves.

When he is ready he steps out into the night, clicking his fingers and gesturing to the guards to bring a lantern. Thomas says nothing as he leads Warwick back through the camp.

When he reaches the picket, the rider has dismounted but Thomas still can't see his face. Warwick moves forward and speaks to him, and after a moment the two men shake hands.

'Right,' Walter says. 'Another tour of the camp. Come on.'

They set off again and by the time they are back, the stranger has left and there is no one to say what has happened. By dawn the rain has stopped. Thomas sits next to Red John on the earthwork and they drink their ale in silence. The bushes are thick with birds and their song is loud in the air. A wagon comes into the clearing, one wheel wobbling, loaded with barrels of ale. It is pulled by four oxen. Another follows, then another.

So Walter is right, Thomas thinks. For all the ambassadors and overtures that Warwick and March are sending to King Henry and the Duke of Buckingham, they know it will come to a fight, and now here it is, the ale the men will need to insulate themselves against the horrors of the day to come.

He slips off the earthworks. If there is any ale going, he wants to be in there early. He takes a full mug from the woman and retires to the bank again. Richard Fakenham appears, the first time he's seen him walking without help since his accident. He steps gingerly, like his father, as if he does not quite trust his feet to hold him up, and behind his new black beard, his face is pinched with pain. He wants to speak to Thomas.

'What was that token the messenger gave you last night, Thomas?' he asks.

'It was a ragged staff, I thought.'

'Did Warwick recognise it when you gave it to him?'

'I don't think so. I think he was confused, to begin with.'

'And what about when he saw this messenger?'

They'd shaken hands warmly, hadn't they? As if Warwick had recognised him, and yet the stranger had said that he wouldn't know him by name. So here is a mystery, but it is not one that will be solved just now, because a trumpet sounds, and the men look up. This is it.

Thomas downs the last of his ale and returns the cup to his pack. He helps Richard back to the tent. Katherine is there, helping load the cart. She is to stay with Richard and Sir John and to keep an eye on the baggage train.

'Good luck,' she says.

'You too. I'm glad you're not coming with us,' he adds. 'Walter says it is suicide.'

There is a long moment.

'He will be there this time, Thomas,' she says. 'I know it. I don't know why. I just do.'

Thomas swings the pollaxe behind him.

'I thought it would be different,' he says. 'I thought I'd meet him alone somewhere and it would be fair. But this?' He gestures to the army around him: the men sharpening swords, packing arrows, testing strings, honing blades. Men of all sizes, shapes, ages, experience. Thousands upon thousands of them. How will he ever find Riven among such a crowd? How will he ever find the time and space to fight him?

'It may not be as either of us imagines it,' she supposes. 'But surely it is God's will that it should happen?'

Thomas nods again. He knows she is testing him, half in jest, half serious. He knows she no longer believes in God's will. But Thomas does, and if God wills it, he will find Riven and that giant of his.

'And then it will all be over,' he says.

She looks at him steadily and he cannot help smiling. She is so slight, yet so fierce. She breaks into a smile too.

'Yes,' she says. 'All over.'

He turns as once again the shouting begins and the army starts to form up, each body of men trying to find the right banner under which to gather.

'I must go,' he says.

She nods.

'God go with you,' she says and she clutches his hand.

'You too, Kit,' he says.

And he watches her as she steps back out of the way and her place is taken by a column of archers in fire-scale steel helmets.

19

'Archers, to the front! Archers to the front! Get over there, God damn you, man!'

'A Fauconberg! Where is Fauconberg?'

'Stafford! John Stafford to me!'

'Where are William Hastings's men?'

By mid-morning Thomas and the rest of Sir John's company are in their battle, ready to move out, two bags of arrows apiece, spare strings, mauls, bucklers, sallet helmets. Lord Fauconberg leads the way with his household men and his knights in their plate, still mounted. Their banners and standards are heavy with all the rain and hang from their battens as if broken. Fauconberg is to take the vanguard of archers and the men of Kent, while the Earls of Warwick and March are to take the other two battles.

They move up the road at the head of a loose crowd, hemmed in on both sides by dense woods of hawthorn and alder, everything vivid green with all the rain. Behind them come the rest of Fauconberg's battle, in blocks of about two hundred men: archers, tramping along with their bows over their shoulders and their arrow bags bumping against their backs; followed by the men-at-arms with their hammers and swords; and then the Kentish billmen, with their bills and glaives. Then come more archers and so on, the pattern repeating itself down the line. Behind them come the naked men in shirtsleeves and hose wielding farm tools, and then the prickers, those old soldiers on fleet-footed horses posted to stop any stragglers turning and running.

Once or twice they are forced off the road as messengers from the front thunder past, hurrying orders from one commander to another, and all the while the drums and trumpets continue.

'Make way! Make way there! Make way for the Archbishop!'

'So Warwick is still trying to make terms?' Thomas asks aloud.

'It's all bollocks,' Walter says again. He is huddled in his cloak, wearing it like a winding sheet, and he is pale and worse-tempered than ever.

Thomas takes up his usual position between Dafydd and Red John, and ahead of them, across a sloping meadow framed by the trees, he can see the spires and watchtowers of Northampton behind its walls.

Above the town there is a thick column of smoke, dark against the rainclouds.

'Is that normal?' Thomas asks.

Walter snarls.

'Course it's not normal,' he says. 'They're burning the town. It's like bloody France.'

When they emerge from the trees and on to the meadow, the rain starts in earnest. They huddle in their damp jacks, and some men tuck their strings under their helmets for the sake of superstition. There is an abbey in the grounds nearby and an ornate stone monument to some long-forgotten event surrounded by camp followers and a local audience, there to watch what happens.

'All right. All right. Move along now.'

More drums and horns and they turn off the road, dropping down into a broad ditch with water up to their knees, then scrambling up and out on to the slope where cows have stripped the lower branches of the few trees. The grass under their feet is soft and tussocky and as they file across the fields that dip gently down towards the town on their right, men begin cursing.

Then Thomas sees why.

Across the meadows, no more than a thousand paces away, down in the crook of a bend in the river, the King's men have excavated a broad ditch that is now filled with river water. The earth they've removed has been piled up and compacted behind the ditch to make a long wall as high as a man's head. It is bristling with sharpened stakes and at regular intervals along its length it is punctured by embrasures from which stick the unmistakable snouts of guns.

'Suicide,' someone mutters. 'That's what this is. Suicide.'

'Bloody Burgundians,' Walter murmurs. 'Just like Castillon. Worse, even.'

'How many have they got?' Geoffrey asks. He too has lost some of his colour.

Walter counts.

'Twenty bombards,' he says. 'Lots more small ones. A whole bloody armoury. And look at all them.'

Behind the bombards stand thousands of men in rank: men-at-arms at the front, so that they may defend the dyke, archers behind, so that they may shoot over their fellows' heads into any onrushing army.

'Haven't got many archers,' Geoffrey says.

'Don't need archers if you've got all those guns, do you?' Walter mutters. 'We'll be dead before we ever come in range.'

Behind the thin line of archers is the camp, a hundred tents, like a village, including a huge two-poled tent above which flies the royal standard. It is the King's tent. Above the troops there must be fifty banners of all sorts, including those long fishtailed battle standards carried by the lords' retainers. After all the rain, even those droop so as to be unrecognisable from any distance, but Thomas is only looking for one: Riven's white flag with its checked edge and rising triangle of crows.

He wishes Katherine was there. She has better eyes than anyone. She might even have been able to see the giant.

'Can you make out any of the banners?' he asks, turning to Geoffrey. Something has caught his eye in the rain. A pale square, towards the back on the left flank, marked with black symbols.

'The King's, I suppose,' Geoffrey says. 'And Buckingham's. And there's Ruthyn's on the left there. Beaumont is there, and Egremont, too, and that one is the Earl of Shrewsbury. Christ, there are a lot of them. Must be scarcely a man left to fight for all those holding flags.'

He tries to laugh. Walter sneers. They can hear the King's men shouting now, a rolling roar, both defiant and taunting, and Thomas looks along the line of men about him, silent in response. Not a face about him shows anything but fear. There is none of the resolution he'd seen in Sandwich, none of the determination they'd shown at Newnham Bridge.

Walter looks as if he's given up his ghost already and a tremor has appeared in Red John's cheek. He keeps clenching and unclenching his hands on his bow. After a moment he turns to Thomas.

'Thomas,' he says. 'I've got a bad feeling about this one. If it goes wrong, will you find me? Make sure I get a decent hole? I don't want the heralds to throw me in the river with the rest of them.'

He holds his hand out and Thomas takes it.

'It's going to go fine,' Thomas says. 'Fauconberg knows what he's about.'

The words sound hollow, and he wonders he has the nerve to say them, when Fauconberg rides along the line out in front of his troops. Raindrops bounce off his armour and the raised peak of his helmet. He undoes the bevor at his throat and turns to address the men.

'Men of England!' he calls out. 'This is an infamous day. Today, through no fault of our own, we are called upon to make war on fellow Englishmen. Those of you who fought with me in France will know my preference for killing Frenchmen, and so today finds me heavy-hearted. Heavy-hearted that we must take the field against the King's army.

'But I say to you that our cause is just. I say to you that God has given it His blessing and though we go against the banner of the King, we do not go against the person of the King himself. So therefore, in the name of God, I command you to spare those whom you may spare.'

'Lord spare us,' Walter mutters.

'Spare first the King. No man among you is to touch the person of the King on pain of death. Where it can be helped, spare too the common soldier where you find him, for he being duped is more to be pitied than despised. Spare him his life so that he may use it more profitably in future.'

As he speaks the rain becomes a drenching downpour. Fauconberg huddles into his armour.

'Kill only those of a noble stamp,' he shouts above the noise of the rain. 'Kill only those in harness under their own banner. You may kill as many dukes and earls and lords as your hearts desire, and for each death, you will find yourself handsomely rewarded. Kill them all, kill them all, save those persons who fight under the banner of Sir Edmund Grey of Ruthyn. Do not harm him or his. The men of Ruthyn fight in red coats and are distincted by their ragged-staff badge, which is similar to my lord of Warwick's save that while his device is white, the men of Ruthyn carry a grey-coloured staff. Spare these men where it can be helped.'

'As if we'll get the chance to spare a soul,' Walter says.

So that is what last night's rider was about. His token was not Warwick's but Ruthyn's. What does it mean though? He turns to Walter to ask, but Walter is just then sick, throwing up his ale in a welter of bile. A vintenar along the way tosses a handful of grass in the air, watching where it falls. The wind is negligible, the rain heavy, and the grass falls swiftly to the ground.

'Just let's get on with it,' Walter says, wiping his mouth. His eyes are bloodshot. 'Let's get it over with.'

But there are further delays. Fauconberg turns his horse and holds his hand out to check on the rain. Behind him, on the plain below them in front of the King's position, Warwick Herald and a party that includes the Archbishop of Canterbury are riding back from the enemy lines across the meadow.

'We have time for a prayer,' Fauconberg continues and he dismounts and passes his horse's reins to a page. He kneels in the mud and a priest appears alongside and the rest of the men fall to their knees too and together they begin the paternoster. When they've finished a trumpet blows in the middle of Warwick's battle. Fauconberg turns and faces the rain and the enemy, then raises his arm and holds his battle hammer high. Men make their last signs of the cross and lower visors.

Another trumpet.

And Fauconberg drops his arm.

The men surge forward, armour and weaponry clinking and scraping as they go. A first man slips in the grass; another follows. The line sags and wavers and they've only gone ten paces before another slips, his feet taken from under him, and yet another. Now the line buckles. Weapons are dropped. Picked up. Carried on. Thomas digs his heels into the soft earth and Black John behind has to use his shoulder to stop himself sliding down the hill.

Walter has forgotten his duties as vintenar and is mumbling prayers.

'Keep a line!' Geoffrey shouts in his stead. 'Keep steady there. Steady, lads. Forget the guns. Forget them.'

They are near the bottom of the slope now, getting into the boggy ground of the river's flood plain. The mud sucks at their boots. There are pools of brown water where the river's burst its banks. Around him Thomas can only hear the din of men beginning to run in armour.

And that is when he sees it.

And this time he is sure.

It is waved, like a signal. It rises briefly in the extreme left-hand end of the wall. Riven's flag.

Thomas stumbles, trips, nearly falls. But he feels as if he is floating, being held up by some unknown force. He feels invincible. The bog beneath him firms and he surges forward.

'Come on then!' he roars. 'Let's go!'

He elbows his way to the front of the archers, splashing through the mud. He cuts across the line and men follow him, bunching up on the left.

'Thomas!' Geoffrey calls. 'Slow down! Let the billmen take the brunt!'

They are six hundred paces from the enemy line now, six hundred paces from those guns, but Thomas runs on into them, his eyes fixed on that flag. He can hear the enemy roaring at them. At him. He keeps running.

Five hundred paces.

The line is stretching to the left, hollowing out in the middle. Thomas is still ahead, mud caked up to his thighs, leading them towards the King's right flank. Whatever plans Fauconberg had for his attack they are of no use now. Everyone is pouring after Thomas.

Four hundred paces.

And then the first gun goes off: a spike of grey smoke that stabs across the ditch towards them. It is followed instantly by a clap of thunder. The boulder cuts through the air behind him, throbbing through the space the archers have just left. It drills into the ranks of the men-at-arms who've moved up to take their place. The noise is shattering. Thomas glances back to see a man in mid-air, his feet above his shoulders, his head gone.

Behind him an alleyway has appeared in the ranks, paved with the dead and the dying, men skilled in the tilting yard, men who'd trained all their lives with lance and sword and hammer, men who can control a horse with their knees and heels, men now bowled over and left on the ground like butchers' spoil.

Another gun. Then another. The sound splits the sky. With each one a new hole opens up between the ranks. Smoke drifts across the meadow and the bitter tang of saltpetre fills the air. Thomas can smell it above his own sweat and the blood and the lush earth beneath his feet.

He falls. He spills his bow and a bag of arrows. A man treads on him, can do nothing else. He is pressed into the mud. Men thunder past. He wrenches himself up, crawls to his knees, and is pushed down again. He hears an oath in his ear; he snatches his bow and then gathers himself and stands and starts running again. He is well back now, but around him men are wavering.

It is the boulders. This is not why they have flocked to the Earl of Warwick's banner, Thomas thinks, to be torn apart by a stone fired from a wall by French mercenaries.

An archer from another company is writhing on the ground, crying out for his mother. Blood is leaching from a smoking hole in his jack.

The archers around him slow. They are in position now and they fumble with their bows. Thomas pulls an arrow from his belt and nocks it. He looses it and moves forward. He sends another, flitting across the meadow at one of the gunners prancing on the wall. He hits the man, knocking him down in a heap. A fourth gun fires and the stone skips across the marsh and decapitates a man so quickly his body stays upright for a moment. The stone ploughs into the mud under the heels of some billmen who've turned to begin back up the hill.

And suddenly there is Walter, seemingly restored, and all is well.

'Loose and move!' he is shouting. 'Loose and move!'

Thomas nocks another and looses it. He is still pulling them to the left.

The billmen are pressing up now, coming through the archers' ranks in their companies.

Then the fifth gun fires, but instead of the expected crack that follows, this one gives a muffled sigh. Walter pauses and lowers his bow.

'A misfire,' he shouts.

Then comes an even softer report as another gun misfires, and smoke billows above the enemy lines. There's yet another low thud.

Walter starts laughing wildly and pointing to the sky.

'It's the rain!' he shouts. 'The bloody rain! God is on our side! They can't light their bloody guns!'

They can see the Burgundians now, throwing their hands up, turning from their guns, trying to run away. One of the King's men, in full armour, slashes at a Burgundian to stop him retreating, knocking him flat. He raises his sword at another, but a third throws something at him, knocking him down, and there are running men everywhere.

'Come on!' Walter bellows. 'Move up! Move up! We've got them now!'

He gestures to a captain of the billmen, a gangly boy in a rusting helmet and greaves he's probably borrowed from his father. They are still two hundred paces from the wall, coming into range of the enemy archers, and just as the men-at-arms and billmen next to them begin their charge, the sky above darkens with arrows.

'Look out!' someone cries.

There is a sudden frenzy of noise, like a hundred hammers falling in succession, and all around him men fall, and arrow shafts are bouncing among them, cracking and splintering. The men-at-arms huddle in their shells, heads down, pushing forward, their vision blocked by their visors so that all they can see is the neck of the man in front. Speed is vital. There is no help for the wounded. To dither is to die. They keep on, charging over bodies, knocking the wounded out of the way, just trying to get through.

And all the time Thomas is nocking, pulling, loosing, three or four steps forward, nocking, pulling, loosing, three steps forward. Then he is out of arrows.

In front of them the boy in his father's greaves writhes on the ground, splashed in his own blood, gagging for breath. He is trying to pull an arrow out of his chest, but he has one through his thigh as well and it is all up for him. One of the vintenars lowers his bow and looses an arrow into the boy's throat.

'Only to shut him up,' he shouts, as if the others have accused him of something, but he too is already moving on, nocking and loosing, nocking and loosing. They scurry through the beaten-down, blood-soaked grass of the meadow, feet squelching in mud and worse. Bodies lie pinned to the ground, and the turf around them bristles with fletches. Thomas steps over a man apparently asleep in the grass, and next to him another one is screaming with an arrow in his stomach.

A hundred paces.

Sweat stings his eyes. He pulls arrows from the ground, nocking and loosing them all in one movement. He sends his shafts thumping into the faces of the men on the other side of the ditch. He is only a few yards behind the men-at-arms now, moving towards the river, moving towards that banner.

Fifty paces.

The shouts from the enemy rise into a solid wall of muffled sound as Fauconberg's men-at-arms reach the wall. Thomas waits for the crash of arms as they meet the enemy, but the impact never comes. Instead of the mêlée, there is another sort of excitement.

After a moment of confusion, he looks up.

Men are roaring with joy.

There are others standing on the wall. Men in red livery with grey badges. They aren't fighting. They are breaking down their own barricade. They are spilling out on to the top of the earthwork and throwing down the logs and stakes to make walkways across the ditch. Fauconberg's men in their blue and white livery are storming up them. They are charging through the gaps in the defences and jumping down into the camp. The men in red are helping them, offering hand-ups. One of them stands on the barricade and waves them forward. He has a grey ragged staff on his chest.

Walter is screaming with delight.

'They've turned! Ruthyn's men have turned. Come on, you fuckers! Let's get at 'em!'

They scramble across the rough bridges, Thomas helped by the outstretched hand of one of Ruthyn's men, and then they are in the camp. Underfoot it is foul with mud, river water, blood and shit. There is a pile of corpses to one side, stuck with broken arrows; already one of Fauconberg's archers is going through them. Thomas tries to push through the crowd of men, to get back towards the river, towards Riven's flag.

But the fight isn't over yet. In the camp trumpets sound, drums beat, and orders are shouted. The rage of the recently betrayed lends the King's men an unstoppable savagery. They tear into Ruthyn's troops, men who only moments before had been their comrades in arms, and begin driving them back.

For a moment it looks as if they'll be cut down or thrown back into the ditch to drown, but as more of Fauconberg's men-at-arms join them, the balance begins to tip against the King's army, who have relied on the guns instead of archers, and on the strength of their wall instead of numbers of men. Now both have let them down. They are outnumbered and outflanked. There are only two things they can do: run and be killed, or fight and be killed.

They choose to fight.

One knight in black and red livery blocks Thomas's way. His plume of exotic feathers bobs and sways as he clears a circle around him with a long hammer, as if cutting hay. Bodies of every hue are piled around. He stands on dead men and knocks a billman's glaive to the ground, steps forward and despatches him with a backhanded chop that passes through his teeth. He is inhuman, sealed in his blood-glazed armour, wheeling and stabbing. Nothing can touch him.

This is no place for a man without even the meanest armour, but Fauconberg's men are crowding forward. Thomas is caught in the crush, his arms pinned to his sides, shunted towards the knight. Nor is the knight alone. His household men are together holding back the blue and white liveried tide.

Thomas pushes and shoves; he tries to slip away, but men push back. The din of steel on steel is louder than in any smithy; iron thunders against iron. He can't get through. He is face to face with one of Fauconberg's men, snarling, but his opponent is stuck too. Thomas turns to find himself facing the man in harness. He drops his bow and swings his pollaxe up. The man lunges at him. Thomas throws himself back. The crowd behind gives. The man in armour slips on a dead body and Thomas catches his dagger with the butt of his axe. The knight is committed, pulled off balance for a moment, and a man on the ground grips his bill in both bloody hands and hooks the knight behind his knee. The knight staggers, tries to right himself, isn't quick enough.

Another of Fauconberg's men-at-arms hammers his halberd down on the knight's shoulder. The knight buckles, rears back again, but his armour is jammed. He can't move his arm. Another billman, smaller, like a ferret, darts forward and smashes the knight's visor up while a third plunges a long spike into his mouth. The knight's retainers have been too slow, and now they turn and run, or try to. But their path is blocked and Fauconberg's men cut them down from behind, hacking at their hamstrings. It is so easy.

Now Thomas can move. He forces his way towards the river, scrambling between two carts. Some archers have discovered the King's ale and are busy trying to drink themselves stupid. Dead bodies lie everywhere in the mud. Wounded men blink at him. Thomas ducks left, down a path between the rows of tents, shoddy canvas bivouacs for the common soldiery, finer for the nobility, his boots sliding under him.

There is another surging cheer from the main field and the percussive ripple of arms as Warwick's men engage, and now the King's men begin streaming back through the camp, ripping off their armour as they come, casting weapons aside. A billman, wild-eyed, half his clothing missing, bounces off Thomas, flinching when he sees the axe, and hurtles away through the tents towards the river. Another's clothes are smoking.

Thomas follows the path and comes to a clearing. Dafydd and Owen and Henry are there before him, crouching pale-faced over a body in white livery. Dafydd is trying to unscrew a ring from the dead man's finger. Unarmed men flash past, right to left. Henry nocks an arrow and follows a man just as a huntsman might follow a bird. He shoots straight through the man's chest and sends him bowling. He laughs.

Dafydd glances up, sees where Thomas is going.

'You don't want to go up there just yet,' he calls. 'A bit hot for the likes of us. Come and have a drink.'

Owen holds up a flask. Thomas shakes his head, carries on.

'Bloody hell!' Dafydd shouts. He drops the dead man's hand, slings his bow and pulls Owen after him. Henry follows. He is out of arrows anyway. Along the path they can see the King's tent, a coat of arms on the canopy, banner flags drooping from both poles. In the clearing before it, over the ashes of last night's watch fire, a crowd of Fauconberg's billmen are gathered around five or six knights in harness, hacking and chopping at them, wearing them down as dogs bait bears.

These are the lords, the dukes and the earls, those too well known to need to bother with livery coats, and they are differentiated only by the decoration on the crowns of their helmets. They have been deserted by their retainers, or perhaps they are all that are left alive of their household men, and their billmen – in red and black livery coats – are being beaten back by Fauconberg's men. Behind them, watching with pale faces that remind Thomas of the monks at the priory, are the royal heralds in their quartered tabards.

And then there is Riven.

He is unmistakable, even in his ornate harness, a long black hand-and-a-half sword in both hands, parrying, twisting, feinting, ducking the thrusts of the billmen with well-practised moves. Thomas is rooted for a moment, watching. Riven steps aside to let a bill glance off his thigh, then grabs it, pulls the billman forward on to the point of his sword and then thrusts him backwards to die on the ground with blood frothing at his throat. Riven never looks at the man again, but hurls the butt of the bill at another one of Fauconberg's men, distracting him for the moment it takes one of the other knights to reach forward and smash his mace into the man's face.

'Christ on His cross,' Dafydd mutters. 'I'm not having anything to do with that.'

But Thomas takes his place in front of Riven. He stares into the dark slits of Riven's helmet. He expects some sort of reaction. He gets it in the form of a lunge. The tip of the sword, flat and round like a tongue, hums past his eyes as he throws himself back. He rolls away and gets to his feet. Then he moves in again and ducks and swipes the pollaxe at Riven's right side.

Riven steps aside, dodging the blow, but the axe's spike catches and runs down his side, rippling over the buckles of his cuirass. It breaks the bottom leather strap and the cuirass sags. Riven feels the change and pats it with his steel-ringed fingers. There is nothing he can do about it.

He waits. Ash rises around his feet. Dafydd is on Thomas's shoulder, Henry sliding around to the left. He's picked up a bill from a dead man. Thomas feints with the pollaxe. Riven lunges. Dafydd steps in with his sword, takes Riven's blade on his buckler, staggers under the force, and slashes at Riven, but his sword bangs uselessly on Riven's vambrace. He skips away with a yelp, clutching his hand. Riven smashes his quillon at Dafydd's head. It hits his helmet and Dafydd staggers back, blood streaming into his eyes. Riven turns, faster than ever, and slices his blade at Henry, aiming for his legs.

Henry takes the blow on his squeaking greave and swings the bill short-armed at Riven. Riven steps inside and crashes his elbow into Henry's face. Now Henry sags, two spurts of blood on his lips. Riven steps over him and lifts the sword. Thomas steps in, jabs at him, the point of the pole ringing on Riven's cuirass, sending him staggering, breaking another of the leather straps.

Henry forgotten, Riven rounds on Thomas, who ducks and runs. Five paces: he turns and comes back. He chops at Riven. Riven blocks, then cuts back. Thomas drops back. One nick of that sword and it will all be over. He comes again, and once more Riven sends him scurrying away. His blade is so quick it defies the eye to follow it.

But the knight next to Riven is floundering. His sooted armour is crimped from some earlier blow, and he is finding it difficult to move. He is staggering as the other billmen lash their pikes at him. He's being beaten down. He doesn't have long to live. Riven is tiring too. Thomas slashes at him again, the point of the axe scraping a weal down the side of his visor, nearly unpinning it. Riven dances aside; his sword flashes and slices through the meat on Thomas's shoulder. It feels as if it has been burned and he gasps with the pain.

Henry has recovered, but his legs are sloppy, and his chin and chest are covered in blood. He comes at Riven from the other side. Riven forms a triangle, back to back with the two knights still standing. There are dead billmen lying in the ashes under their feet. Many more are wounded enough to want no further part in this.

A moment later the third knight goes down under a flurry of blows from the other billmen, but as they move in to finish him off, one of the billmen loses his wrist to the second knight's axe. Blood sprays over their feet in the ash as the billman slides away.

Thomas goes back at Riven and for the next minute they trade blows with blocks and near misses. Riven keeps him and Henry away with sudden feints, swapping his sword from one hand to the other, but after Henry breaks the final leather strap on his cuirass, he begins to move more stiffly. The plates of armour gape, showing a sliver of vulnerability.

Again Thomas attacks, sweat and blood and rainwater in his eyes, his joints vibrating from the blows; but Riven is moving sluggishly now, an almost different creature from before. Each time Thomas attacks him, Riven's sword gives an inch or two. Thomas starts to land blows on his body as well, and Riven's armour is dented. He is still strong enough though: he knocks the bill from Henry's hands. Henry trips over a wounded man.

But now the second knight has killed the last billman. He stands over him with his hands on his knees, gasping for breath. Then he stands and labours around towards Henry, but before attacking he stops for a moment and raises his visor. His face is streaming with sweat, scarlet with exertion, and even his eyes are red. He holds up his hand for a stay.

'A moment, for the love of God!' he gasps.

Henry is on his feet. He has an axe from somewhere and steps in. He chops the knight across the face, knocking him back on his heels, and the man falls screaming into the sky and clasping his pulpy face with both hands. Henry steps over him and crashes the axe down into him like a woodsman splitting a log.

Afterwards he can only move the axe by standing on the man's neck and levering it free.

Riven turns to kill Henry while the axe is stuck, but Thomas lunges. Riven parries, tries to catch him with the pommel, and then a long thin dagger appears in his hand. Thomas feels it pass his ear as he ducks away.

It is Riven's last desperate move, and this time there is no mistake. Thomas feints right, then turns and swings the pollaxe in a blur. A bellow escapes as the pick head hums through the air. It crashes through the gap in Riven's cuirass and stops still.

Riven staggers and drops his knife. He lowers his hands, carefully. Time seems to stop; all clamour ceases.

Thomas pulls the pick out and Riven stands for a moment, his arms by his sides. He takes a step or two, then drops to his knees.

For a moment he stays upright, his arms by his sides.

Thomas drops the pollaxe and falls to his own knees, facing him. Blood is pouring from the slash in his shoulder; his livery coat is sodden with it. He is shaking; his vision is blurred. He stretches to open Riven's visor.

He wants to see Riven before he dies.

He wants to be seen.

Wants to look into his eyes.

But the visor is jammed. Thomas scrapes it open and stares at him.

It is not Riven.

Thomas's insides rebel and he vomits, scorching and sour, all over his hands and wrists, all over the steel plate, all over this knight.

He falls and rolls on to his back. The rain is wonderfully cold. He lets it fall into his eyes, mix with the blood and sweat.

He stares up into the grey rainclouds, watching them coiling and unfurling, gathering in fists and then drifting away like the smoke from a gun, and all the while the rain falls gently, and all around him he can hear the conclusion to the battle as men are finished off with screams and cries in a welter of blood.

Henry is there, still with that axe. He is threatening someone by the King's tent.

'Who by all the saints are you?' Henry asks.

Thomas hears a reply and then a tall man appears, looking down. He is shaking his head, and saying something Thomas cannot understand. He has one of those boneless faces that reminds him of a brother in the priory who'd died from what the Dean described as an abundance of piety.

Then Thomas sees nothing. Sound and vision fade and silent whiteness envelops him.

Later he wakes to find himself propped against the canvas wall of a well-braced tent. He can taste blood and ash. A mug of ale is pressed into his hands but he cannot hold it. Someone takes it and presses it to his lips. He lets it run over his chin. A face looms into view.

'You all right, Thomas?' Dafydd shouts. He is splashed with blood, but alive, and grinning. Thomas's head is ringing and he hears him as if from the distance. He keeps jabbing his arm, pointing at something, but Thomas can only see the backs of men drifting around the clearing between the tents. Dafydd is laughing.

'New Henry caught him,' he shouts. 'Confined him to his tent. Imagine! A bloody archer from Kent capturing the King of all England, Henry the bloody Sixth! In his tent! A bloody archer!'

Thomas tries to move to see what is going on but the pain is too great.

'We've done it!' Dafydd is saying. 'We've beaten them! We've killed all the nobs and captured the King of bloody England!'

Thomas manages to sit up. Owen presses more ale on him.

'What happens now?' Thomas asks.

'We drink more ale!'

Owen pours it till it runs down his cheeks, leaving pink smears in his ash-smutted face.

'The Earl of March's gone down on his knee to the King, hasn't he?' Dafydd says. 'But we all know who's in charge now. There he is: the Earl of Warwick. Look at him.'

Thomas's eyes ache as he inches his gaze across the clearing. A gap in the ranks has appeared and there is the Earl of March, huge in his steel plate, on one knee before the King, the whey-faced, boneless man whom Thomas saw the moment before he passed out. The King looks stricken, mortified. He doesn't seem to know what to do, what to say to this bloodied giant kneeling before him. Thomas can almost smile. He wishes Katherine were there. It would make her laugh and mutter something. Behind the two but standing apart from a mob of other men in harness is the Earl of Warwick.

It does not look as if he has exerted himself in the battle. He is still smiling as he looks up and around the gathering, and then his smile broadens in welcome. He raises his gloved hand and a man on a grey horse slides across Thomas's vision, blocking it for a moment, so that all he can see are the man's cuisses, his greaves and his sabatons. And then the man gets down from the horse and the horse is led away and Thomas sees the man in full for the first time and he recognises him as being the visitor from the night before, who came to see the Earl of Warwick.

It is Ruthyn's man, he who organised the arrangement, and Warwick is turning to him with that smile, crossing the clearing to greet him, and while every other man is now cheering at what is happening, and while Warwick's and March's and Fauconberg's men are celebrating their famous victory at this field outside the town of Northampton, Thomas is gripped by a new spasm, and is spewing such ale as he has drunk in a hot stinging torrent for now he recognises the man.

Riven.

It is Giles Riven, his hands still clasped in the Earl of Warwick's, and there in the background, holding that grey mare, is the giant, and his naked feet are the last thing Thomas sees as the pain swells in his limbs, and once again he passes into a void of echoing whiteness.

PART FOUR

Marton Hall, County of Lincoln, September 1460

20

It is late summer and the air is pungent with ripe fruit and turned earth. Slender stooks of oats are piled by the barn and an old man and his boy are guiding two oxen and a plough across their furlong of rain-blackened soil. Katherine, for want of anything else to do, is helping an old woman comb the brambles for blackberries and she has almost filled her basket when they hear the steady clop of hooves. A horseman coming from the village – a visitor with news of the outside world perhaps. When they see it is only Thomas, the old woman goes back to work.

'You look the part,' Katherine says when he pulls the horse up beside her. He is wearing a travelling cloak and a velvet hat, and he seems even taller and broader on the back of a horse; had she not known him she knows she would have cowered from him. Now he swings his leg over the saddle and drops easily to the ground, just as if he had been riding the horse all his life. His wound bothers him less now, two months after it was inflicted, but his face is still drawn, and there are smudges under his blue eyes. He takes off his hat and runs a hand through his reddish hair, and smiles.

'Would you like a turn?' he asks, offering her the reins.

Katherine shakes her head.

'I can hardly stay on a pony,' she says, 'let alone that thing.'

They both step back to admire the horse. It is a fine animal, a palfrey. It once belonged to the Earl of Shrewsbury, and had been found tethered to the rear of the tents at Northampton, its groom dead or long since fled, and after a pause while lesser lords coveted it, the Earl of

March had awarded it – and Shrewsbury's dented armour – to the man who'd killed him: Thomas Everingham, an unknown archer from the county of Lincoln, of the retinue of Sir John Fakenham.

'What are you doing out?' he asks.

'Fournier is coming to bleed Sir John today,' she says.

Thomas laughs.

'So you've been sent away?'

'No,' Katherine begins. 'Well. Yes. Anyway he has written to say that he is coming, and that the bleeding is in accordance with the movement of the heavenly bodies, or some such, though it is more likely he's run out of money for wine.'

'How's Sir John?' Thomas asks.

She thinks about it for a moment.

'Low,' she says.

Thomas grunts. They turn to watch a flock of starlings behind the plough. A wood pigeon is calling in the trees.

'And you?' she asks.

He raises his arm above his head to show that all is well, but says nothing.

'I wasn't thinking of your wound,' she says. 'I was thinking about – about this.'

She gestures at the soggy fields, the clutch of rough houses under the church's tower and behind them Marton Hall, Sir John Fakenham's manor.

'I don't know,' Thomas admits. 'I am grateful for all Sir John has done for us, and for this life, but—' He shrugs.

It has been hard for him, Katherine knows. She has heard him grinding his teeth in the night. This anguish has delayed his recovery, she thinks, and she is sure he would be healed already if only he did not believe that God had deserted him on the field of Northampton in favour of Giles Riven.

'But you will get your chance again,' she says. 'I am certain of it. God wills it.'

'No,' he says. 'There will be no more battles in England. The country is at peace now, or so Richard says. When the Duke of York comes from Ireland, he will take up his rightful position on the council, and that will be that.'

'No? What of the Queen? What of her? And what of the sons of all those men killed at Northampton? What of all those who took to their heels that day? Surely they will not let this rest?'

'No one even knows where the Queen is. And she's a woman. She has no power. No say.'

She stares at him. Is he joking? Apparently not.

'But she has a son, doesn't she?' she perseveres. 'She must hope to see him on the throne one day?'

'And she will,' Thomas goes on as if it is she who is the fool. 'When our present king Henry dies. Besides. You miss the point. Riven is on our side now. If Sir John goes to war again, so will he, and I shall be standing shoulder to shoulder with him.'

'As if that matters,' she counters. 'You heard Richard's story of the knight called William Lucy? Who hurried to the field outside Northampton too late to aid the King, only be struck down by one of the King's men who had an interest in his wife?'

Thomas thinks back to the battle and wonders how many such incidents there were that day. He can recall pieces of it, distant fractured moments, fleetingly glimpsed. After the fighting was done they had helped dispose of the bodies, throwing some in the river to join those already drowned, dragging others to a pit dug by a farmer and his boys and burying them there. They returned those of the nobles – their weight lightened by thieving hands – to their heralds. A Mass was heard in the nearby abbey, for some show of sorrow was necessary when among the defeated dead were the victors' cousins, uncles, brothers-in-law and nephews.

'This is how it goes,' Sir John had said. 'War: cruel and sharp.'

They'd found Red John lying on his back. Rainwater was cupped in his eye sockets, his helmet tipped from his head and his russet hair washed back in waves. His alabaster skin was cold to the touch, his freckles somehow pale, and when they turned him over they found he was lying on one of the barbed traps used to cripple horses. They'd had to pull hard to remove it from his spine and in the end they couldn't, so they buried him with the caltrop in place in a good deep hole of his own, quite near the abbey where King Henry and the Earls of Warwick and March were saying their prayers. It was not consecrated ground, but it would have to do. Thomas had watched from the back of a cart with tears in his eyes.

When they'd finished they set off back towards London with King Henry treated as he should be, riding at the front of the column, attended by Warwick and March, the Archbishop, the Legate, and even Henry, the archer from Kent, who smiled all the way home.

It was then, on the road south, camped by a crooked cross where two old roads met, that Warwick had decided in Riven's favour. He had given him the right to Cornford Castle and all its lands, and the wardship of Lord Cornford's daughter until she came of age. Sir John had argued that the girl was engaged to Richard, his own son, whom Warwick had nearly killed in a hunting accident, and that Cornford was his cousin, and that he was due the castle and its estates. But Warwick was blithe. In return for the castle, Riven was to give up Marton Hall, the house he had forcefully occupied the year before, and gift Sir John a sum of money in recompense.

'It is because of Riven's part in Ruthyn's defection,' Geoffrey said, 'and the fact he has a hundred mounted archers to call his own.'

It had been a depressing lesson in the power of power.

The journey from there to Marton had taken four days and in all that time Sir John said not one word. He'd sat on the cushion on his trunk in the cart and stared at his feet, a hiss of drawn breath whenever they hit a pothole. Not even the sight of Richard recovering from his wound and able to ride a horse again cheered him that much, and when they stopped in front of Marton Hall all he could do was look at it with tears in his eyes. It was not the sort of homecoming any of them had imagined.

In his absence the hall had been sorely treated. The windows were gone. A wall was broken down so that the joists of the upper floor splayed in mid-air like spread fingers and the roof sagged. Broken tiles lay scattered about the yard and a sheep's carcass poisoned the well. The lead on the outhouse roof had been taken, and there was a pile of shit below the privy that must have been there six months or more.

'Bastard,' was all Sir John had muttered when he saw the bed upstairs had also been stolen. 'Bastard.'

In the weeks that followed Richard set about restoring the old house to a fit state, and now, two months later, a fire burns in the hall and Sir John can lie upstairs in a new-made bed, protected from the draughts by woollen blankets and the yards of blue damask that hang all around.

His archers from the Hundred have returned to their homes, rich men for a few months, while those with nowhere to go have stayed at Marton, helping in the fields when they are not helping repair the house. Thanks to the pardoner's salve and Katherine's attentions, Thomas's arm has slowly healed, and while he is still not able to draw a bow, he has spent his time learning to ride his new horse.

Katherine has been warm and dry for as long as she can remember, and she cannot recall the last time she went without food for more than a day. Marton Hall has become home to her, and the habits of the priory, ingrained like dirt into her skin, have slowly come loose.

But now Thomas is restive.

'If it is not God's intention that I find Riven,' he tells her, 'then I should go back to the Prior of All. I should rejoin the order. I made my vows.'

He is confused, wretched even.

'I can't live like this,' he says. 'Look.' He shows her his hands.

There are small wounds in the palms where his nails have dug in. 'I do it at night,' he says. 'I can't help myself.'

They walk on. She understands Thomas and the way he feels about this: if God wishes him to be His instrument of vengeance, then it will come to pass, and he will find Riven and kill him, but if He does not, then it will not come to pass; and with every flitting day, while Thomas stays in Marton and there is no chance of coming across Riven in battle, this last scenario seems the most likely.

She wants to tell Thomas that if he wants to find Riven, all he need do is seek him out, that it need not be by chance, that it need not be on the field of battle. He, Thomas, must act for himself, not wait on God's whim.

She opens her mouth to tell him this, but caution keeps her quiet. She is learning lessons, she thinks, however frustrating they might be. Instead she says:

'Look around you, Thomas. Look at this place. Take strength from it. Your chance will come again, I know it.'

They are near the village now, down by the piggery, and she finds a stick and leans over the fence to scratch a pig between its russet shoulders.

'And what about you?' he asks. 'We are a day's ride from the priory.'

She is silent for a moment, watching the pig's pleasure. Thomas means for her to return not to rejoin the order, but to discover who left her there as an oblate. She has been worrying over this ever since that day in the dunes below Sangatte when he told her someone must have been paying her way.

'But how can I do it?' she asks. 'I cannot go as I am, for no boy would be permitted into the cloister, and if I were to go as myself, well, you cannot have forgotten I am wanted as a murderer.'

She has dreamed about her arrival at the priory with a particular intensity in the last months. In them she's seen the letters on the paper, felt its texture under her fingertips. There is the hint of a seal at the bottom of the page. She can hear the dull clack of coins in the oiled leather pouch, and can feel her wrist aching from its heft.

'Perhaps you might return as a woman?' Thomas asks. 'Not a sister, but a normal sort of woman, such as Liz?'

Liz is Geoffrey's daughter. She is Katherine's own age perhaps and helps her mother and father around the hall where she is the subject of much speculation among the remaining archers. Katherine has found herself watching Liz closely, studying the way she moves, her ease in society, her clothes. Liz has caught her gaze more than once, and each time Katherine has looked away as she's felt the heat in her cheeks. Liz has smiled knowingly. She tries to imagine herself as Liz, but cannot, though the thought remains vibrating in her mind like a strummed thread.

Now she shakes her head and they leave the pig to its own rooting.

'There must be another way,' she says.

They walk down past the church, both keeping an eye out for the sexton, a busy man, who's had nothing to say to Sir John since their return. There are chickens everywhere, a dog sleeping in the road and across the way a woman is sealing up a bread oven. Katherine and Thomas are familiar figures now, and the woman raises a hand in greeting, as does a swineherd, with no pigs in tow, who turns and points back down the road towards Lincoln.

Three horsemen appear at the end of the village. Thomas instantly stiffens. She lays a hand on his arm.

'Fournier,' she says.

They watch the riders come on.

'Good day to you, Master Fournier,' Thomas calls out.

'God speed you, sir,' Fournier replies, taking off his hat. 'And to you, young man. Not armed today, are you?'

Katherine shakes her head. Fournier can be very disarming, she has to admit.

'You are sent to guide me to Marton Hall?' Fournier asks.

They are not, but it hardly matters. Fournier is wearing a new cloak the colour of Gascony wine, and his tight-fitting cap is lined with fur. He looks to have prospered since Katherine saw him last, and he has acquired a new assistant, another gangling lad with skinny shanks but one with his ears intact. She tugs her own cap down over her ear.

The third in the party is a grim-faced bodyguard, slouched in his saddle, who rolls his eyes as they start the ride back up the road to Sir John's house and Fournier continues a lecture she imagines must have begun in Lincoln.

'The objective of the patient is to be cured, yes? And to that end he will agree to anything. Once cured, though, his thoughts turn elsewhere and, like as not, he will forget his obligation to pay. The object of the physician, on the other hand, is to obtain his money, so he should insist on taking the money in advance. He must never be satisfied with a promise or a pledge from the patient before the cure is effected. D'you see?'

As they pass the field, the man and his boy are still at work, their plough turning neat lines of glossy black turves, but now seagulls the size of cats have chased away the starlings and they screech like the souls of the damned. On the road ahead the old woman is walking home with her basket of blackberries.

'Are these all Sir John Fakenham's lands?' Fournier asks.

Thomas nods.

'As far as the eye can see,' he tells them.

That'll increase Fournier's price fivefold, she thinks, and she marvels again how naïve Thomas can be.

In the courtyard Walter is sharpening his knife on a step. He looks up, sees them, and then goes back to his task, saying nothing more.

'Yes, well,' Fournier says. 'Good day to you.'

Geoffrey's wife, Goodwife Popham, meets them at the door and Fournier asks her to warm some wine.

'To drink or to use to cleanse your instruments?' Katherine asks.

Fournier ignores her and she leads the way up the stairs to find Sir John in his chamber lying in the bed, drinking wine from a pewter cup. Two white hounds lie alongside him, ugly animals too, and all three look up at Fournier with fearful, bloodshot eyes.

'Good day to you, Master Physician,' Sir John murmurs, his pale lips hardly moving. 'Has the time come already?'

His face is powdery, and he looks closer to death than life. When he tries to sit up and put the cup aside, the pain is too much, and he subsides.

'It has, Sir John,' Fournier answers, sitting on the bed and taking the cup from his fingers. 'How is the fistula?'

Sir John squeezes his eyes shut. A tear escapes.

'I cannot walk,' he says. 'I cannot shit. I cannot even cough for the pain of it.'

Fournier nods.

'It is as I thought,' he says. 'Your humours are out of balance.'

Katherine groans. Fournier turns on her.

'You have some new thing to say?'

'No,' she says. 'Only that what ails Sir John is not some misalignment of his humours. It is a sore in his backside.'

Fournier stands.

'Are we to have this again?'

He touches the handle of the knife in his belt. Brave this time, she thinks, but then again the last time she was carrying the pollaxe. Sir John wafts a hand and lets it fall on the sheets.

'Leave us, Kit,' he murmurs. 'Let the physician go about his work.'

Katherine gives Fournier one last look and then leaves the room and rejoins Thomas in the courtyard below.

'This bleeding is barbaric,' she says. 'It is as bad as putting faith in bits of old bone such as the pardoner used to sell.'

'I have been thinking about the pardoner,' Thomas says. 'And the ledger. Do you think his people will know why he valued it so?

He had a son, he mentioned, who died, but is his wife still alive, I wonder?'

They hear a stifled cry through the window above them. Both look up to the eaves.

'How long will he be here?' Thomas asks.

'A week?' Katherine guesses. 'He must see his patient survives, if only to collect his due.'

'So perhaps we might journey to Lincoln, if only to avoid his company?'

She laughs. His duplicity is charming in its simplicity.

'You imagine meeting Riven in the marketplace? In the church-yard? At a tavern perhaps?'

He looks askance. Then he too smiles and they find themselves grinning at one another and a moment later both look away. The next morning they set out at the pink-fretted dawn, Thomas on his palfrey, his axe over his saddle, Katherine on a little brown pony. She is not a natural horseman – there is something about the position, with the legs apart, that she finds to be wrong – and she knows that alongside him she looks more like his servant than his equal. But the pony is fair-tempered and often anticipates her commands, and she is fond of it.

When they emerge into the sunlight, Lincoln lies ahead, the spire of the cathedral all the taller for the flat fenland around. They ride on and all morning the sun shines in their faces, and as they pass under the castle's pale stone walls and through the old arch, the cathedral bell rings sext.

They stop to stare at the cathedral. It is so huge as to be unearthly, beyond their understanding, and there is even something frightening about it. Eventually they can stand it no longer and they turn their backs on it and tie up their horses, handing a boy a coin to water them. Then they stop in the shade for some ale – tasting of hedge-rows and bramble plants, and with a deep head – and a dish of hot buttered peascod in one of the lanes by the cathedral yard. Insects hum in air as thick as honey. Nearby a stationer is selling books and Thomas cannot resist.

The stationer, snowy-haired and bearded, is dressed in accordance with the sumptuary laws, the tie strings of his cap hanging down to his chest; he begins showing Thomas his cheaper wares, holding them out and declaiming the virtue of the limning. Thomas's fingers stray to the leather surface of one and when he prises it open, the stationer exhales approvingly.

'*Problemata Aristotelis*,' he nods. 'In French. You know quality when you see it, young man.'

There is a suggestion of a question mark at the end of his sentence. He eyes Thomas's rough-made boots and homespun clothing.

'Do you know who made this?' Thomas asks.

'Sadly no,' the stationer admits. 'Only that it is from a workshop in Bruges. Copied from an original there, I dare say.'

'You've been to Bruges?' Thomas asks.

'Many times. A most beautiful city. Though the damp penetrates old bones like mine.'

'Many of the best designs come from Bruges,' Thomas tells Katherine, turning the book over in his hands. 'One day, I should like to go. Though it means crossing the sea again.'

When Thomas is excited about something he looks like a boy. He looks at the other books and keeps testing the textures of the leathers, stroking the surfaces of the paper and the stationer lets him place the pad of his finger on one very fine gesso-backed gold-leafed initial letter L.

'A fine piece of work,' Thomas acknowledges.

The stationer is half smiling, but his gaze flicks from Thomas to Katherine and back again and Katherine feels the familiar twist of anxiety twist in her guts. She has never forgotten what the pardoner had said about travelling among strangers, and now she tugs her hat down over her half-ear again. They should never have come. She brings the conversation to an end by asking of the pardoner.

'Old Master Daud?' the stationer says, softening a little. 'I know of him. A fine man and a serious collector. He has been gone these past months, has he not? Abroad, I hear, though the priests still say Mass and ring a bell for his safe return. He has a house on Steep Hill, down near the Jew's.'

A thought seems to strike Thomas.

'Have you seen anything like this before?' he asks, unslinging his pack and unwrapping the ledger. The stationer takes and opens it and studies it for a moment.

'I dare say I have,' he says, 'though I'd not bother to look at such a thing twice. It is an official document: a list of soldiers and their movements in France, is it? Yes. Perhaps of value for scrap? Ah. Though that I like.'

He is pointing at Thomas's copy of the round window of St Paul's Cathedral in London. Thomas has added some colours since: reds and blues and yellows, and the design glows. The stationer offers some money for it, but Thomas shakes his head, and the old man hands the book back and they leave him just as the bells chime the half-hour.

Master Daud's house is down the hill on the right. It looks shuttered and empty, but after Thomas pounds on the door, a blank-faced girl in a kirtle and a cloth cap opens up.

'Is Mistress Daud at home?' Katherine asks. Without a word the girl holds open the door and with quick glances at one another they go in. She shows them across a rush-strewn hall and into a wooden panelled parlour where the shuttered windows let in only a little light. There is a long table against one wall, and cushions on the window seats and tapestries of scenes she does not recognise on the walls. There are even silk rugs under their feet, but it is the books on tables all around the room that draw the eye, for they show up the worst of the dust. It lies everywhere, a pale coating half of an inch thick. It is as if no one has been in the room for weeks, maybe months, possibly years.

'She always said you'd come one day,' the maid says.

'Who?'

'Mistress Daud.'

'But you don't know who we are.'

The girl nods and withdraws.

'Strange,' Thomas says, his eyes on the books.

Katherine thinks for a moment. Then it hits her.

'She doesn't know he is dead.'

It has occurred to neither. Thomas starts shifting his feet and is tugging at his collar when the door opens again and a woman enters. She is tall and slight, with a high forehead, as if her hair is plucked, and skin pale as ivory. She wears a dress dyed the colour of old sage leaves, with sleeves that droop to the floor, and once inside she stands unnaturally still, her only movement from her elbow as she gestures to the maid to offer the wine she has brought in on a silver tray.

'Good day, Mistress Daud,' Katherine begins. Her voice sounds loud in her own ears.

'Good day to you,' Mistress Daud whispers. Her eyes are fixed on Katherine's. They are almost as pale as her face, tinged yellow. For a moment Katherine does not know how to start. Mistress Daud remains immobile while her girl passes them each a silver cup.

'He is dead, isn't he?' the woman says.

After a moment Katherine nods. Mistress Daud closes her eyes. When she opens them such light as was there has faded further.

'It is as I feared,' she says. 'God has not looked kindly on me.'

God has not looked kindly on the pardoner, either, Katherine thinks.

'He had said his prayers,' Katherine lies, 'and was given absolution by a priest.'

Again the woman nods.

'I thank you for bringing the news,' she says. 'If there is something . . .?'

Katherine feels the blood rise to her cheeks.

'No, no,' she says. 'We are in search of no reward. It is no more than our Christian duty. But – he left only this.'

She gestures to Thomas, who hurriedly removes the ledger and offers it to her. Mistress Daud makes no move to take it.

'A book,' she sighs.

'He seemed to think it was of great value,' Katherine says.

Mistress Daud gestures to those stacked on the tables.

'He thought all books were of great value.'

There is a long silence. A cart rumbles by outside: the cry of the carter, the plod of his horse's hooves.

'It is a book of names,' Katherine goes on. 'No more than a list, really.'

'Keep it then,' Mistress Daud says. 'I have no use for it. Master Daud never taught me to read.'

There is another long silence.

'You do not even recognise it?' Thomas asks.

She shrugs.

'He was going to France, he said, to sell something of great value to the King there. At least that is what he told us. But he was always planning to sell things of great value. He had three crossbows belonging to the witch Joan.'

More silence.

'But these books—' Thomas begins, gesturing.

'Are nothing to me. They serve to remind me of my late husband and that is all.'

'May I look at them?' Thomas asks.

'I am your servant,' Mistress Daud says. 'They will all be gone soon. I will have to marry again, and my husband-to-be is no lover of books. Maria will show you out.'

With that she turns and leaves the room. Maria follows. Katherine glances at Thomas. He puts his empty cup of wine on the tray, pours himself another, drinks it, and then starts wiping the dust from the bindings of the books. Katherine says nothing. She realises how cold the room is, even on a warm day.

'Thomas,' she says. 'Let's go.'

'He has everything here,' Thomas says. 'Look.' He holds up a book. 'A psalter,' he tells her.

'As fine as yours?'

'It is a copy of the Utrecht Psalter, you see? Illuminated by a genius. Look. Beautiful. And here, a Life of Julius Caesar.'

He opens the front, made of some hardwood and decorated with gold lace. He sniffs, inhaling the mixed smells of leather, wood, vellum and glue. He turns a page.

'Look at that,' he says, gesturing to an ornately designed letter Q in the loop of which men in madder cloaks are harvesting plump grapes with golden knives.

'It is finer than our ledger,' Katherine agrees.

'I wish Mistress Daud had given us this instead,' Thomas says. 'It is exquisite. Almost beyond belief.'

He lays it down gently and begins moving the books, revealing those that lie beneath, sighing as he does so. She leaves him to it and finds the maid standing in the hallway, staring in silence at the cobwebs that festoon the lamps above her head. The candles are so old they are almost orange. Mistress Daud has disappeared. Katherine opens her mouth to say something but faced by such blankness, she can think of nothing. Thomas has to be called away from the books.

When they leave the maid closes the door on them, and they stand on the steps frowning at one another.

'Something awry, there,' Thomas suggests.

He is right, but what is it? They stop in the sunlit street, the cobbles warm under their feet, the smell of fresh horse dung in the air. Flies and bees drone, catching the sun. Katherine turns and looks up at the windows of the jettied storeys of the house. Mistress Daud is there, staring down at them through a thick pane. After a moment she steps back into the gloom, her face rippling through the glass, and is gone.

They stand in the road a moment longer. Thomas is staring south to where the flat lands that lie beyond the walls dissolve in the summer's haze.

'The priory is a day's ride from here,' he says.

She looks at him.

'And so is Cornford Castle,' she says.

Before he can say more they hear a horse clattering up the road towards them. The rider is standing in the stirrups, lashing at its rump. They step off the road to let it pass. Its flanks are white with sweat.

'In a hurry,' Thomas says.

By the time they reach the crown of the hill a crowd of people is gathered by the cathedral gate. Someone is shouting something. A bell begins ringing.

'What is it?'

The stationer is packing away his wares. He turns to them.

'Have you heard?' he asks. 'Richard of York has come from Ireland. He has landed in Chester this last week and is making his way to London. The rider says he has a man walking before him carrying his sword of state, and it is upright.'

'What does that mean?' Katherine asks.

'Only kings progress in such a fashion.'

'So?'

'The Duke means to claim the throne.'

They turn to one another.

'You see,' she says. 'I told you the fighting isn't done yet.'

21

The next morning, when Sir John emerges from his drink-induced slumber, they tell him of Richard, Duke of York's arrival in England.

'I must get up,' he says. 'We must get to London. We must see him. He will reverse Warwick's decision in the matter of Cornford Castle. I am certain of it.'

Thomas sees Katherine shut her eyes, as if the mere mention of Cornford Castle depresses or bores her, but when Fournier hears that Sir John enjoys a connection to the highest in the land, his eyes brighten.

'However will you get to see him?' he asks.

'Through the Duke's son, the Earl of March,' Sir John says. 'He is in our debt. Come, Kit, help me up. Richard my boy, take Walter and Thomas and summon the men. See if there are any newcomers who might swell our ranks. Goodwife Popham, we need more of the red cloth for our jacks. I do not want to turn up in London with this lot in rags.'

'What's he like, the Duke of York?' Thomas asks Richard as they saddle up.

'I don't know,' Richard sighs. 'But I've heard things. Men say he's gone mad since he's been in Ireland.'

'Mad? How so?'

'He is supposed to be the premier lord of the land after King Henry, and has been regent while the King was inane, but now, instead of taking his counsel, the Queen favours self-interested graspers such as the Dukes of Buckingham and Somerset. It has gone hard for him, but in Ireland, with no one to tell him otherwise, they say he has been acting as if he is King of England in King Henry's place, as if King Henry does not exist.'

Thomas is sent first to Brampton to find Brampton John. Brampton John lives with his mother and three goats in a windowless cot under a thatched roof where two paths cross. Brampton John is pleased to be recalled to join Sir John's service, having had enough of the farming life for the summer, and they celebrate with a pot of his mother's ale.

'Why don't you put some windows in here?' Thomas asks, coughing from the smoky interior of Brampton John's cot.

'Windows? What for?'

'So you can see.'

'Windows won't help. Even if I was ever in here when there's daylight, which I'm not, the last thing I want to see is that bloody field. Spend all my time there, digging, sowing, cutting.'

The next morning they go north to find Little John Willingham.

'You'll not guess who I saw the other day,' Little John says as they begin walking back towards Marton, bows over their shoulders. 'Edmund Riven. The boy with the eye.'

He gestures to his right eyeball.

'Son of that bastard what stole the castle from Sir John. And well, it wasn't me who saw him, it was my ma. Said he was there with ten of his men. Riding north, they were. They stopped and bought ale and asked if she knew everyone in the hundred, and when she says she did by sight, they asks if she'd seen any strangers hereabouts, particularly a girl. She says no and then they asks who owns the land. She told them to clear off as they should know perfectly well who owned it, seeing as how they'd been living on it for the last year or so.'

'And they rode north?'

'Up towards Gainsborough. With a baggage wagon. Only reason she didn't shut the door in their faces is she wanted to sell them her rotten old ale. Disgusting stuff.'

Thomas means to remind Little John to tell Richard or Sir John what his mother has seen but when they reach Marton Hall a cart and two oxen stand in the yard, and Geoffrey and Richard and Brampton John are carrying Sir John down the stairs on his mattress. Thomas and Katherine hurry to help them lay the old man in the bed of the cart while Fournier watches, a cup of wine in his hand, and Goodwife Popham fusses.

'How long will you be?' she asks. Richard shrugs. No one has any idea. Goodbyes are said and the carter cracks his switch and the beasts take the strain.

'Thank God for that,' Walter says, hauling himself up in his saddle. 'Spent far too long here, hanging about, doing nothing, getting fat.'

Thomas shares Walter's feelings, Katherine knows.

'Is it wise to leave Fournier there, though?' she asks. 'He'll drink every last drop of wine and all the ale.'

She is sitting up next to Geoffrey in the cart. The others follow behind, Walter on the pony, Thomas and Richard on their horses, the reins slack in their fingers. They pass through Lincoln where the stationer has moved his stall and then down the hill past the pardoner's old house. Thomas looks up and fancies he sees a movement at the window, and imagines the widow standing there in silence, watching.

As they travel south they collect more news of Richard of York's progress through England. They hear that his wife, the Duchess of York, has travelled from London to meet him in a litter hung with blue velvet drapes and drawn by four pairs of white horses. The next day it is five pairs and curtains of cloth of gold. Whatever the slight variation in detail, it looks as if the stationer heard correctly. Richard, Duke of York, is coming south in royal dignity.

Sir John is troubled.

'It changes everything,' he says. 'Up until now we've been fighting to rid ourselves of the bloodsucking leeches that hang around the court, the sort of men who let us down in France. Men like Buckingham and Somerset; men like goddamned Giles Riven.

Thieves, murderers, swindlers and the like. We were trying to restore good governance and the rule of law, weren't we? So that a man might walk the roads without fear of being robbed, or that he might go to law without the fear of being manhandled by his opponents, or that he might leave his own household to go over the sea to fight for his bloody country and come back to find it still his.'

'And we were right to do so,' Richard says. 'Everyone can see the country was in a parlous state and that the wars in France have ended in defeat and shame.'

'Yes. Yes,' Sir John agrees, flapping his hand. 'But that's all changed now, don't you see? If what we hear about York is right, it will seem that we have been fighting to get rid of the King. To depose him. And replace him. With the Duke of York. I did not answer old Fauconberg's call to do that, and I do not imagine that many others did either.' He shakes his head. 'Worst of it is that it will come as a rallying cry to the lords in the north. We've had a peaceful summer of it, haven't we? Fixed the roof, got the harvest in, got a few girls pregnant too, I dare say, but that's only because young Warwick knows he hasn't the power to interfere with what goes on up north, so he hasn't tried. He's been in Calais, for the love of all that's holy! And that's suited all those northern bastards – begging your pardon, Thomas. They don't mind one way or another what Warwick does in Kent and London, so long as he doesn't bother them. But now York arrives and he wants to be king? They'll be up in arms.'

Richard looks thoughtful. They travel on.

'Do you suppose', he says at length, 'that Riven has heard the news?'

'About York? Of course.'

'I wonder what he will make of it.'

It is Sir John's turn to look thoughtful.

'He will weigh up where his advantage lies,' he eventually says, 'and jump accordingly.'

Richard nods.

'As should we, surely?'

Sir John looks at his son for a long moment, then shoos a fly from his face and turns away.

The road is crowded with carts banked with produce for the London markets and the word of the Duke of York's coming passes up and down between travellers, and with each telling it is given a new twist, so that by the time they enter London through Bishopsgate just before curfew on the evening of their fourth day on the road, they don't know whether they'll find the city in flames, or with celebratory wine flowing in her fountains.

In the event the city seems to be in the same quandary. It is tensed for something, but no one seems to know what. They pass through all the tenter frames and the washing posts on the greens by the road-side and they find space for the cart and horses in the yard of the Bull Inn where the ostler, a fat man with a stained leather apron, tells them the Duke of York is in Abingdon, two days' march from Westminster, and that he has trumpeters to sound fanfares wherever he goes.

When Thomas relates this to Sir John he groans.

'To think of all the trouble taken after Northampton!' he says. 'How we let everyone know the King is still the King, how we bent our necks and renewed our oaths of allegiance. And now this!'

It is to get worse. After a night tormented by the inn's sour beer and then fleas in the straw, the next day they hear from a cookshop owner who'd heard it from a boatman who'd just come from Westminster that all the talk there is of the Duke of York marching with eight hundred men under the banner of the royal arms of England, undifferenced by the strap of white that had marked his own banner from that of the King.

'That's it,' the cookshop owner says. 'When they find out he wants to be king, we'll have those northern bastards rampaging down here again before St Martin's, pissed as voles, nicking every-thing they can get their bloody hands on.'

They return to the inn.

'Our journey has been wasted before it has reached its point,' Sir John admits. 'The Duke won't spare the time to see us now, let alone hear our case.'

They order beer and drink it at the table by the fire.

'Still,' he goes on, 'we've come this far, let us take a barge to the palace at Westminster and see what there is to be seen. If nothing else we will have something to talk about on the way home. Geoffrey, make sure the boys are cleaned up, will you? New livery coats, and as much plate as we possess, shared out, so that we look the part, eh?'

After the battle of Northampton, when the Earl of March had awarded Thomas the Earl of Shrewsbury's armour, Thomas had sold it to Richard and the price had included Richard's old cuisses, greaves and sabatons, and these he now straps on, covering his legs from toe to thigh. Thomas cannot help smiling at the sight of his legs encased in steel, the neat rows of bands that taper across each foot to form a point over his toes. They are almost tolerable to walk in.

After hearing Mass in St Botolph's next to the priory opposite, Geoffrey hires a litter to carry Sir John down to the bridge, five archers ahead, five behind. Katherine runs alongside, her cap pulled low to hide her ear. They find a barge willing to take them up to Westminster and climb aboard and spread themselves out on the broad planks that span the boat, and they prop their weapons on the gunwale. The oarsmen, half-naked and too old for this sort of thing, take up their oars and the master hauls up his patched ochre sail and sets the craft out into the middle of the river.

There is a light breeze. The sun comes out. The water is green. Thomas and Katherine sit together on the last thwart in the stern and stare back through the arches under the bridge where the water roars, to where the Tower's battlements are softened by coal smoke.

The oarsmen row against the current up past the wharves, each one backed by a church or a priory or a friary, and Thomas cannot help but recall the pardoner's words. The church is indeed rich. They row past the square bulk of Baynard's Castle, dour and uninviting, its water gate firmly boarded, and then on past the city walls, following the river as it meanders past Charing, until before them stands the King's palace and St Stephen's Chapel at Westminster.

'Busy day,' the barge's pilot grunts.

The oarsmen lean on their oars and take them upriver while they wait for space on the jetty. A barge pulls away, then another, both heading downstream to London. Thomas thinks he recognises the white-haired old man in the first one, grandly turned out, with a small retinue in red livery. Is it the Earl of Salisbury? Warwick's father?

Eventually ropes are tossed out and they make fast. Richard speaks to the guards and assures them of their bona fides while Thomas and Geoffrey help Sir John up over the side of the barge and then set him on the shore with tears of pain in his eyes.

'That bastard Fournier,' he murmurs. 'A fee of two marks and he's only made it worse, may the saints be my witnesses, and I feel as weak as a kitten. Here, help me, Thomas, will you?'

Thomas takes one arm over his shoulder, Geoffrey the other.

'Not very dignified, but by Christ . . .'

Richard leads them hobbling through the gate and into a courtyard.

The palace is an intricate maze of buildings and precincts dominated by a bluff stone chapel and at every gate are more of York's men, road-stained and bristling with spears and axes and swords, as if on the field of battle rather than in a royal palace.

They regard the red liveries of Sir John's men with suspicion, but there are only ten of them, and at length they are let through to the New Palace Yard, where another mob mills around the doorway to the hall. On the steps there is some confusion among the royal heralds in their quartered livery coats, and there is trouble in the offing.

As they approach, William Hastings emerges from the throng.

His face is pale with fatigue and there is a long stain on the sleeve of his blue vented jacket, but he is pleased to see them.

'Day to you, sir,' Sir John calls. 'I'd shake your hand but I am encumbered as you see. Perhaps you will shake the hand of my man here, Thomas.'

'I'd be glad to shake such a hand,' Hastings says, removing his hat and taking Thomas's hand, then the others in turn. 'I'm sorry to see you in pain, Sir John, but it pleases me to see you here. We are in need of cool heads.'

'When did the Duke arrive?'

'A short while back. And look: there are his heralds now. Did you ever see such a thing?'

Hastings laughs. The heralds are pushing and shoving one another: one side belonging to King Henry, the other to Richard of York. They are indistinguishable except that the Duke of York's heralds' coats are the brighter for being the newer. It strikes Thomas that these men reflect what is happening across the country, and that if somehow the strife could be confined to these fellows, then much blood might yet go unspilled. He puts the thought aside.

'So it is true?' Sir John says. 'We heard rumours but hoped them baseless.'

'It is true, sad to say. My lord the Duke of York arrived with these fools sounding their clarions as if to wake the dead. Then he marched into the hall with his sword held upright before him, his men wearing the royal coat of arms, and he clapped his hand on the throne as if it were his. He turned to the lords expecting a cheer, but, you know, how could they? They renewed their vows to King Henry only months ago. And anyway, besides . . .' Hastings wrinkles his nose.

'Dear God,' Sir John says. 'He has been in Ireland too long. He has caught some native malaise. That is the only answer.'

Hastings laughs.

'At any rate, he has gone to find King Henry. I should love to hear what they have to say to one another.'

'And what of the Earl of Warwick?' Sir John asks. 'What has he to say on the matter?'

Hastings's eyebrows shoot up.

'Nothing yet,' he says. 'He is expected this evening.'

It is now late afternoon and men are leaving the courtyard in clusters, wrapping their cloaks about them and hurrying down to their barges to be taken back to the city, or out through the gates to the road that leads back through Newgate. The Duke of York's men are left in the fading light looking ill at ease and out of place. It is impossible to know what they've been told to expect, but surely, Thomas thinks, it cannot have been this curious anti-climax?

'We should go and find him,' Richard says. 'Appeal for his jurisdiction against Riven.'

'Find who?' Sir John asks.

'The Duke of York.'

Sir John turns on him.

'Have you lost your wits, my boy?' he asks.

'Not at all,' Richard says. 'If we appeal to him now, he will think we do so because we believe he is king. He will be flattered. He'll look favourably on us.'

Sir John is taken aback. There is a pause. Then Hastings nods. It makes sense.

'Well, I suppose we can but try,' Sir John admits.

'Quite,' Hastings adds. 'What's the worst he can say? And I'll come with you, if I may? We share a great-grandmother, the Duke and I.'

They look at him afresh.

'Philippa of Clarence,' he says, as if it is amusing, 'daughter of Lionel, son to King Edward the Third. From there, we part company, though. This way.'

They leave the others in the courtyard and pass through a gateway into the palace courtyard, where the concentration of the Duke of York's troops becomes only denser, and here they see that Richard is not the only man to have had the idea of seeking an interview with their commander. The stairs leading up to his apartments are choked with men waiting for the self-same thing.

'It'll be a long wait,' Hastings supposes. They stand on the twisting stone steps for more than an hour, unable to proceed upwards, and soon unable to reverse thanks to the press of those who've come after them. Sir John begins to flag. Thomas passes him a wineskin. Candles are lit. They can smell the kitchen fires. At last they arrive on a landing. Here are the tapestries depicting Judgement Day and some scenes from the life of Solomon and Nebuchadnezzar. Beyond a barrier of five more guards across the doorway is a clear corridor and beyond that, a solar in which Thomas can see more men in the light of a fire. Stewards in plaincloth pass by, bearing trays of fragrant pies and ewers of wine.

Thomas's mouth waters. None of them have eaten since the morning and to think of pigeon pie and a jug of ale is to think of heaven. He is regretting wearing the plate on his legs.

But then there is a disturbance behind them. There is a surge. Men are shouting on the stairs. A punch is thrown. They are shunted against the five guards; Thomas is nose to nose with a bearded captain of foot in a breastplate and helmet.

'For the love of God step back,' he says. 'Can't you see he is wounded?'

The guard looks at Sir John.

'All right, let him through. You're not to go into the solar though. Stand to one side.'

The guards let them through. They carry Sir John down the short gloomy corridor and into the hall. It is crowded with men but instantly Thomas's eye is drawn to Edward of March, who stands staring into the fire with a cup of wine in one hand, gently scratching his cheek with the long fingers of his other. He is apparently listening to a man dressed in blue, but his attention seems elsewhere and just then a disturbance reaches the landing behind them and March looks up at the noise and catches sight of Hastings.

'William!' he calls, summoning him over. 'Come in, come in! I commend myself to you! But for the love of all that's holy how do you find yourself here?'

They kiss one another. March is taller than Hastings, but not by much, and Thomas wonders if he can see the common ancestor in their faces. No. March is wearing a flamboyant green velvet jacket, with vast shoulders tapering to his waist, cut short to expose his buttocks and the messy bulge of his cock and balls. The toes of his leather boots are extravagantly pointed.

'I am waiting with Sir John Fakenham,' Hastings tells March, 'here to beg the indulgence of a word with your good father.'

March's eye settles on Sir John and then flicks to Thomas.

'By God! You again. Thomas Something! Saviour of Newnham and slayer of my lord the Earl of Shrewsbury.'

Thomas bows his head.

'My lord,' he says.

'Our paths seem entwined, and every time you are near me, something beneficial comes my way. I hope to God you bring good luck tonight, for I believe we'll need it. Is that my cousin I hear coming?'

They turn and see that the disturbance on the steps was the arrival of the Earl of Warwick.

'Oh, saints above,' March murmurs. 'Did you ever see a man so enraged?'

All talk falters and the room seems to draw breath as Warwick stalks into the solar. He pauses, his face pinched. He is looking for someone and everyone knows whom. A path seems to open up between him and the Duke of York, who is leaning against a sideboard with a cup of wine in his hand. He is pretending he has not noticed Warwick, and is talking too animatedly to a youth with long blond hair spilling from under a dark cap.

The Duke of York is a head shorter than his son the Earl of March, and older than Thomas had supposed, about fifty perhaps, with a thin grey beard and a slight and shrunken body. No one is deceived by his show of nonchalance, especially not Warwick, who now strides towards him as if he means to strike him.

'By what right do you choose now to claim the crown of England?' Warwick demands. He raises his voice, broadcasting his fury. The Duke of York turns and affects to notice him.

'My lord of Warwick!' he says as if pleased to see him. His lips are very red and wet and he licks them, but he does not have the stomach to lean forward and kiss Warwick as he might have in other circumstances.

'I demand an answer,' Warwick continues. 'By what right do you now claim the throne of England?'

The Duke of York hesitates, glances at the blond boy, and then finds his voice.

'I am Richard, Duke of York,' he says. 'I am son to Anne who was daughter of Roger Mortimer, Earl of March, who was son and heir to Philippa, who in her turn was daughter and heir to Lionel, the third but second surviving son of King Edward the Third.'

It is a rehearsed speech that becomes steadily more fluent.

'Through this line I claim the right, title, royal dignity and estate of the crowns of the realms of England and France and the lordship of Ireland, by right, law and custom before any issue of John of Gaunt, the fourth son of the same King Edward.'

Warwick stares at him.

'This I know,' he says. 'This we all know. What I do not understand is why you make the claim now?'

'It is my right,' York replies. 'I have set it aside till now. But it has not died. It has not rotted away.'

'Can you not see that we all love our King Henry?' Warwick goes on, raising his voice again for all to hear. 'And that none of the lords or the people of this country wish him any harm?'

The Duke's eyes bulge and glisten like polished glass. The blond boy steps forward and addresses Warwick with a misplaced wave of his hand.

'Fair cousin,' he says, 'don't be angry. You know that it is our right to have the crown. It belongs to my father here, and he will have it whatever anyone may say.'

Warwick stares at the boy. Thomas thinks he might even kill him.

'Oh lord. My brother Rutland,' March breathes. He hurries forward, his large feet making the fresh reeds squeak, and steps between Warwick and Rutland. He puts a hand on his brother's shoulder. 'Brother,' he says. 'Don't say another word.'

Rutland starts, looks up at March, and flushes. He is so young, too young to know what he is doing. March turns and puts an arm across Warwick's shoulder and guides him away and towards the door.

Warwick is stiff-backed with anger, his face blotched, and March soothes him in a low voice, urging some future plan perhaps, as he guides him back through the throng and out on to the corridor.

The Duke of York turns back to Rutland and continues talking as if nothing has happened, but even Thomas can see his hands are trembling, and his brittle smile reveals two crooked front teeth. After a moment, the Duke and Rutland leave the room, and as they go the murmur of conversation flares behind them.

'Well,' Hastings says after a moment, 'that went as well as anyone could hope.' He taps his front teeth with his forefinger, and it is hard to know if he is joking or not.

They spend that first week in London at the Bull Inn on Bishopsgate and every morning they hear Mass at a different chapel before taking a barge to Westminster to attempt an audience with the Duke of York. Every evening they return unsuccessful. By the third day Thomas stops bothering with his leg armour and by the fifth they are all bored.

Sir John and Richard may discuss the events of state as they unfold, but Thomas knows they have no power to influence them, and so they too are condemned to sit idle. Nor does he see William Hastings again, though other lords come and go and meet for long hours in Westminster Hall, each bringing with them their retinues of liveried men, who play dice, practise their drills and drink ale to while away the time.

'It all hinges on whether the right to the crown can pass through a woman,' Sir John is saying. 'If it can, then the Duke of York's claim is superior to the King's, even though the King's father and his father's father sat on the throne before him.'

'Course it shouldn't pass through a bloody woman,' Walter offers.

'But why not?' Sir John counters in the spirit of discussion.

'Why not? Because women are women.'

'But look at the Earl of Warwick. How did he become the Earl of Warwick? He married Anne Beauchamp, Countess of Warwick. So he got the title and the estates through his wife. Why shouldn't the crown pass so?'

'Because it's the crown,' Walter says.

'Well, there you have it,' Sir John says. 'I don't suppose the lords are arguing it any more clearly in there.' He gestures to the hall. 'But it is a shame,' he goes on, 'because on this question men will lose their lives.'

'Lost 'em before; 'll lose 'em still.'

Sir John sighs.

'Thank you, Walter. Of course that's true. But this will divide families. Brother against brother, father against son. That sort of thing. I hope it does not, of course, but whether or not a man has the right to call himself King of England raises dangerous passions that can only lead to more blood being shed.'

The discussion rumbles on all morning, until Katherine can stand it no longer.

'I think I'll take a walk,' she says.

Thomas joins her. The others stay in the square where Sir John labours his points again and again.

'Sir John seems better,' Thomas says.

'Only because he is out of the range of Fournier,' she snorts.

Beyond the abbey walls they find a stationer selling a poor

selection of books, some of them unbound. These are of little interest to Thomas, but Katherine likes them.

'It is as if their author will return at any moment to take up his reed and continue the conversation,' she says.

Not all the books are religious tracts.

'What is that one there?' she asks, pointing. It is a series of folded sheets, roughly hacked at the edges, bound with strips of cloth the colour of shoe soles. Thomas unties the cords and opens it, watched by the stationer. It smells of must.

'Saints,' Katherine says.

On the very first spread of pages is a startling picture of a man in robes with his finger inserted in another man's anus.

'It's a treatise on fistulae,' Thomas reads aloud. 'By a man named John Arderne. He is a barber surgeon of London, it says.'

They study the picture. There are more besides, each as peculiar and gruesome as the first. Thomas flushes.

'So a fistula can be cured?' she asks.

'I think so,' Thomas says, reading on a little. 'Though I should not like to see it done.'

Katherine takes the parchment from him. Over her shoulder he sees there are many illustrations, including one of an owl. A shadow of doubt crosses his mind. Whoever has drawn the bird has obviously never seen one in real life, and has drawn a duck with claws and a pointed beak. Elsewhere are pictures of plants that might be used in cures and a picture of a zodiac man, suggesting propitious times to cut into particular parts of the body, and a wounded man, too, showing the sorts of injuries that might occur in war.

'I wonder if Fournier has seen this?' Katherine asks. 'When was it written?'

'It says in the year of our Lord 1376.'

'Nearly a hundred years ago. Even Fournier must have had time to hear of it, then. We should buy it. How much is it?'

The stationer names his price and without demur Thomas reaches for his purse. Katherine beats the man down to half. As Thomas pays the stationer, the old man hands her the parcel.

'You bargain like a Jew,' he says with a smile. 'Or a woman.'

She says nothing, but takes the parcel and turns.

'Thank you, Thomas,' she says as they walk through the abbey yard.

Thomas is struck with an idea.

'Perhaps, though, we might use it to start your lessons in reading?' he asks.

'Lessons in reading?'

'Yes, why not?'

'It would help pass the time, I suppose.'

So they sit against a wall, shoulder to shoulder, and he begins to coach her in the art of letters.

'"A tretis extracte of Maistre Iohn Arden of fistula in ano,"' he reads aloud, his finger following the line, '"and of fistula in other places of the body and of apostemes makyng fistules and of emoraides & tenasmon and of clisteres: of certayn oyntementes, poudres and oils."'

They look at one another.

'A difficult text to start with,' he admits, 'but it is what we have, so—'

By the end of the second week Katherine is beginning to read, with her finger under each letter of each word, but in the process she has acquired an intellectual grasp not only of the process of John Arderne's operation for the removal or cure of fistulae, but also his various salves and ointments that make use of hedgerow plants such as hemlock and henbane, and his various theories about cleanliness in the surgery.

For all that time Sir John waits patiently, unsuccessfully, for an audience with the Duke, but it is as Katherine is finishing reading Arderne's pages for the second time, beginning to enjoy his lively turn of phrase and his light-hearted boasting, that the lords finally reach their decision in the matter of the Duke of York and his claim to the throne of England, France and Ireland.

Over the weeks the question has been passed to and fro between the justices, the serjeants-at-law and the royal attorneys. They are serious men in black fur-lined coats and each has taken his turn to wash his hands of the problem. It is for the lords to determine, they say, and so in the absence of a clear answer, the lords opt for a compromise that serves all in part and none in whole. The King will remain the king, they say, but the Duke of York now becomes his heir.

'But the Duke is ten years older than the King,' Sir John says. 'He is sure to die first. Why ever would he agree?'

'And why would the King agree to disinherit his own son?' Richard asks.

'If indeed he is his own son,' Sir John counters.

A rumour has been circulating in the Palace Yard that the Queen's son is not the King's son, and that the boy was begotten while the King was indisposed. The rumour, swapped once, twice, three times, hardens into fact. The Queen's son is *not* the King's son. Some even say the Duke of Somerset is the real father. Only Katherine asks how the Queen might react to hear of her son disinherited and called a bastard.

'She will not be best pleased,' Sir John admits.

'So this settlement has solved nothing?' Katherine says.

There is a long pause.

'No.'

'So the Queen will come south with her army again?' she continues.

Again there is a pause.

Finally:

'Probably.'

22

Thomas and Katherine follow Sir John and Richard out through Bishopsgate the next morning and they are not alone on the road. The news of the settlement has spread fast and it seems the whole country is taking stock and getting ready for what might come. Armoured men ride in packs, returning to their estates, while friars and messengers hurry in both directions.

Sir John, who has been enlivened by their time in London, now suffers a reverse. He can no longer sit on his trunk, but lies slumped in the hay in the back of the cart as they follow the road up towards Stamford. Near Ancaster there is a turning on the road that leads towards Cornford Castle and as they pass, all look down its hedge-crowded length.

'I wonder what he's up to,' Richard says. 'I half expected to see him in Westminster.'

Little John Willingham pipes up with the story of his mother selling Edmund Riven ale, of his questions about a girl and how he had been heading north with ten spears. Sir John is asleep at last, but Richard listens.

'Could mean anything,' he says, at length. 'Or nothing.'

When they get to Marton Hall Fournier is still there, still at the table, though his boy and his guard have apparently taken his horses and deserted him. Goodwife Popham says he has been drunk by eleven every morning and asleep in his dinner by midday. Sir John pales when he sees him.

'Why, Master Fournier, good day to you.'

'And good day to you, Sir John. You do not look to have flourished since our last meeting. It is as well that I delayed my departure, so that we may cut you once more tomorrow, and restore the balance of your humours.'

Richard and Geoffrey help Sir John up to his room, leaving Thomas and Katherine and the others to their supper.

'Master Fournier,' Katherine calls down the length of the table, 'are you familiar with the name John Arderne?'

The physician, who has picked up his cup, pauses.

'John Arderne? Why yes. A surgeon. Of the last century, a great talent with the knife, but the possessor of dangerous and ungodly theories concerning the production of the laudable pus.'

'Was he not an expert at curing fistulae?' Katherine goes on.

Fournier takes a long drink and stares at her over his cup. He puts it down and dries his lips.

'He had some small success,' he allows, 'but the intervention . . . Well. It is highly dangerous. I would not advise it. And do you know that Arderne ignored the need for cautery or purgatives? He recommended a clean sponge pressed against a wound to stop the flow of blood and thereafter nothing but bandages, changed only when dirty, and the wound kept dry? Madness.'

'You know of his cure for fistulae then?'

'Of course. Whatever do you take me for?'

'I had you as a barber. A cutter of hair.' She does not add 'a drunk'. All talk has silenced on the table.

'You doubt my skill to carry out such an operation?'

Katherine chooses her words carefully. 'I do not doubt your skill. Only your courage.'

Fournier puts down his cup. He is thinking hard.

'It is not so serious a fistula,' he says, as if to himself. 'And there is only one of them. I have the tools required for the operation in my pack.'

For a moment it seems to Katherine that Fournier will conduct the operation.

'But no,' he says. 'I have none of the notes I need, nor sufficient recall of the details of the procedure.'

He returns to his drink with relief.

'We have his instructions here,' Katherine says. She nods to Thomas, who fishes the manuscript out of the pardoner's pack. He is about to pass them along the table, then sees the greasy thumbs that might mark the pages, and so he gets up and delivers them to the physician himself. Fournier looks at them, casually at first, but then a frown gathers.

'Now you have no excuse,' Katherine says.

Fournier does not look up. He turns a page, folding it carefully. After a long moment he closes it. His gaze flicks around the hall, as if anxious not to settle on one thing too long, before settling on the door.

'It is a pity,' he says. 'I should have done the operation first thing in the morning save that the moon is in Libra, and astrologers agree no operation ought to be undertaken while the moon is in the sign governing the part of the body to be operated upon. The stars are powerful forces in our fates—'

'Yet you said you would bleed him tomorrow,' Katherine interrupts. Fournier's dark eyes deepen in his head.

'Very well,' he concedes, 'I shall conduct the operation tomorrow, first thing in the morning.'

He drains his cup and bangs it down for a refill.

The next morning he is gone.

'At least he didn't charge for the bloodletting,' Geoffrey says, before they discover he has taken a silver cup in lieu.

'I had a dream in the night,' Katherine tells Thomas later. 'I dreamed that it was me who cut Sir John. I cut out his fistula and as a reward he gave me his cushion. For some reason I was pleased with it.'

Thomas narrows his eyes.

'You don't mean to do it yourself? Fournier said it is a dangerous operation.'

She shakes her head.

'It is no more dangerous than any other. No more so than cutting the arrow out of Richard, and I would if I had the instruments. I feel I know it off by heart now.'

Thomas sighs.

'We should find you something else to read,' he says.

Katherine laughs, and is about to go out when Goodwife Popham comes down the stairs from Sir John's chamber. She is carrying a leather bag.

'Surgeon's gone and left his instruments,' she says.

Thomas turns to Katherine. He is staring at her, alarmed.

'It is God's will then,' he says, very quietly, and she can see he wishes it were not.

Goodwife Popham hands Katherine the bag as if it is hers by right and as she takes it, Katherine feels her chest flutter. Her whole body is trembling.

Perhaps it really is God's will?

'There is a chance Sir John will not let me do it,' she says.

'Do you really want to do it?' Thomas asks.

'I want him to be well again. I want to see him walk.'

'But to cut him?' Thomas exhales.

'When I took the arrow from Richard it was as if I had a power,' she tells him. 'As if I knew what to do. I feel the same now.'

Thomas nods, accepting her word, and together they climb the stairs and peer in through the curtains around Sir John's big bed. Richard is awake; his father sleeps; the dogs are muddy-pawed.

'He hasn't stirred all night,' Richard says. 'And now I hear Fournier has skipped off.'

Katherine nods.

'Richard,' she says. 'Do you trust me?'

'What do you mean?'

She holds out the manuscript. Richard takes it and flinches.

'Dear God,' he breathes. 'You can't mean to cut it out?'

Katherine nods. Richard turns to his father. Just then the old man twitches as if in pain, and a grimace tightens his face. Richard passes back the manuscript.

'Are you certain you can do it?' he asks. 'It is more than removing an arrow, you know? More than binding a wound like Thomas's.'

'I feel certain. I don't know why.'

Richard strokes the hair from his father's forehead.

'Leave me to think on it,' he says. 'I will give you an answer soon.'

Katherine nods and leaves then.

After breakfast she follows the others to the butts behind the church, bringing the manuscript with her. They loose their arrows, sending the shafts thumping into the earth banks at the far end of the clearing. They nock and loose, nock and loose. An hour, two hours. By the end of it Thomas is rubbing his shoulder and they are all grimy with sweat.

'Let's do it again,' Brampton John says.

'What's got into you?'

'Just the thought of twenty thousand northern bastards coming this way. I've got a wife now, you know?'

'Have you? I thought that was your ma,' Dafydd says and for once a fight doesn't break out.

Later Richard comes down to the butts. He calls them away and into the church. They leave their bows at the door and assemble in the nave.

'I've paid the priest to say Mass.'

'To what end?' Walter asks.

'Kit is going to cut open my father's fistula.'

Dafydd opens his mouth to swear but realises he is in the house of God. In the dappled light from the glass window their faces are discoloured, and Katherine feels a distance yawn between herself and the others, as if she is becoming something different, something to be feared. The curious thing is that they look to Thomas for their lead. It is as if because he is Kit's friend, he has some special insight.

'He can do it,' Thomas says with a shrug.

Mass is swiftly delivered by a priest impatient to be elsewhere, but the prayers the men send up are heartfelt. Afterwards they troop silently back through the village to the hall. The atmosphere seems to have thickened, and every movement, every gesture is charged with added significance, as before a punishment.

'Thomas,' she says. 'Will you pluck some hair from the tail of your horse? About twenty strands perhaps. As long as you can find them, good and strong and not likely to break.'

She asks Goodwife Popham for some hot wine.

'We'll need plenty of it, in a copper dish, as well as linen and candles and a flask of oil of roses. And the whites of five of your freshest eggs.'

Up in the bedchamber Sir John is awake but only just. His eyes are slots and his tongue is thick. With the treatise by her side, Katherine begins going through Fournier's instruments, picking out those she will need.

She finds the *spongia somnifera*, soaked in the anaesthetic Fournier uses to stupefy his patients. There is an inch or so left in the flask, but is that a lot? Or not very much? She will have to wait to see how powerful it is.

After a moment Goodwife Popham brings a large copper dish of steaming red wine. Thomas shuffles in behind her with the horsehair. Behind him come Dafydd and Owen, then Black John, then all the others. Only Walter remains downstairs.

'You can put the dish on the floor,' Katherine tells Goodwife Popham. 'And can you bring some blood-warm water in a ewer?

And a dish of salt. And as many candles as you have? And, Geoffrey, will you get those damned dogs out of here.'

While Geoffrey shoos the dogs, she curls the horsehair into the wine and places the instruments on them to hold them down. Then she dips the sponge into the flask. She has no idea what is in it, but the scent is heady, almost overpowering the sweet reek that rises from the sheets whenever Sir John moves. She places the sponge under his nose. He looks at her over it, his eyes like a pug's.

'Courage,' he whispers, placing a damp hand on her wrist. 'Have courage, Kit. It is God's will, and He will be at your shoulder, guiding your hand.'

She nods. Sir John's pupils swell as the fumes take effect. Then the lids come down. His breathing eases. He begins to snore.

Everyone relaxes.

'Help me roll him, will you?'

Richard and Geoffrey gently rock the old man around so that he lies face down on the side of the bed, his legs hanging over the edge with his knees among the rushes on the boards of the floor. His bulk is impressive.

'Get a cushion, will you?' Katherine says. 'One that is not too valuable. And some rags, and warm water.'

Dafydd goes off in search and comes back with them and the ewer of blood-warm water. They slide the cushion under Sir John's knees, and then swaddle them with rags. Katherine nods at Richard and he eases the bloodstained braies down past his father's thighs to reveal a pair of pink buttocks covered in a white furze. Just then he farts, a soft wheeze that ends in a rapid blurt. A splash of dark blood stains his pale calf.

'You'll have to spread his legs,' Katherine says.

Geoffrey has finished lighting candles in lamps. He looks at Richard, who swallows.

'All right,' he says. Each bends to take one of Sir John's heavy thighs and they haul them apart. She can hear the gasps of the men behind her. Between Sir John's legs, just above the flopping sack of his testicles, is a dark wound the size of a thumbnail, weeping a pink-tinged, foul-smelling discharge. Buried under the powdery skin on his buttock, she can see a ribbed, slightly nubbled filament of scar tissue.

That must be the fistula.

Sir John moans.

'Thomas,' Katherine says. 'Be ready with the sponge should he stir.'

Thomas climbs on to the bed from the other side, relieved not to have to watch.

'Arderne recommends a clyster first,' she says, talking mostly to herself. She takes the copper funnel from the dish of wine and holds it up. Under it hangs a dog-legged tube, as thick as a thumb, the end of which is punctured with numerous small holes. She fills it, lets the wine run out into the dish and then lets a thin line of the rose oil run over the funnel's end before, taking it gently in both hands, she coaxes it into Sir John's rectum.

He stiffens.

Thomas dips the sponge into the flask.

'Wait,' she says. 'Not too much. Not yet. It can't be good for him.'

Thomas nods.

'Dafydd, pour the water in will you? Steady now.'

Dafydd steps forward and pours some from the ewer into the funnel. It gurgles down the tube.

'Good,' she says. 'More.'

He pours more and water streams out on to the rushes below. She watches the dark head of the fistula bulge as if a worm were trying to escape the skin, and then the wound begins to weep a pale liquid. Small lumps of matter follow, and then uneven rivulets of bloody water dribble down his legs. When the flow slows she removes the copper and more water rushes from his anus.

Then she takes the probe. It is about eight inches long, beaded at both ends, made of fine malleable silver. She shakes the wine from it and then mutters a paternoster before she slowly screws one blunt end into the mouth of the fistula.

Again Sir John flinches and Katherine nods at Thomas. He wafts the sponge under Sir John's nose.

Katherine guides the probe along the canal of the fistula, forcing the corrupt flesh before it, feeling the soft give of rotten tissue until it meets a different sort of resistance, spongy and unyielding.

The probe has travelled perhaps three inches and she guesses it is now in Sir John's rectum. This is the thing she has been most anxious about, the actual slipping of the fingers into the anus. She dips her hand in the wine and then asks Richard to pour a few drops of oil of roses on her fingers. Then she guides them between the cleft of his spread buttocks and into the swirl of hair that marks his anus.

It is startlingly hot, almost burning hot. She nearly pulls them out. She presses on though. She slides her two fingers up to the second knuckle until she can feel the probe pressing through a hard puckering in the rectum wall. This must be the start of the fistula. Blood that is almost black oozes down between her fingers and snakes down her wrist. She puts her fingertips on the end of the probe and pushes from the other side, until something gives, and she can feel the probe's nub against her fingertips. She breathes out.

Then she takes hold of the probe and levers it down, bending it, running it against her fingers so that it pushes its way out of Sir John's anus with a gobbet of thickened blood and other corrupt matter.

Sir John mews in his sleep. Thomas twitches the sponge towards him. Katherine shakes her head. She sits back and looks at what she has done. She shudders, wishes she could give up, wishes herself elsewhere, but now she has started—

She twists a few strands of the horse's hair into a loop and wraps it around the bead at the end of the probe that remains sticking out of the fistula. Then she pinches the anus end of the probe and gently tugs it all the way through, so that it takes with it the horse's tail hair, just as if she were making a stitch in the cheek of his buttock.

She hears the men behind her leave the room one by one. The blood has drained from Richard's face and Geoffrey is green.

'No man should have to see his father like this,' Richard says.

Katherine, on her knees behind Sir John, has a far worse view.

'No man should have to see anyone like this,' she says.

The smell of disease and corruption is powerful and Katherine cannot stop herself softly gagging. She uses a rag to wipe the blood from around the old man's buttocks. His testicles are heavy, bald; the sack is like a pear, the skin whorled.

'What next, Thomas?'

Despite having read Arderne's work three or four times, she cannot remember everything.

'Knot the two ends of the ligature, and then tighten them using the tendiculum, so that you obtain a straight line between the fistula's opening and the anus.' He coughs as he finishes.

Katherine fiddles the horsehair over the brass screw on the tendiculum and attaches it to the other end. Then she winds it tight over its polished rosewood point. The hair bites into the inflamed and crusted flesh around the puckered mouth of the fistula.

She asks Geoffrey to come around and hold it still while she finds the snouted needle, about a foot long, with a groove running its length. She slips this into the hole, following the line of the horsehair. Blood and something else leak out and run on to her shoes.

'Right,' she says. 'This is it. Thomas, be ready. Richard, can you bring that sponge? And Geoffrey, hold the candle steady.'

All three nod, Richard clutching a sponge stained red with wine, thickened by rose oil and egg albumen.

'When I have made the cut,' she says, 'we must first mop the blood. We need to clean the channel as far as is possible. Then we must sit him up so that he presses down on the wound and we must wake him and feed him meat and wine.'

Sir John is still snoring. Drool stains the sheet under his mouth.

She feels in the dish of wine for the scalpel. It is bone handled, beautifully made, the sharpest thing she has ever seen. She touches it to the needle and then slides its blunt edge into the groove.

She gives Thomas a nod and then begins.

Thomas reminds her to insert the cochlea.

She stops.

The cochlea. Of course. She finds the little ivory spoon in the wine, and inserts it carefully into Sir John's anus. She turns it and then takes the snouted needle and taps it against what she hopes is the cup of the spoon. This will stop her cutting too far, cutting into the rectum.

She returns to the scalpel and nudges it towards the flesh. After a moment's hesitation, the skin splits. Blood wells into the cut. She slides the scalpel down, parting the skin and the layer of pale waxy fat below. Blood fills the cup of her hand. She can see no detail of what she is cutting.

'The sponge! Clean the blood away.'

Richard wipes it away and the wound is clear for a moment. She finishes the cut. Feels the tap of the scalpel against the cochlea. The tendiculum comes free in her hand.

'The sponge.'

Richard applies the sponge, smearing the blood. Katherine drops the needle and the scalpel back in the wine.

'Give me that,' she says and takes the sponge. She holds it against the wound, wiping away shreds of black corrupted flesh, cleaning the scar of the fistula.

She discards the old sponge and finds a fresh one to press against him.

Sir John is twisting on the bed.

'Quick,' she says. 'Sit him up.'

She holds the sponge in place as the three men roll Sir John over and sit him up. His head lolls as if he is drunk. Thomas holds him. Sir John's face is very pale and she can feel his breath on her blood-damp hand. He is wheezing, but is still alive – for the moment, at any length.

'Get his trunk,' she says. 'Put it on the bed and sit him against it.'

Richard and William lift the old chest on to the bed and set it behind Sir John.

'How did it go, do you think?' Geoffrey asks.

'The cutting was easy. Now is the hard part. To stop the bleeding and hope for no putrefaction. It is why I put all the instruments in hot wine.'

Geoffrey nods.

'And what does that do?'

It is a good question.

'I don't know,' she answers.

Geoffrey grunts.

They wrap a blanket around Sir John and put his hat on his head so that he does not catch a chill. His eyelids are blue, his pouchy cheeks chalky, each bristle catching the candlelight.

'Poor old bugger,' Geoffrey says.

Time passes. The shadows deepen. The dogs come back and are chased away. Sir John's breathing flutters. Katherine bites her lip. She can feel his heart beating and a surge of fear comes with every irregularity.

'All right,' she says. 'Roll him back.'

They carefully let him down on to his back and then turn him. She dares not peel away the sponge though she wants to. She stares at it. Though it glistens, nothing moves. She thinks the blood has stopped coming.

'All right,' she says. 'Let's get him comfortable.'

When he is lying on his front with his head canted to one side, the sheets pulled up to his ears and two blankets across his back and legs, she wipes her hands on a strip of linen.

Goodwife Popham arrives with more candles, some wine and a cut of beef, and leaves them on a sideboard while Geoffrey gathers together the blood-soaked rushes. Neither can look at Katherine.

'We'll have to watch him,' she says. 'Someone'll have to be with him all the time now. And keep that sponge handy. The pain will be bad.'

'He can stand the pain,' Richard says. He is staring down at his father with the linen bandages piled in his hands. 'He's a tough old bird.'

Katherine nods.

'Thank you for what you've done, Kit,' he says. 'You are a natural leech. You should be out making your fortune, instead of wasting your time here looking after us.'

'We'll see,' she says. 'If he can get through the next few days without putrefaction, then, well. We'll see.'

'You need a wash,' Richard says, and nods at her legs. Her hose are sodden, baggy at the knee, heavy with the enema water and blood. She peels the wool from her thigh. Then she lets it go and tries to stifle her cry.

'What is wrong?' Richard demands.

'Nothing,' she says. 'Nothing.'

She feels her face flame. The blood is not all Sir John's. Some of it is Katherine's. Her time has come to flower.

23

The days pass slowly. To begin with they take turns to sit with Sir John, wafting the soporific under his nose whenever he begins to twitch in his sleep, taking turns to lift his sheets and smell for the signs of putrefaction. On the fourth day the soporific runs out, or he becomes immune to its effects, and he begins to surface. He babbles and murmurs and flinches in his sleep like someone in the grip of a nightmare.

Goodwife Popham brings a dwale of poppy seed, hemlock and henbane, lettuce heart and the root of a mandrake plant, bound together with the bile of the pig and sweetened with wine to mask its bitterness. It is an old recipe of her mother's, she tells them, and her mother's mother before her. To get Sir John to drink it, they use the same funnel with which Katherine gave him the enema and afterwards he sleeps like a dead man.

Katherine is there all the time, sleeping and eating on the bed next to him, only leaving to seek the privacy of the privy. Each time she leaves, Richard panics and tells her that she should use the pot in the room. Each time she tells him that she has eaten or drunk something that has poisoned her guts, and she makes a joke of it.

A week later they can smell winter in the air. Martinmas has been and gone, the winter wheat is planted, the pigs slaughtered and singed, and now cold winds strip the last leaves from the trees. There are flurries of snow in the sky and skeins of geese wing south. Every face Thomas meets in the village is pinched and fearful; the winter dread is on them all.

But a month passes, and it is almost Christmas before they receive the bad news from a travelling friar.

King Henry's wife, whom the pardoner once called a she-wolf from France, is raising an army in Scotland, just as that cookshop owner in London had foreseen, and the Duke of Somerset, her most powerful ally, is back in England, having been ejected from his castle in Guisnes. After Northampton he had promised the Earl of Warwick he would never take up arms again, and yet now he is gathering his forces just across the river in Hull. The friar, a Dominican with a powerful thirst, has heard it said the Earls of Devon and Northumberland have joined him there, along with Lords Clifford and Dacre, with enough men to march on London.

'They'll come down on you like locusts on the fields of Egypt,' the friar says, drinking deep. 'They'll take everything they can, spoil what they cannot. I should be gone, were I you.'

His gaze rests on Goodwife Popham, and on Liz, until Geoffrey bundles him on his way. Afterwards Thomas and the rest of the men spend their days in the butts, enduring rain and hail and sleet, sometimes snow, sending flights of arrows whipping into the leaden skies.

'We'll never be able to stop 'em, you know,' Little John Willingham says. 'There'll be too many of 'em. Our only hope is they pass us by.'

'They won't do that,' Richard says. 'We're five miles off the road from Hull to London. Our only hope is that Warwick sends an army up north.'

'Whatever happens it won't be till spring, anyway,' Geoffrey reassures them. 'No one puts an army into the field in the winter. Hardly enough food as it is, let alone to feed ten thousand archers.'

They walk back to the hall just as the sleet starts in again.

'Never known worse weather,' one says. 'It's as if God means to flood us out.'

On the road they meet a messenger on a skinny sway-backed horse coming the other way. He has been to the hall, he tells them, with a message from Lord Fauconberg. Sir John has been ordered to take fifteen archers and ten billmen and to proceed to Sandal Castle outside Wakefield. There he will find the Duke of York and the Earl of Salisbury and he is to join with them to go north in answer to the threat posed by the army of the Queen and her magnates.

'But it is Christmas in a week,' Dafydd says. 'No one fights during Christmastide, not even the bloody Scots.'

When they reach the hall Thomas drinks a mug of ale and goes up to see Katherine. Sir John is awake, sitting on the edge of the bed, his wasted legs hanging on the floor, loose skin hanging in swags from his old bones. Katherine looks exhausted, but happy – pleased with herself, even.

'Thomas!' Sir John cries. 'Just in time to help an old man take his first steps in many a day.'

With Katherine taking his other arm they support Sir John as he walks up and down his chamber four or five times. The old man tires quickly but for the first time in years he walks with no pain. After a few moments' rest on the bed, he asks them to help him dress and take him downstairs.

'Sick of this chamber,' he says. 'Sick of the bed, sick of the view. Sick of those bloody dogs, to tell you the truth. Put me in front of the fire with some hot wine and a mutton pie and God will reward you even if I do not.'

They take him down to the hall and help him to the table in front of the fire.

'I feel a new man,' he says. 'I feel I can accomplish everything and anything. Within a week I shall be back in the saddle, I tell you. We shall ride to Sandal together.'

'So,' Richard says, placing his cup on the table and swinging his long leg over the bench. 'We have been summoned. Fauconberg wants us. Now we have to decide what we are going to do.'

Sir John looks pained, as if this is not the way he'd hoped to celebrate his return to the hall.

'Do?' he asks.

'Do while Riven remains in Warwick's favour,' Richard answers.

'I don't understand you, my boy.'

'It is only that while Riven is in Warwick's affinity, and while we are too, there's no chance of asserting our right to Cornford, is there?'

Sir John shakes his head sadly.

'It certainly looks that way,' he agrees. He glances at Thomas and Katherine standing there, and for a moment Thomas thinks he ought to excuse himself but both have spent so long with Sir John and Richard in the solar upstairs while the old man has been recovering that there doesn't seem much point. Sir John gestures for him to pour themselves a drink and sit.

'So we have two options,' Richard says. 'The first is to try to create a schism between Riven and the Earl of Warwick.'

Sir John nods.

'How might we do that?'

'It is difficult. We do not know enough about Riven's interests: where they might rub up against Warwick's. I do not think they have any neighbouring properties.'

Sir John tries to think of something. His brow creases. Eventually he shakes his head.

'I cannot think of any way at all. Warwick has shown that he will forgive anyone anything if it suits his needs.'

'The other option then is to take an arrow from Riven's bag.'

Sir John frowns.

'What do you mean? Simply go in there and steal the castle? With fifteen of us and a boy with half an ear?'

'No,' Richard says. 'We change our allegiance. We do not march to Sandal, but instead we find the Duke of Somerset. To join his affinity.'

There is silence at the table for a moment. The thought of joining Somerset is startling. Sir John is the most astonished.

'And fight for him against Warwick and the Duke of York? And old Fauconberg?'

'Yes,' Richard says. 'So long as we support Warwick in power, we support Riven's occupation of Cornford.'

Now Sir John is pink with anger.

'But I am indentured to serve my lord Fauconberg,' he tells them. 'And through him, the Earl of Warwick, or the Duke of York, or whomsoever Fauconberg pleases. God damn it, Richard! You can hardly have me change my allegiance!'

'Plenty of others have,' Richard replies, raising his voice. 'Ruthyn, for one, and Riven himself. He stood for Buckingham in the morning, by midday he was Warwick's man.'

Sir John bangs a fist on the table. A month ago the cups might have jumped but now it is no more than a dusty pat. His fury is real, however.

'Do not compare me to Riven,' he barks. 'Do not say I am like that.'

Richard sits back.

'I am only suggesting options, Father,' he says. 'I was not accusing you of being a turncoat.'

'Good,' Sir John says. 'That avenue is closed to us, d'you hear? Let there be more options, options that do not involve the sullying of the Fakenham name.'

There is a long silence. A log collapses, sending up sparks.

'What of the daughter?' Katherine asks.

They turn to her. She has proven her worth so often in the past that her counsel is taken as equal.

'Which daughter?' Richard asks.

'Lord Cornford's.'

'She is betrothed to that bastard son of Riven's, the one with the gammy eye.'

'How I pity her,' Richard says. 'Fournier says the wound will not stop weeping pus and the smell of putrefaction is strong enough to curdle sheep's milk.'

Thomas cannot help but smile. Katherine avoids catching his eye. No one says anything for a moment.

'But they are not yet married?' Katherine asks.

'No,' Sir John says, looking around for confirmation, his eyes narrowing. 'We would have heard, surely?'

'But, then,' Richard says, 'why hasn't he?'

Sir John frowns.

'I confess I have tried not to think about it since the summer,' he says. 'But it is a good question.'

'Can it be that he does not have her?' Richard asks.

'He must do, surely? He is her guardian.'

'But he only came to that post after we came from Northampton. Only five months ago. She might have slipped away in the meantime.'

Sir John nods.

'And d'you remember that story John Willingham was telling us?' Thomas ventures. 'About his mother seeing the boy on his way north? He was looking for someone. I think it might even have been a girl.'

None can recall that detail of the story.

'I thought you were telling me that Riven was moving north,' Richard says. 'But can it have been they were looking for Margaret? No. No. It is too far-fetched.'

'But all the same . . .' Sir John says.

'How old is she?' Katherine asks.

There is another silence. Richard looks at his father. Sir John is hunched forward, his elbows on the table. He cups his beard in the palm of his hand.

'I recall she was born on the Epiphany,' he says. 'I remember sending old Cornford a barrel of wine in commiseration she wasn't a boy, and then I heard the mother never recovered from the birth, and it didn't seem so funny.'

'When was that?' Richard asks.

Sir John waves a hand.

'It was the same year your mother died,' he says. 'Year of Our Lord '46.'

A long silence follows. The darkness has deepened. The yellow light of the candle makes Sir John look biblical. One of the dogs starts in its sleep.

'But that means she'll be fifteen at her next birthday,' Richard says. 'In less than a month. She's Riven's ward until then, but he's cutting it fine, don't you think? If he's going to marry them against her will?'

'It might not be against her will,' Sir John points out. 'She might have fallen for the boy.'

'But how can she if Riven doesn't even know where she is?'

'We can't be sure he doesn't.'

'It is the only explanation.'

There is another of the long pauses. They can hear Liz Popham laughing through the window in the yard where John Willingham is juggling apples for her entertainment. She's been sewing patches on Geoffrey's coat, red with green thread.

'But then if Riven doesn't know where she is,' Katherine begins. 'Who does?'

Sir John and Richard look at one another, as if realising something.

'I don't know,' Sir John says at last. 'She was at Cornford's place in Wales before he was killed, but after that?' He shrugs.

'But I was betrothed to her!' Richard goes on. 'Surely you should know where she was?'

'You *were* betrothed to her, Richard,' Sir John says, patches of colour appearing on his cheeks. 'And while you were betrothed to her, I knew where she was. Once I had been attainted and made a traitor, once I had been driven from my own house, my own estates, my own goddamned country, I had other matters on my mind, such as your welfare, the welfare of my men, the welfare of my people. Do you understand me?'

Richard lifts a hand. It is not clear if it is an apology, but it calms Sir John.

'Would Riven know of Cornford's place in Wales?' Katherine asks.

'Perhaps. The land came to Cornford through his wife, nothing but rough hill pasture, to hear him talk of it, and full of violent Welshmen stealing each other's sheep and wives and confusing the two.' Sir John laughs gently at his own joke.

'Why did she stay down there then?' Katherine goes on. 'Why did he not bring her to live at Cornford?'

'She was a sickly creature,' Sir John says. 'Something wrong with her chest and Cornford was supposed to be too cold for her. It is draughty, that castle, and the east wind comes straight off the sea.'

Richard tuts, disapproving of someone so soft, but Sir John goes on.

'Cornford never got over the death of his wife,' he says. 'Used to dote on the girl. He was like that. It was why I liked him. He was the only one who understood why I didn't send you off either, my boy, so before you start criticising, think on that.'

Richard raises his eyebrows but drops his gaze to his hands on the table.

'I only met her once,' Sir John goes on. 'When she was about five or six, I suppose. The strangest accent you ever heard. Like Dafydd and the other boy – Owen, is it? Probably had it beaten out of her by now, of course.'

Goodwife Popham comes in with an armful of logs. She drops them on the hearth, and leaves the room again.

'So she might still be in Wales?' Katherine asks.

Thomas admires the way she can stick to a matter, to follow it to its heart.

'I suppose she might,' Sir John agrees. 'Which would explain why Riven hasn't found her.'

'And she is Riven's ward only until the Epiphany?' Richard asks. 'After that she may do as she wishes?'

Sir John nods. A gleam appears in his eye.

'If my grasp of the law is correct,' he says.

'So do we pray he doesn't find her before then?' Katherine says. 'Or is there a way we make sure he doesn't?'

Sir John scratches his cheek. Richard is looking at her intently.

'Ordinarily I would place my trust in God,' Sir John starts, 'and hope for the best, but with men like Riven perhaps it is as well to look into the matter ourselves.'

'But how do we find her?' Richard asks.

An idea strikes Thomas.

'Dafydd,' he says. 'Dafydd used to serve Lord Cornford, didn't he? He told me he was at Ludford Bridge when Riven killed Cornford, and for want of anything else to do, he fell in with the next company in the line, which happened to be yours.'

There is a moment of silence.

'That's right,' Richard says, half smiling at the memory. 'I remember. Couldn't understand a word he said at first, him or his brother – still can't really, but they can both use a bow, so.'

'So get him in here, will you, Thomas?'

Thomas finds Dafydd in the barn playing dice with Owen and two of the Johns. He comes reluctantly, having been enjoying a winning streak, but is happy to be reminded of home.

'Lovely place it is,' he says, when he is given a drink and sits with them at the board. 'Always warm, as if the seawater's heated or something.'

Sir John looks at him sceptically.

'Did you serve Lord Cornford in his household?'

Dafydd scratches his head.

'Not likely,' he says. Certainly, in his sleeveless jerkin and shaggy hair, he looks too wild to be invited inside.

'D'you remember Lord Cornford's daughter?'

'Margaret? Never saw her. Heard all about her, though. Always ill, wasn't she? Gwen worked in the castle, used to have to boil her water and so on.'

'Gwen?'

'My sister.'

'Cornford had a castle in Wales?' Richard asks.

'No,' Dafydd says as if Richard is a simpleton. 'Cornford had a hall, up in the hills, didn't he? Well, it is his wife's, as a matter of fact. But whenever Cornford was away he moved his household into the castle, in Kidwelly, for safety's sake, like. Gwen worked for the Dwnns.'

Sir John is at a loss.

'What are the Dwnns?' he asks.

'The Dwnns? You don't know the Dwnns? The Dwnns live in Penallt. Well, that's their house. Old John Dwnn is constable of the castle. Proper castle, that one. Kidwelly. Towers and a drawbridge and everything.'

'And that's where Margaret Cornford would be?'

'Well, I don't know about that. She was when I left, at any rate.'

They all stare at him. Thomas almost laughs, so simple is the solution to their problem of Margaret Cornford's whereabouts.

'What?' he asks.

Sir John offers him another drink.

'So how far is this place, Kidwelly, from here?' Richard asks after a moment.

Dafydd looks into his drink for a moment, then looks up.

'I don't know,' he says.

'Well, where is it?'

'On the sea. Near Carmarthen.'

Everyone looks blank. None of them have heard of Carmarthen.

'Where's that?'

Dafydd opens his mouth to say something. He thinks, then closes it again. He looks stricken.

'Dear God,' he says to himself. 'I don't know. I don't know where it is. I don't even know how to get home.'

'It's all right, Dafydd,' Richard says. 'Someone'll know. Someone in an inn. A friar perhaps.'

Dafydd nods dumbly and gets to his feet.

'I'll just go and find Owen,' he says, and he stumbles out, leaving the hall door open. Thomas closes it and comes to sit down again.

'We can't just send those two to look for her, can we?' Sir John asks. 'Can we?'

Richard actually laughs.

'Those two? They'd never find her, and if they did, they wouldn't make it back here to tell us they had.'

'We can send Thomas and Kit with him,' Sir John suggests. 'And Walter. And maybe one or two of the others.'

'But what of the summons to Sandal?' Richard asks, still needing to be convinced.

'There will be no fighting until next year now,' Sir John assures them. 'Eastertide at the earliest. So there's no point going to Sandal until then. All we'll do is sit around in that wretched keep, freezing to death if we don't starve, waiting for the spring to come.'

'And in the company of Salisbury and York,' Richard admits.

Sir John shudders and turns to Katherine.

'Would you go to this Kidwelly?' he asks.

She is alarmed.

'If you think it would help, of course,' she says. 'But what should we do if we find her?'

It is a good question.

'It is all a matter of judgement,' Sir John says. 'If she is safe with these infamous Dwnns of Dafydd's, then leave her be, but if you think there is a danger of . . . Well, I am not sure what. Of Riven's men finding her, I suppose. If that should be the case, or she would take our help, then bring her back here. Five of you should be enough, and if you leave after Childermas you'll be back by Candlemas. Neat symmetry, that.'

And so it is agreed.

They spend the next few days preparing for the journey and on Adam and Eve Day, while Richard and Walter buy more horses from a dealer, Thomas and Katherine and the others make the journey into Lincoln to buy clothes from the tailor and fripperer, another bag of arrows, some new shoe leather. While repairs are being made to their boots, Little John Willingham takes the others to an inn to celebrate the start of Christmastide.

'We'll never see them again,' Thomas says as they part.

'I only hope they do not wag their mouths off,' Katherine says. 'Imagine if Riven discovered what we are about and where we are going?'

'He would not, surely?'

Katherine frowns and they walk on. A paradise play is being performed outside the cathedral and they stop to watch and to ask around. How to get to Carmarthen? No one has heard of Carmarthen. Where is it near? Neither knows. Wales? Wales everyone knows. That way. To the west. Eventually they find a wool merchant who knows the country around Gloucester, where he says the best wool is to be found, and which lies that way. He knows of Wales, or at least the south of the country.

'The most direct route is along the Fosse Way,' he tells them in return for a jug of ale. 'From there, you might press on down the road to Cirencester until you find the drovers' route that will take you across the country to Gloucester. Or, some leagues south of High Cross, the road fords a river. Avon it is. Might hire a boat to take you to the port at Bristol.'

Thomas thanks the man and by the time they have found Dafydd and the others it is near dark and the walk back to Marton involves numerous delays as one after the other stops to relieve himself. Little

John Willingham passes out and there is only Thomas sober enough to carry him.

When they reach the hall they find a horse waiting to be unsaddled and, within, Fournier: returned, he says, to collect the instruments he'd carelessly left when called away so suddenly on his last visit.

'And his fee, of course,' Katherine mutters.

Fournier is surprised to hear they are setting out on a journey at this time of year, but is glad to catch them before they leave.

'Because I find myself witness to something of a minor miracle,' he says from his usual place at the head of the table, a new boy behind his shoulder, a cup of hot wine in his hand. 'I find that Sir John is cured.'

He is talking loudly for show, and Thomas can see Katherine stiffen on the far side of the hall where she sits in the shadows.

'It is no miracle,' she says, leaning forward into the light.

'No? An untrained boy with no experience conducting a complex and usually fatal procedure such as that? Come now. Something must have guided your hand. What was it? The Holy Spirit?'

Fournier is sitting very still, and his boy is staring very hard at the back of his master's head. There is silence in the hall now, and every man leans in, each aware that something has been said. Richard throws a piece of bread on the table.

'What talk is this, Master Fournier?' he says.

'I only say', Fournier replies, 'that it is not possible for a mere boy to do what this one has done without some intervention. The only question that remains is whether the intervention is divine, or diabolic.'

PART FIVE

To Kidwelly Castle, Wales, January 1461

24

They leave at dawn on the day after Childermas. The sky above is a perfect scrim of pale cloud that promises snow and under their horses' hooves the earth rings hollow.

Sir John watches them go.

'We shall miss you,' he calls, and: 'We shall expect you back by Candlemas.'

By the time they are through the trees and have raised the spire of Lincoln, Katherine has lost all feeling in her fingers and toes. Dafydd rides alongside, smothered in his travelling cloak with a baggy cat-fur hat on his head. The only way of telling he is a living thing is the smudge of his breath.

'Least it's not snowing,' he says, just as the first fat wet flakes begin to swirl around them.

They ride on, passing up through the grey stone city just as the cathedral bells ring out for sext. Walter leads the way on Richard's horse, Thomas behind on his palfrey, the other three on their ponies with their rough winter coats newly grown. Each man carries his pack and his bow. Walter has a sword, Thomas his pollaxe, Dafydd and Owen a fifteen-foot spear each, Katherine a short sword in a leather scabbard, which she likes wearing. Sir John offered her a crossbow with a goat's foot winding mechanism, but she has rejected it.

'You might need it more than me,' she said, and he took it back and put it by the front door.

'Just in case,' he'd said with a laugh.

They do not talk much, not even when they find the turning on to the Fosse Way and set off down its length. Snow dusts the ridges far off to the north and west but otherwise the road runs straight and level until they reach Newark just as the gates are closing for the night. The Captain of the Watch lets them through and directs them to the Castle Inn, where there is rabbit pie and ale around the fire.

'Not much else I can serve you,' the innkeeper tells them. 'Duke of York's men took it all and paid me bugger all for the pleasure. A turd in his teeth.'

'Have they come through already?' Walter is surprised.

'About five thousand of them, heading north. Not all of them stayed here, but before that we had the Earl of Devon and his men, didn't we? It isn't Christian to be in the field this time of year.'

The next morning there is black pudding for breakfast and the unpopular parts of a pig, long pickled in brine. They linger in the warmth while Walter pays the innkeeper and then it is out into the cold. The soldiers on the Mill Gate watch them pass without a word, and beyond the landscape is softened by fog.

'We'll ride into the sea before we know it,' Dafydd complains.

'Wonder what they're doing in Marton Hall right now?' Thomas asks.

'Probably sitting on their fat arses by the fire getting through another gammon pie,' Walter suggests. 'Christ, I wish I was there. This horse is making me feel seasick, you know? Like crossing the sea. How're you feeling, Kit? Not too cold?'

It is interesting to see how Walter's tone has changed. He has become almost respectful, and she cannot decide if this change is since the operation on Sir John's fistula, or since Fournier's accusation that she was in league with the devil, and her reaction to it.

She mutters something, and huddles down into her cloak.

The odd thing is that when she'd heard Fournier accuse her of sorcery, the blood had rushed to her face and she'd been at a loss for words, but then, when the pushing and shoving started, and she found herself with a knife in her hand, it occurred to her that this was what she had been waiting for ever since the operation. Because it struck her, just as she pushed Fournier back off the bench, that she had been wondering the exact same thing herself.

Thomas had pulled her off before she'd ever really been a threat to Fournier, and she had been relieved of course. She would not have wanted to kill a man, not even Fournier, but she is sure that in attacking him she'd done the right thing. It had been an instinctive thing, a human thing. A witch would have waited, bided his time. A boy with a knife was something to which they could all relate, and it only increased their liking of her.

They reach the city of Leicester that night and find boiled mutton at the inn but the straw for the mattresses stinks as if something has lain dead on it for a week or more and the next morning they can't shake the smell from their clothes.

'Sorry about that,' the innkeeper says, but gives them no explanation.

They ride on, heading south and westwards. Jackdaws clack in the hawthorns and there is an empty gibbet at a deserted crossroads. Owen lags behind, twisting in his saddle.

'What's up with him?' Walter asks.

'Thinks someone's following us,' Dafydd announces.

'Honestly?'

Dafydd nods.

'He's normally right,' he says.

Walter glances at Katherine.

'Reckon you can keep up if we ride for it?'

She nods.

They canter along the road and then pull their horses over a ditch and in between the trunks of a clutch of trees close to the roadside. Overhead the branches knock and scrape and meltwater patters on their shoulders. They wait, leaning forward in their saddles, shivering while the horses steam.

Nothing.

'You sure, Owen?'

Owen nods fiercely.

'Not just travellers?'

He shakes his head.

They wait under the trees until the horses begin to shudder in the cold. Still nothing. After a long while Walter tuts and forces his horse back over the ditch to rejoin the road. They go on, descending a slope, but still Owen keeps turning in his saddle.

'Someone's still there,' Dafydd calls out.

'Kit,' Walter says, 'go back and have a look, will you? Welsh bastard's got me all spooked.'

She drops back to the rear, but Owen's nerves are contagious and she is frightened now, not wanting to drop too far back. She keeps up, touching the handle of the little sword. They ford one river, then another, and ride up the far bank, their horses scrabbling on the stones. Moments later she hears something and they both turn in their saddles. This time they are sure.

'There's someone there,' she calls.

'Christ,' is all Walter says.

Again they stand up in their stirrups and force the horses to gallop. Katherine's pony, cold and wet and hungry for so long, is blown. She sees a priory ahead and, beyond, a dark wood and some sour-looking yews.

'Under them,' Walter calls, gesturing. They ride harder still for a few hundred paces, past the priory, then jump from their saddles and pull the horses under the straggling spread of branches.

'Keep going,' Walter says. They push on through, weaving between the sweet-scented trunks until they are well off the road, sunk in the gloom. They hobble their horses and hurry back towards the road. Katherine leans against a rough-barked trunk and waits.

She tries to think who might be following them, and can only think of one name.

Beyond the priory is the long vista of dead straight road, deserted.

The wind soughs through the branches. One of the horses snorts and they hear some movement. Katherine peers back but can see nothing in the gloom.

'Are the horses all right?' she asks.

'Shhhh!' Walter hisses.

She turns back and peers down the road. Her eyes begin conjuring shapes that cannot possibly be and after a while she has to pinch the bridge of her nose and shake her head. Around her the others are crouching behind the trees, pale faces tense, fingers clasping and unclasping their bows. Each has an arrow nocked. Time inches on.

There is nothing. And yet. So they wait. Still nothing. In the end they give up and gather themselves together and walk back to the horses.

Katherine's pony lies on its side, its flanks unmoving. She cannot stop herself letting out a cry and running to him, but there is nothing to be done. Green-flecked drool coats his black lips and though his eyes are open they are sightless. She kneels and shakes her head. She cannot stop the tears.

'These're graveyard trees, aren't they?' Dafydd asks, looking up into the branches. 'Supposed to be poisonous to cattle, like.'

They look at the remaining horses, out on the edge of the wood, pulling at the dead grasses under the hedge, then back at Katherine's horse, lying under the yews.

She'd not even given it a name.

'Only a horse, Kit,' Walter says. 'Here, come on.' He helps her unload her pack, yanking the leather straps from under the dead weight of the horse. 'You'll go with Thomas then?' he asks. She nods, and he begins loading her pack on to the back of his saddle to spread the weight. Then they lead the four remaining horses back through the yew trees and over the ditch on to the road.

'What shall we do?' Dafydd asks. 'Can't ride all that way with five on four horses, can we? Even with Kit so skinny.'

'We'll have to do as the wool merchant suggested,' Thomas says. 'Take a boat down the river.'

'Which river?'

They look around.

'We can ask at the priory.'

But the Prior won't open the beggars' gate, and one of the brothers shouts instead that they should ride on three more leagues, through a ford and then, a little way downstream on the far bank, they will find a port.

Why had no one told her about the poisonous trees?

They ride up and over a hill and as they are coming down the far slope she hears something again. Owen stops and turns in his saddle.

This time even Walter hears it.

They all look at one another and then press on. It is getting darker, and the temperature is dropping. Whorls of ice are forming on the puddles. Katherine sits with her arms around Thomas's waist, and when no one is looking she rests her head against his back. She closes her eyes. She could sleep if every time she tried she didn't see her dead pony.

At length they find the river, marked by willow trees, and hard by the ford a small hamlet gathered around a siding in the river. Tied at both ends to a mud-slicked platform of logs are three flat-bottomed boats, the same as those that ply the Trent behind the hall in Marton, carrying God knows what where.

A man comes out from one of the cots. He is holding a rusted kindling cleaver. Behind him is a sad-eyed boy with a long stick.

'What d'you want?' he asks. His voice is cracked with fear and his eyes are perfect dark circles.

Walter dismounts.

'The Prior sent us,' he lies. 'We mean no harm. Just want to hire your boat, if she'll float.'

The man lets out a gust of relief.

'She'll float all right,' he says. 'But she might not be for hire. Depends where you want to go.'

Walter looks around for some guidance. No one knows.

'Kidwelly,' Dafydd says. 'Know where that is? Wales.'

'Wales? She's not going to get you there, is she?'

They look at one another in consternation.

'Why not?' Walter asks.

'I'll take you to Stratford,' he says, putting the cleaver aside, but not so far aside that he cannot reach it. He has an accent like Geoffrey. 'You can get a barge from there, downriver to Bristol. Or Gloucester. Last bridge on the Severn. Or first, depending on how you look it at.'

'Can we stay the night?' Katherine asks. 'Or is there an inn nearby?'

The man looks them over. What choice does he have? He gives them what little ale he has and they share some pottage with him and his boy and then they sit crammed together on the ground by the fire in his cottage, watching the smoke rise from damp logs until there's nothing left to burn. Behind them the boatman's goat and dog stare at them, the dismal flame hardly reflected in their eyes.

'You think someone's really following us?' Thomas asks in the darkness.

Walter shrugs.

'No,' he says. 'Course not. Why would they?'

But although no one knows the answer to this, they do not believe him and they sleep only fitfully that night, and in the morning there is a sour gruel flavoured by a badger's bone. The boats' ochre sails are gathered in sagging rolls on their booms and there is an ankle-deep soup of leaves and river water in the bottom of each.

'Not getting in there,' Dafydd says. 'Sink soon as you look at it, that one.'

But they force the horses up the gangplank and in with a barrage of hooves on the hull's thin boards. Ice slicks everything and the boatman gives them each a long pole with which to push against the bank or the riverbed and then he sets the sail just as the boy unhitches the aft rope and loops it in.

Katherine catches Thomas's eye, knowing what he is thinking.

'I half expect to see the giant appear,' she says.

'This time we're ready.' Thomas smiles, and he nods to where Owen sits with his bowstring nocked and a bag of arrows at his waist. The current takes them westwards. After a while Katherine sits in the bows of the boat and her thoughts turn to that evening with Fournier again.

Once Thomas had calmed her down and taken the knife from her, she had left the hall and gone to sit in the yard with Liz Popham, who was having trouble trying to decide whom she should take as a husband: Little John Willingham or John Brampton. Katherine had said nothing. She did not – still doesn't – suppose it mattered which one Liz chose, since both were so similar, but afterwards she spent an anxious night unable to sleep for fear of what Fournier might do next.

The next morning, Fournier had been up before first light. He'd collected his horse and his tools and had ridden south, pausing only by the gate to look back at her, and she had thought he was about to say something when Walter chased him away.

'Good riddance,' Walter had said.

But what had he been about to say, and where was he going? As he'd hauled himself up into his saddle and turned his horse south, he'd sent her a particular knowing look.

The only sound around them now is the dipping of the boy's paddle and the gurgle of the waters.

'Still thinks someone's there, Owen does,' Dafydd calls. 'A boat.'

'What?' Walter bellows. 'For the love of Christ!'

They gather in the stern and stare back along the river. Nothing.

'Kit?'

She can't see anything, but she trusts Owen and as one they find their boat poles to send the boat surging forward, a shunt that makes the horses stagger.

In a little while the horizon becomes dominated by the looming bulk of a bluff-walled castle, flags at every buttress, chimneys leaking coal smoke.

'Warwick Castle,' the boatman's boy tells them. They stop punting to stare up at the castle as they come under its walls, from the top of which men in helmets look down on them.

Thomas stares open-mouthed and even Walter seems impressed. But Owen is still studying the riverbanks in their wake.

'Seen anything?' Katherine asks.

He shakes his head. At Stratford the boatman will go no farther, so they pay him off and the next morning they find a larger barge, crewed by three men who will only leave their places by the fire in the hall of a riverside inn for such wages as make Walter hate them and admire them in equal parts.

'What's your hurry?' one of them asks.

'Just get on with it,' Walter tells him. They load the horses and push themselves off through the river traffic. From here the water becomes busier, with all manner of boats coming and going, sails set, men on the oars, rowing barrels and sacks and more horses up and down the river. Again Owen sits in the back with his bow across his knees. He'd have been easy to ignore if Dafydd hadn't kept glancing across at him.

'What's he got? Some kind of magic sense or something?' Walter asks.

'Never been wrong yet,' Dafydd tells them.

'But there are loads of boats following us!' Walter cries. 'Look. That one, with the patched sail. Cows on board. They can't be following us, can they? Cows. Ever think of that?'

They stop in Tewkesbury that night where they find an inn named after the bells that sound compline from the square tower of the nearby abbey. While the others settle the horses, Katherine and Thomas linger by the dock, waiting in the shadow of some willow trees. There is nothing unusual to be seen, or at least that they notice.

'I'll go upstream,' Thomas says, and is gone for so long that Katherine thinks something has happened to him. He returns in the dark, having got lost in the woods.

'I like this place,' he says.

The next morning they are up at cockcrow, loading the boat to the faint sound of plainchant from the abbey. Owen is back at the aft rail again, looking anxious.

'For all that's holy!' Walter cries. 'No one can've followed us here.'

'Why not?' Katherine asks.

Walter opens his mouth to say something harsh, but then closes it, looks aside.

'It's that Welsh bastard,' he mutters. 'He should go and sit at the front of the bloody boat; least that way we'd be able to have a kip.'

But all through the morning Walter keeps glancing back along the length of the river. At one point he frowns.

'That sail there,' he says, pointing to a green square in the distance. 'Seen it before?'

'Owen says it's been with us since Stratford,' Katherine says, but no one replies.

They are in the city of Gloucester by midday.

'Straight on down to Bris'el now,' the captain tells them.

The green-sailed ship is still with them, five or six bowshots' distance, never farther, never nearer.

Katherine is still not sure.

'Master,' she asks at last. 'Do you know most of the ships on the river? What do you make of that one?'

He stares back the boat, the winter sun catching on the bristles of his chin, as on snow.

'Seen her before,' he mutters. 'From Stratford way. Can't think what'm be doing down this way, though, 'less she's taking some men somewhere in a rush?' He looks straight at her and she turns away.

At Bristol they hug the eastern shore of the river as her two banks part, and they sail towards the setting sun until they swing into the mouth of another river and use the tide to take them up between some towering red stone cliffs. A while later they enter the reach under another battlemented castle where the dockside is filled with boats, more than they've ever seen in Boston or even Calais perhaps; some seem large enough to carry a church. The houses around them smack of the sort of wealth that only comes through the buying and selling of wool.

'Come on, come on,' the boatman calls as they unload the horses, 'don't want to be here when the tide runs out.'

Walter pays the pilot while the others stare downstream to where the green-sailed boat stands off in mid-channel before dropping her sail and diverting, as if after some discussion, to the river's far bank. Without the sail she is quickly lost in the forest of masts.

'Did you make it out?' Walter asks.

Katherine shakes her head.

'We've come too far down the river to cross now,' Walter carries on. 'We'll have to find a ship to take us to this bloody place. Christ, I hope to hell all this is worth it.'

'Just wait till you see Kidwelly,' Dafydd assures them. 'You'll never want to leave it again.'

After some enquiries with the revenue men and one of the harbour master's assistants they find a cog, a single-masted vessel, captained by a man whose accent they can hardly understand.

'He's an Easterling, or something,' Walter says. 'Or he's from somewhere, anyhow.'

The Easterling is intending to sail to Wexford, in Ireland, with a cargo of Gascony wine in barrels, and he is prepared to carry them, though he cannot manage their horses.

'Where you want go?'

Once again they explain.

'Kid Velly?'

'It's on the sea,' Dafydd keeps repeating.

'When you look at sea, does sun shine on face or on side of face, or on back?'

'Hardly ever shines,' Dafydd admits.

'Face!' Owen shouts. 'On face.'

The cog master blinks, and begins to move away as if idiocy might be contagious.

'Is good,' he admits. 'Is south coast you want.'

'You'll recognise it when you see it, won't you, Dafydd?'

Dafydd looks none too sure. They pay the Easterling a share of the fee he demands. Walter shakes his head as he counts out the coins from the purse Sir John has given him.

'We have missed tide,' the cog master announces, gesturing at the mud behind him. 'We sail tomorrow. First light.'

They sell their horses at a stable that smells of river mud. The dealer can hardly believe Thomas's horse, and has to send a boy to borrow more money so that he can cover even half of its real value. Then instead of buying provisions for the journey they pay a boatman to take them across the river where they spend until nightfall looking for the green-sailed boat, but with no luck.

The next morning the cog master and his crew meet them on the foreshore with a large supply of foodstuffs and supplies for the journey, some of which they are prepared to sell to Walter – at a price.

'A man has to make living,' the master says with a shrug. He sells them a clay pot of cooked beans, ale in a wooden barrel and a loaf of bread the size of a man's torso and twice as hard. When they've climbed aboard, each finding a nook around the wine tuns, the crew cast off and two small rowing boats tug them out into the fast-flowing channel that has swelled overnight to refill the muddy reach. Soon they are back in the Bristol Channel. Walter and Thomas join Katherine at the stern and peer back towards the harbour mouth, where the spires of the churches and the towers of the castle are hidden behind the converging cliffs of red limestone.

Between them another boat is just putting out, a green sail hoisted.

25

It is their second day at sea and the Easterlings know the storm is coming because the birds disappear.

'Bad one, I think,' the cog master says.

Then there is an argument. The mate wants to put into port, Thomas guesses, but the cog master wants to ride it out at sea. Eventually the cog master carries it, and the little boat veers out into the emptiness of the western sea, where blue-black clouds boil on the horizon.

The day darkens and the rain starts some time after noon, sharp and cold, stinging like pinpricks. The wind baffles the sail, starts humming through the ratlines, and only gets stronger until it is enough to lift ropes from the deck to stream aside horizontally. The ship ducks and rears and the crew furl the sail and cram it below the deck. The mate ties himself to the mast and shouts at the others to do the same.

Then the sky turns black and sea rises up around them. Thomas is suddenly aware how small the ship really is. It is tossed about, lifted on great scarps of green water, then let go to plummet into frothing troughs. Great slides of water thunder across her deck. Thomas clings to the mast. He prays to God for deliverance. The cog master battles to stay upright. The wine tuns float free. Something falls from the masthead and hits the mate, knocking him either dead or cold, none can tell. He remains tied to the mast, hanging with his hands by his feet, head by his knees, and is thrown back and forth until he surely must be dead.

The cog master bellows all the while: they must bail out; and so they stagger from their perches and set to with anything they can find: buckets, jugs, dishes, an old hat. One of the crew uses a mallet and lever to get the tuns back into place.

The wind rises further, shrieking in the stays, and the sea is battering the cog, breaking her to kindling. Water booms over the gunwales, shoving them aside, its level rising to froth around their knees. The cog feels heavy, unbalanced.

Thomas begins to think that this is how it will end: they will be drowned in a cog with some Easterlings off the Welsh shore, the roar of the wind in their ears and the taste of brine stopping their mouths. It would be easier to cease now, he thinks, to put aside his bucket, to say his prayers, face the truth. It is only the sight of Katherine that pushes him on. Her hair is plastered over her narrow head and her brittle little shoulders are pumping away as she scoops out the water with a wooden bowl.

On it goes, through most of the afternoon and into the evening, until at last the pitch of the wind eases. The rain hesitates, falters. Thomas looks up. Is it his imagination, but is the next wave shallower, the climb less arduous, the subsequent dive less deep, the rush of water across the deck less powerful? He seizes on the difference. Takes new heart. Digs his bucket into the churning broth and begins again. Soon they are managing to scoop more out than is coming in.

The crew give a muted cheer. They too guess the little cog has made it. They carry on bailing through the night, dipping, lifting, pouring, and by the time they stop Thomas is dizzy and his fingers are bleeding, but the cog is still afloat, and they are still alive.

They sleep all that night and the next morning breaks clear, just a bar of purple cloud across a sky the colour of a dove's breast, and a steady breeze from the southwest. There is nothing to mark the passing of the storm except a quantity of driftwood in the sea. Then there is a body, floating face down, a man in a pale coat and blue hose.

'Someone not so lucky,' is the cog master's opinion. 'Keep eye out for survivors.'

But there are none, only more wreckage, a terrified rat on a barrel bobbing in the water, and then a shred of sail. Is it green? Katherine watches it pass, frowning hard, saying nothing.

The land is a shadow on the horizon. The mate, a purple bruise the size of a duck's egg on his forehead, gets the crew to unfurl and set the sail and the cog master shouts a tired order and gives a heave on the tiller. The canvas slaps for a moment, then tautens and the cog collects herself, and turns in the dimpled green water, and they head northwards, back towards the coast.

'How far d'you think we've drifted?' Thomas asks the cog master.

The man shrugs.

'Day, maybe,' he says. 'Maybe two. We see.'

The sailors are still bailing out, but above them the seagulls are back.

'Is good sign,' the cog master says.

Thomas joins Katherine in the bows where she is letting the wind dry the woollen coat she's refused to take off. She is scanning the sea.

'Any sign of it?' he asks. He means the other ship. She pauses, and then shakes her head. She is pale in the early-morning sunlight, her skin almost transparent, her clothes stained, her hair salt-stiffened. Her cut ear is reddened by chafing against the damp wool of her hat. He wants to touch it, but doesn't. He almost laughs as he tries to imagine what she'd say if he did.

The next day the coast reveals itself as jagged green hills skirted by grey stone cliffs and stretches of ochre sand. Clouds are gathered over it and soon it starts to rain again.

'This way, I think,' the cog master says, and the cog heels to the west. They sail on, past a spit, and then turn northwards again, across a bay towards another headland.

'They call Worm's Head,' the cog master tells them, nodding at a low point as they sailed past. 'Is haunted.'

'Haunted?'

'By souls of drowned sailors.'

Dafydd and Owen are together at the gunwale, clutching each other and pointing at a bay that opens before them.

'Is?' the cog master asks.

'Home!' Dafydd shouts. 'Look! There's the house.'

He points. There is not much to be seen: a broad sweep of mud, a sandy bank, then low hills and a river emptying from the north-west. Thomas can't see any cottage. Katherine stares hard, frowning, looking at something else in the sand, but still she says nothing.

'The next bay is Kidwelly!' Dafydd says. 'Just around there.'

The cog master orders the sail reduced and they steer past the headland. Beyond is another river's mouth.

'Never seen so much bloody mud,' Walter mutters. 'It's like there are two seas: the watery one we've just been on, and now this. Look at it.'

Walter's sea of mud stretches to the horizon either side of them and all the way ahead to where the land rises in soft-topped green hillocks. Seagulls wheel overhead, calling to one another, playing in the wind, their feathers the only bright accent against the grey clouds above.

'Not much of a place?' Thomas suggests.

'A shithole,' Walter agrees.

'Wait till you see the town,' Dafydd says, but his words have taken on an ambiguous tone. They carry on through the channel in the mud. A man in the bow shouts instructions to the cog master at the tiller and Dafydd points out a low-roofed grey stone house, set among some scrub on the hills.

'Penallt,' he says. 'Where the Dwnns live.'

'Bloody Dwnns.' Walter tuts. Thomas can't help smiling at this, and seeing him, so does Walter.

The cog master puts them down on the deserted quay, a rotting wooden platform half backfilled with rubbish.

'Happy hunting,' he says, collecting the balance in coins and giving his crew the order to cast off.

After nearly four days at sea they stand on the uncertain ground and watch the cog slip back along the channel.

'Never again,' Walter says. 'I'll walk from now on. Don't care where I'm going, you'll not see me in a bloody boat ever again.'

Nevertheless they'd agreed with the cog master that he will come past on his way back from Wexford to see if they need carriage back to Bristol, but Thomas does not imagine they will see him again.

'Return journey price double,' the cog master said once he'd seen where he was dropping them. 'A man has to make living.'

It carries on raining, soft and constant, but warm – or at least not so cold.

'See?' Dafydd says. 'Told you it was hot.'

'It's odd,' Thomas agrees.

'Come on then, Dafydd,' Walter says. 'Let's see this fabled castle of yours.'

They carry what they can of their salt-stained baggage, and follow a worn path along the river's bank, around a low bluff to the church, above which they see the castle rising up on a headland. It is small, but there is something perfect about it, the way its pale walls cap the rise and lean over the valley.

'See?' Dafydd asks.

'Why's it boarded?' Walter asks. He is pointing to the castle walls, which are clapped in planks.

Dafydd looks anxious.

'I don't know, do I?'

Dafydd leads them splashing through a ford and up into the village that hunkers under the castle's walls. The houses are very low, stone built, with rough thatches, mossy and rotting in parts. Water throngs everywhere. A straw-flecked road takes them past the church up towards the castle and they meet a boy with three goats and no shoes. Dafydd greets him in a language Thomas doesn't understand and the boy returns the greeting just as if he has seen Dafydd the day before.

'That's Dafydd, that is,' Dafydd explains when he's passed on down the road. 'Dafydd the swineherd's boy. Grown a bit, hasn't he?'

Owen moos in agreement.

But there is something strange about the village. They all feel it. There is no smoke in the air, nor any of the workaday clatter they'd expect. There aren't even any chickens or pigs about. Dafydd stops and ducks under the low lintel of a cottage. Inside it is dark, no fire in its place, no swirl of smoke to sting the eye. The straw mattress is gone, too, and when he feels above the door, where the bow and its arrows might be kept on pegs, there is nothing; nor are there pots either, only a broken-handled bucket half full of something viscid.

'Where is everybody, Dafydd?'

Dafydd shrugs. Thomas unconsciously swings his pollaxe so it is nearer to hand. Walter nocks his bow and fishes out an arrow. Farther up the road a bare-legged brewster's girl is washing out a barrel in the rain. She stops when she sees them and waits with her mouth open. She's very ugly. She recognises Dafydd and Owen and they talk a moment.

Whatever she tells him, it makes Dafydd gasp.

'What is it?' Thomas asks.

'I don't believe it! Myvanwy says Jasper Tudor has raised his banner in Pembroke.'

'Jasper who?'

'Jasper Tudor,' Dafydd says. 'The Earl of bloody Pembroke. He's raised his banner and is recruiting men to march on London. She says he's waiting for an army of Irish and Frenchies to come from over the water, from Ireland. Gallowglass and Kerns, and those bastards with guns.'

'What's he want with them?' Walter barks.

'They're going to fight for King Henry.'

Walter curses.

'What about the castle?' Katherine asks.

Dafydd turns to the girl and speaks urgently.

'She says the Dwnns are holding it for the Duke of York. That's why it is boarded.'

They hurry on up through the deserted village until they stand before the castle gatehouse. The drawbridge is raised, presenting them its blank underside, and heads move in the tower and along the boarded battlements above. A moment later and one of the shutters slides open with a bang and a man's face appears.

'Name yourselves,' he shouts.

'Bloody hell,' Dafydd mutters. 'It's old Gruffydd Dwnn.'

He sidesteps behind Thomas, as if afraid to be seen, and Walter calls back:

'We've come from Lincoln,' he says. 'We are of Sir John Fakenham's household and he has sent us with letters for John Dwnn in the hope of his assistance in a matter of property.'

When Walter is trying to sound formal, he speaks as if he has only recently been taught the language. The man in the window cocks his head. Then he starts speaking Welsh and ends with what sounds like a question. After a moment Dafydd calls back. He is blushing as if he'd been caught out at something. The man in the window barks with laughter and the shutter is drawn up again. More heads appear at the battlements, curious, but they are small, and none wear helmets. Boys, girls, women, peering over. Dafydd waves up at them and shouts something.

The drawbridge comes down with a percussive rattle of heavy chains running through stone eyelets, and the planks boom against the stone bridgehead. Suddenly the air is rich with the smell of horses, damp, mud and rot.

They step on to the mossy bridge and wait while another

iron-hooped gate is opened by unseen hands. Beyond is a dark tunnel, barred by an iron portcullis, which rises to admit them with another rattle of chains. Through that a further gate stands open, its daylight portioned by the bars of yet another portcullis. While this is inching its way up into the ceiling Thomas looks up to see faces peering down at them from the murder holes above.

'Pretty tidy,' Walter admits. 'Take a hundred bombards to knock a hole in this.'

A man appears beyond the gate.

'We've no news Tudor has bombards,' he says in an up-and-down accent. 'Only an army of Irishmen. They're devils for rapine, they are, and best killed on sight, like wolves, and as for the Frenchies, well, I expect them to be more busy than bold, as usual.'

He names himself as Gruffydd Dwnn, the constable of the castle, of the affinity of Richard, Duke of York. He is wearing an old-fashioned hood, such as Thomas remembers the pardoner wearing, though this man is an old soldier, flint-hard, his nose a mess, as if he's been hit by a hammer.

He leads them out from under the gatehouse and into the castle's outer ward. Here is a clutch of rough tents and lean-tos and the air between the walls is hazy with the smoke of cooking fires. To one side the entire village's livestock compete for space behind a woven withy fence and the smell is powerful.

'So that's where everybody is,' Walter says.

As news of their arrival spreads, a hundred faces, smoke-smutted and filthy, some of them flame-red-haired, emerge to stare at them through the murk of the smoke. A brindled dog on a rope barks at them.

'Crowded,' the old man agrees with Walter's unspoken observation, 'but these walls make us too tough a nut for all but the largest army to crack. Tudor's men will pass us by in the hope of easier meat in England.'

A woman in a russet sackcloth dress and filthy coif shouts

something, and comes pushing her way through the camp, clearing a path to Dafydd and Owen, still yelling and gesticulating with powerful, heavily freckled arms. She greets Dafydd with a soft cuff and then is folded into a hug by both men.

'Is that Gwen?' Walter asks out of the corner of his mouth. 'She looks like a murderess.'

Katherine asks Dwnn if they might find a vantage point from where they can see the sea.

'Fine view of the sea from up there,' Dwnn tells her, with a sideways glance. He points her to a low doorway in the side of the gatehouse. Thomas follows her up the spiral steps past a doorway into a tapestried hall and on up.

'You don't think it can have followed us here?' Thomas asks. 'It'd be witchcraft, after that storm.'

'I don't know,' Katherine says. 'I just want to make sure.'

After another few turns they emerge out on to a stone-flagged walkway where the wind ruffles the hair of a barefoot boy in a kilt and a leather jerkin keeping watch on the sea. At the very periphery of the broad sweep of the bay, the little cog is just slipping around the headland into the mists that shroud the western horizon.

Thomas feels a twinge of sadness at their departure. He wonders if the cog master knows about Tudor and his army of Irishmen coming from across the sea. Perhaps he does? Perhaps the wine was destined for Tudor in the first place?

Of the other ship though, the one Katherine believes has followed them, there is no sign. The sea is empty, only a sweep of turbulent blue-grey water, and in the far distance, the doughy bulk of some flat-bottomed clouds bringing more rain.

'Seen any boats out to sea?' Thomas asks the boy.

The boy gabbles in his language.

'We'll need Dafydd,' Katherine says.

Thomas peers over into the ward. Dafydd is fending off questions and pats and pinches from a small group of women in rough-sewn kirtles. When Thomas calls down to him about five boys hear their names and look up. Even a dog barks.

While they wait for him to climb the stairs they study the land. The hills here are sodden, fissured with streams, covered in bracken and swathes of vivid green grass. There are stands of wind-twisted hawthorns and small black and white sheep and everything is smudged and mossy.

Dafydd arrives breathless and questions the boy in gasps. The boy confirms the impression that he has seen no ship except the Easterlings' cog.

'Says there's been a storm,' Dafydd says, glancing at them and raising one eyebrow.

'Is the girl even here, Dafydd?' Thomas asks.

'Oh, she's here all right,' Dafydd says.

'What do you mean by that?' Katherine asks.

'Nothing. Nothing. Come on. Let's go and find her.'

They find Walter two storeys below, in the tapestried hall, warming himself over a slate hearth, drinking ale with Dwnn and a bearded man who can't speak English. When Dafydd sees them, he continues down the steps, leaving them to go in together. The smoke has stained the rafters above their heads, and the tapestries, rough woollen things, are the colour of peat water. There is ale in a hooped wooden ewer on a round pewter tray and a boy pours them each a cup. Walter is tearing at some bread.

'Your man is just telling me how it is you came to fall into the company of Dafydd the Sheep-Stealer,' Dwnn begins. 'I'd heard about Cornford being killed, of course, but I'd thought he was killed in battle, not murdered.'

'One of the murderer's many sins,' Thomas says. 'And with God's grace one of his last.'

'Amen to that,' Dwnn agrees, raising his cup. 'I was fond of old Cornford. He had foreign ways of looking at things, perhaps, but we appreciated his company in these parts. In the meantime though, I have his daughter here. He entrusted her to me when he went off to serve the Duke of York last year, as was usual, though I was given to understand she is Sir John Fakenham's ward? I have to say, I expected to hear from him sooner. It has been more than a year since Cornford's death.'

'Been a bit busy,' Walter mutters.

'Well, I am glad you are here, at any rate,' Dwnn says. 'You'll take the girl with you?' There is a hopeful catch in his voice.

This was not the plan. But then: what was the plan? Thomas doesn't know.

'Is she so troublesome?' Katherine asks.

Dwnn looks caught out.

'Not troublesome, no,' he says, not quite quickly enough. 'She is easy on the eye, that I will grant, but she—' He stops.

'What is wrong with her?' Katherine presses.

Dwnn is uncomfortable.

'Her breathing,' he says quickly, alighting, even Thomas can see, on something, anything, other than the real reason. 'It is. Difficult. And. Well. She is – She has a strange temperament. You'll see. She will be beside herself with joy to see you.'

Thomas wonders why.

'Come,' Dwnn says. 'Let us go and find her. You may see for yourselves.'

They put aside their cups and troop down the stone stairs and out into the ward.

'We were not intending to take her with us, were we?' Thomas asks Walter.

'I don't know,' Walter says. 'I thought you knew?'

They both look to Katherine.

'She does not rest with you in your apartments?' Katherine is asking Dwnn. She is surprised.

'No,' Dwnn admits. 'She rests with the priest. On account of the

351

smoke of the fires, and of the villagers themselves. She has not made a point of endearing herself to them.'

They cross into the shadow of the towers that make up the inner keep. Once again there is a gate and a portcullis that can be closed, but in the inner ward there are no tents or fires, only a priest in his robes sitting on the grass hulling dried beans with a pregnant woman and a small child who is obviously his son. Dwnn ignores them and takes Walter, Thomas and Katherine through another low-lintelled door and up a twisting flight of stone steps.

Margaret Cornford stands at the far end of a long unheated solar. She is wearing a dress of indeterminate colour, cinched at her narrow waist, and a close-fitting green headdress with a castellated fringe. She does not move when she sees them, but stands there, waiting. No dust motes swirl in the slices of grey light that fall from the windows and it strikes Thomas that she has been standing still for a very long time.

'Margaret,' Dwnn announces. 'The visitors are from England. They have come from Lincoln. To see you.'

Margaret's face is spectrally pale and her eyes empty, but she is astonishingly beautiful. Thomas holds his breath. He can hardly stand to look at her and he tears his gaze away for fear of betraying himself. Walter opens his mouth to say something and then shuts it again with a dry tick. Even he removes his hat. The girl stares at them and Thomas risks another glance. Christ, she is lovely. She reminds Thomas of the representation of St Mary Magdalene painted on the rood screen in one of the chapels at the priory. She has fine curving brows, high cheekbones and wonderfully smooth, creamy skin, and her lips are plump and seem to promise something he cannot identify.

Then she speaks.

'Finally,' she says.

26

'I have had enough of this place,' she says, 'and these people.'

Margaret Cornford gestures first at the stone walls and the narrow windows with their sliding shutters, then the truckle bed in one corner, the linen sheets and rough woven blankets, the earthenware pots, the chest, the table, the tapestries. As she singles out each item she seems to expect her visitors to agree that her life has been hard. Yet here they stand in bloodstained, salt-crisp, sodden clothes, famished and exhausted.

Gruffydd Dwnn raises his eyebrows fractionally. He is obviously used to such displays of ingratitude.

'Are you strong enough to travel, Margaret?' he asks. 'It is winter, and the cold – you know?'

His tone is ambiguous: half-doubtful, half-hopeful.

'Of course I am strong enough,' she says.

But with this she begins to cough and once she's started she doesn't seem to be able to stop. The cough never catches in her throat, and after a moment her cheeks are aflame and she is hunch-backed and gasping for breath. Katherine steps towards her but Dwnn shakes his head.

Another woman – older, shorter, a nurse of some sort – bustles from a door hidden in the gloom of the far end of the room and takes her and guides her back towards the bed.

'Come,' Dwnn says, gesturing back towards the doorway through which they came. 'It's best we leave her now. These fits come on her for no reason, but they pass, and Goodwife Melchyn makes her

353

drink horses' urine – and bats' blood if she can find it – mixed with some herb or other.'

Thomas half expects to hear Katherine say something about the treatment bringing more harm than the illness, but for once she bites her tongue. She looks worried though.

They spend the night in the hall above the gatehouse, on benches gathered around the board in front of the fire. Dafydd and Owen are not asked to join them, for they have reputations, and they stay with their women out in the ward, but Thomas and Katherine and Walter eat buttery pies filled with some fishy-flavoured seabird. They eat roasted cheese, plenty of it, and drink sweet dank ale until their eyes become pouchy and Dwnn orders his servants to fetch straw for their mattresses.

Thomas shares his blanket and warmth with Katherine as usual, while Walter shares his with the bearded man who can't speak English on the other side of the covered fire. Dwnn retires to his private rooms above.

Thomas usually lets Katherine sleep nearest the fire, but tonight she does not want to and they swap.

'Kit?' he whispers.

She nudges him with a knee to show she is listening.

'Are you all right?'

He feels the straw shake as she nods. She turns over, moves her back towards him, and a moment later he can hear her steady breathing. He lies awake a while longer, his head on the pardoner's ledger, perhaps too tired to sleep, just able to hear Dwnn snoring through that mangled nose of his on the floor above. He isn't thinking of the storm or the horses, but of Katherine. He wants to put his arm around her and touch her. He wants to feel her skin under his fingertips. He cannot sleep. He can hardly breathe.

In the night he feels Katherine stiffen and he wakes instantly but doesn't move. He feels her roll across the straw and hears her getting to her feet among the rushes. Is she going to relieve herself? She crosses the room on careful feet and draws the bar on the window shutters. A band of moonlight bisects the room. A dog is barking in the distance.

What is she doing? She climbs up on to the bench and presses her face into the aperture and stays there, perfectly still, for a long few moments before climbing down again and closing the shutter.

'What is it?' he whispers when she returns to the blanket.

'It's just . . . No. Nothing,' she says, but he doesn't feel her ease before he goes back to sleep himself.

The next morning she is gone. He searches for her and finds her on the walkway in the tower, with the boy still asleep just inside the doorway, cramped into an impossible position. She is in her still-damp travel cloak, her hat pulled around her ears; long strands of hair that have escaped from its brim lash her face.

Over her shoulder the sea has turned green in the rain, and comes right up so that there is now no mud to be seen in the bay. They can hear the waves on the shore from all this way, and even the river below them is full.

She is peering westwards, shielding her eyes from the rain. When she hears him she turns, and then turns back and points. Thomas stares. Away beyond the headland to the west there is the suggestion of something, a long trail in the sky.

'What is it?' he asks.

'Smoke, I think.'

'Have you told Dwnn?'

She shakes her head.

'He is at Mass.'

Thomas rouses the boy with a vigorous shake. He babbles something, still half asleep, so Thomas takes him by the arm and points out the smoke. The boy babbles more, excitedly, and then disappears through the door. They can hear him running down the spiral steps. A moment later they see him threading his way through the outer ward, shouting something as he goes. Thomas recognises the word

Tudor. Behind him the women and children come scrambling out from under their shelters. They stare up at the tower. Thomas turns back to Katherine.

'Is it this Jasper Tudor? Has his army come ashore?'

'It must be,' she supposes.

Thomas feels nauseous. An army of men coming this way. He is not sure he can endure anything like that afternoon outside Northampton again. A moment later he hears feet on the steps and Dwnn and Walter join them.

'That's it,' Dwnn tells them. 'Tudor's ships're here, full of bloody French and Irish mercenaries. Christ! We'd best get ourselves set.'

They begin clattering back down the steps.

'I don't understand it,' Walter is saying. 'Why've they come now? It's the middle of bloody winter. Where are they going to get their fodder? Where are they going to sleep? Just doesn't make sense.'

'Tudor was always a bit like that,' Dwnn admits. 'You know his grandfather thought he was made of glass? Can you believe it? King of France, he was.'

'And because of this his son is bringing an army here to unseat the Duke of York?' Katherine asks.

Dwnn shrugs.

'Seems that way,' he says. 'No soft spot for the Duke of York, after what happened to his brother, and he can't have liked the Act of Accord, can he? His own nephew disinherited.'

Thomas shakes his head.

'But he probably hasn't ever met his own nephew,' he says. 'Why would he care so much as to – to invade his own country with foreign soldiers?'

Dwnn looks at him as if he is simple.

'If his nephew's the king, he gets given positions, doesn't he? Titles, lands, positions and that. Gets to marry his son to the richest woman in the land. If his nephew's not the king, he gets what? A kick in the balls and a push down the stairs. That's why he's here.'

Put like that, it makes perfect sense.

In the ward the women are already hard at work beating laundry in the rain, marking the passing of time with the steady thud of their beetles.

'So what now?' Katherine asks Dwnn.

'My John'll send word of the landing to the Earl of March. The Earl'll want to stop Tudor joining Somerset's army up north, I'll bet. Dear God. If those two get together, I shouldn't like to be living in London right now. A load of Scotsmen, Irishmen, Frenchmen and northerners? They'll steal everything they can't fuck and burn the rest.' Dwnn frowns at them. 'You should be gone if you want to make it back to England before midsummer,' he tells them.

'Today?' Walter asks.

'Today,' Dwnn agrees. 'Tudor's scurriers'll soon be combing the countryside looking for anything they can get their hands on. We can sell you horses and food.'

'We'd ride home?'

''Less you want to walk, or a ship docks, which I can't see happening.'

Thomas and Katherine look at one another.

'We'd best be going then,' Walter says. Katherine nods her agreement.

'I'll inform Margaret,' Dwnn says.

'Why?' Walter stops him.

'She'll want to be ready. She'll have things to pack.'

'You want us to take Margaret?'

Dwnn speaks quickly before they can change their minds.

'Of course,' he says. 'I thought that was why you were here. And it's best that way. She'll come without a servant, if you don't mind? I cannot send Goodwife Melchyn to England, not with

Tudor's men here. You'll be able to move faster that way, at any rate.'

Katherine sighs, and the men nod in reluctant agreement. A boy is sent to alert Margaret and they return to the solar to bundle up their possessions again.

'Do we even know a route home?' Thomas asks Walter.

'We'll take a guide,' Walter says. 'One of the local lads.'

'Where are Dafydd and Owen?' Katherine asks.

'They must be about,' Walter mutters. 'Probably saying their goodbyes.'

Dwnn sells them three strange-looking horses with large eyes and small heads. The best available, he says.

'What about Owen and Dafydd?'

'They can bring their own.'

They look them over in the outer yard while Margaret's pony is brought from the stables, saddled with a side-saddle that does not look to have ever been used.

'She enjoys riding,' Dwnn says, 'but it is her breathing. She seems to find it hard to be around horses.'

'Will she have a coughing fit again?' Katherine asks.

Dwnn shrugs.

'She may do, but Goodwife Melchyn has given her plenty of medicaments. She will be fine. Only——' He breaks off with a glance at the grey sky. 'Only keep her warm, won't you? Her chest, I mean. The cold seems to make it worse.'

Margaret appears in a blue riding coat, lined in quilted wool, and a hat to match. She is as beautiful as ever and Thomas can hardly stand to look at her. She presses a napkin over her nose and mouth as behind her comes Goodwife Melchyn with three heavy leather bags and a leather flask of something Thomas can only guess is horses' urine and bats' blood.

They thank Dwnn and prepare to say their goodbyes.

'So now where are Dafydd and Owen?' Thomas asks.

They are nowhere to be seen. After a search through the castle, it emerges that Gwen has disappeared too.

'Obviously don't want to leave their family,' Dwnn says, with a shrug. 'You can hardly blame them, with Tudor and his Irishmen and so on.'

'But – But they can't just not come back, can they?' Katherine asks. She can't believe it. And them not saying goodbye.

'No,' Walter says. 'No, they bloody well can't. They're indentured to Sir John Fakenham.'

Dwnn shrugs again.

'They'll have gone into the hills,' he says. 'You'll never find them now.'

But how will they live in the hills during the winter? Thomas wonders. Dwnn is evasive, can't quite hold their gaze.

'Where is their cottage?' Thomas asks. They can only have gone there.

'A few leagues,' Dwnn gestures vaguely.

'We'll not take Margaret if we can't find Dafydd and Owen,' Thomas says. 'We'll have to leave her here.'

Walter angles his head in approval. Dwnn hesitates. He needs as many men as he can get of course, but does he want to keep Margaret? The girl is glaring at him.

'All right,' he says at last. 'I'll get Little Dafydd to take you.'

This is another Dafydd, another swineherd, on a shaggy little pony with no saddle. Little Dafydd looks so very like Dwnn that Walter laughs.

'Do you lot do anything else?' he asks.

Thomas turns to Little Dafydd.

'Speak English?' he asks.

Little Dafydd nods vigorously but says nothing to prove it.

'He understands it, at any rate,' Katherine observes.

'Once you find Dafydd, you're to go east,' Dwnn explains, 'towards Monmouth. Dafydd here knows the roads and paths roundabouts, and which questions to ask when he reaches the edge of his world. It should take you three days if you ride quickly, which you must if you wish to avoid Tudor's men. Dafydd will leave you on the Monmouth road, and from Monmouth you can find your way to the river at Gloucester. Tell those you meet that Tudor is landed, but leave it to them to decide if that is good or bad news.'

They hoick themselves up into their saddles. Goodwife Melchyn and Dwnn help Margaret, who takes a moment to spread her skirts and then her cloak. She sneezes wetly and Thomas notices an exchange of glances between Goodwife Melchyn and Dwnn.

'So then farewell, Meg,' Dwnn says. 'We've had some times, haven't we? Is there anyone you'd like to bid farewell?'

'No,' the girl says from behind her linen. 'I shall be pleased to be elsewhere.'

'Right,' Dwnn says, stepping back, raising a hand and smiling weakly. 'Well, farewell then. Safe journey.'

They follow a drovers' path winding through the low hills. Black rainclouds reinforce themselves, coming in from the sea, and a kestrel dithers on the lip of a scarp. Little Dafydd is at the front on his sure-footed pony, then Walter, then Thomas, then Margaret and finally Katherine.

She finds she cannot take her eyes off the back of the girl, watching the way she moves on the saddle, the way her cloak masks her body, even the shoes she wears – red leather, slightly pointed, clean – poking from under the hem of her long skirts. They even match her riding gloves.

And the girl keeps glancing back at Katherine, as if she has divined some mystery, some difference. Katherine rips her gaze away and finds herself blushing, yet a moment later she is back, watching.

After they stop to eat – three cold pigeon pies – Thomas lets Margaret go ahead and drops back to talk to Katherine.

'What woke you in the night?' he asks.

'I was dreaming of Fournier," she says. 'He has often been on my mind since we left Marton Hall.'

Thomas snorts.

'Because he accused you of being in league with the devil? You can forget that we all saw you cut Sir John's fistula. There was no witchcraft there, only a sharp knife, a steady hand and a lot of blood.'

'It is not that,' she says, and she tries to describe the look Fournier gave her as she left Marton Hall the next morning, and why it has stuck with her.

'So what do you think he's divined?' Thomas asks. 'That you are a woman? That you are an apostate? That you have killed a woman? If so, he would have unmasked you to Sir John, there and then.'

'No,' she says. 'It was as if he'd discovered something new and had recently recognised its value.'

'Such as what?' Thomas asks.

'I thought perhaps he knew we were headed here to find Margaret.'

He turns on her.

'But—' he begins, then understands her meaning and breaks off. 'Christ,' he says. 'If he knew that, then there is only one man in the kingdom with an interest in Margaret's whereabouts.'

Katherine nods.

'Dear God,' Thomas breathes. He looks at Margaret. 'And he was riding to Riven's the morning we left.'

Katherine nods. Thomas stops his horse and turns in the saddle and studies the land all around, though what he is expecting to see she is not sure. The sea has reappeared on their right, a grey smear beyond the mossy flanks of the hills. Ahead is another inlet, another river, sand dunes and mudflats. It is the bay the cog master told them was haunted by the souls of drowned sailors. There is the long spit of rock he'd called the Worm's Head, frilled with surf where the waves break.

'But why hasn't Riven already taken her?' Thomas asks. 'If he knew where she is?'

'I've been thinking about that,' Katherine says. 'I believe he doesn't know where she is. He only knows that we know where she is.'

Thomas thinks about this.

'So it was him following us on the way down? Hoping we'd lead him to Margaret?'

Katherine nods.

'It makes sense,' she says. 'They followed us until the storm, and then . . . well, they lost us, or I suppose we lost them.'

'Or perhaps they are themselves lost?'

'Let us pray to God above.'

But still she wonders if she did not see a ship berthed on the sands in the bay Dafydd had said was home. It may have been anything, or it may have been something, she does not know, but now the boy ahead has stopped on the crest of the hill and is pointing at something and they can see the sky beyond is hazed with dark smoke.

They ride up the hill past Margaret and when they get there Walter and the boy are off their horses, crouched like hunters, peering into the valley beyond. Little Dafydd is pointing at a cottage, half hidden in a copse of poplars, smoke sifting from blackened rushes where part of the roof has burned away. In the orchard there is a man lying face down, arms outstretched, and a dog is yapping somewhere.

'God's sake,' is all Walter says.

They watch a while. Nothing moves.

The dog continues barking.

'Tudor's men?' Thomas wonders.

Little Dafydd recognises the word Tudor and nods fiercely, but Katherine wonders. Tudor's army landed far to the west, only that morning. Could they have come this far so soon?

The cottage is next to a ford where the drovers' path runs through the river. The river cuts down towards the sea but vanishes into the dimpled mudflats before it gets there. She starts and squints. Settled in the sand is a wreck of a ship, small, distant, and nearby something, a dead horse perhaps, is mobbed by birds.

She nudges Thomas and points. There is something else lying in the mud down there, attracting fewer birds. It is too far to see what it is. Beams and spars and other scraps from a ship lie scattered about, half sunk in the mud.

'Can it be the ship with green sails?' Thomas asks.

She nods.

'We should see if we can go around,' Walter is saying. 'This isn't our fight.'

'We go around?' he asks the boy loudly, pointing north and indicating walking with his fingers.

The boy shakes his head and gestures forcefully at the burning cottage. He repeats something. Over and over.

'What's he trying to say?'

Katherine suddenly feels cold.

'It's Dafydd and Owen,' she says. 'That's their home.'

27

They return to the horses. Walter and Thomas nock their bows. Katherine looses her sword.

Suddenly Walter swears.

'Damn creeping Christ!' he says. 'Damn creeping bloody Christ! Some turd's stolen them! Look! I've only got three left!'

He holds up three arrows.

Thomas has also been burgled, and is left with two.

'Damned creeping Christ,' Walter says again. 'Five. Five bloody arrows and we've got to get across half of bloody Wales and most of bloody England.'

He stuffs his arrows in his belt and then turns to Margaret.

'Wait here,' he says. 'If we don't come back, ride back to Kidwelly.'

She looks at him with undisguised disgust. He ignores her, and climbs back up on his horse.

'Come on then,' he tells Thomas and Katherine.

They get into their saddles and follow him over the hill and down through the ford. When they reach the orchard they dismount. The dead man is lying on his belly, wearing a russet jack, cheap before it'd become old, and there is a hole in the back through which protrudes the black iron head of an arrow.

'Bodkin,' Walter says, tapping it with his bow. He puts his foot under the man's torso and rolls him over. There is nothing special about him: just a man, now dead, a small scar in among his gingery whiskers, a broken arrow shaft buried in his belly. There is nothing to say who he is or what he did, other than the heft of his shoulders and tell-tale calluses on his right palm.

The dog is still yapping.

'You go that way,' Walter tells Thomas. 'Kit, you stay here.'

Walter goes to the right, Thomas the left, up towards the back of the cottage. Pale smoke floats almost listlessly from the roof. She watches Thomas sidling through the stunted apples, arrow nocked, until he stops at the willow hurdle of a goose pen. He steps back suddenly, as if he's found something at his feet, and he raises his face to the sky.

Walter has reached the door of the cottage. He pushes it open and steps back as smoke billows out around him. When it has dissipated he steps forward and shakes the frame, wondering if the rushes on the roof will fall in on him. Katherine can smell meat cooking.

A moment later and Walter is out again. He looks grim.

'Gwen,' he says, jerking his head.

Katherine approaches. Gwen is inside, on the ground, her skirts pulled up, her heavy thighs marble-white in the gloom, a pattern of blood smeared across each one, the nub of her forearm burned black in a fire still winking. Katherine gags and claps her hand to her mouth as her insides come scorching upwards.

She staggers out and vomits. When she finishes, she starts again until she is retching bile. Thomas comes back. His hands have fallen to his sides and his mouth is opening and closing silently. She forgets her own nausea.

'What's wrong?' she asks.

He gestures. Flaps a hand.

Walter goes over. Katherine follows, her footsteps slow. She does not want to see this.

In among all the shit and the feathers of the goose pen is Owen, thrown on his back, both hands clutching an arrow in his throat. The blood is diluted in the drizzle. More is pooled in the divots in the mud in the pen, in what she now sees are the prints of large bare feet.

'Oh dear God,' she breathes.

She can hardly believe it. She feels numb. Owen. She cannot stop a sob racking her. Walter puts his arm around her.

'It's all right, Girly. It's all right.'

But it's not, and his voice cracks too. Thomas stands by Owen. He is holding the broken arrow from the first dead body, inspecting its fletch.

'Ours,' he says, showing it to Walter.

'At least he got one of them,' Walter says.

Margaret appears. She has run out of patience waiting and has ridden down the hill, but she sees the body and stops before she reaches the orchard.

The dog keeps barking.

'Where's that bloody dog?' Walter asks.

'Where's Dafydd?' Katherine asks.

They look at one another and then follow the sound of the dog, coming from the hovel, around the back of the cottage. There is more wood stored here, carefully cut and stacked in neat piles: logs, faggots, pimps. Another man is lying face down in a leather coat, and then another, lying on his back, his eyes open, arms thrown back, an arrow in his chest. They can smell blood and shit.

Walter steps over them.

Thomas stops.

'Look,' he says.

The arrow sticks from a filthy white tabard and on the chest is a dark badge.

A raven.

She sees Thomas's shoulders sag as he breathes out.

'He's here,' he says.

She nods. She feels cold. Fear grips her.

The dog yips.

Ahead Walter swears.

The dog, a fox terrier pup, is tied to an upright pole and just beyond its reach, in the shadows around the back of the hovel, under the hawthorn where the washing might dry should the sun ever shine, is Dafydd. They recognise his boots, salt-stained, a hole in the sole, and his hose, stitched at the knee after the fight in Kent. He is lying on his back in the dung and the wood chips.

His eyes are shut, the lids folded inwards over empty sockets.

'It is him,' Thomas says. 'That giant. He is here.'

Katherine can only nod. Then she turns and looks down towards the sea where the mud and sand of the beach are only just visible through the twisting valley bluffs. Riven and that giant and the rest of them would have come up here, she thinks, once they'd come ashore. She wonders how many survived the storm? Five? Ten? Twenty? She wonders about their tracks. Surely they'd have left some? She thinks to go down to the sand to see.

'We've no time to bury them,' Walter mutters. 'Take whatever we can use and let's go.'

'We can't leave them here like this,' she says, gesturing.

Walter looks at her.

'If these bastards followed us from Lincoln, then they'll be back here by this evening. How far d'you think we're going to get with the girl here?' He jerks his thumb in Margaret's direction.

'Margaret,' Katherine says, and turns and runs. She is back in front of the cottage in a moment. Thomas's footsteps come pounding after her, then Walter's.

'Margaret!' she calls.

And Margaret peers loftily at her from the clearing before the orchard.

'Yes?'

'Thank God.'

They stop and look foolishly at one another.

'Kit,' Walter says. 'You keep an eye on her.'

She nods.

'But at least put them together,' she says. 'They'd've wanted that.'

Walter grunts in irritation, but Thomas leads the way and they carry the bodies from where they lie and place them together under an apple tree. Then they fetch Gwen from the cottage, Thomas gagging as he goes, and they lay her beside Owen and cover her with a straw mattress, the only thing they can find to do the job, and then they kneel and say the prayers over their bodies, though the smell from Gwen is so bad.

Afterwards they mount up and ride out in silence, following the path as it rises into the hills. Katherine cannot help but stare back over her shoulder, looking for that giant. Thomas does the same and their gazes meet and both nod in understanding.

In a little while the rain starts again. They turn inland, following a valley where dark water froths over a series of rocky falls. Ahead are more hills, barren flanks rising into the clouds, and already the ponies are blowing hard. At one point the boy turns and studies the sky behind them. It is coming on to the evening, and the temperature is dropping.

He says something.

'What did he say?'

'Snow,' Margaret translates. 'He says it'll snow on the high ground tonight.'

'All we need,' Walter mutters.

Katherine is surprised Margaret understands the language. Hadn't Dwnn said she had made no effort to do so?

'We'll have to find some shelter,' Thomas says. It is all they ever seem to be doing, Katherine thinks, finding shelter from something or someone.

'Let's press on,' Walter says. 'More space between us and those bastards the better.'

A while later they join a road with the grass grown high on the berm between the cart tracks. A little farther on, there is smoke in the air and they find a bridge over the river's fast-running black waters and, beyond, a large village with an inn. They stable their horses and gather around the fire for thin rabbit soup and more baked cheese. There isn't much straw in the mattresses but in any case Katherine would not have slept much. She lies listening out for Riven's men, hearing nothing but Margaret coughing.

It snows in the night just as the boy Dafydd said it would and in the morning the hills are capped white and there is ice on the water in the well. More cheese and they set off wrapped around in their travel cloaks, all except the boy, who has nothing, not even shoes.

'Can't even look at him, he makes me feel so cold,' Walter admits.

After a while Thomas can stand it no longer, and they stop and open Margaret's bag to find the boy something warmer. There is a quantity of dresses, shirts, a coif, some documents, gold coins in a blue leather purse, rosary beads, a pair of oak pattens with leather points, as well as fine-spun wool hose, linen underthings, a woollen jacket, and underneath it all a Book of Hours, probably worth more than everything else put together. They give the woollen jacket to Little Dafydd, and Margaret says nothing but shrugs and ignores his thanks.

They ride all day until in the afternoon when they come to a town dominated by its castle. The boy says something and Margaret translates.

'Says this is Castell Nedd,' she tells them. 'He says it is best we stay here tonight, and in the morning take the road north.'

The inn has a stock pond, and they eat fish soup and bread and yet more roasted cheese and despite the brackish ale no one says much. The innkeeper has heard of Tudor's landing, but knows nothing of Riven's party. Katherine sits by the fire watching the steam rise from her clothes and now she misses the solid presence of Owen, the constant jabber of Dafydd.

That night Margaret sleeps on her back, breathing reedily and coughing in her sleep, and Katherine can't sleep because of it. At length Thomas places an arm around her shoulders to calm her, and it is still there the next morning when they wake before dawn.

'More bloody snow,' Walter says.

Outside the snow is a hard crust and as they move off a woman shouts something from the doorway of her house.

'She says we're wrong to be taking this road,' Margaret tells them through her wheezing. 'She says there's bad weather on the way.'

But there seems to be nothing they can do. They ride on out of the village, under the church where the doors are closed and the bell is silent and through the gatehouse beyond which the river flows swiftly under a wooden bridge. Plates of frosted ice spin on its surface.

All that morning they ride north with the river at their side, the snow on their backs. The road gets worse the farther they go, rising into the hills. Bushes grow undisturbed in the middle of the track now, and sections seem to have slipped into the river below. The valley sides rise up around them. It gets steeper and they pass waterfalls where brown water churns in peat-coloured pools and mist rises into the air. Icicles hang from the rocks.

'How much farther, Margaret?' Katherine asks.

'Why do you imagine that I should I know?'

'Ask the boy.'

She does so.

'He says we ought to reach a place he calls Merthyr tonight,' Margaret tells them. 'He says he's only been this way before, once, with my father when he was going to Ludlow, that last time.'

There is silence and after a while they stop for bread in a village and buy warm cheese from a woman who'll only part with it for two of Walter's coins.

'Daylight bloody robbery,' Walter mutters, but he pays because they will collapse without it. They feed the horses and then mount up again. It is too cold to linger.

As they are riding out, with the promise of only a few leagues before they stop for the night, Katherine looks back. Her gaze travels from the village where snow lies thick on the thatch, and all the way along the valley side, back along the dark thread of the road down which they've travelled.

The horsemen, when she sees them, are obvious enough. They

aren't trying to hide. They are riding fast, flashing through the trees, racing to catch them.

'Look!' she cries. 'Thomas!'

Thomas whips around. Walter too.

'Can you see him? Is he there?' Thomas asks.

They are still too far away to know.

'I don't know.'

'How many?'

'Five? Ten?'

The pollaxe is already in Thomas's hands.

'Not here,' Walter says. 'There'll be a better place up there.'

He points ahead to a couple of cottages on the side of the road. Behind them is the suggestion of a path cutting up into the wooded hills behind. They turn and ride hard. Even Margaret jabs her heels and her horse starts a trot. They ride until they reach the cottages and then find the cut through to the trees behind them. It is another drovers' path, though this one is paved here and there with larger stones as if it might have been one of the old Roman roads. The boy burbles something.

'This path leads up to something he is calling Sarn Helen,' Margaret reports. 'He says it takes you to Brecon, but it goes through the hills, which he fears on account of the weather.'

'We'll worry about the weather later. Is Brecon good?'

Margaret talks to the boy and tells them that Brecon is one way to England.

'Come on then,' Walter says. He forces his horse through a ford. They all follow and ride up into the trees, tall, silver-barked, with pale leaf mould on the ground and snow whispering through the naked branches above. They follow the path as it cuts across the slope and then doubles back again.

'Here,' Walter says, getting off his horse where the path turns. It is narrow here, cinched by tall earth banks. Walter steps aside to let them pass.

Thomas gets off his horse.

'Give me your arrows, Walter,' he says.

Walter turns to him, his face oddly placid.

'No,' he says, in a voice to match. 'You give me yours. I'll stay. You two go. You take the girl, understand? It's her he wants dead, isn't it? You saw what they did to Dafydd's Gwen – can you imagine what they'll do to her? So whatever happens, she has to live. Understand? Otherwise, all this is a waste, isn't it?' He gestures vaguely to take in everything.

'No, Walter,' Thomas argues. 'You always say it yourself. This isn't your fight.'

'And it's yours? A couple of servants from Lincoln?'

'We were never servants,' Katherine tells him. She's dismounted and walks up to where they are talking. She feels her lack of size now, standing downhill from them, but she knows the time has come. Both are looking at her. Walter frowns, curls his lip.

'What were you then?' he asks.

'We were ecclesiastics,' she says. 'Thomas is a canon of the Order of St Gilbert.'

Walter swings his doubting gaze on to Thomas. Thomas looks for a moment as if he might try to deny it.

'And I', she goes on, 'was a sister of the same.'

She hadn't meant to tell Walter this way, on a hillside in the snow, with Riven's men in the valley below, but once the words are out of her mouth she is glad. This is no time for dishonesty. Walter's eyes are on her now.

'You were a sister?' he says. 'A nun?'

He cannot believe it. She can see Thomas squeezing his eyes shut.

'I was,' she says.

She lets Walter look at her body.

'I'm sorry,' she says. 'It was . . . easier.'

Walter takes a pace away and then returns. He's pushed his hat back and twists a clump of his forelock in his fist.

'Can't bloody believe it,' he says. 'All this bloody time. Girly! Girly? Ha!'

'I'm sorry, Walter. I didn't want to lie to you, but once it started . . .'

Walter nods, collecting himself, trying to make sense of it all.

'All right,' he says, nodding. 'All right. So you're a girl. A nun. How did you come to be on a bloody boat dressed as a boy, then, surrounded by all those dead blokes?'

'It is a long story,' Thomas begins, meaning that he does not want to tell it. But Walter deserves more than that, and Katherine tells him how she came to leave the priory.

Walter grunts.

'I knew there was something about you. About you two. But bloody hell. A girl. All that time. Holy Christ.'

'I'm sorry,' Thomas says. 'I'll stay, if you like. If that makes a difference.'

Walter looks at him blankly. He is thinking hard. Then he pats Thomas on the shoulder. Tears ring his eyes.

'No. No. It doesn't make a difference. Or, yes, it does. It makes a big difference. It means that I'll stay. You go.' He turns to Katherine. He drops his gaze. 'Sorry,' he says. 'You know. For the things I said. All the times . . .?'

'There's nothing to be sorry about, Walter,' she says, though her throat is tight and she can hardly speak. 'It's me. I should be sorry. I am sorry. All the things you've done for us.'

Walter looks up sharply.

'Us?' he says. 'So you're—?'

But before either can answer, the boy shouts something from up below.

'They're coming,' Margaret translates. 'They're still on the road, but they've found the tracks.'

Walter jumps back down into the path again.

'All right,' he says. 'Go. Get on your horses and go.'

'No,' Thomas insists. 'It isn't your fight.'

Walter shakes his head.

'Course it's my fight,' he says. 'You seen what they did to Dafydd? I'll stay here, hold them as long as I can while you get ahead with the girl. The girls. And the boy. I'll have surprise and the hillside on my side and, with a bit of luck, I'll kill them all. Five arrows. Five men. Then we'll see.'

'And what if you don't kill them all?' Katherine asks.

'You ever known me not to kill them all?' he asks. It is an act. She knows this. He is being Walter the old soldier.

Now she can feel the tears brim in her eyes.

'Walter,' she says, stepping towards him.

'Stop there!' Walter says, backing off. 'Go on. Get away. A monk and a nun. Creeping bloody Christ.'

The boy shouts again.

'They've found the tracks,' Margaret intones.

'Right,' Walter says. 'Go as fast as you can. Find somewhere to shelter tonight and I'll catch you up. Make some kind of signal. An owl. What about that? A couple of hoots, you know it's me.'

They all know he'll never make those hoots.

Thomas nods. There are tears in his eyes too.

'Go on now. Go on. Fuck off,' Walter says.

'Wait,' Thomas says. 'Take this.'

He hands Walter his pollaxe.

Walter looks at it.

'You sure?'

'It's a lend, isn't it?' Thomas says.

Walter barks a laugh.

'Might come in handy. Now, go! And good luck!'

When they look back, Walter is kneeling, applying the sign of the cross and bending to kiss the ground.

28

Little Dafydd leads them straight up the track, one long scour through the forest, wider than the drovers' path but cramped on both sides with blackthorn bushes and straying field maples. Thomas rides as fast as he dares – he owes that to Walter – but the sure-footed cob is nervy, sensing the atmosphere, and nearly goes down just as Thomas is turning to look over his shoulder. He hears the scrape and clash of weapons below. A scream perhaps. Or maybe just a crow.

He puts his head down and they ride on.

Later, he pulls his horse aside where the track bulges and he lets Katherine and Margaret pass. Margaret's face is clenched and she is racked with another coughing fit. Her breathing makes the sound of a saw in oak. Katherine does not look at him. They ride up on up the hill for a league. They ride in silence and all the while he knows he should have stayed and fought the giant.

Later Margaret stops them and has to take a draught of the medicament. She shudders. Thomas looks at Katherine.

'What is it?' he asks. 'What is wrong with her?'

'I don't know,' she says, 'but whatever it is, the horse urine does no good.'

They ride on. The path flattens, dips into a hollow where there are traces of some workings, a mine perhaps, and a stand of fir trees. They ought to stop, he thinks. They might even risk a fire. Get the girl warm. Beyond the hollow, the track rises steadily. Katherine pauses in the copse, perhaps thinking the same thing. But it is too soon. They have not ridden far enough yet.

'We go on?' Thomas asks the boy, pointing up the hill.

Little Dafydd looks anxious. His gaze strays to Margaret, whose cough has not caught, but goes round and round, a constant churn. Katherine looks at her too, then back down the hill.

'What do you think?' he asks.

'We should go on,' she says. 'We have not gone far enough.'

Thomas nods, and turns his horse and uses his heels to set it trudging up the hill. The others begin to follow. The wind strengthens, and the snow stings their eyes. It gathers and hardens in the folds of their cloaks. They lean into the wind and the slope and press on until night is about to overtake them and they can stand it no more.

'We can't go on!' Katherine shouts over the wind. 'It is too dark.'

'But we can't stay here! There's nowhere to shelter. If we get over the top, there'll be somewhere on the other side.'

They carry on, heads buried against the wind. The road continues on up.

'Thomas,' Katherine is shouting again. 'Thomas! What's that?'

She is pointing ahead, on the left where a dark shape looms out of the snow. Thomas reaches for his pollaxe but remembers it's gone. Little Dafydd starts saying something and pointing. The shape doesn't move and they ride on towards it, watching it grow larger through the snow.

'A stone,' Thomas says at last.

'Is there shelter?' Katherine calls.

Margaret is really bad now, her breathing a constant haul. Its noise mixes with the wind.

'We'll have to,' Thomas says.

He dismounts and pulls his horse off the track and up towards the stone. It is a thick slab of grey rock, twice the size of a man and almost as wide as it is tall, placed on its end by who knew what forces? Instinctively the horses huddle behind it, sheltering from the wind, nose to tail.

'We'll have to get Margaret up against it,' Katherine shouts. 'Where there is most shelter.'

Thomas helps Margaret from her saddle. She is rigid and light in his arms, like a strung bow, he thinks, but too hot to the touch and her breathing is a jerking scrape that makes him want to cough himself. He carries her to the side of the rock where Little Dafydd is scraping away the snow with his bare feet. Thomas sits her down, her back to the gritty surface. Her head rocks back and she gasps for breath.

'Dafydd,' he says and points Little Dafydd to the spot next to her. Little Dafydd cautiously sits down next to her, but she is too far gone to care for station or manners and she slumps against him. For a moment the coughing stops and it seems she will be comfortable. Then it starts again.

'We need a fire,' Katherine says.

He is doubtful.

'Can we risk it? What if . . .?'

Neither wants to think about what might have happened down in the woods. It is better to concentrate on getting away.

Thomas rummages in his bag for his flint and steel and the little bag of baked linen for kindling. He looks around for anything he might get burning. There is nothing. Even in the shelter of the great stone the wind tugs at his clothes. Katherine pulls out her extra clothes from her own bag and lays them over Margaret and Little Dafydd. Dafydd looks over her shoulder at Thomas. His eyes are large, and Thomas suddenly wonders if any of them will live through this.

They must have a fire.

He has the ledger. He opens the bag and is about to rip out the pages, all those names, all those dates and moneys paid out, all up in smoke. Would it matter? But Katherine leans forward and takes his wrist. She shakes her head.

'Not that,' she says. 'What about the book in Margaret's bag?'

He is relieved. He packs the ledger away and picks out Margaret's

Book of Hours instead. He knows that it is good by its binding and the quality of the paper, and he fears to burn what might be a work of some beauty. But what choice is there? He closes his eyes as he rips out the pages, one, two, three at a time, tearing them from their stitches and pressing them into balls. He strikes the steel and the flint and after a moment the linen catches. He lets the flame grow, and then builds it a shelter from the balls of paper.

'Keep it going,' he tells Katherine, passing her the book. The others huddle forward, spread their shaking hands over the tremulous heat. Thomas brings Margaret's pattens, then his bow, useless without arrows, then he tears up some thick-rooted snarls of heather, beating them on the ground to knock the snow off. There is a small twisted tree he hacks at with his sword and brings back to feed into the flames. It will not last the night but it will have to do.

They huddle together under a tent of their clothes until one by one they fall asleep, last of all Thomas, his back against the stone, his legs stretched to the fire in front of him, Katherine's back against his chest, her head against his shoulder. He presses his nose into the top of her cap, breathing in the mix of smoke, wool, dirt and that other distinguishable trace that is uniquely hers.

He shifts, so that she rests more fully against him, and he places an arm around her that, after a moment, she grips across her chest. He can feel her breathing and is conscious that his fingertips rest on her inner thigh. He cannot resist and he slowly strokes the worn wool of her hose, not intending anything other than intimacy, or perhaps, from somewhere deep within himself, to test how far he may presume on her. It is what he needs, he tells himself, after leaving Walter to die.

It is a moment before he realises that her breathing has changed and that she is holding her breath. Then she says something, perhaps in her sleep, and she shifts her legs so that his hand falls away, but she rests her head against his chest, and after a moment his own heartbeat slows and soon he too is asleep.

He wakes in the night to silence and registers that the fire is dead and that the wind has dropped and there are stars scattered thick above them. He can't hear the stream any more and it takes a moment before he realises it has frozen.

It is only later, near dawn, that he misses Margaret coughing.

For a moment he is glad, imagines she must be over it, but then in the pale light of dawn, when they come to wake her, she will not move and she is stiff and her face is blue. Snowflakes have melted on her eyelids and then frozen again.

Katherine bends over the girl's bent body and after a moment she looks up at him. He sees tears in her eyes and down her grubby cheeks. Thomas feels sick with guilt. In the night he had been thinking only of himself and Katherine, of himself with Katherine, and he had let the fire die. He had not checked on her. He had heard her silence and was himself comfortable and warm and had done nothing and all the while . . .

'I am so sorry,' he says. 'It is my fault. I should have . . . I don't know.'

'No,' Katherine tells him. 'I did it. You said we should stay in the valley down there. I said let us ride. Oh God, forgive me.'

She begins gathering all their clothes, shaking the snow off them, and he hears her sob. Little Dafydd looks on with no expression.

'There is a pit down there,' Thomas says, nodding towards the river. 'We can bury her there.'

He leaves Katherine to strip Margaret's body. She leaves her in her linen shift and they carry her, sublimely beautiful now she is released from the coughing, down to some workings which Little Dafydd has cleared of snow. They lay her down and after a moment the stiffness seems to leave her body, and she subsides, and even looks at peace. While Katherine and Little Dafydd fetch bracken, more heather, grasses, anything they can pull up, Thomas takes the first page of the pardoner's ledger, and his ink, and he cuts a frozen reed from the frozen river's bed, and he fashions a pen. Then he writes: *Here lie the mortal remains of Lady Margaret Cornford, only issue of the late Lord Cornford, who died on this day, right beloved of God and of all those who knew her. May she rest in peace.*

Then he places the piece of paper on a stone and then places another stone on top to make a simple marker. They cover her body as best they can and they kneel by her graveside and Thomas says a prayer, asking the Lord to look down favourably upon his hand-maid Margaret, to forgive her any sins she may have committed, and for the saints and martyrs to receive her in heaven and guide her to Jerusalem. Tears shimmer on Katherine's cheeks, and she wipes her nose with her sleeve. She is shaking and Thomas has to help her stand and come away from the graveside.

Afterwards Katherine offers Margaret's cloak to Little Dafydd, but he will not take it. They load the horses in silence and then turn their backs on the stone and walk back to the track. There is almost no wind now, and the sky above is very pale. The snow has obscured all trace of their arrival, and ahead the road rises to the two peaks.

When they reach the track Little Dafydd says something.

'I think he wants to leave us here,' Katherine says.

'You can hardly blame him,' Thomas agrees.

They try to give him Margaret's horse but he will not take it, not with the side-saddle, so they give him Katherine's horse, which is the one he wants anyway. Then they say goodbye as best they can and they watch him retrace their steps down the track, hurrying away from the great slab of stone and down over the snowfields, back towards the town he'd called Castel Nedd.

'Whatever will he tell Dwnn?' Thomas wonders.

They are left just the two of them, with two hungry horses, but no bow, no companions and no idea what to do next except follow the road over the hills towards England.

They turn and walk north, up the slope to the crest, where the wind picks up. On the other side the land drops steeply into a valley. The path follows it down, bent like scissor handles, until it straightens out to run alongside a dark line in the snow that must be a river.

'Come on,' Thomas says and they set off down through the snow, still walking as the horses pick their way down behind them. They reach the river, frozen over in parts, rushing in others, and they follow it eastwards, travelling all that day. Katherine rides side-saddle on Margaret's horse, and finds she likes it.

'You look proper, up there,' Thomas observes. 'Well, you would if you were in a dress.'

Katherine does not say anything. She has not said a word since the morning. All around, the land is deserted. They do not even see a sheep until towards late afternoon when it is getting dark and they make out a smudge of smoke above a pair of cottages in the distance. Then there are more houses, and next a small town. They stop at the first cottage and an old man agrees to sell them bread and when Thomas makes the mistake of letting him see the weight of Margaret's purse, his old eyes deepen in his head. He invites them to sit by his fire and they tear at the bread with filthy hands while the man's wife fetches ale.

While they sit, another man joins them, and then another. Neither speaks. They just stare. The atmosphere deepens. Thomas can imagine how this will end.

'Ought to see to the horses, Kit,' he says, standing suddenly, hauling her to her feet before the three men can gather themselves. They hurry outside and haul themselves up into their saddles just as two more men come running.

They ride hard, following the path alongside a river brimming in its banks until they join a proper road. It takes them through some roughly marked furlongs and stone pens where sheep bleat in the settling gloom. The horses are tired though, and cannot run for long. When the road fords the river, Thomas reins in.

'Christ,' he says.

They stare at the river's roiling black surface. Across it they can

381

hear the bells in the town ringing for compline. Thomas turns. Along the road are five Welshmen.

'If I had my bow,' Thomas says, 'even with just those five arrows I could stop this.'

He sees another man join them with a bow and an arrow already nocked. He watches him draw and for a moment cannot believe it. The arrow hums past, its fletch buzzing where it has not been properly set. It disappears into the water beyond with a loud plock.

'Quick,' he says, and he hauls the reins of his horse around and down the cobbles into the river. The water is numbingly cold, deep and fast-flowing. He feels his horse lose purchase on the stones of the riverbed before it starts to swim.

'Come!' he calls to Katherine. Katherine kicks her pony down the bank into the icy current.

Thomas is across quickly, his boots full and his hose wet. The horse exhales loudly, shuddering. He looks back for Katherine. Her pony is struggling to swim, but makes it to the other side, only to stumble as it climbs the riverbank.

'Katherine!'

She falls and is under the water and he thinks she has been hit by an arrow. But no, she clings with both hands to the reins and the pony ploughs on and she is dragged out. Water pours from her and she loses her hat. Her pony scrabbles up the bank on slipping hooves. Thomas leaps down to help her. Over the other side of the river the Welshmen are still coming.

'Quick,' Thomas breathes. He bundles her upright and they turn and run, ducking through the trees towards the town, leading the horses behind them. An arrow skips in the mud behind them, but it is a parting shot, and soon they are weaving their way among the hurdles and pens where geese hiss at them in the gloom. If they can only now find an inn in the town, they'll be safe.

They find one below the castle motte, with a stable lad the innkeeper has to wake with a kick, and the promise of ale to go with a stew of pork and beans and more roasted cheese. The innkeeper speaks English and they tell him how they've been attacked on the road.

'Like that everywhere these days, isn't it,' he says without much concern. 'Everyone's taking advantage of it.'

'Taking advantage of what?' Katherine asks. Her voice is oddly slurred.

'Tudor's coming, did you know? Coming this way with an army of French and Irishmen, and the men of Pembroke of course. Strong arms they've got on them. They're on their way to meet the Queen's army somewhere up north, aren't they? Ha! I fancy they'll knock old Warwick and March and whatever's left of the rest of them back into the sea for good this time.'

He is about to say more, but notices Katherine shivering.

'Like a greyhound, aren't you, hey? You want to get out of those clothes, you do, lad.'

Katherine sits on Margaret's bag, holding her hands over the slowly resuscitating coal fire in the middle of the hall. The innkeeper steps behind the screen and begins shouting at someone in his own language. Thomas meanwhile begins rummaging through Katherine's bag. There is a stained white shirt, a pair of braies, a length of cloth, two old-fashioned woollen hoods and a leather strap, but it has been so cold she's been wearing everything else she owns, and now all that is sodden, clinging to her.

Thomas's eye falls on Margaret's bag. In it are the blue cloak, those dresses, the linen underthings, the fine-gauge hose. A thought strikes him.

'Kit,' he says, half from habit now, even though they are alone. 'You'll have to become a girl again.'

She looks at him and he sees her eyes are bright and feverish.

Dear God, he thinks, she cannot die on me too. Not Katherine. Not her.

'Come on,' he says, and he takes her by the hand and leads her to a corner of the hall where the fire is yet to cast much light, and he begins taking off her clothes. She starts to struggle, pulling away from him, but he is too strong, she too weak.

'Come on, Kit,' he murmurs. 'Come on. It's all right. It is just me. It's Thomas. I'm helping you. You have to get out of these wet clothes. We have to get you dry. Come on.'

He coaxes her out of her wet jack, her woollen pilch, her rosary, Alice's rosary, her linen shirt. Her breasts are no bigger than knee-caps, and she is so thin he could have played a tune on her ribs, but dear God! What is this?

All over her back is a fretwork of tiny scars from her shoulder to the hollows above her waist. He stares at it, horrified, then rubs the thickened skin gently with the dry cloth, trying to work some life back into flesh as pallid as goose fat. Next he rummages in Margaret's bags and finds a shift of thick linen. He spreads it out and pulls it over her head. It falls to her knees. Then he bends and yanks off her hose and her braies, which gather in rolls around her sodden boots. He lifts one skinny shank and hoicks the roll of cloth down around her ankle, removing the boot with a sucking sound and the smell of river water. Then the other boot.

Katherine stands half comprehending, half helpful, mute. He finds a pair of braies in Margaret's bag and lays them on the floor for Katherine to step into. When she's done so, he pulls them up and ties them as best he can under the linen shift.

He rubs his chin. What next? He rummages in the bag, his blunt fingers among the fine-spun wool. A coif. He places it over her head, then rolls back the seams in imitation of women he's seen. He finds a heavy linen kirtle, dull brown, that he drops over her head and laces up at the front. He ties off the strings just above her breast and then steps back. The effect is eerie, but not yet right. She still looks half dressed. What is missing? A proper dress. He finds the pale blue one Margaret had been wearing the day they first saw her, slips it over Katherine's head, pulls it down and then thrusts her arms into the narrow sleeves.

All the while he talks to her, his voice low and reassuring. She sways when he is not holding her, but otherwise cooperates willingly enough. He wonders if it is the effect of the cold. He's never known her so biddable.

He finds a long leather belt in Margaret's bag and wraps it twice around Katherine's waist. Then he finds a hood with a long tail that he places over her head and tucks into the belt. All that remains are the hose and the shoes, which have never been worn outside, let alone seen mud. He bends and picks up Katherine's foot and slips a leg of hose up over her calf. It reaches mid-thigh and hangs loose and there does not seem any way to stop it falling straight back down around her ankle again. It will have to do. He does the same with the other one, and then slips her bony feet into the leather shoes, fastening the buckle just as the innkeeper returns.

The man stops still, a ewer of ale in his hand.

'Oh,' he says. 'Well I never. I took you for a boy, mistress.'

She is – there is no other word for it – striking.

Still Katherine says nothing. She looks at the way the cloth grips her forearms and then she pulls at the coif against her neck. She runs fingers down to the front of her dress, feeling the lacings, which he now sees he's tied poorly, and then she runs both hands down her hips and Thomas can feel his face flush. He does not know where to look and is reminded in a flash of what he had felt the previous night, before Margaret had died.

'So strange,' Katherine says at last. 'So strange.'

The innkeeper pours them ale and leaves the stew on the board by the fire and Thomas watches as Katherine sits and drinks some warm ale and pushes the food away. Now she is dressed as a girl, she drinks more delicately, so whereas Kit made a conscious effort to guzzle ale and then wipe her mouth on her sleeve, here she is, sipping at the cup as might a female. He feels suddenly very anxious in her company, as if she is a stranger, and he does not know what to do when she puts the cup down and leans against the table, holding her head.

'We are the only people staying?' Thomas asks the innkeeper when he brings the straw for their beds.

'No one's about this time of year generally, and with Tudor coming, well . . . Are you quite well, mistress?'

Katherine's eyes are glassy and she sways where she sits at the board.

'Tudor is coming here?' she asks.

'So they say. Coming up from Pembroke around the hills, he is, with six thousand men. Soon set that Earl of Warwick back on his heels, won't he, eh?'

Neither Thomas nor Katherine say a word while the innkeeper takes their bowls and puts them on the floor for a short-legged dog to lick.

'And where are you from?' he asks, turning to Thomas. 'You don't sound to be from these parts.'

'We are from Lincoln,' Thomas stammers. Is it bad to admit they are from Lincoln? He has no idea. The innkeeper brightens.

'Then you'll have further news of the battle?' he asks.

'Battle?' Thomas asks.

'A friar brought news only yesterday,' the innkeeper says. 'There has been a great battle outside the castle of Sandal, somewhere up, you know, north? Near York. It was fought on the eve of the New Year, and Richard of York is killed! Aye, and the Earl of Salisbury too! Have you not heard? The whole of the Duke's army were cut down, to a man, and now the north country lies in the Queen's hands, and all of England soon, too, so they say.'

29

She is woken by the sound of horses on the road outside. It is still dark and though she recognises the noise of men in harness she cannot stop herself slipping back into sleep. When she wakes again her body is heavy, and she peers through her half-opened eyelids to see Thomas in his linen shirt feeding slips of wood into the flames of the fire.

He glances over, sensing a change in her, and opens his mouth and says something, but she cannot understand him, and she drifts back to sleep. She has been dreaming curious swirling dreams, intensely vivid yet bewilderingly vague, and through them all flicker the shadows of the dead: Walter, Dafydd, Owen and especially Margaret. Margaret is there often. At times she is no more substantial than a wisp of river mist at dawn, at others she acquires flesh and becomes all too real.

'She is unwell?' she hears the innkeeper ask Thomas.

'A fever,' Thomas says. 'Nothing more. She was caught in the cold on the hills.'

The innkeeper grunts something about a nunnery being more suitable than his hall and Katherine stares past Thomas up into the roof, at the tiles and the soot-blackened rafters. She tries to stay awake, but drifts back into sleep where the shades of the dead gather about her once more.

How long she is like this she cannot say. When she is awake it is as if everything is at a remove. She sees Thomas, his face swimming towards her, sometimes obscenely large, sometimes in miniature;

and she hears his voice, sometimes loud in her ears and then sometimes as a distant rattle. She knows he is asking a question, or offering help, but nothing she hears or sees has anything to do with her. It feels as if someone else is lying there drifting through consciousness.

On one of the days – she knows it is day because the shutters are open and a breeze stirs the wood smoke – she sees Thomas eating something. Every now and then a servant – a sullen, chunky girl, slow-moving, who'd never have survived long in the priory – comes in to look at her and her possessions, and Thomas looks up from his scribbling. He has placed Margaret's bag where he can see it.

Later Katherine looks down and sees her arms encased not in the mossy, malodorous woollen jacket she's become used to, but in fine linen, and she is surprised to find that she is dressed as Margaret Cornford now. She falls asleep again, and when she wakes it is dark and she is certain she is now Margaret, but once more she drifts off into padded slumber.

It is daylight when she opens her eyes the next time, woken by hunger. Thomas is sitting at a bench, making marks in the pardoner's ledger. He looks careworn and sorrowful. She thinks of him when she first saw him, running in the snow beyond the priory's walls, and then his face with the sun falling on it when they were in Calais, and now this. She finds tears in her eyes. He is such a good soul, she thinks, and has suffered so for the sake of others. Now he turns and is looking at her, with a smile breaking through the worry. It is like the onset of spring, or the sun breaking through clouds.

'Katherine?' he says, his voice cracking. 'You are with us. Praise the Lord!'

He swings his feet and comes to her. She says nothing. Her mouth is foul and her head aches almost as badly as her stomach. He helps her to sit up and she drinks the ale from a slimy leather cup.

'How long have I been like this?' she croaks.

'Days,' he says. 'A week even.' He too has lost track of time.

A moment later the innkeeper comes in with wood for the fire.

'God's grace!' he exclaims. 'She lives.'

The lumpen servant girl appears over his shoulder and looks disappointed. When they have gone Katherine turns to Thomas again.

'Did I dream the news that Richard of York is dead?'

Thomas shakes his head. 'No,' he says. 'And further confirmation has come.'

He tells her how he has heard that Richard of York and his army had emerged from Sandal Castle only to be engulfed by a much larger force led by the Queen's favourite, the Duke of Somerset, and Andrew Trollope, the man who had led the Calais force that switched sides the year before. He describes how the innkeeper laughed as he told him the battle lasted less then an hour and that the Duke of York had his head knocked from his shoulders and set on a pike and carried to York where it is set on the gatehouse.

'"So York can overlook York!" he said.'

They'd even put a paper crown on his head as well, so he looked the part, the innkeeper said. The Earl of Salisbury had been executed the following day and the Duke of York's younger son, the Earl of Rutland, whom they'd seen arguing with the Earl of Warwick in Westminster that summer, was murdered after the battle, and now all three heads were on pikes together. Heralds have named the battle after the nearby town of Wakefield.

Katherine asks about Sir John Fakenham and the others, about Richard and Geoffrey, and all the other Johns who had been waiting to join the Duke of York.

'They might not've been there, you know?' Thomas says. 'They might have stayed in Marton Hall. D'you remember what Sir John said? That they'd go in the spring, when the fighting was supposed to start?'

She nods. It is a slim hope.

'And what of – What of Walter?'

Thomas shakes his head.

'Nothing,' he says, 'but nor have I heard anything of Riven's boy or the giant either.'

'You think Walter might have——?' She cannot finish the sentence.

'I hope so. He was the sort of man who might have liked the idea of selling his life dearly.'

Then Thomas lowers his voice and glances at the screen across the buttery where the innkeeper and his servants come and go.

'Tudor's scurriers have been through,' he whispers. 'The army is working its way around those hills we crossed, from the west. The innkeeper thinks they will be here within the next two days.'

'Then we must be gone,' Katherine says, trying to sit up.

Thomas nods.

'The innkeeper says the road to England runs northeast from here,' he says, 'to a town called Leominster. He tells me to be careful to whom I speak when we get there, for the area is what he calls the Marches, and is supposed to be full of traitors.'

She struggles up on to her elbows and looks down at her clothes. Seeing them, something like relief runs through her, as if something has been decided for her.

'Why am I dressed like this?' she asks as she prises the blankets off.

'D'you not remember? They are Margaret's clothes. They were all that was dry. I sent your other clothes to the washerwomen but they would not touch them for fear of having them fall to pieces.' He pauses, looks at her keenly. 'Are you strong enough to travel?' he asks.

They stare at one another. Both have heard the words before, when they were about to leave Kidwelly and someone asked the same question of Margaret Cornford. *Are you strong enough to travel?* Margaret had given them the answer they'd wished to hear, but it was not necessarily the right one.

'So long as there are no more of those hills,' she says.

Thomas frowns. 'I cannot promise you that,' he says.

She looks up through the bars of the hall's window. Nor can he promise she will not be snowed on. The early-morning sky is white with it, and while the ostler's boy saddles their horses they finish a mutton pie and get the fat girl to fill Margaret's leather flask with ale. Katherine fastens Margaret's beautiful blue cloak around her shoulders and presses the blue headdress over her coif, and she leaves the inn for the first time in more than a week.

Underfoot the snow in the yard is hard and a fat lip of ice hangs from a waterspout. Katherine feels the cold with every breath. She climbs into the side-saddle and settles herself just as she saw Margaret do, and then she waits while Thomas tips the boy for having put oil on the horses' hooves.

After a moment she becomes aware that Thomas is gazing at her. When she turns on him he looks away, as if embarrassed to be caught staring.

'What?' she says.

'You look very different,' he says.

'I am wearing a dress,' she points out.

'I know,' he says. 'Only – only I had not realised how – I had not realised that you would look so good in it, is what I mean.'

He blurts these last words and she cannot help but smile.

They start out through the town gates and follow the road northwards, the country around them clamped in snow, silent except for the river that slides by alongside them like a rill of black silk. Immediately the road rises. The wind picks up, plucks at their hems, ruffles the horses' manes. They ride in silence, Thomas's shoulders hunched. Occasionally he turns to check on her.

She wonders what they will find when they return to Marton Hall.

'What if it is already in Somerset's hands?' she calls. Thomas halts his horse and waits for her to draw abreast.

'I don't know,' he says. 'But Sir John will have left word, and he will want to know what has happened to us. What happened to Walter. And Dafydd. And Owen.'

'And Margaret,' she adds.

Thomas nods.

'Yes. And Margaret,' he says, and they ride on, each wrapped in their own thoughts. Now all Katherine can think about is Margaret. Even her hands in these gloves remind her of Margaret. She is on Margaret's horse, in Margaret's clothes, and sometimes she thinks Margaret is talking to her, telling her something.

A little while later they pass a tower on a hill a short distance off the road to the south. Beyond the next rise is a mean little cottage where there is no one to be seen, not in the cottage, nor in the furlongs beyond. They get off their horses. Inside embers smoulder under pale ashes.

Thomas shouts for the owners but there is no answer.

'Can you feel someone watching us?' he asks.

She senses it too, and looks around, but she finds nothing. The wind soughs in the trees. They eat some of the bread they've brought and pour away the ale for tasting of horses' urine, and then they mount up and carry on over a wooden bridge. Here Thomas stops and gets off his horse. He bends and traces his finger in the frost-stiffened mud.

'Horses,' he says. 'About ten of them, well shod. I have been seeing their prints on the road since Brecon.'

She says nothing. Of course there are hoof prints, she thinks. It is a bridge. Then she sees what he means. There are a lot of hoof prints, all left at the same time, and all going in one direction, northeast.

'Can they be Tudor's scurriers?' she asks.

'Could be,' Thomas says, but there is doubt in his voice.

'Or?' she asks.

He gets back in the saddle and turns to her without a word.

'It cannot be Riven and his giant,' she says, but she knows it can.

'They must know we crossed the hills,' he says at length. 'They must suppose we are trying to get back to Marton Hall.'

'Perhaps we should avoid the road?' Katherine suggests half-heartedly. She looks up at the hills ranged around in a ring, grey with snow, wreathed in cloud. She is not well enough for any more nights in the open; they both know it.

'No,' Thomas says. 'The innkeeper says there is an inn the drovers use. We must make for that tonight.'

They continue on, following the tracks of the riding party until evening starts to fall, and then, after another league, they come to the inn, a yellow light in the gloom, holding out all sorts of promises. It is a thatched hall built on the squint and set back off the road among fields thick with bleating sheep. Even before they've dismounted they can smell meat cooking, and Katherine can think of nothing else, but as they approach they hear the sound of men and ale-fuelled conversation.

'We cannot stay here,' Thomas whispers.

Disappointment settles on her like wet clothing. No, worse than that. It actually hurts. What little strength she has ebbs away, and soon she is shivering and sweating. She is not yet well. They ride on.

'Is it warmer as a man or woman?' he asks.

'Neither,' she says.

He laughs.

Mist is boiling up from the river beside them, overflowing on to the flood plain, dank and penetrative, and they are pleased when the road turns away and heads up a gentle hill. Over its crest they find what they are looking for: a single cottage with smoke seeping through the eaves. A man appears from the gloom carrying a froe and a dead fish. He drops the fish when he sees Thomas, and swings the froe in both hands. He puts the tool aside when he sees Katherine, reassured by the presence of a woman.

He agrees to let them share his fire, but he has no news, not of

Tudor or Riven, or any of the battle of which the Brecon innkeeper told them. He has not even heard that there are any wars, and is only able to tell them that they are still on the right road to Leominster, and that they are in for cold weather. He guts the fish on the floor without much care, throwing the entrails to seethe in the flames. Then he boils the fish in water in a blackened pot that hangs from a bar above the fire. He has no interest in whence they've come or whither they are going and once he's eaten his share of the fish, he falls asleep where he sits by his fire, keeling over on to the hard-packed ground and snoring glutinously through the night.

Thomas spreads his blanket awkwardly over them both, and offers her the ledger on which to rest her head, but she refuses, and in the morning, when they rise the carpenter is outside among low mounds of chipped wood, splitting a log with his froe. Overhead the sky is like milk and the cold fiercer than ever and the carpenter's body is steaming. Within a moment Katherine is shivering in her cloak and her face is burning in the wind. The horses stumble on the iron-hard mud as they cross a low plateau and descend to find another hamlet, also deserted.

'They must have heard Tudor is coming,' Thomas says.

The same is true of the next village. And the next.

'We shall starve if we don't eat soon,' Thomas tells her.

'Is it just us?' she asks. 'Or does everybody travel so uncertainly?'

'Perhaps we ought to return to the man with the fish? We can buy some from him.'

She turns in her saddle just as they crest the next low rise.

'Thomas!'

He turns and stands in his stirrups and peers back over her head. The road behind them, not three leagues distant, is now a line of horsemen.

'Dear God!' he says. 'They have moved up fast. It can only be the vanguard.'

They kick their horses and crest the hill, but the animals are too tired and cold and hungry and they can manage no more than a trot.

'We must not stop until we reach Leominster,' Thomas says. 'The town will shut their gates on Tudor, and the army will pass them by. That's what the innkeeper said.'

'Then let us pray for that,' Katherine says. 'But how far is it?'

'He said no more than two days. We have already ridden one, so . . .'

'Can we outrun them?'

'I don't know.'

They ride on through the morning, the road passing through water meadows skimmed with grey ice, and stands of naked trees. Katherine's muscles ache from unfamiliar exertions of the saddle and she is feverish, half frozen, half broiled. But they must not stop. They ride a league, then another, and all the while Tudor's army seems to gain on them, his scurriers stretching forward along the road towards them, then sliding back, only to come up again.

A mile later she looks around and a riding party is setting out more purposefully along the road towards them. They have been seen, she thinks, two lone dots on the horizon, and someone has given the order that they be hunted down. Ten men she guesses, pale in their livery coats, long spears in their stirrups. There is something about them that draws her up short. A big man, riding what looks like a carthorse.

'Thomas!' she shouts again.

Thomas flinches at her shout and turns to squint into the distance where she is pointing.

'It can't be,' he says. 'It's just another big man.'

'We must get off the road now,' she says. 'There is a turning. Look.'

Half a league ahead is a clutch of cottages at a crossroads, smokeless and deserted like everywhere else in this county. If they can reach them they may be able to leave this road and cut away up into the hills and let the army pass. She hopes that she is wrong about Riven and the giant being among them.

They use their heels hard and though they are done in, the horses are tough, and manage an extra turn of speed. They reach the crossroads between the cottages and strike off to the left, northwards. The path is barely that, but it serves, and takes them through an orchard of crouched apple trees and past a watermill where the wheel creaks and thumps, creaks and thumps above the flare of water in the rill below.

Katherine is numb with cold now, sick with hunger and fatigue, her pony near halt, near dead perhaps. She feels likely to fall from the saddle again, but still they don't stop. Their path runs along the river's bank and then through its water meadows. Hills rise up either side. Ahead is a wood.

'What should we do if they come this way?' she calls.

'I'm trying to think what Walter would do,' Thomas says.

She supposes he will stop and volunteer to hold the road while she rides on. It is the sort of thing he might suggest, just as he had on the other side of the hills in Wales, and suddenly the thought terrifies her. Without Thomas, there is nothing.

She ducks as the path takes them through a small wood of low-hanging trees where dark pools reflect the sky above; then the road dog-legs around a couple of willow trees where Thomas groans and she follows his pointing arm.

This time there is no mistaking them.

The giant, on a huge horse, is following a path down through the tangled woods in the hills above. They must have seen them turn and have ridden to cut them off. More riders follow him, about ten in a file, long spears held upright.

'Dear God,' she breathes. 'How did they know?'

'We might still outrun them,' Thomas says. 'Or find somewhere better to fight.' He looks around. There seems nowhere better than here. He sighs. 'No. Let us have done with it here. I am tired of running.'

She nods. Together they draw their swords, his longer than her short little blade. She throws her cloak over her shoulder and wipes her nose with the back of her hand. Her short hair is loose, the coif hanging like a hood; her ear aches in the cold. Together they watch the riders emerge on to clearing: a man with a bandaged eye and the giant.

'Look,' Thomas says. 'It is the son. Not the father. Perhaps you will unhorse him again?'

The giant sees them under their tree and gestures. Next to him Edmund Riven laughs. Then the giant kicks his horse and begins plodding through the reeds towards them. She hears Edmund Riven draw his sword.

The giant meanwhile is holding something up for them to see. He is laughing.

It is the pollaxe.

Katherine closes her eyes. So Walter is dead. It feels like physical pain, like a punch to the kidneys, a fall from a tree.

'If I can land just one blow, that is all I ask,' Thomas says.

The riders across the meadow fan out shoulder to shoulder behind the giant and Edmund Riven. One or two seem to be carrying wounds. Even the giant seems to have his left hand lying loose in his lap, as if to favour it. Walter's work, she hopes.

The shadows of the hills behind Riven's men stretch out across the water meadow as night fills the broad-bottomed valley, and above them all colour bleeds from the sky. Steam billows from their horses.

'So,' Thomas says. 'This is it. This is what God wills.'

'So it seems,' Katherine agrees. Her voice wavers in her throat, cracks. Her heart is beating very fast. She must try to be courageous about this. Not to fall screaming. Not let herself down at the end.

Thomas turns to her.

'Kit,' he says. 'Katherine.'

There are tears in his lashes; his lips tremble.

She holds out her hand to him. He takes it.

'Thomas,' she says, before he can speak. 'You know that I do not believe in the will of God, but if He wills our deaths now, as it seems, then I give him thanks that at least we will be together at our end. I am glad of that, at least.'

He is silent for a moment. It is as if she's taken his words away.

He rests his sword on his lap and sighs lengthily, a long plume of breath.

'I wish . . .' he begins. 'I wish – we had more time. More time to just be. Like other people. With none of this.' He gestures at her drawn sword and the approaching horsemen. 'I wish we had more time for . . . for everything,' he says.

'I know,' she says. 'I know.'

She spurs her horse to him and stretches up. He leans down and their lips touch. She closes her eyes at the sensation, wishing it could last.

Then they pull away.

'Go with God, Thomas,' she says.

'You too, Katherine. You too.'

30

Even while he can still taste her on his lips, he knows he must kill her.

It is what Walter would have done.

He will do it quickly, so quickly she'll never know what is happening. He will draw the blade across her throat and she will be dead before she slumps from her saddle. It will be so easy and, once done, the giant will never be able to touch her.

He feels the nerves in his fingers prickle and the blood in his sword arm froth. He changes his grip on his sword hilt, draws back his arm. He lifts his arm.

But across the marshy ground Edmund Riven seems to sense what is afoot.

He yells and charges.

As he does so, Thomas sees a movement from the periphery of his eye, down by the woods at the end of the marsh, where nothing should be moving. It is a tiny blur, a blur that a man might register only after it is gone, but an archer would know it for what it was. An arrow shaft.

It slits through the air and catches Riven's horse with a short thud. The horse staggers, cants four or five steps to the left, then dips. The horse's head drops and its forelegs tangle as it runs. There is a crack like burning pinewood and the horse goes down. Edmund Riven is hurled from the saddle. He flies for a moment and then is gone. Behind him the horse rolls through the reeds and the waters.

The giant pulls up. The men behind too. A second shaft hums across the marsh and twists one out of his saddle, bundling him to the ground. A third follows. Thomas slips from his saddle and drags Katherine from hers. He drops to the ground and spreads his body over her, pressing her into the black mud.

'Who are they?' she cries out.

'I don't know. I don't know.'

Riven's men are just as confused. They are shouting the same question. The horse is screaming. The others are trying to turn their horses, trying to get back to the trees. Thomas raises his head above the grasses. At the far end of the meadow he can see the pale spikes of bows among the thickets of sedge. Another arrow skims through the reed tips. It hits something and there is a cry.

Riven's men are pulling back. There is a drum of unsteady hooves as they reach the trees and start up the hill, back to Tudor's army.

But where is the giant? Where is Riven?

Thomas raises his head again. An arrow sighs overhead, missing the horses. He ducks.

'Come on,' he says. He takes Katherine's hand and leads her scrambling back behind the willows. Under the branches it smells sharply of cows. He looks around the rough bark, sees the archers moving up. Three or four empty-saddled horses stand cropping the grass and nearby a man sobs in agony. Reed tops twitch, and an arrow with a broken fletch buzzes noisily overhead in the gloom.

Who are these new men? Where have they come from?

There is a long moment of silence. Then a man shouts in the distance, calling to his own men. Horsemen have arrived from the far end of the marsh and are now cautiously investing the long grasses. They are scurriers perhaps, but whose? Thomas can almost make out their livery, but cannot believe it. Blue and murrey? Isn't that March's livery? Or Hastings's?

'What badges are they wearing?'

Katherine peers through the willows.

An arrow cracks into the trunk above their heads. She screams and he drags her down again.

There is a sudden drum of hooves and a bellow of pain, then another scream that ends in a crunch of something. Whimpering; more silence. Overhead three ducks pass, their wings wheezing as they beat. A man roars. A scrape of steel and iron, a splash, and then more shouts. An archer appears along the road, keeping to shadows, his head bobbing. He starts when he sees them, raises his bow and draws.

Thomas throws aside the sword and holds his palms up. The archer half relaxes his string.

'Who the fuck are you?' he asks. He sounds like Walter.

Thomas stares at him. He can hardly speak. The archer has the badge of a bull's head on his tabard. The bull's head. William Hastings's badge. He is one of Hastings's men. Hastings's archers.

Thomas takes a step towards him and the man tightens his string, but then is distracted by Katherine wearing a lady's fine cloak, but her hair is short and uncovered, and she is like no lady he can ever have seen.

'My name is Thomas Everingham,' Thomas begins. 'A good friend to William Hastings.'

There is another scream in the marsh behind them. All three flinch. They hear a man running clumsily, breaking through the reeds on to the path ahead. He stops and stares at them. Then he turns away and runs and there is a thump as he is upended in a tangle of legs by an arrow. Someone laughs.

'Well, Thomas Everingham,' the archer says, 'if you want to stay a good friend of William Hastings, then you'd best be keeping your bloody head down. You too – ah – mistress.'

He touches his sallet and passes them, moving out into the reeds, stretching his bowstring. The archers have started calling to one another now. They are moving through the marsh like huntsmen clearing a covey from a copse.

'Can they be dead?' Katherine asks. 'Oh, I pray to God they are.'

One of the horsemen comes up the path from the far end of the clearing. He looks young, moving with exaggerated swagger, playing the part of the soldier.

'The devil are you?' he asks when he sees them. He has a long sword in his hand and the bull's head is on his chest too. His long nose and wide mouth lend him a familiar look.

'You are William Hastings's man?' Thomas asks.

'I am. I am John Grylle, of Kirby Muxloe, in Leicester. And who are you?'

'I am Thomas Everingham, of Marton Hall in Lincoln, of the affinity of Sir John Fakenham, and a good friend to William Hastings.'

'Is that so?' Grylle nodded. 'And my lady?'

Thomas turns. Dear God, who is she? They have not thought to decide.

He opens his mouth to say something but Katherine speaks first.

'I am Lady Margaret Cornford,' she says in a clear voice. 'Of Cornford, also in Lincolnshire.'

Thomas opens his mouth, closes it. Why has she said that?

'My lady.' Grylle touches his helmet. 'But why are you here and—?' His gaze travels up and down her muddy dress. 'And who are those men on the road? We assumed they were Tudor's scurriers, but—?'

'They followed us here from Wales,' Katherine tells him. 'We have come from there. From Wales. They are Giles Riven's men.'

Grylle starts.

'Giles Riven the turn-and-turn-again-coat? Ha. But how came you here from Wales? Do you have any news of Tudor and his army?'

'His vanguard is on the road south of here,' Thomas says, pointing. 'Making for the town of Leominster.'

'Ha!' Grylle barks again. 'He will need to negotiate with the men of the Marches before he can have the liberty of that choice.'

'Who are they?' Thomas asks. 'Who are the men of the Marches?'

Grylle looks at him as if he is stupid. 'You are in the Marches,' he says, gesturing to the hills around him. 'All this land belongs to the Earl of March and those who live on it do not take kindly to just anyone coming through, especially not a rabble of Irishmen and Frenchmen led by a treacherous Welshman who ought to be hanged like the common criminal he is.'

'But you are Hastings's man? Is he here?'

'Why, yes,' Grylle says, again as if this is the most obvious thing in the world. 'We are camped by Wigmore, not two leagues up the road. We marched back from Gloucester when we got news of Tudor's landing.'

The men in the marshes behind them are more relaxed now and they are beginning to brag and joke with one another as their nerves unwind.

'Let's see where we are then, shall we?' Grylle says, and he kicks his horse to push past them through the reeds. Thomas and Katherine follow. Thomas still has his sword. They find Edmund Riven's horse first, straining to breathe, eyes rolling and ears flattened with pain. A broken arrow is buried in its shoulder and a ribbon of plum-coloured blood snakes from the wound. One of Hastings's men is silently contemplating it. After a moment he cuts through the animal's throat with an almost tender stroke of his knife, and holds its head while blood seethes from the frilled lips of the wound in rhythmic spurts. Steam drifts in the air, the smell rich, and after a moment the horse is still.

'Sorry about that, old son,' the archer says, laying the head down softly.

Thomas looks away. To think he has come so close to doing the same to Katherine.

Riven has been thrown a little way off, among the rushes, so Thomas pushes aside the reeds with his sword, expecting to see him lying dead or unconscious.

But there is nothing.

He searches again.

Still nothing. There are broken reeds and a scrape of mud to show where he's fallen, but no sign of blood or his body.

He is gone.

The giant too, but of him there is even less sign, since his horse is also missing. As is the pollaxe.

'Must have got out of the bag,' is Grylle's estimation, and he gestures down towards the trees in the south. 'My orders are to picket this approach, though, and not to go chasing their scouts back into camp.'

The archers are disappointed. There are four of Riven's men dead and two wounded, both so badly they will not live through the night, and Thomas and Katherine and the squeamish horse-lover look away as one of the sergeants blesses them with a sign of the cross and then brains each of them with two blows of a lead maul.

'It's a mercy,' one of the archers says. 'I'd hope someone'd do the same for me in that case.'

'Christ,' Thomas cannot stop himself breathing.

'I would have tried to do something for them,' Katherine whispers, 'if they had not spent the last days trying to kill me.'

Grylle sends a man on horseback to the camp with them to report what has happened and they take to their saddles again and follow the path through the valley. They are almost too tired to talk. They pass a hamlet and then a soldiers' camp of tents. Men stare them as they pass. They are Hastings's men, and March's men, and Thomas feels dizzy with relief, but he cannot help but wonder why Katherine said she was Margaret Cornford.

She looks at him helplessly and gestures to her dress.

'It was all I could think of,' she says. She closes her eyes and shakes her head.

Thomas says nothing. What could she have done? Said she was someone else? Who, though? He opens his mouth to tell her that, but then stops. It wouldn't help. Besides, what is done is done. They ride on.

Beyond the camp is a castle: a clutch of grey-stone battlemented towers bosomed with bare-branched trees, on a steep bailey a little off the road to the west. Behind it rises a line of hills.

'Wigmore Castle,' their guide says. When they arrive at the gatehouse he names them to the Captain of the Watch as Thomas Iverington and Lady Margaret Cornford though no one appears to care very much for anything they have to say that does not concern the whereabouts, numbers and disposition of Tudor's army.

'Can we see William Hastings?' Thomas asks after he's told the captain all he knows.

The captain grumbles something about Hastings being too busy to see anyone and takes them to the crowded inner ward where they can hear a flute being played in one of the solars above. Someone is plucking strings too, and a man is singing in a high voice. Thomas asks for news of the engagement outside Sandal Castle.

'It was what it was,' the captain says, scuffing his boots. 'A disaster. Duke of York: killed in the field. Earl of Salisbury: captured then executed by that bastard the Bastard of Exeter. Earl of Rutland: murdered by that black-faced butcher Clifford. And how many men like you and me killed where we stood? Who knows? Thousands.'

'But what about Sir John Fakenham? Do you know if he was there?'

The captain shakes his head.

'Never heard of him,' he says, and he leaves them in a dark corner by a doorway that leads to the castle latrine. Thomas puts the bags down and Katherine leans against him for a moment. Thomas stands stock-still; he places an arm around her, and they stand for a while, neither moving, neither needing to say a thing.

Then a messenger with a candle in a lantern comes for them, and they step apart.

'You the bloke who's just come from Wales? Get your things and follow me,' he says. 'Earl of March wants to see you.'

He leads them up some steps in a tower and along a stone corridor to where three soldiers stand with bills at a door. Through it they can hear the flute and the singing. It is quite unlike any of the singing he's heard in Mass. One of the guards opens the door and ushers them in. A fire is piled scandalously high in the middle of the floor and five or six men are sitting at a board where food and drink are being served by attendants. The flautist and the singer stop and are ushered away behind a screen by a fat man with a linen cloth.

Each of the men at the table looks up from their dishes. One is Edward of March, now the Duke of York since his father's death; he whom they'd last seen the summer before, that time at Westminster.

When he sees Thomas, he gets to his feet, incredulous.

'Dear God in heaven,' he says. 'You.'

'My lord,' Thomas mumbles.

But he can hardly take his gaze off the breasts of the glazed bird that steams on a dish held by one of the servants. The smell makes his mouth water.

'What in the names of all the saints are you doing here?'

'It is a long story, sir.'

'And one best told with wine, I bet, and something to eat.'

This is from William Hastings, who's risen to his feet and has come around to shake Thomas's hand.

'It is good to see you Thomas – ah – Everingham, isn't it?' he says.

Thomas nods. Hastings's gaze flicks to Katherine, and then flicks back again.

'But tell us,' he says. 'Who is this?'

He bows his head in mock salute to Katherine. For a moment Thomas thinks Hastings will recognise Kit, the boy who saved Richard Fakenham's life. And Katherine says nothing. She is suddenly ill, pale as a sepulchre, with glazed eyes that seem to roll into the back of her head. She does not answer. The silence only deepens as Hastings and March take in her filthy face, the stained dress, the grubby headdress with the linen coif tugged down to cover her cropped ear. The other men at the table lean in on the conversation, even the servers are poised, mouths open, loaded spoons in their hands, staring.

Thomas can stand it no more.

'Lady Margaret Cornford,' he says. 'Daughter of the late Lord Cornford.'

As he says it, he knows he has crossed some line. That there is no way back now. Katherine looks at him feverishly, and he wonders if she is grateful, or fearful.

Hastings blows through his lips. 'My lady,' he says, and he lets go of Thomas's hand and takes hers. He leads her to his chair at the board. The men there – in fur-collared coats, one with a chain of gold around his neck, another a priest – stand.

'Friends,' Hastings says, addressing them. 'My lady has had a long and discomforting journey, so I trust you will not begrudge her a place at our table. There is precious little room in the castle to which she may retire, and for those of us who hold Lord Cornford's memory dear, we should extend every courtesy to his bloodline.'

The men nod, but frown. A woman at such a table? Katherine takes her place, grateful only to sit on the chair, her narrow fingers shaking as she drinks hot wine and then gnaws at bread. March, meanwhile, takes Thomas to one side.

'So you have come from Wales?' he asks. 'Have you seen Tudor's army?'

Thomas nods.

'All the talk is of them being Irish mercenaries,' March goes on as if talking to himself, 'with a few Frenchmen for good measure. I cannot decide just how poor they will be when it comes to it. The weather has been bad, I hear?'

'It has been cold, my lord, with snow.'

'I hope they have suffered cruelly,' March says. 'They are camped tonight just off the road to the south of here, where the Captain of the Watch tells me you were picked up. My sources suggest they are short of food and ale?'

'There was precious little to be had on the way,' Thomas confirms.

'We can thank John Dwnn for that,' March says. 'He's warned everyone in Wales to bury their food and take to the hills.'

Dwnn. Thomas hears the name like a slap. John Dwnn will know Katherine is not Lady Margaret Cornford.

'Is John Dwnn here now, sir?' he asks.

'Dwnn? No. He is out; harassing the enemy, he calls it. Murdering their scouts, I'd call it, and thank him for it.'

He raises his cup in thanks to John Dwnn before drinking. Thomas thinks to ask about the battle outside Wakefield, but how can you ask a man about his father and brother being killed?

'So,' March says. 'There will be fighting tomorrow. I hope you will join us? You are my lucky talisman.'

Thomas nods, but he is far from certain. He drinks deeply, burning his tongue but hardly caring. Great God, it is good.

'Tomorrow will be a different sort of fight,' March says, raising his voice, broadening the conversation to include everyone in the room. 'In the past we have always urged our men to spare the commons and to kill only the gentles, but hereafter . . . hereafter we want them all dead.'

This sinks in.

'But, Edward – your grace,' Hastings says. 'You are talking about the lives of Englishmen. The deaths of Englishmen, I should say.'

'I know that, William. But I want everyone to know that if they take up arms and follow that bastard-born Somerset, or bloody old Tudor, or any man, against us, then they will pay for it with their lives. They have shown us no mercy, and so by God we shall show them none either.'

Hastings remains doubtful.

'But who among them has a choice?' he asks. 'Commissions of Array are one thing, but if you owe your livelihood to a man and that man demands you harness yourself and march with him to war, then what can you do? If you refuse, you'll be evicted and your goods given to another who will fight.'

But March is determined. Losing a father and a brother might do that to a man, Thomas supposes. Katherine meanwhile is now sitting with her head lolling on its thin stem. Thomas asks Hastings if there is anywhere he might find for her to sleep.

'Of course, of course. I am sure we can find somewhere. She should take a little wine and then rest.'

'And may I ask if you have news of Sir John Fakenham?' Thomas asks.

Hastings shakes his head. 'I have heard nothing,' he says. 'I sent a messenger to command him to come to Shrewsbury with every man he could raise, but the messenger never returned. I don't know if he was prevented from delivering his message, or waylaid on his way back. All I know is that Fakenham was yet to arrive by the time we marched south.'

'He was summoned to Sandal before Christmastide,' Thomas says. 'I was with him when the messenger arrived.'

Hastings takes a drink and Thomas hears him swallow. There is a telling silence for a moment.

'We can only pray,' Hastings says. 'Pray that he still lives.'

Thomas is not invited to sit at the board, but a servant leads Katherine away to her bed, and she leaves with a wary backward glance, trying to find him, but failing. Thomas finds a spot in a passageway outside the kitchen where a dog lies with his jaws on its paws, the light of the rush lamp catching in its liquid eyes, and the wall is warm from the fire, and as he closes his eyes he wonders where she is, and wishes she were there.

The next morning it is bitterly cold, and the sky is rose-coloured, fretted with fine white cloud. The bells are ringing for Mass but the air is filled with the clink and shunt of men gathering with sharp-edged weapons. Some are drinking ale in hard swallows, others telling jokes and laughing nervously. They compare pieces of equipment, swords, hammers, axes, helmets and harness. Still others are huddled blowing on their hands in front of the fires. The stink, even in the icy air, is strong: unwashed bodies in wet wool, coal smoke, hot grindstones, vinegar and the smog of their breath. And above it all is the smell of nerves, of fear, of anticipation.

When Mass is over Hastings and March and the other commanders emerge from the chapel; they are clutching candles. They congregate at the doorway for a moment and later when Hastings sees Thomas, he is still holding a candle but now has a fold of cloth.

'You will wear my livery today?' he asks, offering the cloth to Thomas. 'I should like you to be with me.'

Thomas swallows. Of all the things he'd rather not do, to take the field is among them. But now here is Hastings, a man whom he might well call a friend when almost all his others are dead, asking a favour.

'Gladly,' he says, taking the cloth, feeling the plinth of the black bull's head badge. 'Though I am hardly prepared for it, and I must look to Lady Margaret.'

'Ah. And where is she now? Recovered, I hope?' Hastings gestures up at the keep.

'I have yet to see her this morning.'

'Does she have any family to speak of?' Hastings asks. 'I knew Cornford, of course. A good man. She looks more like her mother, I'd say, though in truth I never met her. She was supposed to be frail, wasn't she? Died after childbirth.'

Thomas nods, though he hardly knows. Hastings scratches the side of his nose with the candle.

'Interesting,' he says. 'Interesting.'

He is silent for a long moment, plunged in thought.

'Here,' he says at length. 'Take this as well.'

He passes Thomas the candle.

A clarion player tries to blow a call but it is too cold to purse his lips and the noise comes out as a curious squeal. Men laugh. Thomas looks at the candle.

'Candlemas,' Hastings explains. 'Today. Time flies, no?'

He walks off leaving Thomas with the candle and the livery coat.

The footmen are starting to move out of the castle gatehouse to gather in the deer park beyond and in the confusion Thomas finds a loaf and an earthenware ewer of ale that a woman has set aside under a table, and after a moment's consideration he gives in to temptation and takes it. As he hurries away he feels the black eyes of the woman's girl fall on him more in sorrow than anger, and he leaves her the candle in recompense.

He finds Katherine still up in the solar and, with no maid to help her, she is wrestling with her unfamiliar clothes. He gives her the ale and bread and they sit on a chest eating until a messenger sent by Hastings appears.

'You're to come,' he says. He waits while Thomas puts his head through Hastings's fulled tabard and straightens it over his still-damp coat.

'Goodbye,' he says, lost for a moment as to what he should call her. She looks at him with her calm blue eyes.

'Godspeed, Thomas,' she says.

He cannot tell if she is putting on a performance in front of Hastings's messenger, but then she adds:

'I've no fear you'll not come back. You are immortal. How else to explain it all?'

He wishes he were so sure.

When Thomas emerges through the doorway of the keep, the courtyard below is loud with drummer boys and clarion callers and a party of heralds in blue cloaks is gathered by the gatehouse. The Earl of March, now Duke of York, is already mounted, on a destrier.

He is wearing harness of fluted plate with a white feather plume on the crown of his helmet, and in the shade of the curtain walls his harness seems to gather all the available light and distil it into something pure, something angelic almost, except that he carries a cruel beaked hammer over his shoulder and a battle axe at his hip.

Next to him is William Hastings, in less showy armour and no plume, his visor open, his handsome face pale. Behind him a man carries the fishtailed battle standard bearing the picture of a white hairy dog or some such, and behind is a line of perhaps a hundred men in plate armour under their own banners.

The horsemen move off with a tuneless timpani: clonking hooves, the scrape of iron shoes on stone and of men in harness. They pass through the gatehouse and ride out over the bridge to join the footmen waiting across the road south. Thomas walks behind the messenger. What does Hastings want of him? Whatever it is, Thomas knows he'll not be able to provide it. His hands are shaking at the thought of what is to come.

He follows the messenger along the road through the trees and past a little hamlet and a patchy wood of much-coppiced willow, empty pigpens and black mud. Everything is limed white with hoarfrost and breath hangs in the air. Beyond, spilling over into the boggy meadows, are thousands of men: archers, billmen, men-at-arms; their liveries new to Thomas, their flags unfamiliar. Their officers, captains and sergeants are shouting and cajoling men into their places. Drums thunder and trumpets call out and for a fleeting moment there is a festival atmosphere, as women and children mill around the fringes, selling ale and bread, sausages, soup. One woman still in her nightcap tries to sell Thomas a smoked eel, the skin as golden as the leaf he used to work with at the priory, and ale that smells of marsh water.

'Got anything hot?' Thomas asks.

She shakes her head. The messenger returns to his side and almost drags him away.

'Go away now, goodwife,' he says. 'We've things to do.'

Steam rises from both man and horse, and from the ditches where the men are relieving themselves. As they progress down the road Thomas feels nothing but growing fear. He cannot go through it again, not without Walter by his side, not without Geoffrey, or any of the Johns. Here he is with strangers. If he falls who will stoop to pick him up? The crack-toothed billman with those stout chains across his shoulders? The boy with a home-made glaive and no boots? He doubts it. They'd go through his purse before they bothered righting him. They'd leave him in a ditch to freeze to death.

When they catch up with Hastings, the knights have dismounted and their squires are leading the horses back through the lines. Hastings is nervous too. Thomas sees him passing his mailed palm over the pick of his pollaxe, teasing it with his fingers as if he can stroke it into a sharper point. Next to him is Grylle. Grylle nods tightly when reintroduced. He is in a suit of plate armour made for a much bigger man, and seems to be peeking out over his gorget like a creature in its hole. His helmet is painted black. He is, what? Fifteen?

'His first proper fight,' Hastings confides in Thomas. 'His mother'll kill me if anything happens to him.'

His squire has ale in a tubular leather flask. Hastings offers some to Thomas and watches him as he drinks. A frown gathers weight under the shadow of his raised visor where the fog of his breath has frozen into beads of ice.

'You seem underdressed, Thomas,' Hastings says.

All around them are ranged men in full harness, some of it field armour perhaps – the mismatched bits and pieces they've scrounged, looted or had adapted for their own purposes – but armour nonetheless. Every man has steel gloves, a helmet, a staff weapon, a hammer of some sort, a sword. Thomas has nothing save a scruffy travelling coat and a blunt sword.

'It is all I have,' Thomas explains.

Hastings nods.

'Take my horse,' he says, gesturing to the squire, a skinny boy whose livery tabard hangs to his knees.

'Won't you need it?' Thomas asks.

'Not if we triumph,' Hastings replied. 'And if we don't . . . well, I am in no mood for flight. If we lose today, I'd have nothing to fly to, in any case.'

'But what will I do with it?'

'I want you to act as my eyes on the field. Indulge me, Thomas. March and I have come to think of you as our good-luck talisman. Since that time at Newnham – do you remember? – he will not go happily into battle without you.'

Thomas nods. Is this normal? He has no idea. He is pleased to lift himself up into the saddle of the horse though, to separate himself from the fighting men. To feel the warmth between his knees. Over their steaming heads he can see the water meadows, still in shadows, all the way down to the marshy acres and the two willows.

'Ride forward and tell His Grace we are in position now, will you?'

There are trumpeters to do that, Thomas knows, and heralds already riding to and fro, and it would hardly take a moment of Edward's time to turn his head and look to see where Hastings's flag is held aloft by a bearded man-at-arms. But Thomas sees this task is extended as a favour, and he thanks Hastings for his unexpected solicitousness.

'Not a bit of it. Not a bit of it. As I say, my lord of March will want to know you are with us.'

Thomas leaves him and rides forward. Men glance up at him as he goes. Are they envious? He supposes so. He knows he would be. But then these are grim-faced men, shuffling forward as if keen not to miss the chance to swing an axe at another man. He turns the horse southwards just as the sun comes up over the eastern hills, setting the mist that billows among the trees aglow as if on fire.

He rides on towards Edward's banner and soon through the mist he sees Tudor's army. It is spread across the meadows five or six hundred paces away, bulking out, moving slowly up, accompanied by the usual din of drums and pipes. Flags are hoisted above their heads, and there are men in green and white livery but most are in brown and russet. Thomas shields his eyes from the low sun and he searches for Riven's flag, or men of his livery.

He has no idea what he'll do if he sees them. He knows he cannot fight the giant or even Edmund Riven, not now, not this day, but still, when he can see no one in Riven's white livery, he feels the loss.

But then, he wonders, where are they? Where would they have gone? Would Tudor – or whoever claimed their free-floating loyalty – have been able to force the giant to fight? Forced Edmund Riven to mount up and ride into battle? Or having lost those men yesterday, would they have absented themselves? Gone back to Cornford Castle.

He thinks of Cornford. Thinks of Marton Hall.

He is before the first battle now, and turns and rides across its front. Men stare at up at him, and he cannot help but look back at them, their pale faces, some so young. At the centre is Edward, Earl of March, the new Duke of York, standing under his banner, moving his arms, jumping on the spot to keep warm. Around him are his best men, hard-faced veterans with axes, pikes, billhooks and hammers, all well harnessed. They stand waiting for Tudor to make a move, their hands changing grip on the shafts of their weapons, tongues running across lips, all heads turned slightly to March, waiting to take their lead from him.

Edward turns to him.

'Everingham,' he says.

'My lord,' Thomas says, but the sun is shining in his eyes. He raises his hand to block it, but finds he cannot. He needs his forearm.

He is confused. Something is wrong. Instead of one sun, there are three. Each casts a halo of golden light.

'Well?' March asks. 'You have a message?'

Thomas says nothing, He is too confused. He points.

'Look,' he says. March turns to look. He turns and he too raises his arm against the suns. Thomas notices he is casting three shadows on the frosted ground, just as if he were standing before three altar candles. Around him the soldiers start to turn, and do likewise, all with their arms up, peering into the light in the east.

'God's blood!' March mutters, turning to a man next to him. 'What in the name of Jesus is that?'

The man has no reply.

'Anyone? Will no one tell me why in God's name are there three suns!'

There is a note of panic in his voice. The men behind have noticed and everywhere they are asking the same thing. The movement is subtle, a shrinking, a withering, as the army takes a step back, cringing from the freakish light. Suddenly all thought of the fighting is suspended. There is a ripple of movement as men make the sign of the cross. More than one casts aside his weapon and falls to his knees.

'It's an omen!' a man says.

'Of course it's an omen,' March says. 'But an omen of what?'

March looks around at his troops and Thomas sees that for once he does not know what to do, what to say. Then the two outer suns move closer together, nearer the centre sun, the larger of the three, and an even brighter ring of light springs from that central sun, to extend around each sun. The colours are of a rainbow.

'A trinity of suns,' Thomas thinks aloud. 'God the Father, God the Son and God the Holy Spirit.'

March stops and stares at Thomas. Then back at the suns, then at his men as they cower before the strange light.

He starts.

'Off your horse,' he says, half pulling Thomas from Hastings's horse. He gives him his pollaxe and swings himself up into the saddle.

Is he going to run? No. His hands are hard on the reins as he yanks the horse around to face his men. Then he takes his hammer from his belt and uses his spurs to get the horse to rise on to its legs and thrash its head and bellow in rage.

'Men of the Marches!' he cries, his hammer in the air. 'Men of the Marches! Sirs! Be not afraid! Do not dread this thing! It is a sign from God. Those three suns represent the Father, the Son and the Holy Ghost! They are the Holy Trinity, sent as a sign to give us courage, to show us that the Lord God above is on our side, to show us that right will prevail! So let us be of good cheer and let us this day think to acquit ourselves as men, as we go against these His enemies right hard, to drive them from the field, for this is God's will!'

There is a momentary pause, almost infinitesimally brief, before the man standing next to March roars, and as he roars, others join him, and still others, and then all through the army men begin raising and shaking their weapons and bellowing, and March throws himself from the horse's saddle and stalks forward and behind him the army surges forward across the marshes towards Tudor's battle.

31

In the days that follow the victory below Wigmore Castle, named by the heralds after the nearby village of Mortimer's Cross, Thomas and Katherine lodge at the White Hart Inn by the river in the city of Hereford. There are the dead to be buried, wounds to be healed and scores to be settled. All that first week crowds gather in the market square beneath the guildhall to watch as whey-faced wretches are held over a broad green log, already gummed with blood and cross-hatched with axe marks, to have their heads struck off into the bloody straw below. The crowds jeer and whistle and laugh to see it done, but it turns Katherine's stomach.

'They like to see bears baited and women strangled,' Thomas tells her. 'Someone having his head chopped off is nothing to them.'

It is Grylle who insists she comes. He is intent on her and whenever Thomas is absent, which happens whenever William Hastings wants him for some errand or other, Grylle is there. She says no at first, but then is caught by the thought that perhaps this is what ladies do? Watch executions? Suddenly she fears that if she says no, he will see through her disguise, and so it is that she finds herself standing with him watching as the old man Owen Tudor is dragged to the block.

Grylle talks to her as if she is a simpleton, but she is pleased when he explains that Owen Tudor is the man who married King Henry V's widow – which makes him the current King's stepfather – and, worst luck for him, also the father of the Jasper Tudor, the Earl of Pembroke, the man who'd raised his banner in Wales and paid for all those Irish mercenaries now lying slaughtered in the fields above Mortimer's Cross.

When he is standing there by the log, the old man doesn't believe they'll do it.

'Thinks he's English,' Grylle laughs.

But when the guards remove his fur collar to keep it clean for selling on, he realises they will, and he looks wistful, his silver locks and wrinkled skin giving him an almost exotic appearance in a world where few live to celebrate their fiftieth birthday. He mutters something about being used to rest his head in more comfortable places than on the log, and just before he kneels he takes the chance to stand a moment and study the crowd.

'Speech!' someone in the crowd calls. 'Come on, tell us a joke, you old Welsh goat!'

Just then Tudor catches Katherine's gaze and he stops short. It is as if he recognises her. Katherine can feel her face flush, and next to her Grylle is puzzled and watches her reaction. Tudor shakes his head as if he cannot believe what he is seeing, and he takes a step towards her and gestures.

'Do you know him?' Grylle asks.

Katherine shakes her head.

'He seems to know you.'

Before the old man can say anything more, the men behind him seize him and force him to his knees and the executioner – a butcher by trade – hacks off his head just as if he is killing a turtle.

Katherine turns away and Grylle laughs and tries to put an arm around her.

Afterwards someone sets the old man's head on the steps of the butter cross to general laughter. It is done in revenge, someone says, for the execution of the Earl of Salisbury, and the head is canted around so that it faces the city of York to the northeast, 'so that they can look one another in the eye'. Later someone tampers with it, a madwoman who washes his face and brushes his hair and lights more than a hundred candles around the base of the cross. No one knows where she's come by the candles, and since they are expensive, they are quickly stolen, and soon the birds are squabbling over what remains unburied of the late Queen's husband.

Over the following days Katherine cannot stop thinking about him, but nor, it seems, can Grylle stop thinking about her. He is around the inn all the time, usually bringing messages summoning Thomas to the castle where William Hastings and the new Duke of York are plotting their next move.

To escape Grylle's company Katherine has resorted to assisting with the wounded, who lie in the guildhall and in the hall of the inn. The surgeons are doing what they can for the wounded men of rank whom they think may live, but for the others less fortunate, it is the women who've traipsed around the country after them who are called into service, and Katherine assists an elderly, broad-waisted woman who's followed the army to France, she says, and had to repair her man after a fight more than once. She has a wen on her chin, and she says she knows how to concoct all the cures and salves she needs from hedgerow plants, and those such as yarrow, camomile or lavender. It is February, though, and none of these are available, and in their absence she pours hot wine on smaller wounds and then seals them with dry bindings and prayers.

'Sometimes seems to work,' she says.

But other wounds are too serious.

'I have seen surgeons stitch flesh together as a wife might mend her man's hose,' the old woman tells Katherine, 'but I lack the art and these fingers are not so dainty as once they were.'

She holds them up: they are lumpen and gnarled like tree roots.

'You have a go,' she tells Katherine and so Katherine tries her hand, stitching together the lips of a wound an archer has made in his own thigh with his knife while drunk.

'Lucky,' the old woman says, pointing to his inner thigh. 'Been there and there'd be no stopping the blood.'

They wash the wound with the archer's urine and a cup of wine warmed in a pot over the fire. It starts the bleeding again, but it cleanses the wound and then, while the old woman pinches the flesh together, Katherine uses a silver needle and a length of hemp and she stitches the separate parts of him together again. She is surprised at the feel of his flesh. It is firmer than she'd anticipated, and tougher, too, so that when she pulls on the needle the hemp does not cut through it, but rather brings it together in a neat seam.

'Very tidy,' the old woman says afterwards and Katherine thinks of the hours spent at needlework in the priory. She tries to imagine what she would have done had the Prioress paid her such a compliment.

But men keep on dying, long after the battle is over. It is those who seem to be drowning in their own blood who go first, those with wounds in their chests. Then the men with wounds in their stomachs follow, usually in great pain, vomiting endlessly or with their bellies horribly bloated. None survive. Then it is the men with no memory of the fight, men who've lost their helmets and who are dazed. For a while it seems as if they will recover, but they die anyway, later. And all the while the men with flesh wounds are succumbing, their limbs swelling, turning first purple then black, and emitting such a stink that men gag and prefer the smell of tallow; and there are others who convulse and twitch and cry out to the Lord in rigid terror of what awaits them.

It is better to be killed on the field, she thinks, and the old woman agrees.

And again, she wonders about the old man, Owen Tudor. Had he meant anything by the look he had given her? She still cannot decide, and yet she cannot forget it. Why would the old man single her out?

Some days later a physician in the mould of Fournier appears and sends the women away and turns the surgeons to adjusting the humours of those who can afford it by bleeding them, and soon the room is emptied, one way or the other.

She finds Thomas returning from the cathedral.

'There is a room', he tells her, 'filled with wonderful books, each chained to a desk.'

She can see the shadow of the fighting still lying over him. There is a hesitancy in his eyes, a distance in his gaze, as if he does not want to look at anything too closely for fear of what he may find. Still, the discovery of the library has given him some way back into the light.

'Is there any news of Sir John?' she asks.

He shakes his head.

'The Queen's army is pillaging the north,' he tells her. 'A man has come from an abbey south of Lincoln, near Boston, where he says the monks have buried all their valuables, including their vestments and plate.'

'They are looting churches?'

'And every beggar and pauper in the land has joined them, he says, like rats from their holes, and they've been raping women and torturing men to reveal the whereabouts of their valuables. He says they have cut a swathe through the country thirty miles wide in which everything is burned or dead or worse.'

She thinks of Marton Hall.

'But what of the Earl of Warwick?' she asks. 'Where is he while all this is happening?'

'He is raising troops, they say, and is supposed to be keeping London.'

Keeping London. That is typical of the Earl of Warwick, Katherine thinks.

'But I don't understand why we are languishing here,' she asks, 'instead of moving to stop the northerners?'

'There are provisions to be got,' Thomas supposes. 'And men need time to heal.'

Katherine thinks about it.

'Perhaps if people hear how bad the northerners are, they will be more eager to join Warwick? Or lend him money at any rate. Perhaps he is waiting until word spreads.'

Thomas is impressed. They walk on through the streets — Katherine is slowly becoming used to the pattens she has bought — and across the marketplace to their inn. Once more she thinks of Owen Tudor's death, and Thomas is just as preoccupied.

'Katherine,' he begins. 'I mean, of course, Margaret. What are you going to do?'

She shakes her head. Her headdress is weighty, awkward, always threatening to come off. Her dress hampers her movement too, and she has no idea how to behave in front of others, and is aware of their gaze, all the time, raking her body, judging her clothes, the way she walks, moves, tilts her head. Even Thomas judges her, she realises when she catches his all-too-rare glances, and she feels she is somehow failing him, and so a distance has opened up between them. She would dearly love to cast aside the dress and find some hose and a jacket and go about as Kit once more.

'I just don't know,' she says. 'I just don't know. It depends on so many different things. And on what you are going to do.'

Thomas shrugs.

'William Hastings—' he begins and then sees her expression and falters.

They let a cart rumble by.

'I know what you make of him,' he goes on, 'and I cannot say I approve of everything that he does, but he has been a good friend to me. To us. Without him, where would we be now?'

It is an interesting question. Certainly she is grateful for the protection Hastings has advanced, and without young Grylle there is no question that they would be dead. But she is aware of Margaret's gold coins in her bag. With them they could pay their way without incurring any obligation. They might not have had to witness the slaughter on the fields south of Wigmore Castle, when Edward's men used the naked Irishmen for archery practice, or forced them into the river with spear thrusts and axe blows and laughed at their clumsy attempts to swim. They might not have had to see men such as Tudor beheaded in the marketplace.

'So I wondered if we ought not to stay with Hastings's household?' Thomas is saying. 'He has shown great kindness, and to be with a household, to have someone looking out for us – well, we need it. We cannot just go about the country on our own again.'

She feels a flare of anger.

'It is very well for you, Thomas,' she says. 'You have cast off your previous life all too well and anyone can see how useful you have become. But what about me? I cannot put aside my sex forever. I cannot join William Hastings's household just like that and with no purpose. You seem to forget I am Lady Margaret Cornford.'

And she places one hand on her headdress and enacts the sort of curtsey she has seen other women perform. He stares at her, stricken.

'Great God above,' he says, 'you don't – You don't believe you can keep up the pretence? No? Surely?'

She doesn't know either, and God knows she does not want to, but fury makes her reply:

'I do. I disguised my sex for a year, living among you all and not one of you suspected. Not one. It will be that much easier to pretend to be a woman no one knows.'

Thomas is astonished.

'What if someone who knew Margaret sees you?' he asks. 'You recall Dwnn?'

'Dwnn is just one man,' she says. 'And he is back in Kidwelly. So long as I never go back there again, who is there to know I am not who I say I am?'

'And what about who you really are? Have you not thought about that? The family that placed you in the priory?'

She has thought of them.

'I've told you,' she says. 'There is nothing for me there. That truth lies beyond me.'

'But it is just so dangerous! What about Riven? So long as you live, he will want you dead!'

She nods. His concern for her softens her temper slightly.

'I know,' she says, calmer now. 'That is why I cannot do this without your help.'

'My help?' he says. 'Katherine, you know I'll do everything I can to protect you from Riven and all his kind. I'd die for you. But . . . it seems to me you are putting yourself in harm's way and for no very good reason.'

She looks at him for a long moment.

'If I go back to being Kit, then Margaret Cornford dies.'

He frowns. This is uncertain territory for him, but she can see he is trying.

'She is already dead,' he says. 'You are not keeping her alive.'

Katherine shakes her head. She is confused and none of this is easy. It does not make complete sense, even to her, and she cannot explain it to him properly. All she knows is that she must save Margaret Cornford and to do that, she must become Margaret Cornford, with all that that entails. It is her task. This way she might redeem herself in part for the girl's death. She had not deserved to die so harshly, so alone.

'I am, Thomas,' she says. 'I am.'

'But don't you understand?' he says. 'Don't you understand? What it means? If you are Margaret Cornford?'

He glares at her. For a moment she is frightened of him, the way he looms over her, his ferocity.

'If Richard Fakenham is still alive,' he spits, 'then you must marry him.'

She takes a step back and stands silent for a moment, suddenly unable to speak, as if winded. Dear God. Why had she not thought of this?

'Then I must marry him,' she hears herself say, though her voice fades to nothing as she speaks.

Thomas retreats. He no longer glares. Instead there are tears in his eyes. He puts his hand to his hair, pushing back his worsted cap. His face grows pale.

'Marry him?' he whispers.

She can feel her own tears welling over her eyelashes. She nods and they splash her cheeks.

'But . . .' she starts. 'But we must find out. We must find out if he is alive before we – before we . . . Oh God.'

But Thomas is gone. He turns and walks away without a backward glance.

And now the tears really come. They fall from her chin and though she wipes them with her sleeve she cannot help sobbing aloud and so she hardly hears the messenger, mud-flecked, fearful, on a near-dead horse that clatters past her on his way to the castle, though the news, when she hears it from the innkeeper of the White Hart, is a distraction.

The Earl of Warwick's army has been crushed, scattered to the wind.

His troops have been routed by those of the Queen's army at St Albans, near London. The Earl has escaped with his life, it is said, but the King, whom the archer Henry from Kent had held prisoner after that day outside Northampton, has fallen back into the Queen's hands, and now there is nothing to stop her retaking London. And if London falls then everything they've hoped for will be beyond their grasp. The lords among them – men such as March and Warwick – as well as lower men such as Hastings will be attainted for what they have done. It will mean the legal death of their families. It will mean literal death for them.

Katherine looks for Thomas at the White Hart, but cannot find him. His pack is still in the hall with his blanket but he is nowhere to be seen. She needs to talk to him, to try to make sense of it all, and to try to devise a plan. She needs to put things right with him.

She resolves to walk to the castle to find him there. Passing through the faint shadow thrown by the tower of the cathedral, she feels none of that familiar angst when she sees the friars and the priests going about their business. She is Margaret Cornford, in a fine gown, with a cloak about her shoulders, a headdress on her head and pattens on her feet. There is gold in her purse.

When she catches sight of Hastings himself though, she feels a familiar flutter of panic and her legs cease to obey her. He is on horseback, followed by five or six men in light armour, none of them Thomas, and he looks grimly preoccupied.

'My lady,' he greets her from the saddle, and she feels his appraising gaze rake across her dress, and he smiles a particular sort of smile, and then, as if he cannot stop himself, he throws his leg over the saddle and slides to the ground to walk with her. He has the disarming habit of talking to women in the same way he speaks to men.

'You have heard the news?' he asks.

'I have. It has changed things, hasn't it?' She feels her voice flutter. She is not so experienced an actor after all.

'Somewhat,' he agrees. 'But it is not a complete disaster.'

'If the Queen takes London?'

Hastings is blithe. 'We have men on the council there,' he says. 'The city'll not open her gates to those robbers and thieves and, hearing the tales of their excesses, more men join us every day.'

It is just as she's supposed.

'But still,' she asks. 'The loss of the King's person?'

Hastings smiles.

'Two things,' he says. 'First is that having Henry of Lancaster with them will only slow them down. They'll have to defer to him now, and he has never yet been known to make up his mind on any matter you care to name. Do I hold it with my right hand or left hand? See? Second thing is that it has forced our hand, shall we say. Henry's broken with the Act of Accord, which specifically states he must do nothing to harm either Edward or his father, and I think any sane man – or woman – would recognise the breach.'

'So?'

'So now he has forfeited his right to the throne.'

'Ah. And in his place, Edward?'

Hastings smiles.

'Exactly,' he says. 'That is as the Act has it. It clarifies things, hmmm?'

They walk on for a moment.

'Did you delay here waiting to see that exact thing happen?' she asks.

He looks at her sharply, but then smiles.

'No, no,' he says. 'The army is tired. We have no arrows or food. We cannot march on London so soon.'

He lies so smoothly, so engagingly, she finds herself enjoying it.

'It seems strange that the Earl of Warwick took the King with him to the battle. Almost as if he wanted him to be taken.'

Hastings laughs now.

'My lady,' he says, 'you suppose us far too clever.'

'And by not coming to his aid when you could, you have not only enhanced your own authority and reputations, you have left the Earl of Warwick looking less than invincible, too.'

This time Hastings is delighted. He claps his hands together and shuffles the steps of a jig.

'I know you do not mean to, my lady,' he says, laughing, 'but you have cheered me immeasurably. Until we coincided here, I had imagined the debacle at St Albans exactly that, a debacle. Now though? Now I see it as a shining victory.'

She cannot stop herself smiling at his pleasure.

'All you need do now is proclaim Edward as king,' she says, 'and all will be well. Save, of course, the small matter of the Queen's army.'

Hastings's smile fades. He pulls on the tip of his nose.

'Yes,' he says. 'There is that.'

They walk in silence for a few more paces.

'And what of you?' he asks as they near the castle drawbridge. Katherine does not know.

'It is the lot of women', he says sadly, 'to depend on men.'

On that note she asks him about Thomas. She does not quite know how to couch the question, since she is unsure how to express the relationship she has with Thomas. Is he her servant, bringing her back to the man to whom she is betrothed? She supposes he is.

'Everingham?' Hastings says. 'I've not seen him. I have offered him a place with me, but I understand he has obligations to you and of course to Sir John Fakenham. We are all concerned for Sir John. I have sent for news, you know? But so far, none.'

Katherine says nothing. They walk a few paces further.

'Everingham tells me you are betrothed to Sir John's son, Richard?' Hastings continues.

She feels a jolt of pain, as if someone has pressed on a bruise, but she is surprised to hear Thomas has lied to Hastings about her, in support of her claim to be Margaret Cornford. And at some cost to himself, she realises.

'I am,' she says.

'Then I wish you joy of it,' Hastings says. 'I can only hope the boy is alive. I heard he was summoned along with his father to Sandal, before the old Duke of York was killed, but there is now some doubt about him ever arriving.'

'I have heard nothing,' she says. 'But I should dearly love to know.'

'I think we all would,' Hastings agrees. There is something unsettling in his manner, as if he is after the same thing, but for a different reason. She thinks again of Grylle and the attentions he has been paying her.

'I should like to ride to Marton Hall and see for myself,' she says.

Hastings looks at her.

'Strange,' he says. 'Thomas Everingham asked the exact same thing.'

She is surprised again. Thomas has been busy on her behalf.

'But I cannot spare him,' Hastings says. 'He is too useful, and Edward – who will soon be crowned king, you know? He has come to think of your Thomas Everingham as some sort of charm. A talisman.'

Katherine bites her tongue to prevent herself saying what she thinks of this.

'You are of course free to go wherever you please,' Hastings goes on, 'but I should counsel against it. This rabble the Queen has gathered, they are as vicious a crowd you are likely to meet this side of the gates of hell itself. And, for the meantime, they own the land north of London, including your land at Cornford.'

He adds this almost as an afterthought, and then he trails off. She can see him looking at her, calculating quickly, that spark in his eye replaced by something altogether more serious, and she realises with a jolt what he is doing. He is calculating her worth. Why has she not thought this through? As Margaret Cornford she has now become an extravagantly attractive proposition.

In fact, she now realises, Thomas is right. She is just the sort of proposition that men might kill to possess. She recalls Lord Cornford, her supposed father, stabbed in the eye for the ownership of the castle and its manors, and now here she is, heir to that burden.

'Excuse me,' she says. 'I must go.'

'God give you prosperity!' Hastings calls after her, and she does not know if he is laughing at her. She hurries back to the inn, suddenly and completely terrified, so that even the sight of four canons rushing to compline unsettles her, and she arrives back at the inn folded in on herself and consumed with dread.

But where is Thomas?

As night falls her panic only increases. She sits on a chest and waits. She eats supper alone at the end of the table. Hours pass. The innkeeper, gaunt as a gallows, comes to cover the fire and Thomas is still not back. She sits for a while in the bloom of a spitting tallow candle and she hears without listening to them the fearful conversations of those at the table where all the talk is of the viciousness of the Queen's Scottish troops.

'She cannot afford to pay them in anything but booty,' one man says.

Eventually the innkeeper draws the bar across the door and she retires upstairs to the room she's shared with two others, a married couple who sometimes sigh in the night and do so that night while she lies there, listening to the ropes of their bed strain like the timbers of a ship at sea. She misses the heft of Thomas, his curious dusty smell and his arm across her in the night, and she wishes she were plain Kit again, and able to sleep with the others by the fire in the hall.

The next morning he is still not back. She eats in silence, aware of the grey-faced innkeeper studying her from under his heavy brows. Nor is he alone. It seems women do not travel unaccompanied, even in such strange times. She wonders if Thomas will ever come back and for a moment she has another long pang of panic.

What if something has happened to him, some stupid accident? Or can it be something worse? Can Riven or the giant have slipped into town and seen him before he saw them? Can he now be lying in a midden somewhere with his throat cut? His head smashed in? She puts on her cloak and cap and hurries back out into the town. It has started snowing again, heavy flakes from a scudding grey sky that melt on her face, and the streets are full of men in their travelling cloaks, grim-faced, gathered huddled at street corners with weapons over their shoulders and heavy canvas bags on the ground by their feet. Finally the army is on the move. Teams of oxen are being lashed towards the east gate through the mash of straw and dung that covers the road, each pair hauling a high-sided cart loaded with barrels and sacks of beans, spoiling in the snow. Stone-faced men on horseback ride in troops and everywhere they have put on their livery coats and helmets.

But where in all this is Thomas? Katherine dodges through the crowds, a single woman with no maid, attracting stares from the men and comments she cannot even begin to understand. A moment later she is lost. She's taken a wrong turn and is now in a narrowing lane, the way ahead blocked with all manner of foul-smelling filth, the upper storeys closing in on one another so that the occupants of one house could lean out of their windows and comfortably shake the hand of their neighbour. Two dogs and a pig compete for some stinking gobbet on the steps of one of the houses and as she passes the door of another it is slammed shut by an unseen hand.

The snow has turned to sleet, and the air is full of ashes, and someone pours a bucket of something from a window up ahead. She hears a laugh, bitter and humourless, and she picks up her hem and steps around a bloody hank of hair attached to a fragment of pale bone as rats slide away into the shadows. Coal smoke washes down the alleyway, catching her throat.

She turns up another alley and shadows move quickly towards her. She reverses to continue down the first alleyway. Dear God, she wishes Thomas were with her now. She stops. Ahead is a broad ditch, steaming and repugnant, a sewer where not even pigs venture.

Behind her a man is moving, two of them, emerging from the alleyway, one dragging his foot. They call to her and she feels her guts heave. She starts running, her pattens slipping in the filth, her new headdress slipping around her neck. She fumbles for the knife at her waist and draws it now, taking a crumb of comfort in its worn wooden handle. She jags past the dogs and the pig, and then hears one howl as it is kicked aside behind her.

'Come here, missus!'

'We only want to talk!'

She leaps up on to the walkway, slipping on the wet wood, catches a pillar, hauls herself up and runs on. She can feel their feet behind her. She throws herself out into the road, East Street, leading down past a friary to a little church and on through the east gate. A man

432

on horseback has paused by the junction; wrapped in his cloak, a cap pulled down over his eyes, he is watching the processing carts. Katherine grasps his stirrup strap and turns to face her attackers.

He looks down.

'Kit,' he says.

It is Thomas.

'Oh Christ,' she says. 'Thank God it is you.'

The relief overcomes her and she remains gripping his stirrup. He gets down and comes around from the other side of the horse.

'I have been looking for you,' he says. 'I went back to the inn. The innkeeper said you had gone.'

She flings her arms around him and presses her face into his neck. He is awkward, but his arms come around her at last, though there is little succour in his embrace, not as she has experienced before.

'Are you all right?' he asks.

'Thomas,' she says. 'I've missed you. Where've you been?'

'I have been busy,' he says. 'Getting provisions.'

She sees he has a new bow and a sheaf of arrows and that there are stout leather panniers on his saddle.

'We are going to ride to Marton,' he says. 'To see how it is. To see if – if they still live.'

'What about Hastings?' she asks. 'Has he let you go?'

Thomas evades her gaze.

'I have come to an arrangement with him,' he says.

She sees he wants her to ask no more.

PART SIX

To Marton Hall, County of Lincoln, February 1461

32

Thomas and Katherine leave the White Hart at dawn the next day and are at the city's east gate before daybell. Thomas bribes the Watch to let them through and Katherine laughs.

'How we've changed,' she says.

Thomas says nothing and they ride out through the common land deserted at this time of day save for pigs and goats among the wringing posts and tenter frames, and they follow the road that will take them to the east, to the city of Worcester. As the morning wears on they pass men and carts coming the other way, bringing barrels and sacks, and stacks of new bows and sheaves of arrows to Hereford, to provision the new Duke of York's army, and Katherine tries to make conversation.

'It is good to travel so warmly,' she tries, gesturing at his new travelling cloak. She too is wearing a new one, dark red with a fur collar and a deep hood and Thomas can see that she looks beautiful: her sharp features framed by the trim, the cold reddening her cheek and lending a spark to her eyes. Even her cracked lips do not detract. Men stare at her as they pass, some opening their mouths to greet her with a suggestive remark, perhaps, but the joke always dies on their tongues when they see Thomas's expression.

'And will we find an inn in this town Worcester?' she asks. 'There seem to be so many on the road.'

He grunts. He cannot stop looking at her, though God knows he does not want to. He knows he is doing the proper thing in taking her to Marton Hall, taking her to Richard Fakenham, but he can do no more than that. He cannot be as he has always been, because she is no longer as she was. She has left him, taken a different path, and, try as he might, he cannot force his features into his accustomed smile and cheer to see her go.

Even this bare minimum is hard.

He wonders if he should say something: tell her that though the thought of her becoming Margaret Cornford is bad enough, the thought of her becoming Richard Fakenham's wife makes him feel sick. He does not care about the lies he has already told to William Hastings and to the Earl of March; he does not care about keeping the dead girl's name alive; he doesn't care about Sir John's plans for Cornford Castle: all he wants is for everything to return to the way it was.

They find an inn at Worcester, near the cathedral, but he cannot share the bed the innkeeper offers her, and instead he sleeps by the hearth in the hall where the stones in the floor retain the fire's heat. He watches her take the bed, hesitantly, confused by the way he is behaving, and he wishes he could behave as he has always done, or that she would insist he comes with her, or she with him, but she does not, and he turns and feels his spirits twist into a savage little knot.

The next day is better and though they hardly speak, their silence is almost companionable, and they ride to another inn in another town where they must sleep in the hall, and they do so, her back to his chest, though Thomas will not touch her. The next morning he finds he has wrapped his arms around her, and her linen-capped head is just below his nose. He gets up before she wakes and hurries to wash in the well outside while rain falls from a leaden sky.

That day they find the road the locals call Rikeneld Street, where they turn north, and the next day they come across the first signs of the Queen's army's passing: a village where the houses are missing roofs and walls are broken down or burned black. Fences have been pulled apart, hovels destroyed, ovens dug up and windows carried off. The land lies in ruins, and smells of rot and spoil.

So Thomas stops to strap on his leg armour and the plate gauntlets, things he's bought in Hereford, probably looted from the field above Mortimer's Cross, but good enough. The helmet is gouged and the chinstrap stained and when Katherine sees it she wonders aloud what Richard Fakenham would have said if she'd ever have let his plate get so rusty when it was in her care in Sangatte. Thomas says nothing. It is too painful to think of that happy time. After a while he unstraps his bow and warns her to keep her little knife to hand. She does so, and they ride on.

The terrible sights continue as they go north: a convent stripped of everything; a line of new graves under the snow in a churchyard; an ugly man's head perched on a stone wall; three babies in the bottom of a well. Near Lichfield they see a body thrown high in the trees and Katherine asks how he thinks it came to be there. He doesn't know.

And now everyone they meet has a story of the northerners' cruelty, each worse than the last, each defying belief, and hatred of the Queen and her adherents is everywhere.

He wonders how the canons would have survived the Queen's northerners. He imagines them ringing that bell, and then what? They'd probably have opened the gates just as they had with Riven. And the northerners would have come in and smashed everything, stolen what they could, burned everything else. They'd've burned his psalter, he supposes. Or stolen it. He hardly cares. Bloody thing. All that time he'd spent on it. He'd probably have done the same thing. He can picture his table chopped and burned for firewood. And what about the sisters? What would the northerners have made of them?

He can easily imagine.

It grows cold again. The rain turns to sleet and then snow, spindling down from a grey sky, and Katherine pulls the cloak up around her ears. They cross the River Trent at Newark where they had stayed on their way down to Wales, and from the river's east bank they see no more burned buildings, but men still peer at them from their cottages, and everyone is armed with something, and everyone is afraid.

Lincoln has been spared, but the Watch is alert, gathered around their braziers, and when they stop Thomas and Katherine they ask questions about what the Earl of March is doing, what the Earl of Warwick is doing, and the whereabouts of the King and the Queen. Thomas and Katherine can tell them little, other than of what happened at Mortimer's Cross, and second-hand reports of this latest fight at St Albans, which saw Warwick's men scattered and the person of the King returned to the Queen.

'We heard that the Queen's army means to take London,' one of the men says, half asking, half telling. 'But that the city will not open her gates, and we heard the Earl of March who is now the Duke of York is hurrying from the west with his army to relieve the city?'

Thomas nods. That is most likely what is happening, he supposes.

'Will the Queen make a fight of it down south?' one of them asks.

'I don't know,' Thomas says. 'Her army is without supplies or friends down there, and, as you can see, it is cold. If the city aldermen do not open the gates, she might retire northwards, back to York, to make the Earl of March come to fight her up there.'

This is how he has heard it from William Hastings, and the men of the Lincoln Watch think that fair enough, and they let Thomas and Katherine through to the city. Thomas and Katherine walk their horses up the hill past the pardoner's house, still silent and ghostly, and up past the cathedral where the stationers have cleared their stalls and the doors are barred from within. They pass out through Bailgate and under the old arch on to the Roman road that cuts north. They climb up into their saddles again, and as they leave the city behind, there are crows cawing and loose balls of mistletoe in the trees and old snow on the fields.

They have travelled this road many times, often in happier circumstances, and once more he asks himself the same question he has been asking for the last four days: why? Why are they doing this? Of course he wants to find Sir John and Geoffrey, to find the others, to see if they are still alive, and of course he needs to tell them about Dafydd and Owen and Walter, and if that was all they were doing, then that would be bad enough, but Thomas must also lie to Sir John and Richard, tell them that Kit is dead, and that here is Lady Margaret Cornford to marry Richard. He can imagine Richard's face when he sees her. How pleased he will be that she is not plain, but in her own way beautiful . . .

And he – Thomas – will have to lie again, and again, and again. Forever.

'We should have brought an escort,' she says. 'Some men from Lincoln at least. What if there are still some of the northerners about?'

Thomas drops from the saddle and nocks the string of his new bow and then sticks some arrow shafts in his boot, in the style of Walter. He can feel the steel bodkin heads against his ankle and he wishes he still had the pollaxe. He mounts up again and they ride on, Katherine with her cloak around her ears so that all he can see of her is her red-tipped nose, sharp, like a beak.

Eventually they reach the turning and she stops her pony.

'Thomas,' she asks. 'What are you hoping for?'

He looks blank, as if he has no idea, but she does not believe him.

'I don't know,' he answers after a while. 'I want the hall to be exactly as we left it. I want Sir John to be sitting by the fire, with Geoffrey on hand, and Goodwife Popham still fussing about her daughter's marriage. I want to smell apple-wood smoke and that mix of roasting pork and baking bread and those herbs she used to put in the bed upstairs. I want, I suppose, everything to be the same. Something calm and orderly amidst all this. All the things we've seen. Everything that's happened.'

Still he cannot tell her what he really wants.

She smiles weakly.

'It has become what people call home, hasn't it?' she says.

He nods.

After a moment she asks the question he has been avoiding all through the journey.

'And what of Richard?' she asks. 'What of him?'

He kicks the horse on and they ride for a moment before he feels he can control his voice.

'I imagine him out riding,' he says, at length. 'I imagine him out riding with a hawk on his fist. A hobby hawk or something.'

He tries a smile too, but feels it's more like a grimace, in keeping with the wintry landscape. He will stop at the gate, he thinks. That is what he will do. He will stop at the gate and turn and ride away, back to Hastings and the Earl of March who appreciate him, who would not expect him to stand and watch while a lie is practised.

'They will see through me in an instant, won't they?' Katherine says. 'They will see me as merely Kit in a dress.'

'No,' Thomas says, and he is right, for she no longer looks like Kit in a dress. She looks beautiful, and not merely to him. He saw the way other men reacted to her on the road, and in the inns. Yet half of him is hoping Sir John and Richard will see through her, and will think she is someone other than Lady Margaret Cornford, and will therefore not risk the marriage, lest someone else discovers the truth.

'How do I look, Thomas?' she asks. 'Tell me.'

He looks at her again. His eyes are slow, as if he has a cold, and he cannot mask his misery.

'You look like a lady,' he says. 'He will not think you are Kit in a dress. Only—' He stops.

'Only what?'

He takes a deep breath.

'Only I will think that,' he says. 'I will think it for however long that lasts.'

She does not answer for a moment. He thinks he has said too much, or perhaps too little. Then she turns and there are tears in her eyes and she looks more awkward and more beautiful than ever and he feels his heart gripped with pain.

'I am sorry, Thomas,' she says. Her face has softened. Her eyes are wet with tears. 'May God forgive me but I am sorry. Sorry that it is like this, and not as it should be. I wish we had done things differently. But we have – We have to, don't we? For her sake. It is my – our – a – penance, I think? For all that we have done.'

'A penance,' he repeats. And suddenly he sees it *is* a penance. But it is not a penance for the death of Margaret, but for the death of the nun in the priory, the one with glass in her back, the one whom Katherine pressed down and killed; and that because of this nun's death, Katherine has endured everything, and she will go on enduring whatever may come at her until her end.

He wants to tell her not to marry Richard, and that he does not know how he will live without her, and that God would not want her to suffer any more, nor make him suffer any more, but he finds he cannot. He cannot find the right formulation, cannot think of all the things he wants to tell her, and so instead he looks away to hide the tears that prick his own eyes, and he says:

'The village is ahead.'

And they ride on towards a sky white with the threat of more snow, and soon they will be at the hall and then it will all start.

Only there is something wrong. Thomas pulls up his horse. There is no smoke above the village, nothing to show that anyone lives there.

Katherine feels it too.

'Where is everyone?' she asks.

There are no prints in the snow, as if no one has passed this way since the last fall. Thomas slips quickly from his saddle and nocks an arrow, taps his sword hilt. He passes Katherine his horse's reins and then skirts up the road towards the butter cross. The church is intact, its windows in place, its door sound and shut, but again, there are no tracks on the steps. Where is its sexton? A cottage ahead is likewise undamaged, likewise deserted. She watches Thomas duck past the tiled bakery. He can smell something claggy and cold. A dead body. Man or animal? One or two? He follows the road up past the pen where Katherine used to stop to scratch the pigs' backs. Empty. Still no tracks.

He crosses to another line of cottages, pushes a door open. Inside it is dark. He bends over the fire. The ashes are cold, even the earth below is cold. No one has been here for days.

Katherine is outside, holding the horses. She looks at him. He shakes his head. They both know what this means.

They carry on up the road until they find the first body in the furlong beyond the apple trees. It is being bothered by five or six crows. Thomas steps across the ditch into the field, stops, takes aim with the bow and sends an arrow humming across the furrows to knock one of the birds cartwheeling. The others clap their wings and take flight, off across the fields.

The body is lying face down, a substantial mound, covered in a thick crust of old snow. The man had been wearing a jack, faded red, much repaired, the elbows patched with more red cloth. Green stitches. His fingertips are eaten down to the bone. Thomas squats and studies the body without touching it. The crows have found their way in above the kidneys and the smell is strong, the sort to coat the tongue.

He can feel tears prick his eyes and he feels a sense of desolation. He stands, steps back, crosses himself, murmurs a prayer. It is short, for he intends to return to bury the body himself, properly in the churchyard, and then he finds the dead bird and pulls it from his arrow with the sole of his boot, wiping the arrowhead in the snow.

He walks slowly back to Katherine.

'Who is it?' she calls.

He can tell she knows. It is just that she does not want to be right.

'Geoffrey,' he says when he is near, and he can hear her draw breath.

'Oh dear God,' she says and she squeezes her eyes shut. 'He was – Oh God.'

He almost takes her in his arms, but dares not. Instead he nods and walks past her and she follows him silently up along the road through the orchard to the little copse where they hobble the horses. Here they find the second body, leaning with his back to a tree trunk under the naked wands of the coppiced willow. He has his hands clapped around a crossbow quarrel lodged in his cheek. His fingers are swollen; the flesh is blue and mottled, streaky with dark blood. Snow caps his helmet in a point, too, and it has mixed with the blood on his livery coat to turn it rose. Thomas bends and brushes the snow away with the back of his fingers. Above the man's heart, picked out in felt and clumsy stitches, is a badge. A raven.

They stare at it for a moment.

'One of Riven's.'

They stop in the trees to watch the back of Marton Hall. One end of the roof is scorched and blackened, just as Dafydd's little house had been, and the yard smells of soot and human waste. The shutters are up, and there are no prints in the snow. It looks deserted. They walk behind the outbuildings and the woven fence until they are at the front of the house. An arrow is buried in the daub by the door. Below it, another body is stretched out in the mud, his feet facing the house, as if thrown from the doorway. His helmet lies some way away and something thick and stubby sticks from his throat. Another crossbow quarrel.

Thomas is about to step out of the trees when she stops him with a hand.

'Wait,' she says. She is studying the hall's rush roof, which is clear of snow, and from which water drips. 'It means it is warm,' she says.

Nothing moves, though, and after a moment Thomas gets up again and is about to cross the yard when a shutter in the house drops with a crash and there is a shout. Thomas jumps, throws himself back. A quarrel zips past, catching his sleeve with a bang that almost pulls his arm off. He scrambles back behind a trunk. Katherine is crouched staring at him, her eyes wide.

'Christ's sake!' he breathes, rubbing the wrist. The sleeve is torn to shreds. The crossbow quarrel lies in the snow. 'Who's in there?' he calls. 'Who are you?'

There is no reply.

'We come here in peace,' Thomas shouts again. 'We are looking for Sir John Fakenham.'

There is the slightest movement in the house. Someone is being cautious.

'What do you want with him?' someone shouts from within.

'We are friends of his,' Thomas shouts back. 'We are of his household.'

There is a long silence. Then someone calls:

'Who are you?'

'My name is Thomas Everingham,' he shouts. 'Thomas Everingham and – and Lady Margaret Cornford. I used to live here. We are looking for Sir John Fakenham. Or Richard Fakenham. Or anyone who might know their whereabouts.'

There is another crash. Another shutter slides down.

'Thomas Everingham?'

The voice is louder now and there is a face between the bars in the upstairs window: white-haired, flabby, red.

'Sir John?'

'My boy!'

Sir John disappears. Thomas glances at Katherine. From the house comes a grate as something is dragged across stone flooring and then a deep thunk as the drawbar is slid back. Then the door opens on unoiled hinges and Sir John stands in the shadows, still cautious.

Thomas crosses the yard.

'Dear God,' Sir John cries. 'It really is you.'

He is looking hellish. He's grown a beard, and is unwashed and filthy, like the lowest sort of villager, but Thomas hurries the last few steps and throws his arms around the old man. They pound one another on their backs, pulling each other close.

'Great God above, it is more than wonderful to see you,' Sir John cries. He leaves off the hugging to hold Thomas at arm's length. Then he embraces him again. Tears are flooding down his grimy cheeks.

'What news?' he asks. 'What news of Walter? Of Dafydd? And where's Kit?'

He peers over Thomas's shoulder but Katherine has stepped back into the shadow of the trees and is waiting, watching.

Thomas shakes his head. He is crying too now.

'Dead,' he says. 'They were killed in Wales. We were trying to get back, back to you, to this house, but— It was – It was Riven. Riven's boy. And that giant.'

Sir John makes a noise somewhere between a groan and a scream.

'Oh dear Christ!' he says. 'Oh dear Christ!'

'Riven's men followed us to Wales,' Thomas goes on.

Sir John pulls his ears. 'Oh God!' he whispers. 'Oh God!'

'And you?' Thomas asks. 'How have you fared? Where is everybody else?'

'Us? Christ above. We have – Well, you see for yourself. We have had quite a time of it and have had to withstand Riven's attentions as well. I thought you might be one of his men, back for more. But, Thomas, who is with you? Did you say Lady Margaret Cornford?'

Thomas can feel his pulse in his ears. He is about to try to gull Sir John, to defraud him. Dear God, what if he just laughs when he sees Katherine? What if he just says, 'That's not Margaret, that's Kit'?

He opens his mouth to stop all this, to say no, that is not Lady Margaret, that is Kit in a dress, when Katherine emerges from the trees in the corner of his vision. She has taken off her cloak, so that it might be more easily seen that she is wearing a dress, so it might be more easily seen she is a woman, and she has plumped up her linen headdress. Despite everything, despite her thinness, her grubby clothes, her worn shoes, or even because of these, she looks, to Thomas's eye at least, wholly beautiful.

Sir John stares. Katherine falters. She glances at Thomas, seeking reassurance. There is a long tense moment.

Sir John seems dumbfounded. Then he recalls himself.

'My lady,' he says. 'Welcome to our house.' And he steps towards her and takes her hand and kisses her, a frown flickering across his brow, perhaps because she is wearing no gloves or rings and her hands are still dirty from the road, and despite himself, Thomas is relieved.

'Sir John,' Katherine says. 'It is an honour, though what is . . .?' And she hesitates nicely, her gaze flickering across the house's façade, the arrow in the jamb, Sir John's wild appearance.

'Yes,' Sir John admits. 'You find us somewhat unprepared. For guests, I mean.' He laughs weakly, but then he tails off. He is staring at her openly, rudely, and he starts crying again. His eyes screw tight and the tears flow into the silver threads of his beard. He begins to sob, and Katherine looks at Thomas for guidance.

Thomas takes the old man's shoulders.

'Sir John,' he says. 'What is wrong?'

Sir John cannot speak.

'Where is Richard?' Katherine asks, her tone sharp and urgent, out of her new role.

'Here.'

A new voice joins them. Coming from the doorway.

Both turn.

Standing there, gripping the lintel with both hands, is Richard Fakenham. He is in soft leather boots and a rough blue jacket and wrapped around his eyes is a long length of grubby linen bandage.

'He is blinded,' Sir John says in a low voice. 'In both eyes.'

33

It is after dark and they are sitting in the hall by the damped fire.

'It was that giant of his,' Sir John tells them. 'They caught him and Little John Willingham by means of trickery. They killed Little John. With an axe, Richard says, and then when he was dead, they took Richard and they held him down and – well.'

Sir John cannot go on. There is a long silence.

'Is he asleep?' Katherine asks.

Sir John shakes his head.

'I hear him crying sometimes,' he says. 'In the night. It is not a sound a father wants to hear.'

'Why did they do it?' Thomas asks.

Sir John shrugs.

'Because they could,' he says, 'and to send me a message, I suppose.'

Katherine sits and listens, unable to contribute, seeing again how awkward this pretence will be. Sir John glances at her now and then, and she imagines he thinks her shy, but in truth she does not know what to think or where to put herself.

When Richard had first emerged from the house, she had stood rooted while Thomas fumblingly reintroduced himself. They'd hugged and kissed and Richard had said that it was good to see him and a silence had fallen and then Richard had said it was good to know that he was alive anyway, and he had asked about Walter and then Kit. Thomas had glanced her way without moving his head and, after a moment's hesitation that might have been mistaken for misery, he'd told them that both were dead, and that of the five men who had set out for Wales, only he remained alive.

She saw how much the lie cost Thomas. She wishes she could somehow undo all this, and go back, and deal straight with the world – or as straight as she ever had – and have Thomas as he was.

Richard had wailed when he'd heard the news and had taken himself off, fumbling up the steps.

'Should we try to help?' Katherine had asked Sir John.

Sir John had shaken his head.

They'd heard him thump around in the chamber above and then it had gone quiet.

Now Sir John pours himself some of the ale, and speaks of the past month.

'We didn't go to Sandal,' he says. 'Didn't want to spend all winter in a castle with so many men cooped up behind those damned walls that it'd be a job to find somewhere to shit without another man doing the same on your lap. And thank the Lord I didn't go. I suppose you heard? York and his men went charging out of the castle gates – leaving the bloody things open, can you believe it, and the drawbridge down – to relieve a foraging party that had, quite against the rules of the Christmas truce, been attacked by some of Somerset's men.

'The next thing they know the woods are heaving with more of the bastards. It was over in moments, I heard, and anyone of any quality whom we had on our side – gone. The Duke of York, of course, and that young fool Rutland – do you remember him at Westminster? Arguing with Warwick, he was – he was murdered by Clifford after it was all over, with the lad trying to get into Wakefield. As for the Earl of Salisbury, well. He was taken to Pontefract. I thought they were going to ransom him to Warwick. Can you imagine? An Englishman paying another Englishman for the return of his own father? But in the end one of Exeter's bastards dragged the poor old sod from his rooms and chopped his bloody head off. Right there and then. The Earl of Salisbury!'

He asks Thomas about the battle Edward of March has won – he cannot stop calling him the Earl of March – and what he thinks will happen in London.

'I have it from William Hastings,' Thomas says, 'that since King Henry's adherents killed Richard, the old Duke of York, at Wakefield, then the Act of Accord is void and that Edward, the new Duke of York, is free to claim the throne as his right.'

'Then what will happen to King Henry?' Sir John wants to know. 'Will he resign?'

Thomas does not know.

'Not if he is with the Queen,' Katherine cannot stop herself answering.

Sir John squints at her, then tugs on his beard. It sounds raspy. She takes a sip of the ale, which is disgusting, and she tries to do it delicately. There is a silence until Sir John turns to Thomas.

'You know Giles Riven has switched sides again?' he asks. 'Gone back to the Queen after Wakefield. By Christ, I'd love to have one last try at him. For all that he has done to me, for all that he has done to mine, I wish he were dead and already enjoying his time with the devil in hell. Do you suppose he will be there? With the Queen, I mean?'

Of course Thomas has no idea.

'He has cost us sorely.' Sir John goes on. 'Sorely. But we have taxed him too. His men came to surround the house, you know, to drive us out. As soon as we heard the news from Sandal, we knew those northern bastards'd be coming our way, so we were ready, we thought. Then they went through Newark instead, and they were so keen on plundering the south they didn't bother to ford the river. We thought we were safe. Life was getting back to normal, or as normal as it could be.

'And then they came. They caught Goodwife Popham. Down in the village.

'Geoffrey and Brampton John and Little John were here in the hall, and Elizabeth, you remember her, Thomas? Geoffrey's daughter. She came running to fetch help. I reckon now that they'd let her go just to come and get us. We snatched up whatever we could, thinking it was just a party of latecomers gone wild on their way south.

'We didn't bother with harness or anything, and Geoffrey, well, of course he was worried. It was his wife they had. So we ran down to the village. We could hear her screaming in one of the cottages, but there wasn't anybody about, so, well, I suppose we should have seen it for what it was. The first arrow knocked Brampton John off his feet. The second went straight through Geoffrey's eye. Dropped him just like a bull. Christ. He'd been with me forever, you know? And they killed him, just like that.' He snaps his fingers. 'Bastards,' he says.

There is a long silence. Katherine wipes away a tear. She knows she is not supposed to know these people Sir John speaks about, but she cannot help herself.

'I killed one,' Sir John goes on. 'The bowman, thank Christ, before he could loose another arrow. And Richard got another. The others rode away. Richard took the bowman's horse, Little John the other horse. They went after them. Then I thought, too late: My God, it's a trap. To get us out of the house. I ran back. Fast as I could.' Sir John's face is grey with shame and regret. 'I got back just in time to see them riding off with Liz over a saddle. They'd set a fire in the roof and one in the stables and the horses were screaming. I had to make a choice.'

There is silence in the room. A log on the fire lets out a long sigh.

'I have that girl's life on my conscience,' Sir John says. 'And God will be my judge in the next world.'

Both murmur amen.

'I let the horses go, and I put out the fire. Then I waited. I thought when Richard and John got back I could send one of them to Lincoln to raise some more men. I heard horses in the yard and I ran out. But it wasn't them. Or rather, it was. It was Riven's men. They dropped Richard in the muck and rode away laughing. He was screaming and kicking and there was blood in his eyes, and I knew straight away what they'd done.'

There is a long silence. Sir John pinches the bridge of his nose.

'But what about the dead men outside?' Thomas asks.

Sir John seems to brighten.

'Them? Riven's scouts. They were taunting us, shouting the foulest things. About the things they'd done to young Liz, and to Richard. Thank God for that crossbow. D'you remember Kit left it when he went? He said I'd need it before he did, or something. The boy was usually right, wasn't he, Thomas? Anyway, I wounded one or two more over the course of the next day and by Christ I hope they died miserable deaths. Then they said they'd just wait. Starve us out. But their hearts weren't in it. I think once they'd done that to Richard they knew they needn't worry any more.'

It made sense, Katherine supposes. Once Riven heard he'd missed the chance to take Margaret Cornford in Wales, he must have changed tactics. He must have thought she'd never marry Richard if he was blind. She wants to ask why Riven had not simply killed Richard, but she cannot betray her knowledge. She wishes Thomas would ask, but perhaps he is too sensible to ask a father why his son hasn't been killed, only blinded.

Sir John turns to address her.

'I'm sorry you find us this way, my lady. I'm sorry my boy is the way he is now. He was a wonderful young man before this. A wonderful swordsman, wasn't he, Thomas? And a fine huntsman. He had such a love of life. To know him was to love him. I know every father says that, but . . . Had you met him properly, I am sure you would have admired him. He was kind, too, of course, wasn't he, Thomas? Hmmm?'

Thomas nods but cannot lift his gaze from the table.

'Will he not join us?' Katherine asks.

Sir John shakes his head. They are silent for a long time. Katherine is aware of Sir John's gaze on her, but when she looks up he is smiling with tears in his eyes.

'Where is Riven now, d'you know?' Thomas asks. His voice has taken on that hard flat tone. Sir John shakes his head.

'He has not bothered us for days. Weeks even.'

'Then he must be with the Queen's army,' Thomas says.

Sir John nods as if to allow it.

'Then this time I'll not fail,' Thomas says. 'This time I'll go and find him and I'll put an end to it. Put an end to him. He cannot be left to live after this, not now, and we cannot go on living like this either.'

Katherine wonders if anything is ever that simple.

She sleeps that night in Sir John's bed, Sir John sharing with Richard on the smaller truckle bed by her side, Thomas downstairs by the covered fire, keeping watch. The sheets are filthy and there is dog hair everywhere. She's forgotten the dogs. Talbots, they were, absurd-looking things. She supposes them dead now. At some point Richard gets up in the night and fumbles his way downstairs.

What must it be like, to be blind? she wonders. To be constantly in the dark? She tries to imagine what Richard must be feeling, even apart from being left blind. She recalls Thomas's face the moment the giant pressed his thumb into his eye on the ferryman's skiff. It had been filled with naked terror, a sensation that surely no man would ever forget. And for someone like Richard, who thought himself a soldier, it must be doubly difficult.

Would it have been better for Richard to have been killed? Probably, she thinks. Which is why the giant didn't do it.

Dear God! Thomas has talked of the mistake of sparing Riven's life, but what of the giant? Even at the time she'd known they should have killed him, when he was lying stunned by the boat that morning, but they'd never have been able to do it. They were too innocent then. Now, though, she would happily crash that pollaxe into the giant's face, happily cut his throat. For a moment her body is thronging with energy.

She feels the constriction of her shift, wrapped tight around her legs and her waist, and she wishes she were wearing a shirt and braies as she used to when she was Kit. She thinks of Thomas downstairs by the fire, wrapped in solitude, and she feels a flare of anger. He is a stubborn fool, she thinks. If he'd said just one thing, or if he'd tried for a single moment to dissuade her from pretending to be Margaret Cornford, then she would have thrown off her cloak and swapped it for some ragged boy's clothing, and she would have resumed the life of Kit in an instant.

But now it is too late.

And the tears come, silently sliding down to her temples, when she thinks about how they are betraying Sir John and Richard, people who have only ever offered them kindness, and she curses herself for ever thinking to remain Margaret Cornford.

And so what is to become of her? she wonders. To what life has she condemned herself? A life that serves as its own penance? A better life than she might have expected at the priory, perhaps, but one shot through with deception and heartbreak, one in which anything she does to serve herself will wound those whom she most loves.

And it is just as she is drifting off, gripped by the sorrow of these thoughts, that her eyes fly open and she is suddenly wide awake.

She thinks she can see the way out of this. She thinks there is a way.

The next morning they are up before cockcrow. Thomas is away all morning, burying Geoffrey's body in the churchyard, dragging the others away from the house, and it falls to Katherine to resuscitate the fire and to make soup with such supplies as remain. She knows her way around the buttery and the kitchen and she knows how to haul the bucket up from the well. She is about to start shovelling the excrement from the back, just as she used to when she was Kit, when she sees Sir John squinting at her, and she leaves the shovel where it is, and she wipes her hands on her skirts and comes to sit at the board where Richard is grinding his fists into his eye sockets.

'Do they hurt?' she asks.

Richard grunts.

'Let me see,' she says. His bandages are grubby and stained and since the bleeding must have stopped, she wonders what they are really for? She moves close. Richard stiffens but she places a hand on his shoulder and a moment later he relaxes. She is conscious that Sir John is watching as she unwinds the filthy linen.

'Tied it myself,' he says. 'I wished we'd had Kit with us still. He was – well, he had a gift that one, didn't he, Richard?'

Richard grunts.

'He cut me,' Sir John continues, addressing Katherine now. 'This last autumn. Before all this. I had a fistula. You know what that is, hmmm? Nasty, anyway. Could hardly walk for the pain of the thing. Anyway. Kit learned to read, can you believe? Only a boy, but he learned to read, and then got hold of some old leech's instructions about how to cut out a fistula, and he cut mine out. Simple as that. Bloody miracle it was, wasn't it? Richard? A bloody miracle.'

Katherine blinks away the tears that gather in her lashes. Richard says nothing. She peels away the last wrap of linen and there are his eyelids, sunken and gummed together, crusted with what looks like sand and blood. A smell rises from them, a sort of sweet fug.

Sir John sucks his teeth.

Katherine fetches the last of the wine and some fresh linen from the coffer in the room above and she washes Richard's eyes, wiping away the crust and the traces of blood with a good pad of the material so that she does not have to feel the emptiness. When she has finished she sees that there is no real need to cover his eyes, except that it is such a terrible shock to see the empty sockets. So she cuts some dry linen with her knife and reties it around his head. She can smell Richard now and she thinks how he needs a wash, and she wonders whether it will be her task to insist on this kind of thing in the future.

'Where did you learn your skills, my lady?' Sir John asks.

She does not answer. She does not understand that Sir John is talking to her.

'There,' she says. 'Better, I think.'

And now Sir John is looking at her through narrowed eyes, but then Thomas returns with some wood for the fire and the body of a heavy duck with a limp neck. Sir John cackles and they set to work gutting and plucking it.

'Your swineherd is back,' Thomas tells them. 'And he says the others will be back soon.'

Sir John nods.

'To my shame I sent them to Lincoln,' he says, 'since I could not guarantee their safety with Riven and his men in the Hundred.'

The next day Katherine catches the scent of wood smoke in the air and there are some women bent-backed in the fields and a sense that everything might return to the way it was. She gets Thomas to carry the linen up the old lane to the river, where she rolls up her skirts and sets about the washing. It is so cold she can stand it for no more than a few moments at a time and is pleased when one of the women from the village finds her way to the riverbank and agrees to help for a cost Katherine would gladly double. At the end of the day they wring out the not very much cleaner linen and spread it on the hawthorn branches and when Katherine returns to the hall exhausted, there is soup and ale and news from the south.

The Queen's army has not taken London, but has turned and is making its way back up north, to York, just as William Hastings had hoped.

'Praise Jesus,' Sir John says, 'thought we had better ready ourselves lest they come this way.'

'Won't they take the shortest route?' Thomas asks.

Sir John grunts to admit the possibility but the following days are spent anxiously. They have hoarded as much food as they can buy: apples, smoked mutton, dried peas and beans, three barrels of ale. Thomas has his new bow and two more sheaves of arrows and he has collected up the quarrels and the crossbow stands by the door, ready for use.

Then they wait by the damped fire and hope the smoke does not broadcast their presence and Katherine sleeps, and thinks, and prepares herself.

As the days pass, the tension slowly tightens, and they take turns at the windows and one of them is always awake through the night, but then there comes a point when nothing has happened and they begin to believe the Queen's army has passed them by, and then, the next week, when it snows again, there is a day afterwards when the sky is clear and blue, and they gather outside to listen to distant bells, from as far away as Lincoln perhaps, sounding in the icy air.

'Is it a warning?' Thomas asks, his breath fogging his face.

'Too fast,' Richard says. It is good to hear him have an opinion on something. He looks better now that he is shaved and washed and his eyes trouble him less since Katherine washed them, and while the others cover their eyes from the sun on the snow, he stands perfectly still and faces south.

'I think they must be to celebrate something,' he says.

'But what?' Sir John asks.

They must wait until the next day to find out. It is another friar, in grey this time, garrulous and travelling south, who has met a man travelling north, a Scot, who robbed him.

'I thank St Matthew that he did not take my beads,' the friar says, touching the loop at his belt. 'Though he took all I had to eat and shared my fire to cook it over.'

In exchange for the food the Scot had shared his news though, and once they set beans and ale before the friar, he divulges it as if it were worth gold.

'Only that in London Edward of March has been proclaimed king!'

Sir John whistles.

'Edward of March is king!' he says. 'So that is what the bells were for.'

'Aye,' the friar agrees. 'They did not ring them sooner for fear of attracting the attention of the Queen's army.

There is a long moment while they consider this. Katherine remembers the lanky boy with the big feet and the strange leer she could not understand at the time. What has God seen in him that he should be king? Something that Henry lacked, she supposes: some vigour, some youth. A fresh start perhaps, a new green shoot in the garden, but then what about the old growths? What will happen to all those dukes and earls and lords that fought for Henry in the past?

'And what about King Henry?' Sir John asks. 'What will become of him?'

'King Edward's affinity says that King Henry broke some Act of Parliament, and that because he's done so, he is rightly deposed, and that from now on we are to call him just Henry of Lancaster.'

'Henry of Lancaster,' Sir John repeats, his voice soft with regret. 'Don't suppose he'll like that. Still less his queen.'

The friar nods.

'No,' he says. 'The Scotsman says the Queen has retired to York and has gathered a power of nobles such as has never been seen in England, and that she means to smash this new king Edward, and put his head up on a spike along with his father's and brother's.'

'And what is King Edward doing?' Katherine asks.

There is a moment's silence while the friar eats another spoonful.

'Oh,' he says, wiping his mouth on his sleeve, 'he is at the head of his own army, marching north to meet Henry of Lancaster in a battle he says will prove God's will once and for all.'

Katherine notices Thomas is gripping his cup too hard and that his face has grown pale, but it is only the next morning, as they are walking to the churchyard to say prayers over Geoffrey's new-dug grave, that they have a moment alone together.

'Did you know this would happen?' she asks.

He nods.

'And I must go,' he says.

She stops. It is the most senseless thing she has ever heard.

'Go?' she repeats. 'Go back to the fighting? No. No. You cannot. Thomas. You cannot.'

'I must,' he says, and looks away, suddenly evasive. 'William Hastings—' he starts. 'William Hastings has asked me to take command of some men. Some archers. A hundred of them. And I said I would. I gave my word. It was why he let us leave Hereford and ride up here to find Sir John. And Richard.'

She is aghast. She nearly grabs his jacket.

'Dear God, Thomas,' she says. 'You cannot go. You will be killed.'

'Don't say it, Katherine.'

'No. You are right. I will not. But— But what about us? You cannot leave us here. If Riven knew we were here—? What then?'

Thomas sighs lengthily. His feet are heavy on the snow.

'What would you have me do?' he asks, just as if he has already discarded all other options. 'What else can I do?'

'Stay,' she says. 'Stay here. Where you are needed most. You can see: Sir John, Richard, me. We need you. As Hastings and March and Warwick do not.'

'Riven is with the Queen's army,' he says. 'I will find him this time. Put an end to all this. Finally. For good. Then I will come back. We will plant the fields or whatever it is you want me to do then.'

They are at the churchyard now, and Geoffrey's grave is below a yew by the gate. Katherine wonders where Goodwife Popham is buried, and Liz, but there is nothing to be gained from thinking that way, she knows, and so she closes her eyes and kneels next to Thomas on the icy earth and while he repeats the prayers for the dead, just as he did over Margaret Cornford's body in the hills in Wales, all she can do is pray that he will not leave her.

When they get back to the hall, Sir John is sharpening his sword on the same step that Walter used.

'I am coming with you, Thomas,' he says. 'Or rather, you are coming with me.'

Thomas frowns.

'No,' he says. 'There is no need.'

Sir John stands up. He has lost weight since this ordeal started, but he is still a formidable presence, with an old soldier's heft and a cunning cast in his eye.

'There is every need,' he says. 'I can no longer live like this, huddled away, waiting for news, and you forget I am indentured to my lord Fauconberg. I promised to provide him with fifteen archers, and if I cannot do that, then I must do what I can. Besides, this battle will be the greatest yet. It will end this for once and for all, and I want to be there, Thomas. I want to see if I can find Riven myself before it is too late.'

Thomas almost laughs.

'Sir John,' he says, 'these battles – they are not like that. You will not know if you do find him. You will just find yourself face to face with a man in harness who will try to kill you as quickly as he can. He will try to open your face with a hammer. Something like that. Or his men will use their bills to pull you over and one of them'll stab you in the balls while you cry out for mercy.'

Now Sir John laughs.

'So it has not changed so very much from my day,' he says. 'Come on. Get your gear. We must make ourselves ready.'

'What of us?' Katherine asks. She is standing beside Thomas and her pulse is hammering and she feels faint. Sir John turns to her as if he has only just noticed her.

'Ah,' he says, and she watches him glance back at Thomas. 'Ah. I thought, perhaps, you would stay here with Richard? To maintain the house? I have asked one of the women in the village to come. Also called Margaret, though she is Meg. She will be here.'

Katherine feels like shouting at him, like grabbing his neck and wringing it.

'No,' she says. 'You cannot leave us here alone. What if Giles Riven is not with the Queen's army? What if his son is not? What if that giant of his is still here? What then? It is just me, and Richard, and this Meg.'

Sir John is ashamed but his shoulders are already in mid-shrug.

'My lady—' he says.

'We are coming with you,' she interrupts. 'We will not stay here to be murdered.'

Sir John is stricken. He looks at Thomas. Thomas nods slightly.

Sir John lets out his breath.

'Very well, my lady,' he says. 'Very well. We shall leave at first light tomorrow.'

PART SEVEN

To Towton Field, County of Yorkshire, March 1461

34

It is a clear morning and the sun comes up behind them, throwing their shadows long across the frosted mud of the road. Thomas is up front, then Sir John leading Richard by a rope, and then Katherine. Thomas has packed everything he owns because he does not think he will come back to Marton Hall, and just before he loses sight of it for the final time, he turns and tries to remember the happy times. Then he rides on.

The land north of Marton has been spared, and it is only when they cross the Trent at Gainsborough that they encounter the waste left by the northerners again: buildings pulled down for firewood, pens and sties emptied of livestock. There is that smell of something left to rot and ungainly crows squabble in the lower branches.

They ride on through the day towards Doncaster. The road improves, but a sheet of pale cloud obscures the sun and later it begins sleeting again. Sometime in the early afternoon they see a band of eight men on horseback riding ahead. Thomas notches an arrow and waits. Then Katherine recognises Fauconberg's blue and white livery.

'Good eyes you've got, my lady,' Sir John says without looking at her.

Soon the men reach them. They are a picket, riding from Pontefract Castle, in full harness.

'How many men has Fauconberg?' Sir John asks their captain, a big man who keeps his eyes on Katherine.

'Six thousand?' the man guesses. 'Archers, in the main. King

Edward and the Earl of Warwick are bringing more men-at-arms and what have you, and the Duke of Norfolk is expected to bring yet more from the east. We should number something like twenty thousand in the field.'

Sir John whistles admiringly.

'Such a host!' he says.

'Perhaps,' the captain agrees. 'But the Queen's power is greater yet. Almost all the lords are with her. Somerset, of course, Northumberland, Exeter, Dacre, Roos, Devon, Clifford . . .'

He continues naming men of whom Thomas has never heard, but Sir John looks steadily more wintry. When the man finishes the list, Sir John does his best to sound confident.

'Have no fear, my boy,' he says. 'I've been in worse binds than this. So long as God is on our side, and He is, then we shall prevail. Besides, we are coming to join you. And look at us! An old man, a blind man, a woman and a single archer, though he is a good one, mind. What more could you need?'

Sir John laughs. No one else does. They ride up towards the crest of a hill together, and the captain asks Katherine what she is doing, riding to war.

'I am with William Hastings's retinue,' she tells him. 'I am to attend to the wounded.'

The captain looks askance.

'You are some sort of barber surgeon?' he asks.

'Of course not,' she tells him, 'but after the battle by Mortimer's Cross this last Candlemas I extracted arrowheads from many a man's body and stitched many a wound. I can staunch blood, apply salves, tie bandages as well as any man. Better, in fact.'

Sir John raises his eyebrows but the captain is charmed.

'Well, you'll have your work cut out, mistress,' he says. 'Look.'

They have crested the hill and in the valley, following the old road north through the distant trees, is the long line of men and wagons. It stretches from one snow-filled horizon to the other.

They rein in their horses and watch for a long moment.

'What is it?'

This is from Richard. The captain turns and stares at him, then turns away again and crosses himself.

'It is the new King's army,' Katherine tells him. 'They are riding north, so many of them as you would not believe. There are thousands. Thousands and thousands. With wagons and horses and God knows what else.'

'Any cannons?' Richard asks.

'I can't see any. Perhaps they will come towards the rear of the train?'

'Like young Kit,' Sir John goes on, turning in his saddle. 'Remember him, Richard? He could see for miles and miles, couldn't he? Saved us a scrape or two. That time we nearly attacked old Warwick's ship in the Narrow Sea. And didn't you say that time at Newnham . . .?' He tails off. A wind is getting up, shaking the alder branches above them, hustling the sleet. 'Anyway,' he says, pulling his cloak around his chin. 'A good lad, and much missed.'

Thomas watches Katherine as she tries to find the right expression to meet this remark. In other circumstances he might almost laugh at her discomfort, but not today, not here, sitting on his horse, watching the column of Fauconberg's men winding through the bare crowns of the trees with the wind in his face. The captain of the picket leaves them with a salute and spurs his horse down the incline. His men follow.

'Come on,' Sir John says after they've watched them go. 'Let's find old Hastings then, shall we?'

They set their horses after the picket and join the column on the road. Companies are walking behind their carts, moving with all the speed the carters can manage, but the oxen are no longer fresh, and the road is bad. Progress is trudging slow. By the time they reach Doncaster, they are told that Hastings has already moved on to Pontefract.

'In a hurry, isn't he?' Sir John asks himself. 'Don't suppose they can spare a day, feeding this lot.'

All around them men are pale-faced, pinched, hungry, anxious and cold. Winter is no time to fight a war.

'We must catch him at Pomfret, then,' Sir John says.

'Can we make it by nightfall?' Katherine asks. The sky above is uncertain, but Sir John is adamant and they set off riding alongside the column once more, leaving Doncaster behind, constantly having to step off the road where it is blocked, broken or flooded. Messengers pass them as best they can up and down the column's length, carrying missives from the front to the back, a full day's ride apart.

After two hours they raise Pontefract Castle. It towers over the surrounding countryside, the squared crenellated towers drawing the eye from distant miles, surrounded by outbuildings and pastures and paddocks, all crammed with tents, carts, flocks of sheep, lines of horses and oxen. The snow here has been churned to thick mud and there are so many men milling about looking for food, ale, anything to burn, that it is impossible to move within bowshot of the gatehouse. The gloom is banished and then made worse by a thousand smoking fires, and any peace made impossible by men talking, shouting, singing, hammering on armour, sharpening weapons, playing drums, flutes and tabors. Dogs bark incessantly.

They push their way through the throng, looking for badges they recognise, flags they know, asking for Hastings. Eventually they find men squatting by a fire under the sodden slough of Hastings's flag. Thomas recognises their captain, another Thomas, a Welshman, who looks tired and hungry, and his men no better – worse in fact. They are sitting on their helmets in the mud around meagre fires of smoking green wood. At least the Welshman has a hunk of bread. He brightens when he sees Thomas.

'Thomas! There you are! Haven't got any food, have you? No? Any ale? No? Oof. Stupid question. Stupid time of year to be out in the field, this is. We should all be at home. Tucked up, like. And we aren't allowed to take anything without paying for it, you know, are we? On pain of death. Drowning, it is. And then when you do manage to scrape together the money they're asking for it, the bread' – he holds up a piece of dark loaf as evidence – 'the bread is bloody disgusting.'

He throws the lump in the fire where it sits for a moment until one of the archers hoicks it out with a broken arrow shaft and takes it for himself.

Sir John steps into the firelight.

'It's still Lent, man,' he barks. 'It's good to be away from daily temptations. Good to be on your mettle. Now, where can we find Hastings?'

The captain stands. Sir John has that effect on some men.

'You've just missed him, sir. He's gone up to the river with Lord Fitzwalter—'

'Fitzwalter?' Sir John demands. 'By God! I've not seen him since Rouen. What's he doing here? Is he with Warwick?'

'Yes, sir. He's taken the bridge – after a bit of a scrap, I hear – and now he's got all our carpenters and coopers trying to repair it.'

'How far is this river?' Sir John asks.

The Welshman shrugs.

'Half a league? That way.'

He gestures northwards. Sir John wonders if they ought not to go up and find this Fitzwalter, but the Welshman is unsure.

'No place for a lady,' he says, nodding at Katherine, 'nor a blind man, if you'll pardon me. You can stop here by the fire, such as it is, until William Hastings returns? If it is him you want to see, my lady?'

Just then the first wounded men limp back from the mêlée at the bridge, and behind them there is a cart carrying those who cannot walk. Men get up and clear them a space, but they stare, stock-still when they have done so, and there is silence now. Arrow wounds mostly, Thomas sees, but also some men clutching their faces with blood on their hands. He can smell it, and he feels that familiar fear again. He does not want to be here.

'Had to clear a few of Somerset's men from the bridge,' a blue-liveried vintenar tells them. 'And they didn't want to go.'

The wounded men are unloaded from the cart and placed in the mud by the fire. Some need to be carried in their cloaks.

'What d'you want me to do with them?' the Welsh captain asks the vintenar.

'Haven't you got a surgeon?' he replied. 'Heard you had.'

The Welshman scratches his new-grown beard.

'We had a surgeon, all right,' he says. 'Lovely fellow he was, but we buried him outside Leicester.'

There is a pause. Both men look down at the wounded and Thomas can see them thinking that the sooner they die, the better.

But now Katherine is among them.

'Are there many more to come?' she asks.

'That's the lot. For the moment,' the vintenar supposes. He stares at her with his mouth open and Thomas sees the effect she has on men. She bends over each of the wounded and makes a quick decision on each.

'Fetch the priest,' she says, and, 'This one is already dead,' but there are also some who she thinks will live. She turns to the Welshman. 'Where are the barber surgeon's tools? His bags?'

'I don't know,' the Welshman admits. 'He has a servant, though.'

'Find him then, and get him to bring the bag.'

'Right,' Sir John says, rubbing his hands and turning to Thomas. 'Let's go and find Fitzwalter, shall we? He's usually got a pot going.'

Thomas turns to Katherine. She has heard what Sir John has said and is now standing still among the wounded men, staring back at Thomas. Her face is ashen. They stare at one another and Thomas can feel prickles all over his skin and tears in his eyes and he wants to run to her and take hold of her and tell her that – dear God! – he loves her.

But. But Sir John is there and the Welshman and so instead he stands with his hands by his sides and he says nothing, but watches as her eyes mist and she wipes away a tear with a grubby hand. She sniffs and she says, finally, very quietly:

'Go with God, Thomas.'

And he cannot stop the tears leaking from his own eyes and nor can he speak for the lump in his throat but he whispers:

'You too, my lady. You too.'

And then they have to go, and he turns and buries his head in some little task to do with his leg armour before helping Sir John into his saddle and climbing into his own. He looks at her from the saddle and raises his hand; then he lets it drop and he covers the noise of a sob by jabbing his horse to take a few steps.

'We shall see you in the morning,' Sir John says, and, 'Look after her, Richard.'

Thomas turns the horse and follows Sir John into the smoke and darkness. As he goes he feels he is leaving something behind, something from within him, winding it out through a wound in his chest. His legs do not feel strong enough to control the horse, and he wonders if he will fall.

By the time they reach the river's bank, the fighting is over and the enemy dead have been looted and left in the snow. Thomas does not know their livery: a badge like a pilgrim's shell on rough russet hessian. Warwick's dead are laid on their backs next to one another by the roadside, as if for inspection, and down by the bridge the air is thick with the smells of chipped stone, fresh-cut wood and hot iron where the carpenters, masons and coopers are working bent-backed, steaming in the cold.

Fitzwalter's men in their blue livery jackets are across the bridge, on the river's far bank, burning a broken cart for warmth. The flames are beautiful in the gloom, flaring and leaping, and the column of smoke rises crow-black and silent against the late-afternoon sky.

'What river is this, anyone?' Sir John asks.

No one has any idea. It is about fifty paces wide, strong-flowing, fringed by snow-laden poplars and willows. The bridge across is stone-built, wide enough for a man and a cart, with low parapets supported by a succession of broad arches and at the far end a chantry chapel. Halfway across, though, the enemy have levered the stones apart and broken two of the spans.

'But why did they not hold the crossing?' Sir John asks again, nodding at the far bank. 'Makes no sense, unless they're drawing us further into a trap, but, Lord, aren't we already in one?'

'And if they wanted to do that, why break the bridge in the first place?' Thomas asks.

Sir John grunts and rests a foot on the low stone wall. A breeze is picking up. It is hard to tell if it will snow again tonight or in the morning. Possibly both. The land beyond the river fades into the sombre distance and just to look at it is to feel cold.

'He's there,' Sir John mutters. 'I can feel it in my bones, you know? Him and his bastard stinking son. That goddamned giant. This time we'll find them, Thomas. This time we'll make them pay for what they've done.'

Thomas can only feel the cold and the bruise of having said goodbye to Katherine so badly. He shivers and stamps his boots. He is thinking he must find Hastings first, to tell him he is there, and to take up his responsibilities, but Sir John is adamant.

'Hastings can wait until tomorrow. Come on. Let's go and find young Fitzwalter, shall we? See if he's got anything to warm us.'

Thomas Fitzwalter is one of those big men, broad-shouldered, barrel-chested, with an unfashionable black beard, and in the umber light of the flames he looks like a piece of seasoned hardwood.

'Fitzwalter!' Sir John booms when he sees him.

Fitzwalter steps back.

'By all the saints, Fakenham! Sir! What're you doing here?'

The two men clasp one another and kiss. Fitzwalter is half Sir John's age, but he was born old, with all the certainty and the knowledge of the right thing to say and when to say it, and the two of them square up as old friends.

'And look at you,' Fitzwalter goes on. 'God damn it! You're walking properly. What's happened to the old fistula?'

'Had it cut!' Sir John announces, as proudly as if he'd done it himself. 'By my surgeon. Completely cured.'

He walks one way and then the other. He holds his hand up to take that of an imaginary dance partner. In Fitzwalter's company Sir John is a changed man, as if relieved of the weight of recent sorrows.

'Dear God!' Fitzwalter laughs. 'Who is this miracle? Give me his name.'

'I would,' Sir John says, the mood changing for a moment, 'but he is gone the way of all flesh.'

They call for drink and Lord Fitzwalter clears a place for Sir John by the fire under the shelter of a flap of canvas stretched from a tent behind. Thomas stands listening as the two swap meaningless gossip about their time together in France. They mention Rouen and Thomas thinks of the ledger hanging from his saddle. Would Sir John's name be in it? Probably.

They are joined by another veteran, whom Sir John calls 'Jenny', and to whom he offers commiserations on the death of his father. Who is his father? Thomas has no idea. Here is just another man who's lost a father, and who is coming north to settle a score.

Once they've exhausted the subjects of their mutual friends, Sir John brings up the bridge.

'It was a stroke of fortune to find the crossing so poorly defended,' he ventures.

'It was,' Fitzwalter agrees. 'A good old-fashioned military blunder, I expect. They only left a picket, and when they saw us, half of them ran for the hills. The other half stayed on and, I have to say, inflicted more wounded on us than I'd hoped. A score of men killed, too. We couldn't cross to get at them in any great numbers, see?

The bridge being so narrow. We had to thin them out one by one with arrows. Took most of the afternoon.'

Sir John nods. While they have been talking a light dusting of snow has fallen to refresh the earlier fall, and all around the camp men are asleep by the fires, snow gathering in swags in the folds of their cloaks, in peaks on their hats.

'And you've left men on the other side now?' Sir John goes on.

'Twenty archers and the same again of bills.'

'Is that enough, d'you think?'

Fitzwalter shrugs.

'To tell you the truth, I can't send any more,' he says, 'or they'll start to fight among themselves. It's the old puzzle about the boatman trying to cross the river with a hen, you know? With a fox and a sack of grain.'

Sir John looks blank.

'They fought over some dice on the way up,' Fitzwalter explains. 'Jenny's men and mine, and now if we leave them together for a moment they take up cudgels and batter one another. I clipped the ear of one of them for breaking another man's arm in the original fight, but that didn't seem to work.' He takes a drink.

'We could always hang a couple,' Jenny supposes.

'There is that,' Fitzwalter agrees. 'Anyway, I've sent word to Warwick explaining the position, and tomorrow the whole host'll be here, so we'll not want for reinforcements then.'

Sir John looks doubtful but Jenny yawns.

'Nothing will happen until the morning anyway,' he says. 'So we need not fret.'

It turns out Jenny is almost right.

The first Thomas hears of it is running feet and a man crashing through the tent flap. It is still dark, well before cockcrow, and the watch fire is low. The man falls to his knees and spits blood on Fitzwalter's sheepskin. Fitzwalter levers himself up and for a moment does not know where he is.

'Come,' is all the wounded man will say, pointing over his shoulder. He grips Fitzwalter's leg and spits more blood through broken teeth. His fingers are a mass of blood too and he is shaking dark drops of it on the yellow pelt. A guard comes running and catches the wounded man by the shoulder.

'Sorry, sir,' he tells Walter. 'Too fast for me.'

'Come!' the wounded man splutters again, and points towards the river.

They hear more shouts, the scrape of weapons, and a distant bellow of rage or pain. The guard hesitates, looks to Fitzwalter. Thomas rolls to his knees. More shouts.

'What is this?' Jenny barks from his blankets. Sir John is raised on his elbows, opening and closing his mouth, his cap gone, his white hair on end.

'God damn it!' Fitzwalter roars. 'If those bastards are at it again!'

He surges to his feet and snatches the pollaxe from the guard and storms out of the tent. He does not even bother to put on his coat, let alone his jack or any plate. Jenny follows, likewise underdressed. The guard drags the wounded man away, promising to kill him.

The tent returns to silence. The canvas canopy bows under the weight of snow and an icicle hangs from its centre.

'Any ale, is there, hmm, Tom?' Sir John asks. Someone has been evicted to provide for him, and he looks to have slept well, for his eyes are deep in their creases.

Thomas smiles.

'I'll find some,' he says.

'And a pot, too, would you?' Sir John goes on. 'I find I need to piss more often these days.'

In the clearing outside a boy is helping a man scramble into armour. The mud has stiffened underfoot during the night. There is still more shouting from by the river, and the fighting continues. It sounds like more than a couple of companies hitting one another with sticks. An archer comes racing through with a bow and two bags of arrows bouncing on his back.

'The bloody northerners are back!' he shouts. 'Come on. Get your things.'

Thomas ducks back into the tent.

'God damn it!' Sir John groans. 'Come on, help me up, my lad, and let's get to it.'

Thomas helps Sir John into his armour. It is a snug fit. He has changed shape since the armour was made, and the straps pinch.

'Hang on,' Sir John says, stopping him from strapping on the gorget. He takes a last mouthful of stale ale.

'Always get so bloody thirsty,' he says.

Thomas straps his own plates on, foot then shin then thigh, and then the same for the left leg. Next he gathers up his bow, arrow shafts and helmet. He takes his new cloak, looks at it, knows he'll never be able to loose his bow while wearing it, and so leaves it with the rest of his things. He is just about to leave when he turns and slings the ledger over his shoulder. He unwinds a string from his wrist and nocks his bow.

Wounded men are coming back from the river's edge by the time they are ready, some with blade wounds, one retching blood while another clutches his handless arm in the crook of his elbow, pressing it to his chest, his eyes rolling into his skull. The spilled blood still steams in the bitter morning chill.

'It's the Flower of Craven,' one says as he limps past. 'The bloody bastard Flower of bloody Craven.'

'Who're they?' Thomas asks Sir John, who is looking grim.

'Butcher Clifford's men,' he says. 'He's the one who cut down young Rutland after the battle outside Wakefield. His household men call themselves the Flower of Craven, though not everyone else is so kind. Saints! This is going to be a long day.'

On the riverbank the bodies left overnight are invisible under a shroud of snow, but now there are new corpses under the trees and the bridge is choked with the dead and wounded. Men in Fitzwalter's blue and Warwick's red liveries lie entwined together, studded with arrows. Those who have not been killed have been driven off the bridge and they are now sheltering behind the trees and the spars and barrels left by the carpenters the night before.

On the other side of the river the northerners have piled up the carts and barrels and spars to make themselves a fortified wall.

'Christ's cross,' is all Sir John says, and: 'We'll never get across now.'

Five or six billmen are wheeling a cart towards the bridge, cowering behind it as arrows boom through its timbers.

'Not going to do them much good, that,' Sir John says as the cart's front right-hand wheel jams against a dead body in the road. A man behind the cart peers around to try to work out what to do next and an arrow hammers into the frame by his ear. He leaps back and looks around for guidance. There is none on offer.

'We have to shoot back,' Thomas says. 'We have to pick them off.'

Sir John looks at his sword.

'No,' he says. 'Get enough of us together, men-at-arms at the front, archers and naked men at the rear, and then we'll unstick the bastards that way.'

'We can do both. Come on.'

Thomas runs forward and dodges behind one of the willow trees. An arrow shaft hums past, low and flat, missing him by an inch. Another goes skipping across the snow behind. One more cracks quivering in the trunk by his head.

That is good shooting, he thinks, and he peers around the tree. He can see only one man, in a painted helmet, peering through a gap in the wooden barricade. This is tricky. How to shoot around a tree? He takes a step back, stretches the string to his cheek, leans out and lets go. He hurls himself back in time to feel an answering shaft slice past his face. He doesn't even see where his own arrow goes.

Another archer is lying with his back against the trunk of the next tree along, about ten paces away. He is in the livery of the Earl of Warwick and is clutching his bow across his chest. He is chanting a prayer and his eyes are clenched tight and Thomas thinks he's soiled himself.

Behind them, a hundred paces or so, everybody has pulled back beyond bowshot range of the northern bank, all of them spectators now, waiting for some action, up to their ankles in the slush of the fields. They have a fire going and someone is selling ale. Sir John has a cup. He raises it at Thomas. Thomas curses his luck. Why did he run forward?

Another shaft bangs into the bark above his ear. Men are working their way along the northern bank to prise him out. He slides down the tree as the other archer has done. What are they to do? He is stuck, completely stuck. Through the bent brown tips of the grasses he can see the bridge. Bodies are piled on one another, three, sometimes four deep, like reaped wheat stalks. Many have fallen with their backs to the enemy, trying to run. They would have taken arrowheads in the backside, or in the backs of their legs, where archers aimed for the tendons. He can hear whimpering and a constant moan. Men are calling out for help and there is a sudden cascade from the bridge as three or four bodies of men in plate slip over the walls and splash into the dark waters. They'll never be seen again, and their families will be left to guess what has happened to them.

He peers forward. On the other side of the river the defenders' wall is like that of a castle, and the only way to get to them is across the narrow span of the bridge, now broken again. He sees the beauty of it. It hardly matters how many troops King Edward musters on this side of the bank because it can only ever come down to a front no wider than six men abreast. And before this front can engage with the enemy, they will have to endure withering volleys of arrows from both left and right. Even the dead on the bridge have now become an obstacle. The only hope is that the enemy will run out of arrows.

Some men-at-arms now start out towards the bridge, a small phalanx of them, heads down against the expected arrow storm. They move down the road stepping over the bodies, huddling close. There are about fifteen, twenty of them, household men, Thomas supposes, wearing Warwick's livery but probably Fitzwalter's men. They shuffle their feet in small steps, each man's knee in the back of the man in front's knee. They pass the first cart, then another. No arrow fire. They are nearly at the line of the trees now, almost on the bridge. Still no arrows.

The formation negotiates the first hurdle of the dead men, and still no arrows. They open and close around a wounded man who is still crawling, trying to grab the legs and ankles of anyone near enough to help him. Still no arrows. Then they start up the stonework of the bridge, weaving their way through the course of barrels and timbers to the pile of dead and wounded men. Here their formation must loosen.

Thomas hisses to the other archer, who is still clutching his bow.

'Come on,' he whispers. 'Get ready.'

The archer ignores him. He is beyond anything now. Thomas slithers to his feet, nocks an arrow and waits.

There are still no arrows as the men near the central span, stepping up, stepping down, and now there are gaps in their armoured wall. Then, on the far bank, someone shouts an order and there is a flurry of movement. Heads bob, arms rise, bows appear above the walls and the arrows come. They flicker across the waters, so slight and lithe in flight, and yet so heavy.

Thomas closes his ears to the sounds of the men on the bridge for it is too terrible to hear. Arrowheads crack into them from close range, and from such a distance, few stand a chance, no matter how well their armour is fluted or tempered. The first is knocked off his feet. The second is thrown clattering over the lip of the bridge. Another crumples and trips those behind. A fifth and then a sixth fall and instantly those at the back are clumsily retreating. Men are staggering under the hammer blows of the arrows.

Thomas ducks around the tree to loose his own arrow, sending it to vanish through a small space in the jumble of timbers. He imagines he can hear it thump into the glimpse of white livery wool. He nocks and looses again, a snatched shot that makes the string on his bow ring like a bell. His arrow finds a mark, a man standing, taking great care with his own aim. The arrow hits him in the throat, jerks him backwards and he's gone. Thomas turns and draws again, loosing from the other side of the tree. He watches his shaft fade into the grey sky above the fortifications on the far bank, and is drawing again when an arrow buzzes past his nose.

He slips behind the trunk and waits.

After a long moment it is all over. None of the men make it off the bridge and by the time the last falls, the crowd has stopped cheering and the only sound is a wounded man whimpering with pain and the sough of the bare branches of the willows as they float in the wind.

There is a loud laugh from the far bank.

Thomas slumps to the ground. He can smell cooking, his own sweat, the dankness of the river, the archer by the other tree, and blood. Moments wear by: the sky lightens; the cold creeps into his bones through his sodden jack. He dare hardly move now for attracting the attention of the enemy archers. His stomach aches with hunger and his mouth is gummy for want of ale. He needs to relieve himself.

Behind him he can see men organising themselves again. Someone has taken command. The archers have spread in a line, two or three deep. Behind them some haggling is going on. Plate is being swapped, and passed up to those at the front. Threats and money are being exchanged. There is going to be another push across the bridge.

Thomas feels for his arrow shafts. He has five left. The archer behind the next tree is asleep or dead.

After a few moments the men-at-arms set off again, the same formation as before, down the road, stepping over bodies, each with his hand on the shoulder of the man in front. Their heads are bowed, backs braced, hammers and axes held upright as if they might afford some protection. He does not think Sir John is among them. One man has a flag he does not recognise.

Someone is shouting orders to the archers and a bell starts ringing in the town across the fields. The men-at-arms are on the bridge before the arrows come from the far bank. As they do so, Fitzwalter's archers move up fast in a broad line on the southern bank and they loose in return. Their arrows leap into the grey sky, clatter through the treetops and crash down on to the men on the far bank. Arrows thump into the wood of the carts and beams, a rolling drumbeat that wavers like rain across the heads of the defenders.

Thomas hauls his string, bobs around the tree trunk and looses. There are plenty of targets, for they are brave men, standing to send their own arrows towards the men-at-arms on the bridge. Thomas watches an archer fall back with a silent cry. He has killed another man.

Those on the bridge are nearly at the gap where it narrows to a few spars. One slips. The wood must be slimy with blood, treacherous in the snow. Thomas nocks another arrow, aims carefully into the gap in front of the advancing men-at-arms. A head appears behind the wall, axe raised. Bang. The arrow catches him, snaps his head back, drops him out of sight.

Another man appears. Thomas bungles the shot and the arrow is wasted. It is a crossbowman. Thomas watches him level his bow and snap the quarrel into the face of the man at the head of the attack. The bolt throws him back, and he tumbles already dead through the gaps in the bridge, where he is caught in the spars, his legs trailing above the water. Another crossbowman appears; this one Thomas catches, on the shoulder, turning him. A good shot. The men-at-arms step up, and there is a moment when it looks as if they will succeed, but then the moment passes and they have not, and it is suddenly obvious that they never will.

Arrows throw them back, the balance tips, they turn and try to run and soon the bridge is empty, swept of life, a peninsula of bloodied armour and dead men, creaking and sliding as wounded men try to move. A man cries short juddering yelps.

There is a long silence.

Thomas sits and waits.

What will happen? No one seems to know. Confidence leaks from them and it is very cold.

Then, behind, there is the sound of trumpets blown and drums beaten. Across the fields the archers start moving aside. A party of heralds, then the banner of King Edward and then the standards of Warwick and of Fauconberg, riding up from the castle at Pomfret.

Edward, lately the Earl of March and the Duke of York, now the King, is gigantic in his plate and a long blue riding cloak with a ruff of some dense-looking fur. Next to him is Warwick, also in full harness, riding a brown horse. Thomas wonders what has happened to his famous black charger. Warwick's household men are buzzing about him and men everywhere are looking to them for guidance. And there they sit in their saddles studying the terrain, and the cost in men so far. Thomas can see Fauconberg and the King are arguing about something, Fauconberg gestures forcefully one way – to the west – while the King gestures another – down to the bridge – while the Earl of Warwick is setting his horse to pace in tight circles around them.

A new attack is planned, the third of the day. Orders are shouted, trumpets sound, companies of men move up, companies move back. Men in plate arrive on horseback to talk to King Edward. Sometimes he listens, sometimes he doesn't. Fauconberg keeps gesturing. Eventually King Edward says something and Fauconberg rides off with a few of his men.

Companies of archers under their vintenars are fanning across the fields in the footsteps of those who'd supported that second push across the bridge. Now and then arrows sail at them through the grey sky, lofted on a wind that hums through the trees from the north.

Thomas watches while King Edward says a few words to the men gathered in the roadway. Some encouragement, he supposes. There is a ragged cheer and off they go, down the road towards the bridge. This time there must be a hundred of them, and they move as a woodlouse, left right, left right, in step, shouting messages to one another, keeping close. They must all be of one household, behind one lord under one banner. Who are they? Thomas doesn't know.

And anyway, after a moment, it doesn't matter. When they reach the bridge, the arrows thunder down on them and soon there are none alive to return to their estates and their manors. They are all dead, watched as they depart this earth in blank-faced silence by King Edward and the Earl of Warwick and a thousand weary archers hunched over their bows and empty bags. They'd made it farther than the first two attacks, almost to the end of the bridge. One of them had clambered on to a cross beam and even raised his axe, but he'd been pulled forward by one of the northern billmen and it isn't hard to imagine what they would have done to him then.

No one on the southern bank of the river moves. It is as if they are frozen. Arrows flit from north to south still, and after a moment a lightly armoured man struggles up from the river, water streaming from his creases, only to be sent bowling by an arrow from the opposite bank.

As morning gives way to the afternoon they try two more attempts. Each fares worse than the last. There are too many bodies on the bridge now, blocking the way. Each attack Thomas watches from his vantage point in silence.

Farther back Warwick keeps turning his horse around. His nerves are evident for all to see. Around him men are standing as if resigned to failure. There is no food being passed around, no drink, and men's faces are dabs the colour of old linen. Starving, frozen, halted by a river crossing they cannot force, confronted by the sight of hundreds of their fellows lying dead in the snow, and with only the prospect of the long march home through an empty countryside, who could be blamed for wishing to be elsewhere?

And now the wind is picking up, gathering weight. Pale clouds scud overhead. King Edward looks up and all of a sudden he is young again, too young for this sort of thing, and Warwick, well, he's ridden from one battle, hasn't he? And lost another. Who can put their faith in him now? And he is still on horseback, isn't he? As if ready for the flight. Would he stay if the northerners came over the bridge now? Or would he fight with his heels again?

A long moment follows. There is no plan for this and Thomas is conscious that in this moment, everything hangs in the balance. Men are stepping back from the fight; some have even turned to look for their horses. More will go soon, and if one goes, then they all will. This is the moment when something must happen.

And it does. Warwick pushes his horse forward into the clearing at the head of the road so that all can see him. He stands in his stirrups for a moment, holding up his sword. Now he has the attention of every man who can see him, and the ears of those who cannot. He is looking about as if coming to some decision of his own.

'My lords!' he cries. 'My lords! Let those who wish to fly, fly. But let those who wish to tarry, tarry here with me!'

Saying this he swings his leg over his horse and drops lightly to the ground. Taking hold of the bridle, he holds his sword to the horse's neck. Everyone is still. They watch. Warwick is looking at them all. The horse takes a step away, and another. Then Warwick pulls the sword towards him, slicing through the flesh, cutting the knotted veins that run alongside the horse's throat, setting a torrent of blood seething across his fine plated sabatons. He steps back to let the horse fall in a loud struggling curl on the ground.

Except for the dying horse there is silence.

King Edward, who was Earl of March, stares at the Earl of Warwick. He does not seem to know what to do. He looks about, for Lord Fauconberg perhaps, but he is not there.

Warwick's own men know what to do. They start cheering and they push to the front of the crowd, and soon they are launching another attack down the road to the bridge.

35

William Hastings has assigned Katherine and the barber surgeon's assistant a rush-roofed barn among some elms, a league or so from the river crossing they call Ferrybridge. The barber surgeon's assistant has found a moon-faced girl to show them where.

'It's a wonder she's not been strangled as a witch,' he mutters. 'But she knows the way.'

His name is Mayhew, and he is nervous around horses and anyone in command. When they get there they find the barn is occupied by men sheltering from the cold and it smells of cow shit and mice.

'But it's filthy,' Katherine says.

'What did you expect?' the girl replies. 'It's a barn.'

She is about twelve, Katherine supposes, with an accent she can hardly decipher.

Grylle arrives to evict the soldiers, and despite herself Katherine is pleased to see him, though he is shocked to see her.

'Are you quite well, my lady? You look . . .?'

He tails off with a shrug. She has been crying, and imagines her face smutted with smoke mixed with tears.

'I am fine,' she says and Grylle leaves it at that.

'I am sorry it is so basic,' he apologises. 'The hospital in the friary's already full.'

She imagines this to be false, and that it is being kept as a billet for the better class of commanders.

'But the friars are on their way,' he goes on, brightening, 'and the surgeons from the other companies will be here by the by. They'll bring more supplies and so on, I suppose?'

He has no idea. She has no idea. No one has any idea. They are so keen on fighting one another they have forgotten to think what to do with the wounded.

'Is it always like this?' she asks Mayhew when Grylle has ridden off.

'Usually,' Mayhew agrees, staring up at icicles hanging from the roof. 'Any lord of quality wants a physician, doesn't he? But only really to fix him up. They're expensive, you see? No one wants to waste his balms on a dying billman, does he? Be like ministering to a cow, or a dog. Mind you, William Hastings is a good man. Sees to his men, where he can. Hence, me.'

He points at his chest. He has jug ears and a red face, fully freckled like Red John, and his arms hang from narrow shoulders almost to his knees. Katherine cannot help smiling at him.

'Come on then,' she says and together they help Richard from the wagon and into the barn.

'Is there anything to eat?' he asks.

There is a hunk of hard rye bread and a half-full leather bottle of thin ale, but that is all and when that is gone, they'll have to think again. Together they help the walking wounded into the barn and then three grey friars from the friary join them, bringing with them long strips of linen, a glass jar of leeches, a selection of balms in clay pots, some rose oil, a tubby barrel of wine, six dozen eggs and a crucifix.

'You deal with them,' Katherine tells Mayhew.

At first they regard her with suspicion that only deepens when they see Richard sitting blank-eyed against the low stone course of the barn wall.

But then the wounded are brought in and laid in a line along the barn's northern wall. Mayhew knocks out some of the crumbling infill in the southern wall to let in the day's dying light, but it also lets in the cold, with flurries of snow, so they start a fire in the middle of the barn, burning what they can find, and soon the smoke is thick in the air and they are all red-eyed and coughing. They warm the wine and crack the eggs and Mayhew collects as much urine as he can. Then they unpack the surgeon's instruments and start on the wounded, cutting away the clothing and washing the wounds with the urine and the hot wine.

Katherine's first patient is a boy with an arrow in the meat of his thigh. He is pale with the fear of pain, and looks up at her with large eyes, soot-black and oily in the orange firelight. She studies the leg and considers him both lucky and unlucky. The arrow has not hit the bone. That is lucky. Nor has it hit the artery that carries all the blood, the one that when it is cut means a man will bleed to death.

But the arrow is buried deep in the muscle and the lips of the wound, now cleaned with a sponge, are pursed around the shaft of the arrow.

A shadow appears at her shoulder and she looks up.

'May I?'

It is Mayhew. He has put on a blacksmith's apron and he crouches over the boy and feels along his leg, rolling the sliced hose down to his knee.

'Hmmm,' he says. 'Hmmm.'

'Will you pull it?' she asks. She remembers cutting out Richard's arrow in France.

'More likely to pull the shaft from the head,' he says. 'Seen that happen a thousand times.'

He measures the arrow, or the amount of it that protrudes from the leg. Then he sits back on his heels and looks at the boy's thigh from another angle. He nods to himself.

'Only one thing for it,' he says. He stands up.

'Ready?' he asks the boy with a smile. The boy looks up at him with complete fear. His mouth opens and closes but before he says

489

anything, Mayhew crouches again, grasps the arrow with both hands and leans his shoulder on the notch, forcing it through the leg and out the other side with a rush of blood and splitting flesh. The boy screams. He bucks and levers himself up to punch Mayhew.

'Hold him!' Mayhew cries. Katherine throws herself on the boy, trying to pin him down. One of the friars hurries over. Mayhew girds himself and breaks the arrow shaft just above the wound while the boy gasps and thrashes on the ground. There is blood all over the place, mixing with the straw and the mud and whatever else. Mayhew runs his fingers over the break in the arrow to remove any splinters, pours a little of the urine he has in the clay pot on to the wound and then asks the friar to lift the boy's leg.

The black bodkin arrowhead protrudes just below the boy's buttock, where the blood flows in a thick line. Mayhew takes it between his fingers, rolls it, and then eases it through the wound and out. A sudden rush of blood makes him frown. He nods at a wad of linen soaked with still warm urine.

'Press it hard,' he says.

Katherine holds the pad to the wound. The archer has fainted. After a moment the bleeding slows, and Mayhew nods with satisfaction.

'Hah!' the friar exclaims. 'Nicely done.'

Mayhew stands and inspects the tip of the arrow. There is a small cluster of woollen threads, viscous with blood. Again he nods with satisfaction and tosses the arrow on the fire.

'More fun than couching for cataracts, hey?' he says. 'And if we bind him now, I think he'll live to fight another day.'

The boy is very pale and sweat beads his forehead. Katherine washes the two wounds and binds them with linen strips. Every day: a lesson.

More wounded are brought to the doors: a boy in blue with an arrowhead in his stomach, the broken shaft emerging from a rip in his jack. He is carried on a web of cloaks by his mates, five of them, and his face is also very pale, like alabaster, or ivory, and his lips very red. Once again Mayhew appears. He looks at the boy and shakes his head almost imperceptibly. Together they guide the men to a space on the ground near the fire where they lay him with unexpected gentleness.

'You'll be all right, son,' one says, and Katherine sees from their likeness that he is indeed the father talking to the son. 'Surgeon'll soon have you fixed up and we can go back to Mam, hey? Good as new, with a fat purse apiece.'

Tears break from his eyelids though, and he turns away with a final shake of the boy's hand. His mates take their cloaks, sliding them from under the boy's body, and they cluster around the older man, guiding him away, back to the field.

There is a lull as the evening comes on. The friars have more bread and ale and they sleep by the fire. She shares a blanket with Richard and in the middle of the night he sits up, but does not move. It is as if he is staring at the moon. She says nothing.

In the morning they come again. It is all arrow wounds. Not a single blade injury. Katherine washes them, and occasionally cuts an arrowhead free when she knows where she is cutting, usually deferring to Mayhew, who's only ever been an assistant but seems to have a rare gift for his craft.

'Where are those other bloody surgeons?' he asks. He has a spray of blood over his freckles now, and his leather apron resembles that of a butcher. 'Taking their leave until the nobs get involved, I dare say,' he answers his own question.

A priest has come from Pontefract and is moving quietly among the wounded, guided by one of the friars, and now more friars have come and they begin taking the bodies of men out of the barn as well as bringing them in. The men are mostly archers, brought in by their friends, but now and again a few men-at-arms appear, brought on horses by their squires and servants, who linger to help remove the plate armour, and who try to get them preferential treatment – 'My master is a personal friend of Sir Humphrey Stafford,' one will say – and always Katherine ignores them in favour of the most needy, thinking of Thomas and who might bring him in if he were wounded.

A little after noon a surgeon does appear and within moments he has reorganised everything and everybody, so that a large area is set aside for the quality, while those without the appearance of means are set outside in the bitter cold. He is not a surgeon, he says, but a physician. He wears a long coat and a pointed oily fur hat that he never removes. He stands in the centre of the room next to the fire and sets Mayhew the task of bleeding those from whom they have spent all morning removing arrows.

'It is a mercy the commons can't afford it,' Mayhew mutters, nodding at the poor archers and footmen who are banished to the cold.

The physician turns to Katherine, confused by her presence.

'Who are you?' he asks.

'I am Lady Margaret Cornford, daughter of the late Lord Cornford, personal friend of William Hastings,' she says, looking him in the eye. 'I am here at the request of William Hastings, and I will not be party to the bleeding of any man, nor the cauterisation of wounds, nor to the application of any of your sow-gelder's creams.'

Hunger makes her hands tremble, but she means it.

'I will however wash wounds,' she continues, 'where I can, with warm wine and fresh urine, and I will suture them afterwards with hemp or silk, and then I will dress the wound with clean dry linen. No more. No less.'

He is taller than she by a head, with a long rough-skinned nose from which hair erupts in two damp explosions. He stares down at her, calculating her worth and so her power. After a moment he licks his thin lips. 'Very well, my lady,' he says. 'But you keep your ministrations to the commons. I shall deal with the gentles.'

'They'll not thank you, you know, for killing them.'

The physician looks bitter and turns and walks away, his long coat a soft half-turn behind. Mayhew chuckles, watching the physician leave the barn, but he carries on with his knife and bowl, cutting into a man's hand between his fingers and holding him while he bleeds into a clay bowl.

The boy with the arrow in his stomach dies in the early afternoon and by then Katherine is bloodied up to her elbows and across her skirts and she is nearly faint with hunger. She supposes she might have treated a hundred wounds, and she is hopeful for them all, for when he is not bleeding the gentry, and when the physician is not there, Mayhew is everywhere, making instant judgements on whether a man will live or die, and assigning them accordingly, so she finds herself treating the lightly wounded, while the friars deal with those whose grasp on life looks unsustainable.

At about four o'clock, as the daylight begins to leach away, there is a let-up in those thought likely to survive, and for the first time since waking she thinks of Richard. She finds him sitting where she left him that morning. The moon-faced simpleton is staring at him from a distance of only a few inches, and Katherine chases her away.

'Did you know she was there?' she asks.

He shakes his head.

'I thought I sensed something,' he says, 'and I shouted out, but there has been so much coming and going, so many different sounds, that I could not be sure. Your man Mayhew has just asked me to piss in a cup for him, which I do gladly, but is there any other way I can help? I am frozen to the marrow out here.'

Before she can think of some soothing answer there is a thunder of hooves. A great party of men is coming towards the barn. They ride under a saltire flag.

'Dear God,' she breathes. 'The Earl of Warwick.'

'He is here?' Richard asks, struggling to his feet.

'He comes now.'

'Is he wounded?'

'It may be.'

'Don't let that bastard of a physician see him. Save him yourself. It will be the making of you.'

She glances at him. Whatever does he mean?

Warwick's household men tear across the fields to the barn and the first arrival leaps from his horse before it has stopped moving.

'A surgeon!' he cries. 'My lord of Warwick is wounded.'

The physician is still absent. Mayhew appears.

'Is it bad?' he asks.

'An arrow. In his thigh.'

'Is he bleeding?' he asks.

The man looks at him. He has lost his helmet and has blood on his livery coat.

'Of course he's fucking bleeding, begging your pardon, my lady.'

'Is he bleeding a lot?' Mayhew emphasises.

The man-at-arms gestures with exasperation.

'Here he comes. Look for yourself.'

Warwick is on another man's horse, leaning back in the saddle, the broken stub of an arrow sticking from the inside of his right thigh. His proud face is screwed up in pain and with every jounce of the horse he winces and mutters something ungodly.

Mayhew is struck dumb by the sight. It is as if he is looking at a saint or a martyr and not only does his touch desert him, but his voice too.

Katherine intervenes.

'Get him down,' she says.

The men-at-arms help their lord down off the horse and he puts his arms around two of them and hobbles into the barn.

'Where's my physician!' he shouts, his voice rising into a scream on the last syllable. 'Get him!'

'Lay him here,' she says, kicking aside the bowls of blood. They lower him on his back in the space the physician has reserved for those able to afford bleeding.

'Get his armour off,' she orders. The man-at-arms bends and cuts through the leather laces and the straps. He frees the plate and tosses it aside. The arrow has broken through the rings of the mail skirt and lodged itself in the meat of Warwick's thigh, just below the groin.

'Don't just stand there,' Warwick mutters. 'Do something.'

Warwick's hose is soaked with blood but there is not too much. She cuts through the material and rolls it down to his knee. The arrow is in the soft part of his thigh, lodged in the muscles at the back of his leg. Great God he is lucky.

'Have you the rest of the arrow?' she asks.

The man-at-arms looks at her as if she is a fool.

'Can we have someone here who is not a juggler or a clown?' he says. 'This is my lord the Earl of Warwick, for the love of *Jesu*, not some nameless peasant. Get on and cure him.'

She returns to the wound. This is difficult. How far has the arrow gone in? She collects one of the silver-snouted needles, a long one, rinses it in a jar of warm wine and then probes the wound beside the shaft, inserting the sliver of metal into the lips of the wound and letting it trace the path of the barb. Warwick grimaces.

'Wine,' he demands.

She shakes her head.

'We need it for other purposes.'

He is unused to being denied anything he requires and he looks at her properly for the first time.

'The devil are you?' he asks.

Instead of answering she presses the needle farther in. She wants to distract him with the pain, and it works. Her fingers are in the wound now. It means the arrow is deep and it will be easier to push it through, just as she has seen Mayhew do earlier. She withdraws the needle and wishes Mayhew were not suddenly so shy.

She will have to make a short shunt with the heel of her hand on the broken shaft and hope that she can force it out in one move. But what about the wound on the other side? She has an idea, looks up. A crowd has gathered, nine or ten men including a herald in the quartered livery of the King. All are in plate armour and the man-at-arms is on his knees. He is wearing thick leather gloves.

'Give him the wine,' she orders the friar.

The friar holds the jug of wine to the Earl's lips.

'Wait,' Katherine says, and she leans forward and swirls the surgeon's knife in the jug.

'All right,' she says, removing the blade. 'He can drink it now.'

They watch as Warwick drains the wine. He grimaces and spits something out.

'Roll him on to his left side, will you?'

The friar and the man-at-arms take him and move him, complaining, on to his left side.

'Hold him steady. And fetch a candle.'

One of the friars brings an altar candle of good beeswax, casting a true light. In it she can see the Earl has large spots on the cheek of his backside, and she thinks of Sir John and his fistula. Is that how such things start?

'You,' she says, addressing the man-at-arms. 'Push on the arrow. Slowly.'

He is horrified.

'Do it,' Warwick says.

The man shuffles forward. He looks around, seeking approval.

'Come on,' Warwick says.

'Slowly,' she adds.

He bends and grasps the arrow. Warwick gasps.

'Sorry, my lord.'

'Just do it.'

He pushes the arrow through the Earl's flesh. The Earl stiffens. Clenches his teeth.

'The candle!' she calls.

The friar leans over her.

She watches the growth swell on the back of Warwick's thigh, sharpening, turning pale. She snicks it with the blade. She feels a tick of the knife against the arrowhead. Blood seethes from the wound and the arrow comes slithering through. Warwick bucks and shouts with the pain. Mayhew and the friar hold him tight, the man-at-arms taken by surprise. There is blood all over the ground. A great pool of it, expanding fast. Katherine feels a grab of panic. She's cut the artery! She panics, doesn't know what to do, where to turn. Then she calms herself.

'Sponge,' she demands. 'Linen.'

She pulls the arrow free and tosses it aside, then she presses the urine-soaked sponge into the wound and then the wine-soaked linen. She holds it until it is blood-soaked. 'More,' she says. Mayhew passes her a new piece. She presses that down on the first and when that second piece is sodden, she finds a third. By the fourth pressing the blood is slowing and by the sixth it seems to have stopped. Katherine continues pressing, holding the pad down. Moments pass. The men around her grow bored. Finally Mayhew nods.

Katherine almost collapses. She has not cut the artery.

'Well?'

This is from the man-at-arms, and he speaks for everybody.

'He'll live,' Mayhew says. 'He'll live.'

36

When the bridge is finally taken, in the gloom of the early evening, after Fauconberg's mounted archers have forded the river upstream and come around behind the defenders, Thomas sits on the bank and opens his bag to see if he has any food. The ledger is in there. He opens it again, and looks at all the embellishments he has added since he first acquired it. There is the window of St Paul's, the name of Red John, the drawing of Katherine he made while she was ill in Brecon. She looks like the Virgin herself.

He wishes he did not have to carry it with him, but now that he is separated from the wagons, there is nowhere to leave it. He slings it over his shoulder and goes in search of Hastings's men. There is no sign of Hastings's standard, but across the blood-slicked stones of the bridge, Thomas finds the Welsh captain, looking as pleased with himself as if he personally put the northerners to flight.

'Came through a ford up the way,' he laughs. 'Unguarded it was. Old Fauconberg's a fox. He's riding up the north road with his lances and hobilars now, chasing after the rest of those bastards.'

Ahead the fields are grey with snow. The wind gusts in their faces. Thomas feels nothing but dread. He should not go any further: none of them should. Nothing good waits for them. Of that he is sure.

'Well,' the Welshman says. 'We've got to get moving at any rate. A village called Saxton. Up there somewhere. Hastings's orders.'

'How far is it?' Thomas asks.

'Three or four leagues?' the Welshman guesses.

Thomas turns and studies the army filtering across the cinch of the bridge.

'What about the wagons?'

'They're to come through the ford.'

'So we didn't need to take this bridge at all,' Thomas says.

Across the river, through the trees, they can see men digging burial pits in the fields.

'No,' the Welshman says.

They watch the men digging for a while, and the priest shivering by the graveside.

'Got any sons?' the Welshman asks.

Thomas shakes his head.

The Welshman grunts.

'Lucky,' he says. 'I've got two girls; Kate and Katherine, named after their mother. I used to want boys, you know? I used to imagine how that would be. Doing this kind of thing together. But now, maybe, maybe it is better not to. They'd only end up like that.'

He gestures across the river and Thomas nods and then they turn and join the road where the column is moving north through the slush. As they go trumpets sound and drums are taken up, and all around them captains do their best to organise and encourage the men who move slowly, with cramped and weary expressions on dirty faces. They follow the road northwards to the village of Saxton, and arrive in the dark. No wagons have caught them up, so they face a night without food or shelter, and while the captains cram themselves into the church and the surrounding houses, the men are left without.

Before curfew Thomas strides to the edge of the village to relieve himself. Men are gathered there, doing the same thing, staring northwards, to where the sky is tinged orange with the light of a thousand fires.

'It'll be tomorrow then,' one of them says. 'So say your prayers and get some sleep.'

Thomas lays his head on his ledger under the eaves of a nearby cottage, and prays. He prays for Katherine and Sir John. He prays for himself. He prays he will find Riven and that he will not lack the courage to fight him, or his giant. He prays that he will not lack the courage to kill both.

After he has said his prayers, he lies awake, crouched with cold, listening to the soft sound of the men around him: the occasional snore, the whispers, the prayers, the little movements in the dark. This is when they are at their most honest, he supposes, when they are skinless, and when you learn what sorts of men they are, and they learn what sort of man you are.

He must have fallen asleep for he wakes shuddering before first light, his hair stiff with ice. Outside the horizon is growing pale, the first birds are starting to sing, and the land is beginning to emerge indistinctly from the milk-grey morning light. Still there is nothing to eat, and one of the sentries tells him that Fauconberg is supposed to be in a little village called Lead, away to the west. His lances and mounted archers caught the Flower of Craven in the dark, in a little valley farther north, a dint in the dale, the messenger says, and killed every last one of them.

'They weren't looking for that,' the messenger laughs. He'd been there, he says, and taken part in the ambush, and shows Thomas a little gold ring; its design is that dragon with the curled tail. His face is grey with fatigue, and there is a ring of blood around his nostril where he's picked his nose with a bloody finger.

'Give it to you for a loaf of bread?' he asks.

'You'll be lucky.'

'What about a coat?'

Thomas laughs. The bells of the church ring and they both instinctively look up. Behind the church's tower pale snow clouds move south.

'Palm Sunday,' the messenger mutters, tucking the ring away. 'Easter next week. Probably never live to see it.'

'Now don't talk like that,' the Welshman says, appearing at Thomas's side. 'Bad for morale, that is.'

'You seen how many men old Henry of Lancaster's got?' the messenger says. 'No? Well, I have. Went up to the ridge last night. Must be thousands and thousands of 'em. Northern bastards. And I'll tell you what: they've got all the quality. All the lords, the nobles, all the men who can fight. Not like us. Who've we got?'

'The King. We've got him.'

The messenger looks at the Welshman for a long moment.

'Do we?' he asks. 'Do we really?'

'And God.'

Now the messenger spits.

'We've got Warwick,' Thomas says.

'Warwick,' the archer allows. 'Though I hear he's wounded.'

They hear the slow squeal of cartwheels on the road to the south and everyone gets to their feet and they move to meet the carts.

Arrows. Eight wagonloads of them.

'No bloody food? No bloody ale? How're we supposed to fight like this? Can't draw a bloody bowstring with no food in your belly.'

'Kill the oxen,' someone recommends. 'Cook them on their own carts.'

The first carter tries to protest, but his whip is quickly wrestled from his hands and the other seven are glad to leave him to it, and while they unload their carts on the road, one of the men swings his axe and kills the animal and the noise reminds Thomas of the Dean's murder. Before they can butcher the ox or break up the carts to set them alight, there are more trumpets, the sound curiously thin in the cold grey air, as if it might break at any moment.

It is one of Fauconberg's captains and a group of his household men, about twenty of them. There is no sign of Sir John. Thomas wonders where he can have got to. He hopes he is warm, in any event. They pull up in front of the dead ox, their horses shying from the brassy smell of the blood, and begin shouting orders.

Every eye is on the ox, its fat tongue lolling, but the men are driven away, shuffling, stiff and grey-faced and it only gets worse as they leave the shelter of the village and begin the slog up through the furlongs where the wind scours the land in urgent flurries. Every man walks with one eye on the flags that are stiff in the breeze, like pointers, stretched southwards, telling each one to return whence they'd come.

Thomas picks his way among the men William Hastings has assigned to his command, checking each has his bow, at least one spare string and a bag of shafts apiece. Most wear tight-fitting helmets, pitted with rust now, and each man has some other weapon hanging from his belt: a maul, a dagger, something like that. They smell damp and fungal.

They stop again, huddled in the road. The snow starts, tiny balls of it, like hail.

'Will there be many?' one of his men asks. He is younger than Thomas, with a bow of yellow yew. He reminds Thomas of the boy Hugh, who ran away before Canterbury. He has not thought about him since.

'A few,' Thomas says. 'Enough, anyway.'

He tries to see himself through their eyes, as someone who's been in battle, who fought at Sandwich, and at Northampton, the man who'd killed the Earl of Shrewsbury, then fought through the rout at Mortimer's Cross. They look at him as if he knows what he is about, as if he is supposed to lead them, when all he's done so far is ignore them and leave them to their own devices while he wallows in his own misery.

'What's your name?' he asks.

'John,' the boy answers. 'John Perers, of Kent.'

Thomas nods. Another John.

'Well, John,' he says. 'You got good eyes?'

'All right. I can pick out a target all right.'

'No, I'm looking for a flag. Six ravens, like this.'

He marks out Riven's badge in the thin snow on the mud by his feet.

'Black on white.'

Perers nods.

'On our side?'

'Theirs.'

A knot of men on horseback is gathered on the hillside directing the companies to their positions. The wind whips the horses' manes and tails. It plucks at the hems of their clothing, dashes the snow in their faces.

'You lot, over there,' one shouts. He gestures and they step off the road, following other companies across furlongs where the earth has been left in frozen furrows by the passing of autumn ploughs. Below them, down the slope, filtering in vast numbers through the village, come the men-at-arms, the billmen, the naked men. They make up the mass of the army, roughly organised in companies, gathering in the fields around the village, each one following three or four horsemen under their lord's flag.

There must be ten thousand, fifteen thousand. It is impossible to guess. They are uncountable. Boys are leading strings of horses away, back to the rear, and all around them men are manoeuvring up the slope into position.

They stop when they reach a company already in place.

They are in the middle of the field. They turn and face up the slope to where a solitary tree crowns the ridge. Thomas spreads his men out, the usual harrow formation, as more companies filter into the line around them, and they stand seven men deep across a broad front.

'I can smell them,' one of the men says. He is a bitter, bitten old man with grey whiskers. He fiddles with his strings, licking his lips, his gnarled hands shaking.

No one says anything.

'I can smell them,' he goes on. 'I can smell men who've slept under roofs by fires. Men who've had their bellyful of meat and ale.'

Still no one says anything.

'I can smell men with the wind at their backs,' he adds.

'Oh shut up,' the Welshman snaps. 'For the love of the virgin Mary, for the sake of her seven bloody sorrows, will you just shut your bloody mouth.'

There is silence for a long moment. The wind hums and buzzes and the snow softens and starts to fall as fat flakes. The tree on the ridge top is lost to view. Behind them in the village there is a commotion of drums and trumpets. A party of horsemen come slowly through the throng and up the road, heralds clearing their way, three or four of the long-tailed banners above their heads.

'Must be King Edward,' the Welshman mutters.

Behind the King's party come the Earl of Warwick and his men in red, and then Fauconberg, with his own retinue in blue and white. Thomas wonders again where Sir John might be and whether Katherine is safe.

'Heard old Warwick was wounded?' the Welshman asks. He is sauntering around the ranks of his archers, checking his men are sorted, his nerves seemingly made of ice.

'In the thigh,' Thomas confirms. 'An arrow. It must have been a glancing thing, though I saw it, and it seemed well stuck.'

'Probably got the world's finest physician, hasn't he, the Earl of Warwick? An Italian gent, I bet, who's cured the Pope of dropsy.'

'Does the Pope have dropsy?' another man interrupts.

'Not any more,' the Welshman says, barks a laugh, and goes on his way.

Thomas wishes he could be like that.

There is more shouting from the vintenars and the officers, tough men on good horses, and the men-at-arms begin spreading across the fields to find their places behind the rows of archers.

'Where're you from?' a captain of the men behind them shouts. He touches his visor with the plated knuckles of his hand. He is a boy, sixteen perhaps, gangling in his antique plate. He carries a slim and useless-looking sword, but his men are armed with halberds, glaives and hammers and they wear the same red and white livery.

'All sorts,' Thomas replied. 'Yourselves?'

'Huntingdon.'

Thomas has never heard of it.

'North of London,' the boy says. 'We could have come up with the Duke of Norfolk, but we came this way instead. Thank God we did. Wouldn't have wanted to miss this.'

The boy gives him a smile that is closer to a grimace, and then peers back over his shoulder as if he is expecting someone.

'Still, he should be here soon,' he goes on, gabbling with nerves now, his touch flitting from his cheek to his neck to the pommel of his sword and back again. Even in the cold he is sweating. He offers Thomas a drink from his flask.

Thomas takes it gratefully. Wine.

'Yes, he should be here soon,' the boy repeats. 'My father is with him. With the Duke of Norfolk. Coming up from the east. With five thousand men. If not more.'

Thomas hands him back his flask. So they are five thousand men fewer than was thought.

'Well, God go with you, sir,' he says, 'and thanks for my drink.'

'You too. Perhaps we'll share another after the battle?'

'I'd like that.'

They stop and listen to something. It is a low roar, coming and going like the suck of waves on the beach below Sangatte.

'What's that?' the boy asks.

'I think it must be them,' Thomas says.

The boy swallows and nods.

Trumpets blow along the lines.

Thomas returns to the front. He looks at his own hands. They are shaking again and he clenches them around his bow. Christ, how he yearns for more wine. Or ale. They all do. Thomas catches the Welshman's glance. The Welshman nods. Here we go, he thinks.

Fauconberg's officers are riding up and down the line, shouting instructions to the sergeants and the vintenars. Above them their flags flap briskly. One of them stops before Thomas's company. It is Grylle, in his distinctive helmet, his armour still too big. Grylle pretends not to recognise Thomas.

'The top of the hill flattens out,' he shouts, gesturing behind him. 'Then there is plateau, a stretch of flat land rising slightly. Lancaster's men are there, at the far end.'

Thomas cannot imagine missing them, even in this snow.

'They will be two bowshots away,' Grylle goes on, 'and they will be above us, on the rise.'

No one says a word but Grylle knows. They all know.

'We cannot choose everything,' he says. 'We must fight the enemy where we find them.'

One of the archers behind Thomas spits noisily.

'Are there many?' someone shouts.

Grylle is silent for a telling moment and the sound of shouting comes again, washing over them from the north. If he had not been wearing a gorget Thomas imagines he would have seen Grylle swallow.

'God is with us!' Grylle reminds them. 'God is with us, not those usurping northern bastards.'

He nods, and then rides on to deliver his message down the line. Thomas lets his eye run along the ranks. The front stretches four hundred, five hundred paces away from the road, the same again the other side. There must be thousands of archers alone, and twice that number of men-at-arms. And yet the enemy has more? It does not seem possible.

The snow lightens and a priest on a horse appears ahead, away near the road in the centre of the army. He is backed by three or four heralds and a handful of men in plate. Is it Coppini? Has the Legate ridden all this way with them? He is too far away for Thomas to be certain.

The Bishop – if it is him – dismounts, holding his headgear in place, and hands his horse to a squire. The heralds' banners, unreadable at this distance, flap heavily in the wind, and the Bishop holds up his hands and begins saying something.

'Speak up, for the love of St Ives,' someone shouts, and, 'What's he saying?'

'A prayer,' Thomas tells them.

'A prayer? What sort of prayer?'

'One that'll help us win.'

'What? He's praying for the wind to back around and those northern bastards to come off their bloody hill?'

'Something like that.'

The men laugh. Thomas warms to them: to joke about their own deaths. Now the priest has his arms out and those around him kneel. The movement ripples along the army, spreading from the centre and the front ranks, all the way to the flanks and the rear. Men get off their horses and go down with one knee in the snow. Still they can hear little or nothing, but they bend their heads and each man makes his own prayers.

Thomas prays again that he will not be killed, that he will not be wounded, that he will not be left to lie out there and bleed to death, stiffening in the cold, but that if he is, if it is God's will he should die, then that it will not be painful. He prays that he will find Riven and that when he does, that he will be able to punish Riven for all the evil he has let loose in the world. He prays that Katherine will make her way safely in life, and that Sir John will survive to return to Marton Hall. He prays for Richard. He prays that he will come into whatever is best for him.

In a moment of stillness he hears the priest's voice.

'And so we beseech your help, Lord, in ridding this your land of these vile traitors who would destroy our dread liege Edward and those whom he loves. We—'

And the wind snatches the voice away again. Then returns it.

'Into your hands, O Lord, we commend our souls in the certainty that what we do is right . . .'

But there is something else now. Thomas feels it at his back: a stirring, a restlessness that spreads through the archers, the questioning hum of conversation as men look up from their prayers, and turn their cheeks to feel the wind. They begin looking to the skies, peering up at the pale snow clouds, checking the flags on their poles.

'Look at that,' the Welshman says, pointing.

Thomas has seen it. Above the priest's hat, the herald's fishtailed battle banner has fallen slack. It hangs there on its beam, as if broken. Others join it, settling down. The ribbons on the Bishop's hat settle. He removes his hand and it remains in place.

The wind has died.

Thomas can feel the archers holding their breath, not daring to move, not daring to speak, not daring to do anything lest it break the spell. No one moves. Even the priest has stopped his tongue and is looking up, waiting.

The snow still falls from the grey sky, each flake as large as a penny, exquisite and delicate, but they float, they drift. They no longer pitch in Thomas's eyes.

The archer who has doubted the efficacy of the Bishop's prayer stands up.

'Fuck me,' he says.

Then the rest of the line, all of them, stand as one, staring, mouths open as the real miracle occurs.

The banner above the priest flaps, once, twice, and then it twists on its lance and, unbelievably, it slowly swings on its hoops, turning from the south, to the west, and then all the way around to the north, where the wind picks it up again, and it becomes a finger, pointing northwards, pointing towards the enemy. Showing them which way to go.

And the flags all along the battle slowly turn on their lances to join it.

The wind has turned.

'It's a miracle!' the Welshman shouts. He seizes Thomas and shakes him. 'A bloody miracle!'

And now the priest is on his feet shouting and gesturing to the flags. No one can hear him for the din of men in armour and the roar of voices. Instantly Grylle is there, thundering up from the flank to take new orders. There is a surge of energy in the ranks. Men seem to forget their hunger, their thirst, the filthy snow. All they can think about now is how the wind will carry their arrows further than the enemies'.

'This won't be so bloody bad,' the Welshman says. 'We can fucking win this!'

But how long will the wind last?

'Come on,' Thomas finds himself muttering. 'Come on! Advance, damn you! While the wind is with us.'

Drums ripple into life. Pipes pipe up. Trumpets signal. More messengers canter to and fro across the front. The archers are impatient, trying to press forward.

'Come on,' someone shouts. 'Come on!'

But the wind only seems to freshen on their backs and the snow only seems to thicken, and Grylle is back, stopped in front of them and turning his horse so that all they can see is its powerful rump and dressed tail. He raises a hand and checks along the line where more officers in Fauconberg's livery are stationed, about a hundred paces apart from one another.

They drop their hands as one, and as one the men start up the slope.

37

As they breach the ridge, they are able to see across the plateau for the first time, and the line comes to a rippling stop. A man pushes into Thomas's back.

'Piss and vinegar,' someone murmurs.

There must be twenty thousand of them, standing in deep ranks, divided into three battles. They are standing on the higher ground, under their banners and flags, and they are shouting and crashing their weapons together.

Thomas feels his bowels liquefy.

'Dear God!' he breathes. Then he tries to imagine what Walter would say. 'Steady,' he whispers. Then more loudly: 'Steady!'

One man turns to run. It is the boy Perers. Thomas flings an arm out, catches him, spins him around. Walter would have punched him. So Thomas does so too: across the face, a backhand to make his knuckles sting. Perers slumps in a twist of limbs.

'Up.' Thomas bends and hauls him to his feet. 'Come on,' he says. 'The wind is with us. God is with us. Didn't you hear the priest? If we can just get our shots off, we'll live to tell our grand-children of this day.'

Perers stares at him. Blood and snot leak from his nostril. There is a long moment, before Perers nods and smears his lip. Thomas nods too, then picks up the lad's new bow and passes it to him. His own hands have stopped trembling.

Grylle has turned his horse. Facing them, he has to shield his eyes from the snow.

'We'll carry on to within a bowshot,' he shouts. 'Then loose a ranging shot.'

The archers understand. They are touching their weapons, their helmets, what armour they have. They tighten the points on their jacks, buckle belts, finger rosaries. They begin settling themselves, taking deep breaths. Those with the sense or experience to have kept something back to drink do so now, tipping their heads quickly. Thomas settles the ledger in the small of his back. It is a comforting weight, but still an unwanted burden.

Then they begin forward again. They start stretching their shoulders, rolling their arms over. Thomas nocks an arrow and keeps walking: twenty paces, thirty, forty. All the while he hunches and relaxes his shoulders, gently easing the string back, flexing the big-bellied bow, trying to get some life into the frozen wood. He makes a hundred unconscious calculations as to the wind's strength, its direction, the way it gusts. He thinks about the snow, the flurries. He thinks about the field. He looks for advantage, for disadvantage, for anything that might influence the course of the day to come.

The plateau is not flat, but tilted slightly, from the east down to the west, and from the north down to the south. He can see what looks like a stand of trees away across to his left, and there seems to be nothing beyond, as if the ground drops away, down into a river valley, perhaps.

Thomas sees how well the northerners have chosen their spot. The valley protects their flank, and there will be no chance of Fauconberg's riders turning them as they had done at the bridge the day before. He wonders if there are any bridges over the river, or if the northerners have broken them down as a precaution.

And there ahead, arranged in deep ranks across the high ground, is the mass of the enemy archers, scarcely visible in the snow.

What must they be thinking? This morning they'd been in the

perfect position, almost unassailable, with the wind at their backs and a falling slope at their feet. They'd have been wondering how they could lose. But now?

'Here!' Grylle calls.

They are now within a long bowshot of the enemy.

Each man finds himself the space he needs. They shout to one another to spread that way and this way, forwards and back. They loosen the strings on their arrow bags and shake out the shafts. Thomas nocks his own bow. Puts a few shafts in his belt.

He can hardly see the enemy. The wind is not strong, but the sky is full of snow.

Each man stoops to take a piece of the frozen earth in his mouth, just as his grandfather might have done at Agincourt, and to make his sign of the cross on the sod where he'll stand and possibly die, and for a moment there is silence. Thomas fiddles a nugget of frozen black soil and places it in his mouth. It is tannic and gritty as it melts on his tongue. He holds it aside in his cheek.

Grylle signals and all along the line the captains and the vintenars call out:

'Nock!'

There is a swathe of movement. Thomas nocks a shaft.

'Draw!'

'Loose!'

There. It is done.

The first arrows shoot away with a drumming of strings and grunts of six thousand men. The sky flickers and darkens. He stops and watches, peering through the snow. Will they land on the enemy? There is a distant drum roll. Misty figures twitch in the enemy lines. They are within bowshot.

'Nock!' he cries. 'Draw!' The fletch of his second shaft tickles his cheek. 'Loose!'

Walter once said you could tell who was going to win a fight after the first three or four salvoes. Whoever got the most in first would win. They nock, draw and loose three times. More than fifteen thousand arrows.

And in return there is a ripple of something thickening in the snow ahead. The northerners' arrows land with a sudden spitting patter. They are like bristles in the ground, like a strange crop that no one'll ever want to eat. They are fifty paces short.

The men laugh. They are delighted.

'Move up!' the vintenars bellow. 'Move up!'

And already the men are charging forward. They stop shy of the ground where the enemy's arrows are burying themselves with low puffs of soil and ice.

'Nock! Draw! Loose!'

They repeat the process until they are out of arrows. Thomas's back is burning. His fingers are skinless and raw. All around him men are grunting with the effort. The rate of firing is fast, ten a minute, but slowing. Men become clumsy as they tire. Soon they are done and are left scarlet-faced, heaving for breath, hands on knees, one vomiting with the effort. Sweat stings his eyes and the fog from their bodies blurs his vision.

'Arrows! Arrows! More shafts! Quickly now!'

And how is it with the enemy? Over the field he can see and hear the impact of the arrows. He can see their line buckle, thin and bunch, but it seems the poorly armoured enemy archers are paying dearly.

'They'll not take much more of this,' Thomas shouts. 'They must come at us!'

No commander can stand to watch his men take such punishment. Already there is a low wall of the dead at the northerners' feet and everywhere wounded men disrupt the living. The northerners will have to break one way or other, he thinks, forwards or backwards, and it would be better for them if they broke forwards.

Around him men are still crying out for more arrows. They begin reusing the northerners' shafts, plucking them from the ground and sending them back the way they've come. The damaged arrows thrum and throb in the air. The broken fletches buzz like wasps, each one with a dying fall as it speeds out of earshot.

But now the boys are running forward, each weighed down with five or six damp linen bags full of arrows. They duck through the ranks and drop them at the archers' feet. The archers rip them open and get to work.

'Nock! Draw! Loose!'

They do not need to be told.

And yet the northerners still hold their line. They continue loosing their arrows, and all the while their arrows fall short.

'They cannot see,' Thomas guesses. 'They cannot see their arrows are not reaching us.'

Every man is loosing just as he can now, scrabbling for arrows from the ground and from the boys as they pass. Thomas has no breath to order the salvoes, only enough to nock, draw and loose.

On it goes, on and on. How can they stand it?

Then the boys slip away, some sixth sense warning them to go, and across the fields the trumpets blare and the flags move forwards and the colours of the enemy line change. The line solidifies. Gone are the muted buffs and russets of the archers' jacks, and now men in heavy armour and bright livery coats begin moving through.

They come forward in companies under their flags but first they must negotiate the corpses of their archers strewn thick as autumn leaves on the blood-slicked ground. The snow is in their eyes as they tramp forward, down from their hill, away from their advantage, and Thomas shouts at his men to use every last arrow they have.

'Back!' he shouts, gesturing. The enemy front is a hundred paces away. 'Come on! Leave them be.'

They turn and run, Thomas with them, bunching up and streaming back across the field towards the gaps left between the battles of Edward's men-at-arms. He is spent, weak as a kitten, his arms and back afire. For a moment he can hear nothing above Edward's men roaring and bellowing and banging their weapons as they advance against the oncoming northerners. Trumpets shriek and drums thunder and everywhere men are shouting their cries for Warwick or Fauconberg, but the mass of them are shouting out for King Edward, and above all other flags and banners, it is the King's standard that draws the eye. Under it is the huge figure of Edward himself, wielding a pollaxe as if it is a toy, a mere stick, and all around him his men are hurrying forward to meet the enemy.

Soon Thomas is in among the men-at-arms and then he is through the lines, where the archers are wild, savage with the glee of having survived. They are roaring with laughter, suddenly very physical, hugging one another, kissing one another, thumping one another, congratulating themselves on a thing done well. Every man is steaming, as if on fire, but they've suffered not one casualty. Not one.

The archery duel is over, and there is no question which side has carried it.

But the laughter stops and each man is silent as back up the slope the two lines meet. The din is a savage rippling crash, the shriek of steel sliding against steel and the drumming thunder of a thousand hammers falling on their fellows.

Now the ale has arrived, dragged up the slope from the village on the beds of three wagons pulled by teams of six long-horned oxen, and there are fires being lit. Ale and bread and soup, chilled and viscous, better than anything Thomas has ever tasted, drunk from his helmet. Men are letting ale pour down their chins and into their clothes, laughing again. One ale woman has fists bigger than Thomas's, and in one of them she carries a stout club with which to keep order. She opens the spigots on the barrels but keeps her gaze fixed on the hillside behind them, ever alive to the sway of the fighting, knowing that she'll never see another dawn if it goes badly.

Thomas gulps his ale and tears at his hard black bread. Christ, it is good. John Perers appears at his side, looking crafty, pleased with himself. He has to raise his voice above the noise of the fighting and the shouting men, the constant wall of noise that rolls back from the front like a physical force.

'Saw that flag o' yours,' he shouts.

Thomas lurches, pours away his ale, puts aside the bread. Takes Perers's elbow.

'You did?'

'Think so. Not sure. With the snow and that.'

'Where?'

'That way, up the slope.'

He points eastwards, with that bow of his, which Thomas notices is not so fine as he'd first thought, but weighted wrong, top heavy, rushed from the bowyer's bench perhaps. Perers points it towards the tree on their right flank, where the ground rises.

'You sure?'

'No. I said. Hey. Where are you going?'

Thomas is up and running, up the slope towards the King's right flank, across the fields towards where Fauconberg's blue and white fishtailed banner is held aloft at the back. Before he has gone far his way is barred by more men moving up the slope in a block and behind them, coming up from the village, many more in blue and white livery. The reserve, held in blocks, is waiting for the order that means it is their turn.

And already the wounded are starting to emerge from the battles, dragged clear by their fellows, making their unsteady ways back, down towards the village. What are they hoping for? Is there a hospital there? Thomas has no idea. A party of men carry their wounded commander sitting on a chair made of polearms. He is gasping and rolling his eyes with the pain of some unseen wound, and all the while he thumps one of his bearers' shoulder, as if this helps. More bloodied men keep coming, with dented plate, their faces sordid with blood: one with his arm pinned stiff to his chest; another with no helmet, his eyes startlingly white in a face dark with blood from his opened scalp; another staggering in loops as if drunk, unable to get his balance until at length he crashes headlong to the ground, and no one moves to help.

Above them arrows wicker through the air, so light in the sky, so heavy on impact. They fall everywhere, anywhere, all the time, any time. Men who one moment are doing one thing are suddenly doing another as they stagger and bellow; others are knocked flat. Some are instantly still; others flail at their wounds and scream for their mothers, their wives, for the help of the saints. Survivors step over them.

Thomas hurries on. Archers in Fauconberg's livery are gathered on the slope behind his men-at-arms, and they've started returning speculative volleys over their own men's heads, trying to drop their arrows through the slanting sleet into the northerners' faces. They'll be aiming for the flags and the banners, hoping to hit the commanders. His own men must refresh themselves and then begin to join Fauconberg's, drawing and loosing, drawing and loosing . . .

Thomas takes a new bag of arrows and drifts up the slope towards the front. He peers ahead, to his right, looking for Riven's flag, but can see nothing above the shoving ranks in the sleety snow. He nocks an arrow and looses it, guessing where Perers might have seen Riven's flag, then another, and another. He imagines each one striking Riven or the giant, and he takes pleasure in every loosing. When he is out of arrows, a centenar is there with a boy carrying another bagful of shafts. Thomas takes it and ducks around behind the rearmost archer, and is gone.

Here is a man in good plate, lying stretched on the ground with his eyes unblinking as snow and ash flakes fall on his waxen face. He has been left there by his people, and already another man, one of the naked men, vicious as a stoat, stands over him, going through his things, taking what he wants, discarding what he does not. He tosses aside a glove almost at Thomas's feet as he passes. Thomas stoops for it and slips it on. It is still warm, the leather wet with the man's sweat, the steel-plated knuckles bloodstained. After a moment's hesitation, he takes up the second glove where it has been cast aside.

And here a bill, lying abandoned in the grass, a rough-made thing with a chipped blade on a bent staff. Thomas picks that up too, and then with a moment of regret, he sets aside his bow, and so now he is a billman. A billman in bloodied gloves, with an unreliable glaive and an archer's helmet.

He starts again, moving eastwards, up towards the right flank, but across the field down to his right the trumpets are blasting with real urgency, and men are bellowing at one another, and down in the village companies of footmen are surging into life, hurrying up the slope to reinforce the left flank.

Something is happening. The next development of the day.

The army's left wing – Warwick's battle – has canted around, taken a step back. The dead and wounded are thicker on the ground down there and they are streaming back from the line in numbers. The boys are running too, and the prickers are moving up fast, circling like sheep dogs, using sticks and staffs to herd the men back into the fight. He can see the flags of the enemy. They are close to breaking through.

This is the crisis point. The day hangs on the next few moments. Bugles and trumpets sound and messengers ride hard across the back of the battles.

Thomas turns and finds himself in the path of a company of Fauconberg's reserve billmen, being harried down the field to join the fight, to prop up Warwick's battle on the left. He tries to step aside but the sergeant catches him by the arm and swings him around.

'On! On!'

Thomas pulls away. He opens his mouth to say something but the sergeant raises a hammer.

'Get the fuck in!'

Thomas has no choice. He turns and joins them, the sergeant pushing him on. They retrace his steps, past the man from whom he'd looted his gloves, past his own company loosing shafts over the heads of the men in the centre battle, past Perers and the

Welshman, and then down through the ditches and across the road. Footmen in Warwick's livery hurry up from the village, their sergeants howling at them, purple-faced with fury and urgency.

Warwick's banner is a long red tongue. Beyond it the line thins and sergeants are flailing at their men, driving them forward, forcing them to fill the gaps. A man in Warwick's livery shoves Thomas to where men are fighting over a great berm of fallen bodies, three or four men deep. It is a long slug of bristling steel that divides the armies. Men are climbing on the wounded and scrambling over corpses to get at one another. Toe to toe they grapple, punch and elbow one another. They butt and gouge. There is no space to swing a sword. It is all about pointed weapons, thrusts and short-arm blows. Daggers, hammers, axes. He would give anything for that pollaxe now.

Thomas is pushed forward by the press of men. He thrusts and jabs with his glaive, aiming for faces, for eye-slits, for fingers on weapon shafts. He is barely defending himself. The noise is deafening. Rough steel and iron blades are everywhere. He can smell terror and blood and men who've soiled themselves.

The man before him has a helmet that encases his face and a sword he holds with both mailed gloves. He is straddling a body, standing on the chest of another dead man. Over his shoulder more men thrust glaives at Thomas's face, and from below men are crouching and stretching to hook his legs away. He tries to push back, to get away, but the sergeants are there behind him, pushing men into the maw.

Thomas's glaive is caught by the big man in the helmet. He wrenches it free. It is caught again. Pushed down. He is defenceless. Using his sword quillon as a mace, the big man raises it to bring it down to kill Thomas but the man next to Thomas surges forward and drives the blade of his bill under the big man's armpit. He kills him with a roar. Then an axe or a maul swings through the air from the other side and catches Thomas's saviour in the teeth, snapping his head back. Thomas is blinded with blood, and there are broken teeth and fragments of bone from the wreck of the billman's chin.

Neither of the dead men falls. They are held upright by the press of bodies. They are pushed forward, chest plate to chest plate. Thomas seizes his glaive and wrenches it free, but another man throws himself forward and crashes something on to his helmet.

Dear God.

The blow rips down the side of his head, glancing off his shoulder. He is paralysed by the pain. He can hear himself lowing like a bull. He wants to die. He stares down the length of a bill's shaft. A whiskered old man is coming at him. He has a long spike and his eyes are red with fury. Then Thomas's glaive comes free. He endures the pain, thrusts his own blade into the man's face, feels it bite, nag at something, rip free. He stabs again, grinding the blade into the old man's face. He can feel the blade in the hole behind his nose. He jerks at it, turning the old man.

Blood is everywhere, like rainwater. It mixes with the snow. It rises as steam from the ground.

How many men does Thomas strike? How many does he kill? He cannot say. There are always, always more. His fingers are ringing with pain, and at last he can stand it no more. His strength ebbs so suddenly that one moment he is slashing at a man in a green and white livery, and the next he can hardly raise his newfound hammer to break a clumsy blow from a farmer's bill. Then he feels himself being plucked from behind, roughly shouldered out of the way, and thrust backwards. All he can do is obey, follow where he is sent. He lurches away, every ounce of will drained.

One of the sergeants is there, standing among the bodies of dying men, the same one who'd thrust him into the line.

'Get some ale,' he shouts, grabbing another man and forcing him up to the front. 'And get back here!'

Away from the fighting his body rings. He is deafened by the noise; his arms vibrate from the tip of his numb fingers to his shoulders; his back burns; and the blood of other men is mixed with sweat to sting his eyes. His legs are shaking, and when he drops the hammer his fingers remain curled, and the ale woman has to press the greasy leather beaker into his hand.

He drinks. Ale courses down his cheeks and his neck. It runs down his chest under his jack. He doesn't care. He wants to drown in it, to let it fill his mouth and throat.

He holds the cup out again and the ale woman splashes in more watery ale.

He drinks; then the ale woman takes the cup and passes it to another man, pressing it into his hands also. The man remains blank-eyed, his gaze fixed on the distance. Blood trickles from his helmet. He drinks just as Thomas has done.

Thomas turns and stares back at the line where Warwick's banner still flies. Though the line has given, though it has taken a pace back, it has not broken. They have held it, saved the flank. Men still hurry from the rear to stiffen it, but the job is done for the moment. The crisis has passed.

And just as he thinks this, there is a further great shout of dismay and a shrinking of the line, as if peeling back, and Thomas feels the thunder of a thousand hooves through the soles of his boots. From the stand of trees to the west, half hidden in the mist and swirling snow, hundreds of horsemen are thundering up the slope towards Warwick's position. For a moment Thomas can only think they are on King Edward's side, but no, it is an ambush, such as they tried that day at Newnham.

The horsemen are a bowshot away from where Thomas stands. They ride with their fifteen-foot lances and their hammers, two hundred perhaps, more even, and in their path Warwick's men can do nothing other than break.

Seeing this, the ale woman throws down her jug and runs for the seat of the wagon. Her man throws aside the turnip he is eating and jumps to his feet. He begins thrashing the oxen with stinging slashes of his whip. The wheels of the cart pull free of the mud with a jerk and the cart rolls down the hill. And suddenly the prickers and the sergeants are back among them, shouting and screaming and forcing men back in the line. Trumpets blare and messengers set off.

'You! In! Now! Go! On! ON!'

The horsemen come in a wedge. They crash into the fleeing remnants of Warwick's left flank, scattering them, using their spears, riding men down, killing them with hammer blows. The shock of the ambush travels down the line, and just when they are most needed, there are no archers to hand, no one to knock the riders from their horses, no one to kill their horses under them.

A sergeant is there. A big man with a red face. He thumps Thomas with a staff, screaming at him, pushing him back up the field. Thomas has no weapon but it hardly matters. The line is breaking. They need numbers.

New companies come running from the village.

'A Warwick! A Warwick!'

Thomas finds himself pinched between those falling back and those coming up. The men running back are wild-eyed and slack-mouthed and there is no way to hold them. They've cast away their weapons and torn off their armour.

Thomas can do nothing other than join the rest moving up to brace the line. He snatches up a bill with a bloodstained shaft.

The horsemen are slowed only by the number of dead on the ground. The northerners' footmen have taken fresh wind from the spears too, and they're pushing through the wall of bodies and clambering over it to press Warwick's men everywhere and Warwick's men step back, back down the slope up which they came.

Where are the archers?

Everywhere the northerners are gaining the upper hand and what had seemed like the crisis point earlier that morning now reveals itself to have been the first in a succession. Everywhere they are knocking Warwick's men back, stabbing them as they fall, hooking them forward and killing them with hammer blows. Men on horse-back are forcing their mounts forward, battering men from above.

Thomas is drawn back into the fray and all he can do is try to defend himself, breaking their spear thrusts and turning aside their blades with now a bill. But for every point he beats aside another swings across, jabbing always jabbing. A blade flashes at his eyes. He ducks. It strikes his helmet. He seizes the shaft and pulls. Another point wavers across his vision, a sharp side-to-side chopping motion. He lets go of the first shaft and sways back, battering the second point away with the back of his arm. Then another point, straight into his jack. He edges sideways, but his linen is laid open to the skin, his hip scorched by the passing blade. He lashes out, catches someone with his bill.

He takes a step back. And then another.

They are losing the fight, and soon they will not be able to hold the line.

And then suddenly the air is thickened with arrow shafts. A horseman lurches in his saddle and throws himself back while another horse screams and claws the air with an arrow deep in his mouth. More horses go down. The riders turn their horses. Some dismount. Others are knocked to the ground.

A cry goes up to suggest King Edward is coming.

'Hold fast! The King! The King!'

'Thanks be to sweet St John!' a man yells. 'The King!'

And now it is the northerners' turn to waver.

For there is the King's standard and under it perhaps twenty men, in best plate armour, almost impenetrable to sword thrust or hammer blow, swinging their pollaxes and driving the northerners back.

But where the King goes, so does the fiercest fight. Everyone wants to be the man to kill him, and soon ranged on the other side of the new wall of corpses are the enemies' noblest lords. Men with plumes on their helmets, fighting with their own household men under their own banners. These are the proper soldiers. These are men who've trained to fight all their lives, and there is none of the clumsiness of the billmen.

Instead there is a rippling fluency of precisely delivered and shockingly powerful blows. Hammer flukes crash down and blades are thrown up. For every attack there is a defence and for every defence an attack, and the noise is one long percussive roll, like the beating of a drum, and to watch it, it is even elegant in its way, like a dance, save the men are so monstrous in their armour and the price of missing a step is a dagger point in the eye or the groin or the armpit.

And in the middle of it all, under his banner, King Edward is supreme. None can match him. His height and range are immense and he scatters all before him, throws them back, clears them out. He wades into the crowd and swings his axe, crushing hands, helmets, heads and faces, knocking weapons aside and driving on. He kills a horse with a single blow and despatches its rider with the return swing of his axe.

Beside him his men are a blur of calculated speed, defending his flanks, darting forward to finish off anyone on the ground so that he will not be stabbed from below. Thomas watches as a man in plate falls under the King's hammer and lies stunned for a moment too long. His visor is ripped off and a dagger is punched into his face and that is that.

But no man can fight like that all day, and soon even King Edward is forced to retire, exhausted by his efforts and the heat trapped within his armour. His space is taken up first by his household men and then a succession of lesser knights until, suddenly, Thomas is back in the line again, fighting for his life once more, swinging and thrusting at the pale faces of other men. His arms are burning, his ears are ringing and his hip throbs. But on it goes, the endless furious flurry of steel, until his strength flees again.

Thomas turns and forces his way through the throng. Blood is running freely from a wound on his scalp as he limps back towards the ale wagon by the road. At the sight of the crowd of men gathered there waiting for ale he almost weeps.

But eventually he gets some, poured into his stained and dented helmet. He doesn't care about the taste, only the fact of it. It is wonderfully strong. He sits in the snow by the side of the road and drinks it down and then rests his head in his arms and tears fill his eyes and he cannot suppress a sob though he does not know for what or whom.

He pulls off his gloves, holds out his hands, each palm stained with blood, some his own, some belonging to others, and the snow-flakes melt on them, thinning the blood. His greaves are splashed royal purple where blood has hardened in a glaze and there are shreds of something else caught in the web of his sabatons. One boot is filled with warm liquid, and his toes swim in it, though whether this is blood or water, he cannot say.

At length he stands, picks up his gloves and finds a hammer lying bloodied in the snow.

'You all right, mate?' someone asks.

Thomas ignores him. He wonders what time of day it is, and how long they have been fighting. He wonders that there are still more men left to kill, and still more men willing to kill them. But here they are, more of them, and still more of them, moving up from the village, fresh men, yet to fight, though it seems that that is all he has been doing all day. That is all everybody has been doing all day.

But now the din of it seems to have faded, and as Thomas stumbles eastwards, he sees events as if through a pane of thick glass. Men are blurred and then sharp, their sounds are muffled and then loud, and even the sleet takes on a curious sort of beauty. He is warm, for the first time since he can remember, and as he walks gradually everything is suffused with a golden aura, as if leaking sunlight. He's stopped shivering, he realises, and he walks on, no weapons to burden him, even his greaves and sabatons turned so light and easy to walk in. And his jack too, which has been stiff with damp and dirt for a month or more, now seems like a linen chemise floating lightly on his shoulders.

It occurs to him that perhaps he is dying.

A priest passes him and starts murmuring something but Thomas laughs and makes the sign of the cross in the air as if he were blessing a congregation and he feels light enough to dance away from the priest, and a little farther on he notices blood is dripping from his fingers and that he cannot really move them, and then he thinks that this does not matter anyway.

All he can recall is that he has to move to the King's right flank, for that is where he is wanted, or that is where something awaits him. He knows he must get there and that when he does everything will reveal itself. He is moving up across the back of the King's army, through the mess of wounded men. People step aside for him, stare at him as he passes. A pile of corpses is laid to one side and there are dead horses and there are women with more ale and water and a man is stumbling from the fighting, groaning like a bullock until he falls on his knees, and then to his face, and lies twitching in the snow until he is dead and no one even watches.

Thomas walks on until he finds himself stopped by a roadside and ditch brimming with a slurry of faeces, and beyond is a snow-filled marsh where black boggy lakes are skimmed with grey ice. There are stands of sedge grass and crouching alder trees misshapen by the wind and he realises he has walked the width of the field, and that he is now on the King's right flank, behind Fauconberg's men. A memory stirs in him again. He turns and looks down the field, watching the thousands of men fighting and dying under the broad snow-filled expanse of the sky, and then – he sees it.

The flag.

Six ravens.

Riven's standard.

38

The sense of wellbeing is gone in a snap but Thomas feels a surge of power within him, and suddenly he knows what to do.

He is running. He is jamming his helmet over his blood-soaked cap. Then he is forcing on the steel-knuckled gloves. He finds a rondel dagger lying on the ground, a foot-long tapering point of rust-flecked steel, and he snatches up a bill, a nicely made thing, with good weight and balance, and he is pushing forward, shunting men aside, and his eyes are fixed on Riven's flag.

He is not afraid of being killed. He is too fast, too strong. He has a good weapon. He has a helmet. He has gloves. His blood is thrumming in his ears and he can hear himself roaring again.

He is shoving between the gaps in Fauconberg's lines until he is before Riven's flag. Alongside him are three or four of Fauconberg's junior knights in modest harness. They are fighting with pollaxes and bastard swords. The give and take of blows is swift and practised. This is no place for a poorly armoured archer, yet Thomas forces himself forward.

Riven is unmistakable now. In fine plate, he is fighting with a long-handled hammer. He turns to trap a bill under his arm and slash its poorly protected owner across the face. Then he spins to take a blow on the languet of his hammer and he switches hands and drives the helve into a man's face. In the single moment, he has killed two men. It has cost him almost no effort, no thought, and he is preparing to do it again. But now Thomas is before him and for a brief moment Thomas imagines Riven recognises him and hesitates.

But if he does, he does not hesitate for long.

He launches himself at Thomas and Thomas moves to parry the blow, but of course it is a feint, and Riven is on him from below. Thomas throws himself inside the blow, flinching as the hammer fluke slides across his chest, and he crashes his bill into Riven's steel elbow.

Riven is beaten back but comes again. He goes high but hits low, catching Thomas on the knee, sending a barely manageable jolt of pain up his spine. He cracks a short-armed blow in Thomas's face, but Thomas ducks, and then the hammer glances off his helmet. It rattles his teeth and he tastes blood but he is not dead. Riven seems surprised. Thomas goes at him. He feints, lunges, draws him left then right, and thrusts for his armpit. But he trips. Staggers. Is down. The bill is gone. Riven rears over him, raises his hammer in both hands. Thomas is down among the dead, nearly one of them. He rolls. The bodies around him trap him, hold him fast, but before Riven can bring down the hammer one of Fauconberg's men intervenes with a jab. He catches Riven and turns him, distracting him long enough for Thomas to hurl himself forward with the rondel dagger in his fist. He can drive it up under Riven's steel skirt. But Riven grips him and hauls him upright. They are face to face. Thomas presses his cheek to Riven's visor to stop him butting him. He forces his right arm free and slides the dagger up his ribs. He will stab him in the armpit.

Then the giant arrives.

He has the pollaxe. The pollaxe he reclaimed from Walter. He swings it at Thomas's spine and connects with a force that rips Thomas from Riven's embrace and casts him across the heaving layer of steel-clad bodies that cover the ground. He twists with the pain and falls on his back. He lies there, unable to move for the agony. He stares up at the crisscross of weapons above him, watching the giant batter away at two of Fauconberg's men, watching Riven kill the billman who'd earlier saved his life. He feels the man sprawl across his legs and then he feels nothing. It is as if he is floating in warm water, his head swaddled, his hearing muffled.

He wonders again if he is dying.

He thinks of Katherine. He wants thoughts of her to be his last. He wants to tell her that he is sorry. Sorry for dying here, sorry for leaving her.

Above him the fight continues. Men fall by his side. There is blood in the air, scraps of metal and shards of splintered wood, a tooth, something gory.

Thomas watches the swings and blows, back and forth. He watches the snowflakes fall, and he wonders if this is what death is. No triumphant entry through heaven's gate, or agonised descent into hell, only this: detachment, an eternity spent on the field where you died, an eternity spent ruing all your sins of commission, and all your sins of omission.

But now he finds he can move. His fingers are coming to life.

Can it be that he is not dead?

He moves his head.

He lurches, rolls over. There is a brief lull in the fight. Men are pulling back, taking stock. Exhausted men are retiring. New men are coming up.

Thomas is on his hands and knees; he has only one thought in his mind: to get away. He begins crawling, one hand after the other, slithering through the blood, back across the armoured corpses that are covered in gore and shit. Dead men stare up at him with noses smashed and mouths and chins slashed open. Some are still alive, spitting blood, bleeding through their ears. He gasps for breath and the pain is a burning band around his chest.

He can hear himself moaning like a beast in agony as he crawls through the line of Fauconberg's men and slumps against a corpse. He rests his cheek against the dead man's breastplate and closes his eyes.

He saw the giant. He knows that pollaxe. He should have a broken spine. He should have a fluke buried a handspan in his back. And yet. Here he is. Alive.

He raises himself and crawls on. The blood is pooled between the bodies, deep enough to drown a man. Everything is sodden with it. Everything is red. He finds a bill in the crook of a dead man's elbow and hauls it out. He stabs it in the bloody slush and levers himself up on to one knee.

The pain is terrible, yet not as bad as it should be. He inches his arm around behind his back to press against the wound. Then he wheezes a laugh. So that is it. The ledger. The giant hit the ledger. Thomas swings the bag around to see where the fluke has punched a hole through the leather, and he puts his finger in the wound up to his bloody knuckle.

It is the pardoner's final lifesaving gift.

And now sound returns and Thomas can hear the crash of steel and the shouting of men as the fighting continues. Fauconberg's line is giving once more, bowing towards him. Riven and his men are forcing their way through and if Fauconberg's line is thinned any further, then the northerners will break it. They will have won and the battle will be over. Once this flank is turned, then the whole army will be wrapped up, pushed down the hill and murdered at will. Some of them may try to run, he supposes, but then he remembers the bridge. That is as far anyone'll get. That's where the remainder will die. Perhaps that is why the northerners broke the bridge in the first place: not to stop them coming, but to stop them leaving.

There are no trumpets calling for men to bolster the line, for the trumpeters have fled, or they've been forced to throw down their instruments and join the line, and anyway even if they were there to blow the signal, there are no men to obey it. There is no reserve left.

This is it.

He whom they call Edward Plantagenet, formerly the Earl of

March, then the Duke of York, had wanted God's judgement on his right to be king, and God has delivered it: he has no right, and so now all his men must pay the price of that gamble.

Riven's flag is carried high as he comes between the ranks: Thomas can see him, hacking through; and there is the giant, just behind him, crashing men aside with that pollaxe. Thomas wonders whether his one-eyed son is there too, his wound hidden under his visor.

He thinks back to the moment he first saw Riven, when he first saw Katherine. He thinks of their time in Calais, and then the summer at Marton Hall. He thinks of the hills in Wales, and that week in the inn in Brecon. He thinks of Walter, and of Dafydd and Geoffrey, and all the Johns. He thinks of the Dean. Of Margaret. And now it is over. He will never avenge any of them now.

He swings the ledger back over his shoulder and unplugs the bill from the sloppy earth.

He stands.

He will at least die on his feet.

And then from behind him comes the sound of trumpets, faint, distant, thin. He turns. Along the road is a mass of men coming through the snow, grey and indistinguishable at this distance. There is a lull, infinitesimal, a let-up in the constant clash of steel as men turn to face the new arrivals.

'It's the White Lion!' a man shouts. 'It's the Duke of bloody Norfolk! Blessed be God!'

It is the men that boy had been waiting for, his father among them. There is a surging cheer along the ranks of King Edward's men as the news spreads, and Fauconberg's men are heartened and they rejoin the line with renewed vigour. Men in blue and white run past him, hurrying to wade back into the fight, hurrying to hold the line.

'On! On! A Fauconberg! A Norfolk!'

The new contingent in red livery is fast. They join King Edward's line at its eastern end, up by the marshes, and they crash into the northerners' line, and for the first time that day, the northerners are forced to take a step back. They step back over the bodies of the men they've killed and over those who've died to buy them their advance. Their left flank, previously grounded on the boggy marshland beyond the road, is now overwhelmed by Norfolk's men, fresh to the fight, and soon the battle lines are canted around, so that they run from north to south, and it is the northerners' turn to call on their reserves to shore up their wavering wing.

Thomas is breathing more easily, and he gathers himself. He feels redeemed. Released. He must return to find Riven. But now he cannot get to the front for the press of these new men; he can no longer see Riven's flag above their helmeted heads and the forest of their bills and spears, and the fighting is slowly moving away. He follows it, stumbling in its wake where between the corpses the ground is an ankle-deep soup of blood and snow, and every man is coated in it, so that liveries are not easily distinguishable.

The line is slowly advancing.

Those who fight for Henry of Lancaster are being beaten back by those who fight for Edward of York. Thomas follows, through tumuli of bodies creaking where wounded struggle to escape.

And then through the swirling snow he glimpses Riven's flag again, he is sure of it. It is farther back, and he pushes forward. He tries to get between the broad backs of Norfolk's men, but their number is too great, and the resistance of the northerners too fierce.

They fight on, and the quality of light in the sky changes, and it is now nearer the eve than the morning; for the first time in the day it seems the King's men might have the numbers, and the balance of battle is weighing in their favour.

And now there is a great cry. A roar that surges around Thomas.

'A Warwick! A Warwick!'

Men are fighting with desperate intensity, knowing that to yield an inch now will be to yield the whole day. For a few brief moments Thomas is forced to the front again and is hacking and chopping at men in bloodied livery. They are exhausted, and Thomas is aware – also for the first time – he is attacking them and they are defending. The balance has swung.

One turns, and runs. The next likewise, and the man Thomas is trying to kill is struck down by a fat-bladed bill and goes down and behind him there is no one, only the backs of men, fleeing the fight.

Just like that the northerners have broken, and their line is disintegrating along its entire length.

It is as sudden as that.

The battle is won.

And now the trumpets sound behind King Edward's lines again. They are blowing a shrill call, and boys hurry forward with strings of horses from the park and the King's spears and lances are suddenly there, mounted men coming up from the rear, and they are joined by the prickers who've reclaimed their mounts, and every man with access to a horse is forcing his way through the press to get at the fleeing northerners, and to cut them down.

Thomas stands numb and watches the northerners throw aside that which might slow them – their weapons, their armour, everything – as they begin a pell-mell rush northwards, pushing one another aside, stamping on their fellows to get away. But it is no good. King Edward's horsemen are everywhere, riding them down, running men through with spears, breaking skulls with hammers, slashing at them with swords.

And so now the killing really begins. What was a contest becomes a slaughter, butchery, closer to commerce than to sport or battle. Archers are there with mauls and daggers, hacking at the backs of the fleeing men. Those with arrows loose them at men as they run, knocking them over, hobbling them so they can be killed and robbed at leisure.

Some northerners don't run, but try to sell their lives dearly, and they huddle together in groups and turn their weapons outwards, but they do not last long. Surrounded, they go down in a hail of blows and they are set upon as soon as they've bowed their heads; knives jammed into eye-slits, visors ripped open and the contents gouged out, swords stabbed into groins and armour stripped off. Even the dead are mutilated.

Some try to flee back across the field towards the woods, but Warwick's lances cut them off and herd them towards the valley beyond where the rest of the King's men crowd forward to kill them.

Where is King Edward to demand mercy for the commons?

There is no sign of him. He has ridden northwards after the fleeing men.

Where is Riven?

Thomas is running now, tripping on dying men, stumbling clumsily through the corpses heaped like islands in a sea of blood. Here and there some of the King's men have already broken off to loot the dead and Thomas starts searching the bodies himself, seeking that livery badge, but everywhere they are the Duke of Somerset's men with their portcullis, or the Duke of Exeter's, entangled with those of Warwick, or Fauconberg, or the King's men with their white rose. The points of bloodied weapons make it a dangerous exercise.

'You don't look too clever,' a voice says.

It is Perers, alive, looking well even, carrying his bow unnocked and a single arrow in his belt. He is studying Thomas as if trying to work out why he lives when he should be dead.

'So, did you find that bloke with the flag?' he asks.

Thomas shakes his head.

Perers sniffs.

'He'll be down there then,' he says. 'If he's still alive.'

He gestures across the field to where King Edward's men are gathered on the lip of the plateau to the west. There are thousands of them and the noise of fighting persists, a constant grinding.

'Take a look, if you like?' Perers offers.

Thomas nods and Perers shows him how he's been using the bodies as stepping stones.

'Don't tread on them in armour,' he says. 'Too slippery. Just tread on them in jacks. And for fuck's sake mind out for those caltrops. You stand on one of them, you'll know about it all right.'

The caltrops are scattered where the northerners' right flank had started and Thomas follows Perers across the field, stepping from body to body, wary of the spiked iron balls that lie under the snow.

At the lip of the plateau the King's men are ranged in a crowd, three or four deep. Beyond them Thomas can hear bellowing and screaming and there is the dense rattle of hammers and blades beating on well-fixed armour. When he reaches the fringe, men turn to look at him, and he sees they are furtive and guilty, as if they have been caught out at something.

He pushes his way through.

In the valley below are the northerners: Somerset's men, the Queen's men, Henry of Lancaster's men, thousands of men in colours Thomas does not know, and ranged along the crest of the valley around him are the King Edward's men, and Warwick's men, and Norfolk's men, and they are beating down on the heads of those below, killing those they can reach, and driving those they cannot down the slope into a swift-running river that has burst its banks and laps the trunks of alders on the far side.

It is a trap as tight as a barrel.

There must be many thousands down there. Not one will live through the next hours unless King Edward returns to grant mercy for the commons.

The press of Warwick's men is impassable. They all want their moment at the front, they all want vengeance, and they push forward to get their chance to kill a man. They are wide-eyed, as at bear baiting, and Thomas knows he will never forget the sight or sound of this moment.

He turns and pushes his way back through the throng.

John Perers follows.

'Bit bloody strong that, ain't it?'

If Riven is in the valley he will die, of that Thomas is sure. Someone will kill him or he will be drowned. But what if he is not?

He leads Perers northwards. They pick their way through the corpses that clot the field. Looters are bent-backed everywhere, using hatchets to remove rings from men's fingers, stuffing their bags with weapons, purses, the silver livery badges that men wear, jewelled collars. Cruelty is everywhere. Mercy has fled.

Below to the left the ground gives way sharply, down to the river. It is too steep for men to climb up, and from their vantage point Thomas and Perers can look back and see the horror of the thing. While those higher up the slope are trying to escape the blades of King Edward's men, those at the bottom are being forced chest-deep into the icy waters of the beck. They have cast off their armour where they can and are clinging to their companions. Some trust themselves to the flood and perhaps one or two make it. Most do not. Their linen-wadded jacks are blood- and water-soaked, heavier than armour, and they disappear under the waters with a final despairing wave to life.

Thomas cannot see Riven among their number, but that does not mean he is not there.

Still he walks on, something guides him, and farther downstream some of the northerners have managed to get across the river. Men are struggling to cross a ford, waist deep, shoulder deep, slipping on the treacherous stones under the surface. All order has broken down, and they are fighting one another to get across, turning their weapons on their friends, forcing one another down into the waters, and in the gloom it takes Thomas a moment to understand what he is looking at.

It is not a ford, but a dam of bodies.

So many of them have been drowned or killed and thrown into the waters that they are now piled the one on the other. They have risen above the river's waters in a pile and now men are fighting to get across it, cutting and slashing at one other, trampling on the fallen, forcing them into the water the better to keep themselves dry.

Even Perers is aghast.

'Dear Christ,' he breathes. 'Dear Christ.'

There is something about this concentration of cruelty that makes Thomas sure this is where Riven will be.

And that is when he sees him.

Not Riven. The giant.

He is forcing his way on to the dam, knocking down those before him with that pollaxe and then treading on them, battering them down into the waters. Building up the bridge for himself. Thomas remembers the giant's fear of the water. Behind him is another man. For a moment Thomas cannot be sure. In the gathering gloom it might be anyone, but then, after a moment, he is certain of it.

Riven.

He has removed his harness, and now wears only bloodstained linen and hose, and he is using a short-bladed sword to stab any who impede him.

They are getting away.

Thomas has to stop them, but between them stand a thousand desperate northerners, too tightly packed to move their arms, let alone let him pass.

He turns to Perers.

'Your bow,' he says. 'Let me have your bow.'

Perers shakes his head.

'Worth more than my own wife, it is,' he says.

'Give it to me, now!'

It has come to this, this last moment. If Thomas does not do this now, he will never see Riven again.

Thomas stares at Perers. Perers hands the bow over. He is very reluctant.

'A string! Quick! A string.'

Perers unwinds the string from his wrist.

'You'll be careful with it?'

'For Christ's sake! The arrows!'

But Perers only has one.

The giant is on the far bank now. He is stretching back to help Riven.

Thomas notches the arrow. He holds the bow down. Looks at Riven. Looks at the giant. He draws the bow, feeling that top-heaviness. It is an ugly bow, he thinks, unloved, rough. Perhaps that is perfect for this last thing he has to do? He raises it, holds the string to his cheek, his arms fluttering with the effort, and just as Riven scrambles past the giant up the far bank, he looses.

He misses.

But the giant pauses. He takes two staggering steps to his right, arches his back and drops the pollaxe.

'God in heaven!' Perers murmurs. 'That was some shot.'

The giant tries to scrabble at something caught between his shoulder blades. He can't reach it. He falls to his knees, then on to all fours. Riven turns back — perhaps the giant has shouted something?

'Get an arrow!' Thomas yells at Perers.

His eyes are fixed on Riven, who hesitates by the fallen giant, and for a moment Thomas thinks he might help him. But then Riven snatches up the pollaxe, turns and runs. The giant collapses in the snow.

'Find an arrow!' Thomas screams. He looks about too, but keeps one eye on Riven who is moving northwards along the far bank, scrabbling through the bare-branched undergrowth, slipping in the snow, leaving a trail of bloody footprints.

He is getting away. He is escaping.

Thomas casts aside his helmet and runs along the valley top, shadowing Riven. The ground is too steep to descend.

Perers follows.

'My bow,' he says.

Thomas ignores him. There is a great pile of corpses blocking his way, and there are caltrops scattered on the ground. He scrambles over them, still watching the shrinking figure of Riven, still looking for another arrow. He finds one, but the head is bent and curled back on itself. It will never fly true. He throws it aside. Runs on.

It is dusk now.

He will soon lose Riven in the dark.

He begins a prayer. '*Pater Noster, qui es in caelis* . . .' Then he gives it up. Prayers are for later.

On the far bank Riven's run is clumsy with fatigue as he stumbles through the trees, scrambles along the banks and wades through the river's broken water where the valley walls press too steeply.

At last Thomas finds an arrow, sticking out of the ground in a rare patch of sodden earth. He pulls it out and runs to a spot between two low trees on the lip of the plateau.

Riven will pass below on the opposite bank any moment.

He notches the arrow and takes his stance.

The wind here is fitful, uncertain, blustering around the valley, gusting up the rise. He will have to be careful. He has but one shot, and then it will all be over.

For a moment he thinks he has lost Riven, but then he comes, a dark shape against the snow, moving like a spider. He climbs over a fallen bough among the trees on the edge of the copse. He seems exhausted, as if he will fall at any moment.

Thomas draws the string with the last ounces of his strength, getting his back into the bow, and he holds the stance for a long moment, and he waits, waits for the perfect moment, concentrating on nothing but Riven, who moves into line.

And then the bow explodes.

The arrow flits into the gloom and a chunk of the bow's belly lashes against Thomas's temple.

Darkness swallows him whole.

39

They moved up to the village of Lead in the morning and took over the little church surrounded by fishponds, and they have had nothing to eat or drink all day, and so when two of Hastings's men bring in Sir John at dusk, Katherine is exhausted and so hungry that she does not at first recognise him.

His face and beard are crusted in blood. He cannot talk, and no one can tell what is wrong with him. Hastings's men have removed his harness to lighten their load, they say, and they'd found it dented, but there seems to be no wound.

'Face down he was,' one of them goes on. 'Almost drowning in the soup.'

She recognises him when she peels off his linen cap. He does not appear wounded, yet he lies there with waxy skin and anyone looking at him would have given him up for dead.

'Let us find him somewhere more comfortable to lie,' she says.

One of the friars looks up from the other side of the chapel.

'A space here,' he calls, and he stoops to close the eyes of a dead boy. Mayhew summons the other friars to take the body away, and they carry Sir John across the blood-smutted straw. In the light of a rush they stare while Mayhew runs his fingers over the body. What is wrong with him? She cannot say. There is no obvious wound, yet his breath is quick and shallow, and when they remove his arming jacket they find his chest is sunk.

'I have seen something like this once before,' Mayhew says, though he does not look happy with the thought. He rinses water through

Sir John's white hair, washing the blood away, and then runs his fingers over the skull.

'Here,' he says. 'Feel.'

He stands beside her and guides her fingers. She can feel nothing at first; then there is a slight depression. She wonders if she can feel the slightest sensation of grating bone when she applies pressure.

'A blow,' Mayhew says. 'He came in without his helmet, but he must have been wearing it when he was hit.'

'It saved his life,' she says.

Mayhew looks doubtful.

'Perhaps,' he says.

'So what can we do?'

'There will be a sanguineous swelling within the orb of the skull, I have no doubt,' he says. 'It is usually – always – fatal. It is something to do with the brain. It cannot work with the swelling.'

She cannot bear it.

'No,' she says. 'Not Sir John.' Then she thinks, and asks: 'How do you treat sanguineous swellings elsewhere on the body?'

'A leech, sometimes,' Mayhew says. 'Or we cut it open and dispose of the blood.'

'Why?' she asks.

'Why? Because. Because we do.'

'If we cut open the swelling now?'

'It is – behind the skull,' Mayhew says. 'We cannot get to it to cut it.'

'The bones are broken, I am sure of it.'

Mayhew frowns. He looks down at Sir John.

'You would have to cut open the scalp,' he says, 'which is easy enough, of course, but then you would have to crack the skull if it is not cracked already.'

'I think it is.'

'But the swelling might not be where the break is. It might be on the other side of the brain and – no. You do not want to touch a man's brains.'

'It is worth a try, surely?'

Sir John looks closer to death than life.

'It cannot hurt,' Mayhew says. 'But let us call a priest first.'

While Mayhew fetches more wine Katherine finds Richard. He is sitting on a step talking to a wounded captain and tearing linen into strips. She touches his shoulder.

'Richard,' she says. 'Your father is here. He will die unless we cut him. But it is not easy and of course the cutting may kill him.'

Richard stands up.

'Take me to him,' he says.

Katherine does so and leaves the two together while another man is brought in with a wound in his chest that makes a noise and within a few moments he is dead. She glances over at Richard and Sir John when she is holding the dying man's hand and Richard is gently feeling his father's face, cupping his bearded chin, letting his fingertips play over the nose and eyes and forehead.

'Will you do it, my lady?' he asks when the priest is called and she is standing next to him. He is offering her a courtesy, since she knows Sir John.

'Thank you,' she says. Mayhew nods and takes a step back.

Richard holds Sir John's hand and the old man mews in his sleep. She has a blade, taken from the barber surgeon's bag, which is sharper than anything she has ever seen. She holds it up to the candle that the murmuring friar is holding.

'Should I shave his head?' she asks. 'It will help with the stitching afterwards.'

Mayhew raises his eyebrows.

'Good idea,' he says. She turns the knife and slices through the white locks. Underneath there is a silver furze, nicked here and there by tiny scars. She had imagined that people have round heads, but of course they don't. Sir John's is long and fluted with angles, slightly asymmetric, with a ridge here and a point there. She clears away the sodden hair and wipes the bristle with some linen soaked in wine. Now that the hair has gone it is easy to see the indentation and there is even a greenish tinge to the skin. Again she presses her fingers to the skin and she can feel the grating of the bones.

'There is nothing for it,' Mayhew says.

She nods and cuts, holding her nerve even while blood pours from the wound.

'Scalps always bleed mightily,' Mayhew says.

The skin wrinkles around the cut, pulling back. There is a thin veil of pale pink flesh that she needs to slice through. Then there is the bone, the colour of old teeth.

'Linen,' she says, and she retracts the blade. Mayhew wipes the wound with wine and for a moment they see thin cracks in the depression, such as on an egg. He nods. With the tip of the knife she touches one of the pieces of bone. Sir John gurgles and moves his tongue.

'Hold him,' Mayhew calls and he grabs Sir John's head to keep it still. Katherine touches the bone again, this time letting the tip of the knife slip to the edge of the fragment. She probes further. Her hands are steady though her heart is fluttering. Then she attempts to lift the fragment away, to prise it from the skull. It comes, but with it comes a splurge of blood, thick and dark, that wells from the wound and pours down into Sir John's ears.

'Good,' Mayhew says. 'That might be the sanguineous swelling.'

Sir John makes another noise, deep in his throat, more like a dog than a man, and she fears the worst, but Mayhew has placed the clay pot of wine on the old man's chest, and concentric rings appear in its surface to let them know he lives and breathes. After that there seems nothing else to do but stitch Sir John's scalp back together. She uses her own hair and makes the smallest stitches she can, taking her time while Mayhew sees to the rest of the wounded as they come limping in. When she has finished she wipes Sir John's wound with more wine and egg whites and then his face with the last of the rose water.

His eyes flutter and he opens them and for a moment he is terrified.

'All is well, Sir John,' she says. 'All is well, only don't move.'

She takes his hand and they are like that for a moment, still and silent, and then his eyes focus on her and he smiles.

'Kit,' he whispers through dry lips. 'Kit. Praised be, you are here.'

She feels a jolt, and the blood runs to her face. She cannot help herself glancing at Richard, who is sitting there, his face expressionless. Has he heard? She supposes not.

She bends over the old man.

'I am Margaret, Sir John,' she whispers. 'Margaret Cornford. Do you not remember?'

Sir John opens his mouth in close little gasps.

'I know what I know,' he whispers. 'By my truth, I know what I know. And where is Thomas? Where is he? You should be with him.'

'Hush now, Sir John, hush now and all will be well.'

He shuts his eyes and drifts away again.

She stands abruptly and walks away.

Her plan! Dear God, in all this she has forgotten her resolve, and now there is no time for it, but Sir John's words have stirred her again, thickened the brew, decided her. She looks down at her bloody dress and knows she cannot be Margaret Cornford. She cannot be like this. All at once it has become a stupid pretence, as crude as it is dishonest.

But has she left it too late?

And what of Thomas?

She has seen so many dead men this day, how can she believe there are any still living? Yet, somehow, she is certain that he is.

With the dusk the steady stream of wounded that has lasted all day begins to dwindle, but later a man comes in on his own, limping badly. Though he has lost his bow, she can tell he is an archer, and he wears the blue and white livery of Fauconberg.

'Trod on a caltrop,' he tells her, 'just as I was coming off the field. Went through all that, fighting all day, and I slip at the last moment. It hurts, oh Christ it hurts.'

He holds up the sole of his boot for inspection. It is filthy with the manure of every animal she can name, dyed up to the ankle in human blood.

'There is nothing I can do for you,' she tells him.

'I can pay,' he says.

'It is not that—' she begins but he has a leather bag slung behind him and when he tugs it around and opens it up, she feels a flutter in her chest as sharp as a stab.

'Look,' he says, pulling out the pardoner's ledger. 'Got a hole in it and that, but still. Must be worth a penny or two.'

Her ears are roaring and her hands come up to snatch it from him, but she collects herself. He holds it upside down and back to front so that she can see that the hole does not go all the way through.

'Reckon it must have saved his life,' the archer says, exploring the hole with his finger.

Katherine can say nothing for a moment.

'Come on,' the archer says. 'You can have it if you fix me up. Stop it hurting. Make sure it doesn't go bad.'

'Sit by the fire,' she says.

She hurries to get Richard, who is sitting over his father.

'There is an archer by the fire', she whispers, 'who has Thomas's ledger.'

'Have you asked him where he got it?'

'No. He can only have stolen it.'

Richard nods.

'Take me to him,' he says, 'and get Mayhew.'

Katherine waves Mayhew over and together they lead Richard to the archer's side.

The archer glances up as Richard sits next to him.

'What's this?' he asks.

'I'm blind,' Richard says. 'But I have a good sense of smell.'

'Really.'

The archer goes back to staring at the fire. He is clutching his foot.

'Yes,' Richard goes on. 'And I can smell a thief.'

Now the archer looks up. He has been in situations like this before, that much is clear.

'A thief is it, blind man?'

Suddenly there is a knife in his hand, but Mayhew kicks his wrist and the knife flies across the stone floor of the nave. And now Mayhew has his own knife out, and he threatens the archer with it, though he looks confused. Then Katherine steps on the archer's wounded foot.

He cries out.

'What is this? What're you doing?'

'What's your name?'

'John. John Perers. County of Kent.'

'Where did you get that book?' Katherine asks.

Perers looks mutinous. Katherine applies some pressure.

'On the field,' he says. 'All right? I took it from a bloke.'

'Which bloke?'

'Just some bloke.'

'Is he dead or alive?'

'I don't know. Dead, for God's sake. Probably. Everybody is up there.'

'Take me to him.'

'What? No. Don't be so stupid. I'm not going back up there.'

'If you do not get treatment for that wound you'll die. Death will take you bit by bit, starting with the foot, which a surgeon will have to cut off, with a saw, but that will not stop the putrefaction. The surgeon will have to take more off your leg, piece by piece, and each time the saw bites, it will feel as if you are being roasted by the fires of hell.'

Perers is pale with all he's been through, and now the pain is great, and here is this woman, a blind man and physician's assistant trying to force him back up to the field.

He moves to leave. He'll find another surgeon, easy, with all the money he's picked up.

Richard moves like a ferret and his hands are suddenly on the archer's neck. The archer tries to scream and lash out, but Richard's thumbs dig into his throat.

'Take us, now,' he says.

Perers waves his arm to suggest that he will.

'Bloody hell fire,' he says, rubbing his throat after Richard has let go. He is too terrified to look at him.

'Give me the book,' Katherine says.

He hands it over.

'It's a long way,' he says. 'Can't we wait until morning?'

'He is still alive,' Katherine says. 'I am sure of it.'

She cannot stand to think of him out there, just one more man dead or lost. She does not want to number him among men like Dafydd, or Walter, or any of the Johns, whom she has known and now – are gone.

'Look,' the archer goes on, 'I'm sure he's dead. One night isn't going to hurt him any more than he already is, is it?'

'I will cure you if we go now. Tomorrow may be too late, for both of you.'

Mayhew will come with her, carrying a torch, and Richard too.

'What difference will the dark make to me?'

They follow the hobbling archer up the road and on to the dale. The wind has died and the snow has settled and the stars are out, and it is cold enough so that touching metal strips the skin from fingertips. All across the field men have lit fires, burning old arrows and bows and anything else they can find to give them the light with which to see, and everywhere shadows flit as they go about their business. Even now there is still the noise of men hitting other men.

'It was over there,' the archer says. 'Mind out for the bloody caltrops.'

The field stinks like a shambles, and underfoot it is soggy and still warm with the spilled blood. Katherine walks with her hand over her mouth and nose. When she becomes aware the banks she thought were earthworks are jumbles of corpses, ready to be interred in pits, she is glad Richard cannot see. After a moment, Mayhew lowers the burning torch so that none of them can.

'Dear God,' she says. 'How will we ever forgive ourselves for this?'

'Are there many?' Richard asks.

'I can't tell you. Thousands. Many thousands.'

They carry on up towards the fires on the plateau.

'I never did fight in battle,' Richard says quietly. 'All that training. All those hours in the tilting yard and at the butts. It was all I ever dreamed of.'

'Why?' Katherine asks. She wonders why she has not asked before.

'I don't know,' he says. 'It is what you do.'

'Here we are,' the archer says. 'About here.'

They stop by the side of the road, near a broad barrow of corpses. Blank faces stare at them from the pile, and men are twisted among one another, like the frayed edges of a carpet.

'He was sitting here,' the archer says, gesturing in the dark. 'His head was bleeding.'

'You are lying.' She just knows.

'No, as God is my witness.'

'Remember your foot.'

There is a long moment. The dead seem to be letting slip some kind of miasma, thick, like breath, but cold.

'All right,' he says. 'A little bit along.'

She gathers her cloak around her and they make their way along a pathway that has been made between the corpses. Mayhew is reduced to silence. Her shoes are letting in liquid. She does not want to think what. Richard stumbles and someone cries out in the darkness.

'Hurry,' she says.

'All right, all right. My foot. It's hurting.'

'It will only get worse.'

'Christ.'

They go on. At one point Katherine trips and steadies herself by clutching a man's face. It is cold and gelid. She wipes her hand on a man's tunic, but it comes away even darker with gritty blood.

'Where is he?'

They have moved beyond some trees where the land slopes sharply and, over the lip of the dale, dead bodies are piled in acres, three or four deep, and in among them, walking above them, are parties of looters, crouching over the corpses, each one lit by a boy holding a flaming torch as they burrow among the dead. She watches a man twisting at something and chopping at it with a hatchet and she feels a great sorrow.

'May God forgive us,' Mayhew whispers.

Beyond is a river, emitting mist, and there is a weir down there over which the water flares and seethes. Bodies choke the valley. It is unbelievable. They stare so long that they do not notice the archer slip away.

When she does so she can think of nothing good to say.

'We will never find him now,' Richard laments.

'No,' she says. 'He is here. He is not dead. I know it.'

There is a long silence. All they can hear are the furtive rustlings of the looters and the sighing of the dead, the rush of the beck below, and the wind luffing across the dale.

'He is here,' she says, but her voice is no more than a whisper.

'Come,' Richard says. 'Come.'

'No.'

'My lady,' Richard says. He fumbles for her arm. She tries to resist but he is firm.

'He must be gone, my lady,' Mayhew says. 'No man would willingly stay out here if he could leave.'

'I know he is here.'

'Then he must be dead,' Mayhew says.

She cannot believe it. She cannot believe this is what the Lord had in mind for Thomas when he survived all that came his way before.

'Come,' Mayhew says. 'We cannot stay here. The miasma—'

'He is not dead,' she says.

She pulls free, grabs the torch from Mayhew and holds it high above her. She illuminates only more corpses.

'Thomas!' she calls. 'Thomas Everingham!'

There is nothing. Only the wind and a flurry of blows in the distance, short and sharp, where the looters are finishing off yet one more.

'Thomas!' she cries again. 'Thomas! Thomas Everingham!'

But still nothing.

'Where is he?' she demands.

There is another long silence.

'I know what he was to you,' Richard continues. 'I know.'

She does not wonder what he means. She thinks only of Thomas. Of how they left one another.

'He was . . .' She is going to say 'everything'. She bites back a sob. Tears are pouring down her cheeks. She feels she could catch them and fill her palms.

'Perhaps it is right that we don't find him, do you think?' Richard goes on. 'That he is buried with the men who died with him? A sort of fellowship?'

Katherine nods in the dark, but she snivels. She remembers burying Red John and she knows how that felt. Then:

'No,' she says. 'No. He is here. Thomas!' she shouts. 'Thomas!'

'My lady . . .' Richard begins.

She wipes her eyes, her cheeks, her nose, her chin. Tears are everywhere.

Again: 'Thomas!' and her shout is racked by a sob. 'Oh God, Thomas!'

And this time, nearby, there is a movement on the edge of the pile of corpses. A man holds up a bloodied hand. He is hidden, half buried by another man's body, and they cannot see his face.

'Katherine,' the man whispers.

At first she does not hear it.

'Katherine,' he says again, louder, calling.

And this time she hears him, and she turns.

Acknowledgements

This novel has taken a shamefully long time to finish, and in that time I have been shown so much kindness by so many people that it would almost be quicker to list the people who haven't helped me (you know who you are . . .) but I particularly want to thank some of you – and mention you by name – for putting up with me, encouraging me, lending me money and an ear, for buying me lunch when we all knew it was my turn. I'd like to thank you, Kazzie, first and foremost, for continuing to bear with me through uncertain times, remaining cheery and lovely while doing so; Marth, for being a very weird, but very perfect, early reader; Mum, for absolutely everything; Dad, for you know what (the cheque's in the post), and Nick and Lil for all your amazing kindness and support over the years. I'd also like to thank Tom and Max, too, for being so special, in every way. You have all been marvels of patience and generosity – I could not have managed it without you.

I'd also like to say a huge thank you to each of Rooster Clements, Nick Clements, Justin Thomson-Glover, Kate Summerscale, Sinclair Mckay, David Allison, Jake Werksman, Alex Sarginson, Wayne Holloway, Johnny Villeneau and Tessa Dunlop too, for your tolerance, guidance, generosity and support in so many varying guises, the less said about which, perhaps the better. You have been top friends in this matter and I can't thank you enough.

In addition, I'm also very keen to thank Timothy Byard-Jones for reading the manuscript and for picking me up on my many fifteenth century-based mistakes; Graham Darbyshire of the Towton Battlefield Society for walking me around and for sharing his knowledge all those years ago, and the expert and enthusiastic bowyer Les Wigg for his advice on bows and arrows and the mysterious craft of loosing them. All are founts of knowledge, and each has tried his best to teach me what I didn't know. If any mistakes have crept in, they are mine and mine alone.

I'd like to thank Toby Mundy, too, perhaps oddly, for letting me dance on his dollar for a time (and HMRC as well, who have shown inexplicable but blessed patience in the matter of my return for the tax year '10-'11, not to mention '11-'12), David Miller for all his help, and Laura Palmer for her early guidance in the story of Thomas and Katherine. I'd like to thank my terrific agent Charlotte Robertson who helped me finish the book and then got it onto the desk of my terrific editor, Selina Walker – thank you Selina – and I'd like to thank Richenda Todd for her almost unbelievable detail and plot juggling skills. This is a much better book for their input, for which I am very grateful indeed, eternally so.

Read on for a sneak preview
of the next instalment of
the *Kingmaker* series.

Kingmaker:
Broken Faith

CORNFORD CASTLE, CORNFORD, COUNTY OF LINCOLN, ENGLAND, MICHAELMAS, 1462

It is the hour before noon on the second day before St Luke's, late in the month of October, and in the grey light slanting through the castle's kitchen doorway, Katherine inspects the small, skinned body of an animal lying on the scrubbed oak table. It is gutted, headless and footless.

'Rabbit, my lady,' Welby's wife tells her. 'Husband caught it yesterday. Out near the Cold Half-Hundred drain.'

Katherine knows only one thing about rabbits, but she knows the Cold Half-Hundred drain, and she knows Welby, who sits with his broad back turned, eating bread so that she can hear him chewing. He says nothing, doesn't even grunt, but his brawny shoulders are up and she can see him waiting for something, so she prises open the narrow trap of the animal's ribs and counts. She makes it thirteen pairs.

'Not a rabbit,' she says. 'A cat.'

Welby stops his chewing. His wife holds Katherine's stare for a moment, then drops her gaze to the rushes. Katherine notices the skin under her right eye is puffed with a bruise. Her husband swallows his bread.

'It's a rabbit,' he says without turning his head. There are creases of pale skin in the dirty fat of his neck. 'As wife told you. Killed it meself.'

Katherine knows she still seems odd to them – an interloper in a good dress, small, thin, with her hat pulled down to hide her ear and her already sharp features honed by sorrow and privation – but it has been like this ever since she arrived at Cornford Castle more than a year before, since the first time she led Richard Fakenham on his horse over the two bridges and in through the gatehouse to take possession of her late supposed father's property.

The curtain walls had seemed taller then, rough grey stone, stained with damp even in the summer months, weeds growing from every crevice and all sorts of filth underfoot. Welby's wife stood on an unswept step of the kitchen, washing beetle in hand, while unfed dogs snarled on chains and the air was sour with the smell of their waste.

'What is it?' Richard had asked, wrinkling his nose. Welby's wife had stared at his bandaged eyes and then looked away, quickly crossing herself and whispering some prayer.

'A welcome,' Katherine had told him. 'Of sorts.'

'Where is everyone?' he'd asked.

'Dead,' someone had answered. This had been Welby, the castle's steward, emerging from the lower door of the gatehouse from where he'd been watching them cross the fen. She did not like him from the moment she saw him: broad and squat, with fleshy ears and small, mean eyes; and he did not like her.

'Dead?' she'd asked.

'Aye,' Welby had said. 'Every man save meself went north with Sir Giles Riven before Lady Day, back in March, and we've given up on 'em coming home now.'

Welby had said this as if it were somehow her fault, as if she, Katherine, had been responsible for their deaths, but she had ignored him and had taken the moment to look around at the castle, to note the accretion of filth, the dilapidation of the stone, the rot in the wood. There were jackdaws in the roof, and a bush of some sort springing from between the stones up by the crenellations. Apart from the new stone badge of Riven's crows that had been put in place of the old Cornford arms, she supposed, the castle looked to have been falling to pieces for some time. It was strange to see how little it had been valued, while Sir John Fakenham and his son Richard had spent so much time, energy and blood to acquire it.

She had not thought it would be like this. Nor had Richard.

They had come up from London with some of William Hastings's men, ten of them, keeping guard over them and a wagon loaded with wedding gifts they'd received, mostly from the newly ennobled Lord

Hastings: two feather pillows, a bolster, a standing coffer, two small chests of oak, a hundred carpet hooks, three pounds of wire and a hemp sack of shoe nails. There had been two gowns of kendal green, one of damask, a bolt of russet and a pair of stockings. For Richard there was a velvet jacket and a doublet, a horse's harness and a short-bladed sword. Not much, Hastings had admitted, but what else do you give a blind man?

They had come along the same road they had travelled with Sir John and the others the summer before, and to console themselves for their losses and for the absence of men they loved, they had tried to imagine what they would find when they got to Cornford: something sound and well-founded, with slate roofs, stout walls and three glazed windows in the solar. They'd pictured a steward out collecting dues. They'd imagined beehives, orchards full of geese and chickens, fat pigeons in the dovecotes, a water mill chunting away, a saw pit perhaps, and a priest at the door of his church. There would be breweries, a baker, a smithy and an inn. There would be men to keep the oxen straight and to sheer the sheep. There would be boys to fetch in wood from the forest and girls to mind the goats. There would be women in woollen dresses with babies on their hips and barrels of ale fermenting in the cellar's cool.

But it was not like that. Instead there were only widows and orphans. The millwheel was broken, the priest unpaid and gone, and such crops as had been planted before the men had left for the north now lay rotting in the sodden fields.

Katherine had thought at the time that perhaps Richard was lucky not to be able to see any of it. And now, a year later, here she is, standing in the kitchen with the body of a cat in her hand and a mere twine of smoke from the twigs that make up the fire in the hearth. She looks down at the little body and thinks of asking to see its head, to see its fur and feet, but she has too often demeaned herself with Welby in the past, sinking to his level and later finding herself begging him to accept her apology so that there is food on the table for Richard to eat. She has promised herself she will not do it again and so she won't now, and besides, what is so bad about eating a cat?

She places the body back on the table and leaves Welby and his wife there, closing the door behind her. Outside it is cold, the first day of winter perhaps, and her ear begins to throb as she hurries across to the keep and ascends the stairs to the solar where Richard is sitting just as she left him, on a bench by the piled ashes of a cooling fire. He seldom leaves this spot. He is too anxious to face the unfamiliar, but in place of his absent sight his other senses have sharpened.

'Is he trying some fresh fraud?' he asks.

'How did you guess?'

'Your gait. You walk as if you are angry.'

She laughs quietly and crosses the threshes to touch his shoulder. He turns his face to her, smiles blankly, puts out a hand.

'Margaret,' he says.

Katherine knows she must take his hand. She does so, looking down on her husband. She wants to change his dressing; the linen is grubby and there are sooty finger marks where he has adjusted it after fiddling with the fire or something. He pulls her to him, puts his arm around her waist. It is always like this. He cannot just – be. He has to clutch at her, paw at her. Even now his palm drifts from her waist to her hip and she cannot help but stiffen. He feels it, and his already absent smile slips and he lets his hand drop. He is like a whipped dog.

He has declined sharply over the past year, lost the muscle he'd acquired from all that fighting practice he used to do, all that riding with the dogs and the hunting with those birds. It turned to fat in those first few months, but now the fat is gone too, and his skin hangs from his bones. There is no one to shave him, no one to comb his hair, so Katherine has learned.

'Shall we go for a walk?' she asks.

He sighs.

'Yes,' he says. 'Take me somewhere high from where I may slip and fall to my death.'

'Come on,' she says. She takes his arms and he needs hauling to his feet.

She indulges him and leads him out of the solar, stumbling up the circling stone steps to the top of the tower. On the way up there is an unglazed window through which she can see the castle's one remaining touch of ornament: a gargoyle in the shape of a lion's face, dripping water into the courtyard below. Everything else of value is gone, stripped and sold, and she supposes that the gargoyle remains only because it is too difficult to reach. It is not clear whether it was Riven's men who carried everything else away before they left for the north, or if it is Welby and his wife who have been slowly stripping the place and selling it bit by bit.

When they emerge on to the walkway at the top of the tower, she guides Richard across the treacherous flagstones to stand facing into the brisk east wind in which she imagines she can taste salt from the sea that lies just beyond the horizon. It is cold enough to bring tears to her eyes, but not his. He stands and grips the edge of the stone merlon and rocks himself backward and forward, backward and forward. He is like a simpleton in his misery.

Katherine looks away and watches the land beyond the castle, seeing all the things that require attention: the silted moats and flooded furlongs, the sagging fences, the fruit trees in need of pruning, the hazels in need of coppicing, the willows in need of pollarding. Nearby, across the first bridge, the roofs of the cattle shed and the hayloft are sunk-in and green, and beyond them the wheel of the mill remains jammed while water flares through the broken rill below. There are a few houses by the causeway, some of them occupied, their roof lines softened by a haze of pale wood smoke. But there are others there too, abandoned, and their roof lines are softened by their neighbours having pilfered their beams for firewood.

'Soon be winter,' Richard says.

She wonders what in God's name they will do then.

'How does it look?' he asks.

'Sad,' she says.

He tries to encourage her.

'We've no men to work the place,' he says. 'And Welby – if I had eyes in my head I would kill him now.'

'Then we'd have one fewer,' she sighs, 'and be in an even worse state.'

She remembers again his high hopes as they'd ridden here. Richard had asked her what they might find, since she was supposed to have passed her youth in the castle, but she told him she could remember almost nothing of it.

'It is a castle,' she'd said.

'Yes, yes, but Windsor is a castle. The Tower is a castle. What is it like? My father said it was well set up, though cold, and there are two moats.'

'There are moats,' she'd agreed. 'Yes. Yes. That is right. Moats.'

Although she'd thought, why have more than one moat?

'And who will be there?' he'd pressed. 'The steward and the reeve, of course, but do you remember them? Or I suppose it is too long ago?'

She'd agreed again.

'And anything might have happened to the place,' she'd cautioned. 'Or to them.'

In truth she'd had no idea what sort of welcome to expect. For the first few days after their arrival she had looked in the village for anyone so old they might have been able to recall Margaret Cornford as a girl, but there was no one above ground to do so. The longer she remained, the more confident she became.

And so now she takes Richard's arm and leads him to face northward. They say nothing for a while. She watches the river, a snaking grey ribbon among the reeds. It is motionless and looks broken too.

'Do you miss Marton Hall?' she asks.

He cocks his ear, his way of glancing at her.

'Marton Hall?' he says. 'No. Or not exactly. I miss . . . I miss the people. I miss my father, of course. And Geoffrey Popham, the steward, and his wife. They were – well. You never met them, did you? You came after it. Other than Thomas, of course. You met him. And the others. Do you remember Walter? He was a brute, wasn't he? But by Great God above, he was. Anyway. And Kit – I think about him sometimes. I don't remember where he came from. I think we found him on a ship, can you believe it? But do you know he cured my father's fistula? He was no more than a boy, but he cut him like a surgeon, and we all stood by and we knew it was the right thing to do. By all the saints, when I think of it now. That summer. Everything rang with life.'

She thinks back to Marton Hall and remembers the long summer she spent there answering to the name Kit. It is a happy memory, dominated in the main by Thomas, but it is inevitably spoiled by the thought of the winter that followed. Since then she has learned not to sniff when the tears come, so she can weep silently.

'But,' Richard continues quickly, just as if he knows, 'they're all gone now. And anyway, why have a hall when you can have a castle?'

He is half in jest. He gestures, little knowing he is opening his arms to a vista of burdensome and ruined countryside, peopled by worrying responsibilities and petty shames. She twists the ring on her forefinger and together they pace along the tower's walkway to where she stops and forces herself to stare westwards, across the fens to the huddle of grey stone buildings scarcely visible in the distance.

It is the Priory of St Mary at Haverhurst. In the year she has been in Cornford she has never been along the causeway that leads to its gates, never even left the castle in that direction. All she can manage is to make herself look at it at least once a day, and every time she does so she still feels a hot flare of panic. Looking at it now, she can see there is almost nothing to the place: a church, a few low buildings encircled by that wall, and it seems absurd that for the larger part of her life it encompassed her entire world. She wonders what they are doing there now, and knows instinctively the sisters will be gathering to observe the Hour.

She is relieved when there is a flurry of barking from below and she can look away. Welby's wife is down there, using that washing beetle as a walking stick, feeding the dogs God knows what. The head of the cat perhaps. Katherine wonders how many days she can have left. She has asked Welby about his wife's lying in, but Welby laughed in her face and told her that women such as his wife did not lie in. He told her that it was not her concern anyway, and he told her that he had delivered cows of their calves and ewes of their lambs, and that there was nothing very special about delivering a woman of her baby.

Katherine had then tried to talk to Welby's wife, to avoid the fore-staller as it were, but the woman had been fearful and backed away, shaking her head as if she did not want to hear what was being said. Katherine could not tell if it was the prospect of the birth that frightened her most, or the prospect of her husband. Katherine asked if there was a woman in the village who attended births.

'There was,' Welby's wife said, 'but she is in the churchyard since St Agnes's last year and her daughter alongside her, so now there is no one.'

From her vantage point at the top of the tower, Katherine watches Welby's wife and wonders how she can work on like that. She must be due any day. She may even be overdue. She imagines her fear. What must it be like to know what is coming? She has seen men's faces as they troop to battle, the grim set of their mouths, their distant gazes, their skin the colour of goose fat and trembling hands that can only be stilled by wine or ale. But what about women as they prepare for childbirth? Their chance of death is the greater, and terrible pain a certainty.

'We must do something for her,' she says. 'And soon.'

Richard grunts.

'Perhaps we should send for the infirmarian at the Priory?' she asks.

Even as she says the words she feels that familiar flutter in her chest, her breath comes a little faster and she feels unsteady.

But Richard is dismissive.

'St Mary's is a Gilbertine priory, remember?' he tells her. 'An enclosed order. The women are only supposed to see the outside world through an aperture that must be no thicker than a thumb, no taller than a finger. Did you know? It is supposed to be brass-bound, too. To prevent the sisters enlarging it over time. So their infirmarian could not come out even if it were worth her while because, after all, what experience can she have in childbirth? Among those women who have not seen a man in – ever?'

Richard knows little of the sisters in the Priory, she thinks, but he is not really thinking about them: he is thinking of himself and Katherine, and once again the subject of their own missing offspring is between them, dark and heavy. It is not as if she has not tried. They were married in the first month after King Edward's coronation, when she had given up on Thomas Everingham, and since then they have lain together as man and wife on occasion. She does not care to recall those first encounters, but since then they have reached not so much an understanding as a way of doing things. Yet still there is no child, and she feels there is none on the way either, so she wonders if their way of doing things is the right way after all, or if such a union, forged in hidden sorrow, will ever be blessed.

Welby's wife has now fed the dogs and is retreating slowly towards the kitchen.

'I could find some woman myself?' Katherine suggests. 'Have her here when the baby comes.'

'Is there someone in the village?' Richard asks.

'No,' she admits. 'But at one of the other villages? Or I might go as far as Boston. I need to sell such russet as we have left. You could come with me?'

Richard nods but they both know he will not come. He does not like to go out, to be seen abroad as a cripple, just another useless mouth to feed. So the next morning Welby waits alone for her across the first bridge with two horses in the falling rain, making her walk through the courtyard, past the dogs, quietened now with a bone apiece, and the kitchen door where his wife leans against the wall. When Katherine sees her she is brought up short. The woman's skin is taut and her eyes bulge almost grotesquely. She is breathing noisily, too, almost panting, and when she raises her hand Katherine can see it is horribly swollen.

'Good day to you, Goodwife Welby,' Katherine calls. 'We will be back as soon as we can. Rest until we return. Do nothing, do you hear?'

Welby's wife does not speak, but nods stiffly, as if she cannot move her head for the swelling in her neck. She looks terrified, Katherine thinks as she hurries out through the gatehouse and across the first bridge to where Welby looks unhappy in his wet straw hat.

'Your wife—' Katherine starts.

'Will be all right,' he interrupts.

She makes up her mind. She will find someone in Boston. She pulls herself up into the saddle and settles herself. Then they ride out across the second bridge to the causeway.

'Needs mending,' she says.

There is a pause.

'Hard to mend a bridge when you've no wood,' he says. 'Or nails. Or a hammer. Or anyone to use it to drive them in.'

'Is there really no one?'

He lifts his hands off his reins and gestures at the houses along the road ahead. There are five or six of them, low and dark, with rotting, green slicked daub, and farther on is a boy, the oldest in the hamlet yet still beardless, wrestling a pig into a pen while his sisters look on. The detritus of rush weaving is in a pile all around their ankles, and baskets and mattresses are heaped and hooked on the fences. The boy is smacking the pig with a stout stick now, and if the pig turns on him they will have one fewer pair of hands to help them.

'Help him, Welby,' Katherine says.

Welby slouches from his saddle and joins the boy. Together they kick and hit the pig until it retreats into its pen.

'Thank you, lady,' the boy says. He is breathless. Then he adds a thank you for Welby but there is some side there, and Katherine notes it.

'He's a big one,' she approves.

'Aye,' the boy agrees, 'and I'll be sorry come St Martin's.'

Welby mounts up and she says goodbye to the children. They kick their horses on. Farther along the causeway a skinny-looking mother – their mother? – with a bald-headed newborn sits in her open doorway and stares at them as they pass. Katherine smiles but receives nothing in return. She wonders who delivered the baby.

'My wife,' Welby tells her when they are out of earshot.

Welby rides with his head down, hunched under his hat, letting the horse lead the way. She imagines he is probably thinking of all the men who used to live in the hamlet, the men who did all the work and kept the place alive. But they went north with Giles Riven in spring that year and never came home again. She supposes they must have been at the shambles on the fields of Towton, and she shies away from recalling the day, from her memories of it, but even here they come back, almost crushing her.